THE LIMIT OF THE LONELY MAN

THE KING'S SWORDSMAN BOOK 3

BECKY JAMES

First published in paperback in 2022

A CIP catalogue record for this book is available from the British Library.

Paperback ISBN 978-1-9168774-6-7

Book cover design: Timea Schwinger at Fantastical Ink

Editor: Clem Mouleart

Section break illustrations: Angharad Bater

Clarkenhome Press

Gloucestershire

GL2 5DR

www.clarkenhomepress.com

ALSO BY BECKY JAMES

THE KING'S SWORDSMAN

Upper young adult / new adult sword and sorcery portal fantasy.

The Tenets in the Tattoos
The Bind of Blood and Bonds
The Limit of the Lonely Man
The Tempered Turns of Time
The Mettle of the MasterMage

DARK TIDES

Fantasy romance co-authored with Wren Murphy.

A Dram of Freshwater (prequel)
The Shadow of Death

For news from the author, check out www.beckyjamesauthor.co.uk

For Ed.
Some assembly required, but you never hesitate
to put in the work.

PROLOGUE—THE HEARTBROKEN MAGE

Pushing her curls out of her face and under the headscarf with one hand, Liara hurried out of the city limits. Calling this place a city was a stretch; the capital was a collection of tents surrounding the ostentatious palace, itself in the depths of the desert.

She rejoined her caravan, smiling fleetingly at the leader. He was not under her enchantment, merely paid well. Nodding once, he opened the back door of the wooden wagon. Weather-worn with paint peeling on the outside, the cramped interior was pleasant at least, strewn with cushions to make the journey more comfortable and the warm smell of cinnamon to combat the stench of horses.

It had been a hard mooncycle and a half. Liara used her power sparingly and kept to the sand, away from any stone. Who knew what sort of reach that witch Tuniel had; she had to be powerful to map the caves of the Labyrinth under Spiritshere and find the Oberrotian royal family, and do the same under the Palais. And then to defeat Waker…

Liara put her arms around her shoulders, trying to breathe deeply and evenly. *I will fix this.* Only when the rocking started, signalling that the caravan was underway, did she relax.

"Well met, Liara."

Liara cried out, flinging herself to the back of the caravan.

A figure sat at the front of the wagon. It wore the full Rushia man's headscarf, but the voice had been female and young, speaking Dinahen as fluently as if it were her native tongue.

Pressing a hand to her chest, Liara sent out her senses. She should have felt the beating heart and active mind of another, the nascent and the deep-seated desires and wishes that floated out from all beings, but her magic slid off the side of this figure.

As if she were an Earthian.

A torrent of feeling overtook Liara. "So, you show up at last," she said in Dinahen.

The figure inclined her head. "I come with a warning."

Anger lapped against Liara's broken heart. "Your warnings are less than useless. You led Waker down the pathway to a terrible fate and did nothing when that witch killed her!" She dropped her head into her hands. "You were using us. I'm done listening to you."

The other woman sighed. "Waker would have prospered if she had stopped where I told her to. When she took hold of the Lonely Man to punish the Spirit Shaper, that's when her fate was sealed." The hooded figure seemed to study the caravan slats, as if searching for cracks. "As yours nearly was when you did the same."

"The lonely... what? What are you talking about?" Liara shook her head fiercely. "I'm not treating with you any longer."

The figure clasped her hands in her lap. "Liara, that spirit you hold won't bring Waker back. There's only one person who can, as we say, jump the tracks of time, putting events back toward a different direction, and you've..." The woman clucked her tongue. "What's the phrase? Ah yes. Pissed him off."

Liara shook her head. "I'm not relying on anyone else. I will do what I must." *For Waker*. Liara's love burnt as fiercely as any flame. "I will march deep into the Labyrinth to bring her back." Liara dashed the tears away. They would not help. Action would.

Liara would do anything to get Waker back. Even dabble in Rushia death magic.

"You'll be together soon," the woman said distantly. "And actually this... this might be interesting." Standing up, the woman shook out her skirts and raised a hand.

A hole tore through the side of the wagon, but instead of sand and wind, it contained only darkness. Warmth blasted out from the hole at the same time that Liara felt it dragging at her clothes and hair.

Liara backed away, against the side of the wagon.

Without a further word, the woman stepped into the tear. It closed behind her, and Liara's ears popped.

Liara stood frozen, heart beating hard against her ribcage, until she gathered her resolve and courage. She was done with fortune tellers and future gazers.

I will make my own path from now on.

She lifted her right hand. On it was a ring, and the jewel glowed darkly. A black smoke curled and coiled around her fingers, writhing around her wrist. It was cold where it touched skin.

"You will cooperate with me," she ordered in Rushia. A bead of sweat trickled down her forehead. "You heard your mistress, the Princess of Rush. You will help me get her the Earthian."

CHAPTER 1

I WAS GETTING USED TO THE NOISES TRAINS MADE, THEIR PARTICULAR SNORTS and screeches, and how they acted, with their gentle rocking and uneven temperature throughout the interior. I could accomplish entering or leaving at the familiar bidding of the doors to open, as well as finding a seat without drawing attention to myself. But while I was adept at feeding the tickets through the turnstile, I had to rely on Aubin to read the flickering information boards as the text revealed and hid itself by some secretive scrolling. We also had to navigate customs and quirks of culture. Aubin was quicker to notice social norms and adapt to the point that he became unobtrusive, while I was better at assessing the mood of a person and engaging them in conversation. Though I could talk to them, and in Oberrotian no less, I was painfully aware that I came from a different world.

On this train beast, a man sat across the table from us. He looked somewhat pale and thin for a warrior, but he sported plentiful tattoos that festooned the left side of his neck and across his face up to his temple. I sat straight-backed; everything I knew and understood about the codes every swordsman and woman carried etched into their skin screaming at me that this man was a seasoned warrior and I could learn a lot from him. Some designs even echoed insignias I knew, mocking me with their meaning. It took all my self-control to bite my tongue and not beg him for training, but I managed it.

Aubin could make portals, having learnt them from my soul companion Evyn, and travelling on the Earthian side allowed us to reach destinations almost as quickly as using magic and with no forewarning to potential enemies of the kingdom of Oberrot. These were enormous advantages, outweighed by the drawback of having to endure this form of torturous transportation.

And now without our disguises. We had taken our Earthian clothes and the spare Earthian lodestone—phone, I reminded myself—but those must have been stolen, as they were not in the hiding place we had devised for them when we tumbled back out of Oberrot.

The last train we needed was overcrowded when we sat down, eight or so stops before. People filtered on and off, so we could eventually claim a table, but a press appeared as the sun touched down against the horizon; men and women in sweat-stained shirts, tutting angrily at each other but avoiding direct confrontation, preferring to fluff and fan their newspapers. Some men with their neckties askew nursed cans of beer, and most people either shouted into their hand-held lodestones that they were going through a tunnel, or stared enraptured at them as the surface flickered and changed.

A fresh line of people surged in, all drenched as if they had been swimming, and a crackly magical voice chirped that passengers should move right down inside the cars. But there were no car beasts in here, and if there were, it would be hideously dangerous.

My stomach churned. *What should I be doing?* I jerked my head to avoid a direct hit to the face from a sodden umbrella, trying not to jostle Aubin.

He sat curled in on himself, head tipped against the warmth-leeching windows. His shadowed face was slack with deep sleep at last. *Good.* He had been hard pressed to recover during the mission to Skien. I understood why; it was a learnt trait to completely hand over my safety to the watch duty, letting go any need to stay alert in enemy territory. It was hard to do, but something I had considered safe enough to do with my contingent for turns. Aubin hadn't grasped that fully yet, and so any rest we had snatched proved far too paltry for him.

An Earthian in the corridor turned in place, her bag swinging around and into my right side. I bit back a wince as it struck my recently injured arm, tamping down the flare of anger, working to keep tight control of any feelings that could escalate into a bout of uncontrollable rage.

I looked up at her. Hair plastered to her face, the Earthian's lower lip trembled. She looked as tired as I felt. Mouthing sorry to me, she slung her bag into her arms, then attempted to stretch over my head to place it on the shelf above me. Her arms trembled, and she had to bring it back to her chest.

Would it be considered out of the ordinary to help?

I cleared my throat. "Ma'am? I can take that and put it up there for you."

Her eyes widened. "Oh, would you? Thank you." A flush flashed across her cheeks.

Pleased I hadn't committed some kind of crime, I stood and took her bag one-handed, favouring my injured right wrist. On top of that, my right shoulder ached again, just where Amare met my muscle. The cap of my shoulder had been hurting recently, as if it were a training pain that did not recede with rest. I swallowed a grimace and stowed her bag where she had been trying to place it overhead.

"Thank you," she said with heartfelt intensity, swaying a little as the train beast banked.

I gestured to my vacated seat. "Would you like to sit?"

"Oh, thank you." Her face seemed to glow as she slid next to Aubin.

He startled alert, eyes snapping open. "Thorrn?" He stared at the woman next to him.

"Here." I waved the fingers of my left hand to signal *At ease* to him.

His amber eyes went round, but he nodded. He patted his side closest to the window; my father's sword was hidden there and, judging by how he relaxed, was still safely stowed. His leather back-pack sat on the table, the paltry remainder of the supplies we had set out with.

The woman looked me up and down. My leathers moulded to my body, buttoned up to my jaw to protect my throat, normally from blows but right now from the cold. Metal had been sewn into strategic locations, such as the thighs and chest, to protect against strikes from enemy weapons, but these were not visible. I was pleased to note the colour on her cheeks, the sparkle of interest in her eyes. *Even when I stink with sweat and my leathers caked with the dirt of another world.* I shifted my stance, unfamiliar feelings of discomfort rising. The old me would have accepted all female atten-tion, but now that I had a promised match with Tuniel, I felt I had to rebuff all others quickly. Especially as my promised's soul companion sat right there, watching me with his analysing gaze.

The Earthian put a nail to her mouth, then swore, sucking at some blood. My gorge rose, and Aubin's lips twisted. Delving into his pack, he produced a weft bandage. Tearing off a strip with a ripping noise that startled the Earthians immediately adjacent to us, he passed it to her. "Here."

"Thanks." She wrapped her finger without a further care. Earthian blood was still the same colour as ours, but its properties were revered as some kind of accelerant or magical enhancement on Oberrot, and mages and mancers would kill to obtain it.

She looked between me and Aubin. We wore matching leathers

of dark red, marking us as Rangers. "Are you in a band?" she asked me, trying the bandage around her thumb and pressing it.

A band. *What did she mean?* I would refer to a collection of bandits as a band to report them. Perhaps she meant a group? "Yes," I answered truthfully. The Rangers were an additional element to the army of Oberrot. A pair for now; King Gough wished to trial the arrangement, and I was determined that the Rangers would be a success. The Rangers would be beyond reproach, a dedicated and disciplined force, unmatched in the world.

Eventually. The mission to Skien hadn't exactly gone to plan. I shifted my weight.

The woman smiled. "Oh! What do you play?"

Play? The smile froze on my face. Oh no. Did bands engage in games over here? Which ones?

Aubin sighed. "He plays the drums. Very good at hitting things."

I nodded, frowning, but Aubin turned his gaze away, cutting off further conversation with the woman beside him.

She saw and closed her mouth, facing me again. I should also stay quiet, lest I inadvertently reveal that I had no business being in her world, but ignoring someone galled me. Aubin might be able to do it, and thus fade out of the interest of anyone and everyone, but I found doing that harder than attempting to pull information out of papers.

"I play the saxophone," she whispered with a small smile.

That seemed to require an answer, one that was noncommittal and could not reveal my ignorance of what that was. "Do you enjoy it?"

Smiling, she told me all about learning to read music, which I didn't understand as surely sounds could not be placed on paper, but conversed easily enough that I was comfortable asking further questions about her quest. Many people loved talking about themselves and their accomplishments, and I could keep her on that path.

Outside, darkness had fallen, rain collecting in rivulets to stream down the sides of the window. The glowstones inside caused ghostly reflections of the people riding the train to appear superimposed on the conurbations and their collections of light. *People here need light. It draws them, the same as we are.* My stomach relaxed slightly.

The cheerful magical voice announced Evyn's town as our next destination, and I scanned the environs outside with renewed interest. Perhaps I could pick out her home from here? I had felt little from my soul companion; the bond was new, and recently strained by my stupidity besides. It would likely take turns to embed and develop to the point where I could discern her mood, even at a distance. The spirit that drove us both, separated so it could experience extremes in one lifetime, was bolstered by physical proximity at the moment.

I murmured "uh-huh" to the woman I conversed with, only partly paying attention to the conversation, when an arc of red sped into the sky. A trick of the light, perhaps? My hand gripped the shelf above as the red dot expanded into an explosion, heart thundering in my ears. I sucked in a breath as I called the calm of battle down.

A fire mage or mancer, perhaps, but I'd only ever seen them attacking at close range. Another flare went up, this conflagration comprising greens and blues. The buildings were not on fire that I could see, but shadowed bulks shrouded the terrain further away from the train. *Where is Evyn's house? Is she in the line of fire?* I tried to trace the source of the explosions, but the train was still moving and I couldn't grasp any landmarks.

Fingers clicked in front of my face. I glared at Aubin, who sat back down in his chair, fingers flickering. *Stand down*, he signed. He nodded toward the Earthians around us.

They were all as they had been before, content in their malcontent. No one had traces of panic or fear. "Pretty!" the Earthian I had been speaking to cooed. "Someone must be getting married!"

My knuckles hurt. I released the tension in them, letting go of the shelf. Whatever the lights in the sky were, they did not herald an attack or represent something any of these Earthians were worried about, and so I had to act in the same manner.

When the train eased to a stop, a great deal of people exited with us. I held my father's blade to my chest to leave, stepping out onto a hard surface scoured blank by wind and rain. Stripped of warmth immediately, I pressed forward, Aubin's hand on my back reassuring me he was with me.

We regrouped in the lee of a small shelter. "What is that?" I asked him, pointing at the sky where the fire flowers still bloomed, erratic and accompanied by a snap that cracked across the sky.

He stamped his feet to warm them up. "Something for decoration. A wedding, she said, so perhaps it's traditional to the culture."

"What, explosives at a wedding?" I couldn't fathom it.

Aubin shrugged. "Does it matter? It's not an attack from a mage or mancer. We need to move or we'll freeze. These leathers block knives, not the cold."

I waved him to walk in lockstep with me. "I'll ask Evyn."

"Mm." He thrust his hands under his armpits. He kept his Battlemistress blades in holsters along his forearms usually, but we stashed them in his backpack for now. "Keep away from the train guards with that sword. Press it against your leg, don't let it swing."

"Of course." Fortunately, we joined a teaming throng queuing en masse to get past the barriers, and I smiled at a guard as I fed my ticket into the mouth of the machine.

The man shook his head at me.

"Perhaps we are becoming fixtures here," I noted to Aubin.

"Mayhap. I am certainly getting more familiar with the habits of the number ten bus, so I regret to inform you that we've missed the last one."

I scuffed my boot on the polished floor; tiredness dragged at every limb. "So we have to walk it?"

He shrugged, the movement stilted rather than his usual flowing grace, where every move was calculated three stages ahead. He was tired too.

I forced myself to think, even though fatigue dragged my thoughts to a standstill. Evyn knew we were planning on returning today, but not at what time, and without our own phone, we could not contact her now.

Resigning myself to a march, I straightened up. "It's not far."

His gaze strayed toward my right hand, tucked under my left armpit. It pained me, but I pushed that behind the grin I stretched across my face.

We had engaged with a small band of rogue men on the Skienien border only this morning. Pushing them back, I'd moved to defend our right side when Aubin came spinning into me, leaping into the space I needed to occupy. Sword and blades tangled, and I had stupidly kept hold of my father's sword rather than dropping it as we were taught, wrenching my wrist. That had given the rogue men something to laugh about, but after I switched to my left hand and they found it just as strong as my right, they had fled. We hadn't really broached the subject yet, but Aubin kept looking at my hand as if weighing whether to say something.

We had hardly taken thirty paces when a car beast hooted at us. "Oi!" a woman shouted.

"Do we respond to that?" I asked Aubin.

He shook his head. "How do you usually respond to an impolite hailing?"

"Issuing a challenge, usually." I rolled my shoulders. If it came to a fight, I would have to summon more energy than I currently felt capable of, but my heart rocked my chest and strength surged in my limbs as battle-readiness kindled in my stomach.

Another shrill howl sounded along with a roar as the car beast glided up to roll abreast of us. The window slid down. "I said oi." Grinning at us with a gap-toothed smile was Teresa, her hair now an ashy blonde colour and pulled back severely. "Want a lift?"

I smiled back. "I doubt you'd be able to lift me, but if you're asking if I would like to ride inside the car beast, yes ma'am, we would."

Teresa rolled her eyes at me, lined with some kind of dark powder, and exited the beast, leaving it shuddering and growling with discontent. She opened the door on the other side, pulled a lever and bent the seat in half. "Small guy in the back. You wouldn't fit," Teresa told me. "Jess, say hello."

"Hello," a small voice said in response. I put my head in to smile at the boy, sat on a smaller seat fashioned for him, cloth in hand and thumb in his mouth.

"We're not all that clean, ma'am," Aubin said to Teresa.

"No, you're not, you're stinking to high heaven. What you been up to? Actually, save it, we're in a rush. I've got towels in the boot, one sec." She went to the back of the car beast. Another vehicle grumbled at her; she waved back in return. "Won't be a mo'!"

"Park in the pick-up and drop-off area, love!" an angry man said.

"Won't be a mo', I said!" she screamed back.

Maybe it would come to a fight. I drew myself up to my full height, glowering at the middle-aged Earthian behind the wheel of his muttering beast. "Does this brigand inconvenience you, Lady Teresa?"

Teresa shook her head. "I'm technically in the wrong, but talk tidy and don't go nerdy on me. It's well embarrassing."

"Let's get out of here as quickly as we can, Thorrn, and avoid any altercations. Move out of the way." Aubin sidled past me and slid gingerly onto the seats. "Hello, Master Jess."

"Master Jess, this is Aubin Tabreksson. Aubin, Jess... Dansson?" I hazarded, recalling fighting the man and his henchmen a mere day into my first foray on Earth.

Teresa pulled herself into the front seat. "Well, don't stand around like a lemon, big guy. Time is money and all that, and if the station guard picks up my numberplate I'll get a fine, which I'll get Evyn to pay."

The words made sense individually, but the combination flummoxed me, except she urgently wished to depart and feared consequences if we didn't. I gingerly pushed the seat back upright, alarmed at the clicks it made, and folded myself in to sit next to her.

"Right, we're off to the races!" With a gleeful roar, the car beast leapt forward, and we were travelling.

Rain traced down the windowpanes, but in the front they were smoothed off by two sticks working together in concert. I had travelled in a car beast before, with Luc and his soul companion James, accompanied by Tuniel. Aubin had not, to my knowledge, and I watched his face using the small mirror that seemed to form the car beast's ears.

He appeared outwardly relaxed, a face he presented in most situations. He was tired now, his cheeks drawn down, but his amber eyes were active, almost feverishly roving over our surroundings.

These changed from black and grey washed with an obsidian shine, bright colours of yellow and red reflected in pools that the car beast hissed through, to trees lit with single yellow lamps. It was a season where the foliage shed its leaves and the branches were denuded and skeletal, but that prompted the Earthians to put up decorations of lights instead.

Aubin put his chin in his hand, and not for the first time I wondered what was going on in his head. The dreamlands had shown part of it to me, a chink in his armour; he wanted to find some kind of belonging, whether in a traditional sense of husband and wife forming a family or something else. He seemed to hold himself back from the brink of declaring that, however. Perhaps he was afraid it would be denied or, worse, taken from him.

Teresa executed a turn that made me slide to the far side of the car beast and forcing me to cling on to the belt with my left hand. She shifted the mirror inside the car. "What were you two up to, then? You're filthy, and not in a good way. Ev said you was role playing, which sounds well nerdy, playing characters and that."

I wondered how to respond when Aubin spoke up. "Yes. Everyone needs a hobby. It gets us out and about." He leant forward in his seat. "How did you know when and where to retrieve us?"

Teresa was chewing something, rolling it around her mouth. "Ev gets this text message from a random number and said it had to be from you, cos no one texts like that, all 'I hope this finds you well' and 'kindest regards' and stuff. She checked all the times of the trains you'd likely take, factored in a delay what had just been announced, and asked if I wouldn't mind picking you up cos the number ten switches over to night service and you might not know that, she said."

My smart soul companion. "She is very clever." Pride filled my chest to overflowing.

Teresa inflated a small white bubble from her lips, popping it with a snap. I glanced in the side mirror at Aubin, who eyed Teresa carefully and shrugged one shoulder at me.

Once she had recovered the white substance, chewing it again, Teresa asked, "So go on then, nerds. What characters do you play?" She turned her head toward me. "You've got a sword, so a knight of some kind, right?"

I fought the urge to encourage her to keep her eyes trained forward. "Yes. A swordsman."

Jess clapped his small hands. "I like swords."

Teresa grinned into the middle mirror at her son. "He's gonna be a big nerd, aren't you, Jess? Yes you are." She said it fondly, although I knew she had previously wielded the moniker as a weapon against Evyn.

Aubin gave Jess a half-smile. "Thorrn is the hero with the silvrine armour, fighting for justice and truth."

Jess just stared at him.

"And who do you play?" Teresa asked, meeting his eyes in her central mirror, one drawn-on eyebrow raised.

Aubin leant back slowly, folding his arms tight across his chest. "Well. I'm still figuring that out."

I turned around in my seat. "You're *you*."

I couldn't quite see his eyes in the dimness of the car beast's interior. "Precisely," he murmured.

"Maybe you could have a bow, like Legless in *Lord of the Rings*,"

Teresa mused, popping that white stuff around her lips again. "Or do sword fighting too, like that Ranger bloke."

"A Ranger?" I clung onto the handle on the door as Teresa took another turn at a cracking pace.

She flushed, as if I had caught her at something she should not be doing. "Or something. Hey, I've got to be honest with you and get something off my chest. You know me, say what you see and all that." She fixed me with a steady look. Again, the skin on my neck crawled as I wished she would face forward. "Evyn's not that into you, mate."

My stomach swooped. "Er. Look out in front."

Teresa attended, muttering, but glanced at me out of the corner of her eyes. "Sorry to be the bearer of bad news and that. I'd offer a shoulder to cry on, but I've sworn off hot pancakes. Gotta be a mum and myself for right now." She jerked her chin up in the mirror, meeting Aubin's eyes. She raised her voice. "It's you in the back she's all about, mate. Aubin said this and Aubin did that. He said something funny the other day, or he did something what made me think." She made a gagging sound.

Aubin's eyes widened slightly. My chest warmed. To hear it from an outside party cheered me, as Evyn kept her feelings open with an unreserved patience that I had never before seen, but only for certain people. One certain person in particular, right now. I smiled for him even as my heart hurt for myself.

"I told her men are bad and she should stay away or she'll get her heart broken, but I can tell she ain't listening. She's got it bad." Teresa shrugged at me. "You're chopped liver in comparison, Thorrn mate. Sorry."

I nodded once. My recent actions had not served to strengthen the bond between the spirit that Evyn and I shared; quite the opposite.

Teresa curled her hands around the steering wheel. "How is she, really?"

True concern trembled under her words. I responded with

honesty, even though admitting it hurt me deeply. "I do not think she is hale and well." The claws of self-recrimination tore at my breast. "How was she when you saw her?" I braced myself for her words, baring myself to endure the full thrust of them.

"She conked out about eight times with me, just falls where she is, fast asleep. Then when she wakes up, she tries to pick up where she left off, but, like, time has passed for me, so it's awkward as heck. Oh, she fell up the stairs too, thank goodness she wasn't going down, but she just sort of collapsed where she was."

Despair clawed at my throat. I whipped around to face Aubin. "That's worse than when we left."

His mouth formed a grim line. "Indeed. I need to investigate further. I've done all the tests I can immediately think of, though, so I don't understand what's causing this."

"Mm." Teresa clucked her tongue. "What does she have, anyways?"

"No one knows yet," Aubin said.

Evyn's doctors had no diagnosis, and we couldn't go to any medimage or mancer for assistance for fear they would detect the power in her Earthian blood. Tuniel said there was one she might trust, but the prevarication made me reluctant to bet Evyn's safety on them.

"Is this an effect of..." I shut my jaw. Teresa did not and could not realise that we were not from this world, so I dared not pursue my line of questioning in front of her.

Dread and self-loathing crawled up my stomach and into my throat. Gavain had convinced me to administer a sleeping draught to Evyn to allow Special Forces to haze me back into the ranks as they wished, and like an idiot I agreed with his logic. He had doctored it with bruswurt, a benign substance for Oberrotians, fatal to offworlders like Evyn. Aubin had told me the Dinehan medimancer was able to save her and there should not be lingering effects; he remained perplexed over her continuing symptoms.

"We'll talk later," Aubin signed, the flashes of yellow light pooling in from the tall poles outside affording me the gist of the signals.

Teresa bit down again on her meal. "Anyways. Maybe the doctors can, like, electrode her or something and figure it out."

I doubted it. Bruswurt was a substance from our world, not this one. The more Evyn tried to seek a diagnosis here, the more chance of someone discovering that Oberrot and indeed other worlds existed, and cause complications. King Gough had vowed that Earth would stay a secret on Oberrot to protect this world from mages and mancers using Earthian blood to enhance their magics; having Earthians eagerly trying to get in was counterproductive.

The car beast turned again and finally slowed. The roads became familiar to me, and I sat up in my seat. "Ah! The park."

"Yep. Nearly there, gents. Thank you for travelling Teresa taxis. We'll charge next time, won't we, Jess?"

"Yes," the little boy said with a drowsy sigh.

Teresa pulled the beast to a halt outside the path to Evyn's front door. Bright light spilt out of the bottom windows, suggesting someone was awake downstairs. Truly it wasn't that late, but full night had set in, along with a drizzling rain that seemed to be the prevailing climate for this region.

Teresa did not move, the car beast muttering away. "Well, nice to see you. Gotta get home and give Jess his bath before bedtime."

"Thank you, Lady Teresa. We are in your debt." I saluted her, opening the car door and unfolding myself. My spine popped as I took a deep breath in, the air overlaid with some kind of miasma here. The street that held Evyn's house, shoulder-to-shoulder with the other similar-looking houses, was quiet.

I leant back in to work the lever, allowing Aubin to exit. Teresa shook her head at me. "Do you ever act normally, or are you always this weird?"

Shrugging, I held out my arm for Aubin, but he slid out without my assistance. Just as he pushed the seat upright, Teresa's hand snaked out to snatch his wrist.

She looked pensive, chewing thoughtfully. "So, like, I debated about saying anything because, like, Ev and I don't have the best history or whatever, and, well, I'm getting out of that life and that involves changing my way of thinking and whatever, but..." She leant over the central controls of the car. "Just know that if you mess with Ev's heart, I'll be the first to kick you into next week." Her mouth settled into a sincere scowl.

Aubin could have broken her hold and probably knew scores of moves that would tip her out of her vehicle, belted in or not, but I knew he wouldn't hurt this Earthian. He patiently waited until Teresa let go of his arm.

"Thank you for the ride, Teresa." His voice was even and sure. "I do not ever intend to hurt Evyn." Slinging the backpack onto his back, he let his arms drop to the sides.

Teresa's jaw worked whatever it was she chewed, eyes narrowed at him. "As long as we understand one another. Say hi to Mrs R for me, tell her I've gotta get Jess to bed. Night!"

"Go well, Lady Teresa," I called, shutting the door. The car beast grumbled on its pathway, a jaunty flash of yellow lights perhaps its own way of saying farewell.

Rain already coated my hair and leathers, but something more than mere physical discomfort pulled me onwards. "Let's get in there, but we have to be careful. We lost our keys with the rest of our Earthian supplies, didn't we?"

"Yes. Let's try knocking on the door before you scale the walls. Hopefully Evyn is awake..." Aubin frowned.

I nudged him through the garden gate. "Come on, I want you to check her over before we bed down for the night. She was hurt, Teresa said." And I had known nothing. Our bond was still forming, but I should have felt some strong emotions or sensations from her, especially pain.

"Yes, I know, but—"

I sighed. "Yes, you're holding yourself back from declaring her the queen of your heart because you don't think you're worthy or some such rot." Taking his elbow, I hustled him along the path toward Evyn's front door.

"That's not... Well, if you must know, it's because she deserves better, and she has it, in Prince Gerlay." He practically rammed his hands underneath his armpits, locking his arms down over them. "But to forestall a pointless argument, I actually meant to draw your attention to Teresa's words. She mentioned a Mrs R."

I ground to a halt as the front door opened.

CHAPTER 2

Evyn's mother Rose tapped her foot. "Get in, now." She pointed at the floor in front of her. She looked like an older version of my soul companion, with the same small stature, turned-up nose and pale lips. Evyn wore her hair long and flowing, whereas Rose preferred hers short, and right now it was put up into a messy tail, strands escaping to frizz in the damp air.

Saluting, I smiled at her. "Lady Rose, good evening. I was not aware you were back from Oberrot."

She hissed at me, jabbing her finger at the doormat as an unspoken order for me to brush the dirt off my boots. "I want this door shut before I shout at you. The neighbours have enough to gossip about as it is."

She was genuinely angry, high spots of red in her cheeks and hands shoved into her jeans pockets. My stomach clenched.

All three of us together filled the small corridor, standing at the bottom of the stairs to the single upper floor. I had to turn my head slightly so as not to scrape my scalp against the ceiling.

She shut the door and I braced myself as she poked me in the chest. "You do not get to wander around Earth as you please, using it as your own personal travel mancer or mage to get to places in Oberrot faster. Someone could ask questions. It's too dangerous."

"Lady Rose, we take all precautions. We have trained to use public transport and are inconspicuous en route." I fought the urge to stare over her head, as if I were getting a dressing down from King Gough or Captain Barlay. Gough and Rose were soul companions, sharing the same spirit, and right now it felt as though my king was displeased with me. "Gough has authorised our movements here, ma'am, and he takes the safety of this realm extremely seriously, as do we."

Rose's lips twisted. "Well, it seems that he has failed to inform me of that. If you're lying to me—"

"Lady Rose, I would never lie to you." I looked from one of her angry eyes to the other, willing her to see my sincerity, as if she were some kind of Reader mage and could discern my thoughts. "I promised Gough I would obey you as I would him, and that includes my complete honesty and integrity."

She swept her hair back from her forehead, letting out a low breath. "I'll take it up with Gough, then." She glanced up at me. "I take it you didn't cause any incidents, as Teresa dropped you off and not the police."

"No, ma'am." I ventured to smile again, relieved when her lips turned upwards at the edges.

Then her mouth trembled. "I'm sorry, but you're supposed to... to be here. With Evyn, helping her."

Heart wrenching, I marshalled my thoughts. "I am trying to help, Lady Rose," I said quietly. "Whatever is happening to her is either something Liara the ex-Sinjorina Majestica of Dinahe is doing or... the bruswurt." I dug my fingernails into my palms, relishing the pain, my tendons creaking.

If I have caused this... if it is irreversible...

Aubin put his hand on my shoulder. "I'll figure out if it's the bruswurt through a mechanism I'm not aware of yet, though I have been pursuing that line of inquiry. I suspect it's more likely to be

Liara and her magic. Tuniel thinks she might be using Rushia magic to increase her reach, and she's looking into that for us."

I nodded to him. "Meanwhile, Lady Rose, we can confirm that Liara isn't in Skien."

"I never thought she was." Aubin pulled off one boot, balancing on one leg to do so and staying rock steady.

I maintained my ready pose, frowning at Aubin. He was essentially a civilian still, but surely he should realise that he couldn't see to basic needs during a report.

"Liara is a mage. She shouldn't go anywhere near Skien," Rose said, forehead wrinkling as she frowned. "Don't they kill people who use magic?"

"Chase them out of the country, mostly." Aubin put his boots neatly to one side of the corridor. "It might make sense for Liara to hide there, as she could enchant a great deal of rugged men for her to use, but there is another large upswell of anti-magical sentiment there. I will inform the king, who will through official channels inform Tuniel." Aubin kept his face expressionless; I knew he and Tuniel rarely spoke, despite being soul companions themselves. It would perhaps be faster for Gough to tell her.

Not that Gough stopped Aubin and Tuniel from speaking with one another, or Tuniel and myself for that matter. We were trusted now to act in the best interests of our country and indeed the realm, and I was determined that we would uphold a high standard and be worthy of that unprecedented level of faith in us as Rangers.

I put my hands behind my back, taking a reporting stance. "There are rumbles of unrest in Skien that I will report to the king immediately on my return. It was the right choice to send Rangers to investigate it, but we will need assistance if we are to go again."

Rose nodded once, flapping her hand. "Talk to Gough about that. And you can stop being in soldier mode and get your wet coats and shoes off. I'll hang them up in the wet room to dry."

I didn't know that a wet room was where things could be dried.

Nodding once, I pulled off my jacket, scraping my boots off by the heels and digging my toes into the warm carpet.

"How did you get around, as two men?" She looked between us. "Don't you need a matriarch, a woman with you at all times, or you're considered dangerous in Skien?"

I shifted my weight. "Ah. Well." Now I lifted my gaze over her head, unable to meet her eyes. "We innovated around the issue, ma'am."

Aubin took a step closer to me, and a green glow fired to life at my right shoulder, blazing through my red shirt. The soul jewel that Tuniel had given me, embedded in my silvrine armour Amare, responded to her bond with Aubin. She used it to be able to remotely recall Amare when I deployed it, and I liked having her soul jewel so close, a clear sign of her wishing to enter a marriage contract.

What I didn't like was the fact that it responded to Aubin too.

Rose's face flushed. "Ah." She bit her lower lip. "So, you used that as proof you were the third segment of Skienien society. I get it."

I raised my gaze even higher, studying the ceiling. "Yes, ma'am. Subterfuge was necessary in this instance." A pair of men could get around fine, as long as they remained only a pair.

"I gather Special Forces do it a lot when they are sent to investigate." Rose's eyes glittered, her smile widening. "Gough always says, whatever goes on in Skien, stays in Skien. I get it now." She put a hand over her mouth.

She lowered it to turn to Aubin. "Alright. I've heard from him, so now it's your turn. I'm very surprised that you can open portals between the realms of Earth and Oberrot. How did you learn to do that, and why?"

Aubin folded his arms slowly. "I put the procedure together over many occasions watching Evyn. It does not require magic or special attributes; it's a skill. I used it only when in need in Dinahe, and sparingly ever since."

Rose sucked in breath between her teeth. "And are you going to tell anyone? Your soul companion, perhaps?"

"He has sworn to secrecy, ma'am," I asserted. Surely that would have been the first thing Gough made him swear after the first tenet, which was to obey the royal family without question.

Aubin's gaze flicked to me. "I am not going to put Lady Evyn's home at risk, Lady Rose."

"Hm." Rose drummed her fingers on her crossed forearms. "Thorrn, can I have a word with you? Cup of tea?"

I nodded. She spun on her heel toward the kitchen, and I followed, raising my eyebrows at Aubin.

He inclined his head, turning for the stairs. "I will check on Lady Evyn."

Rose turned around sharply, and I drew to a halt lest she collide with me. "Ah, she's in the lounge, sleeping. She's fine for right now. Why don't you have a bath?"

Aubin nodded once. "Very well. Thank you, Lady Rose." He padded up the stairs. He could successfully sneak back to find Evyn or listen in to whatever Rose wanted to bend my ear about, but he knew I'd give him a full report anyway.

Rose sighed, beckoning me through into the dining room, but that was the opposite door to the lounge, where my soul companion rested. Reaching back, I touched the closed door. Perhaps she was lying on the sofa, cheek pressed to the armrest. She was just beyond the threshold, within my reach.

Turning away, I obediently followed Lady Rose.

She pulled two mugs off their hooks, loading each with a small fragrant bag. As I took a stance near to their small well-worn table, the kettle began to shudder with the force of the heat trapped inside it, and Rose lifted it. "You take two sugars, don't you?"

"Saccrine? Yes."

She sniffed. "Sugar, here." She handed me a cup, coils of steam curling from its mouth. Wrapping her hands around her mug, she perched on the edge of the table and nodded approvingly as I took a scalding sip. "You're looking well. Healthier. I'm glad of that."

"Thank you, Lady Rose." I eased my shoulders. The scars across my back troubled me only occasionally, usually if I held myself too tense or if I pushed harder than usual in training. "Aubin says I need to stop eating, or my armour won't be able to wrap around me." I patted my stomach.

She looked down at the mug cradled between her hands. "I know Gough still feels terrible about it. I've been trying to find a moment to talk to you, but what with Evyn..." Straightening up, she put her mug down with a firm clack. "I wanted to apologise. I thought Gough had it all under control, and I know your world handles things differently. I should have realised he was being too reactive and not thinking things through. And then, I... I'd never seen something like that, you realise, I didn't recognise how hurt you were. I wasn't fair to you while you were recovering, I was too focused on Evyn, but you're a part of her as well, now, and I should have done something."

I turned that over in my mind. "I don't know that there was anything you could have done, Lady Rose. Gough had to apply the law. Ten lashes..." I swallowed hard. "A mere ten lashes should have been a firm lesson, but not life threatening." I held up a hand as her mouth opened. "One moment to finish my thoughts, Lady Rose. We both learnt from the experience." I gestured down at my Ranger reds. "We had to go through the really difficult times to tease out what was important to all of us, to end up here, in a perfect middle to suit everyone."

She sniffed. "Can't make omelettes without breaking eggs, you mean?"

"I... perhaps?"

Laughing, she wiped her eyes. My chest lifted at the sound. "I'll make you an omelette tomorrow morning. You'll like it," she said.

"Oh, is it like pizza?" My stomach growled hopefully.

"You're going to turn into a pizza at this rate." She bit her lip, tears glittered in the corners of her eyes.

I passed her a pocket square; she noisily blew her nose into it.

She sighed. "I suppose that's one way of looking at it, but I can tell Evyn sees me differently now because of it." She screwed the cloth into her hands. "Mm. I won't say that there are lines one can't cross, because of course, they can be overstepped. But everything is different after that. You're different after that."

That settled in my stomach, spreading a sour sadness that felt like nostalgia. "Yes. There isn't usually a way back, but there is always a way forward."

Rose nibbled her little finger. "I'm glad you're feeling better, but I'm even more worried about Evyn. She sleeps all the time, tossing and turning with bad dreams that she won't tell me about. Do you know about those?"

Setting my mug down, I laid my hands flat on the table. "No, she hasn't mentioned dreams to me." Could it be another dream mage or mancer? Tuniel assured me she kept tabs on them all.

"The sudden sleep issues are getting worse."

I clutched the edge of the table. "Lady Rose, I'm... doing everything I can think of to do." I closed my eyes briefly, self-hatred welling up to tighten my jaw. Anger flared against whatever unknown entity was harming Evyn, but there was nothing I could attack, no lead, nowhere to go, nothing I could do. Impotent rage boiled in my stomach. I tamped it down through long practice, breathing deeply and settling myself. *Not yet.* But as soon as we had a single clue, I would not rest until it was defeated.

Rose tutted. "There's one thing you're not doing."

My eyes flew open. "What is it? Do you have a lead on Liara?"

She gazed at me sadly. "No, Thorrn. It's something else." She tapped the mug in her hands, rings clinking against the rim. "I know you found each other late in life, and it takes a good deal of time for the bond between each half of our spirits to settle. That usually happens in late childhood and adolescence, so you develop and mature together after that." She put her mug down. "But you are technically adults, learning independence. You're both trying to stand alone because that's all each of you has ever known." She frowned at me. "Are you feeling much from her at all?"

The question was a thrust at my vulnerable spot. I forced myself to examine it fairly and answer it with candour. "No, Lady Rose."

She tightened her tail of hair. "I had a feeling Evyn would be good at shielding."

My stomach fell. The act of shielding or pulling one's emotions away from the bond was a good tool to keep unavoidable pain away from one's soul companion to prevent them being affected by it. I was poor at it; I had waited so long for Evyn that I couldn't draw away from her. But was Evyn shielding me, protecting me from her pain, or was she pulling away from our bond?

I lowered my head. "I want to strengthen our bond, Lady Rose."

She nodded. "Good. It'll take work to get Evyn to open up. She's had a rough few months. You both have." She patted my hand. "How are you, after everything that has happened to you?"

My chest tightened. Did she mean the lashing, or did she mean Evyn's illness, potentially caused by me? Or what Liara did to me and to us? Bile surged into my throat whenever I thought of that woman.

I took a sip of the bitter tea. "I'm hale and well, Lady Rose."

She sighed. "That's part of what I mean, how you two think you have to stand independently all the time. You are allowed to not be perfect to everyone all the time, you know. You can let your guard down here for a bit, if that's what you need."

I imagined telling the king that I had sole protection over his soul companion and instead fell fast asleep. "I try not to let my guard down, Lady Rose. There's no watch posted here." Even if she did this regularly, it still sat poorly with me.

She rolled her eyes. "Well, it's not me you need to open up to anyway. But..." She swirled her tea in her mug, the exact same way that Evyn did. It pierced my heart. "Bolster her with your bond. When I'm sick, I can feel Gough pushing over some kind of energy, and vice versa, I reach out to him when he's feeling under the weather."

I rubbed the centre of my chest. Where was the soul bond located? I tried to feel something else, something different to me.

Except Evyn was a part of me, we were complements to one another, two halves of a spirit to make one whole. When Evyn Found me, it felt like her light touch on my shoulder, not anything inside me. Evyn was the Finder in our pair, able to point to the cardinal direction in which I happened to be in relation to her. I was the Caller, only able to cause a compulsion in Evyn to come toward me. Where did she feel that? I had never asked.

Rose watched me. "We need to do something, anything. Magic won't work on her, and we can't let medimages or mancers too close in case they feel the power in her blood. The doctors here have no idea, and we can't tell them about other worlds." She bit her bottom lip to stop it from trembling. "I can't do anything. Do you know how powerless I feel?"

I feel the same way. Grasping after traces of Liara had not yielded results, and Evyn was getting worse over time, not better as we had hoped. "I will fix this, Lady Rose. I will defeat whatever is draining her, and I will stop Liara." *Unless her condition is the after-effect of me poisoning her.* My stomach lurched. Hopefully this was reversible, and she could be restored to health.

Rose tucked a stray strand of hair behind her ear. "Well. Let me know if I can be of any use apart from being a worrywart."

I saluted. "Yes, Lady Rose."

She pursed her lips. "Onto the second thing I wanted to discuss." She lowered her voice. "Gough said that *he*—" she pointed toward the kitchen door "—tried to murder the man who poisoned Evyn."

I nodded once. Aubin had stabbed Gavain, enraged by how he had brought Evyn into our dispute. No, that was not quite right, because he had remained outwardly calm in order to approach Gavain. Aubin's rage wasn't like mine, where I could be suddenly pushed into mindless violence; his anger was severe and sharp as a scalpel, excising risk with no leniency or second chances.

Rose huffed. "Wonderful." She shook her head. "I know you live in a world where that's the done thing, but let's just say I am not comfortable."

Judging from Evyn's reaction to Aubin stabbing Gavain, it wasn't hard to extrapolate that other Earthians would look askance at it as well. I straightened up. "Ranger Tabreksson is no danger to you. He is trusted to the highest levels by the king, and by me," I said firmly. "I put my life into his hands, and I know he would give his life for Evyn's in a heartbeat."

She levelled a look at me. "This isn't exactly new for me. Gough might not hold the sword himself, but he sends out others to do... things." She swallowed hard. "I suppose you've killed people too."

I nodded. Rogue mages and mancers for the most part.

She bit her lip. "How do you cope with it? Do you get support?"

Support. I had thought I had the support of my unit, the corps, until I was disabused of that notion. "I... am reconciled to it. My father's guiding hand helped me get strong enough to manage the burden that I must carry now. The king I serve is just and has reasons for his orders, but the actions are mine." I would have to take my deeds with me as I walked.

"Do you talk to Evyn about this? That could be a way to open up."

My immediate reaction was one of horror. "I would not wish to weigh Evyn down with it." She had enough to think about for herself and her situation, let alone shouldering my problems as well. "I am strong enough to bear this."

"She won't say that she understands, but she can empathise. She's good at that." Rose sipped at her tea, watching me carefully. "Talking to people isn't pushing your burdens onto them. It can help you frame what you're going through and put it into perspective for yourself."

"Thank you, Lady Rose." I needed to encourage Evyn to open herself to me. Asking her for help again and again would feel like I was trying to drain her, to take from her. That couldn't be replenishing. How could it be?

Rose drained her mug and set it aside. I took that as a suggestion that the conversation was drawing to a close and did the same, the hot liquid warming my chest and cutting through the cold wet shirt clinging to me.

She took my mug. "Let's go face the music. No doubt Aubin will guess we were talking about him."

"No doubt," I said. Aubin was very perceptive.

She swilled water around the mugs. "If you trust him, then I'll try to get on with him," she said grandly.

"My thanks, Lady Rose. He will not disappoint you." Aubin was an amazing asset to any team. My right wrist twinged. Well, he would be, once he learnt how to work in one.

I padded after Rose. Aubin sat on the stairs outside the lounge door, long fingers tapping his kneecaps. He looked warmer at least, pink cheeked and dressed in the Earthian clothes we stashed here, but his red-rimmed eyes held a smouldering intensity. He was dragged beyond the bounds of exhaustion, held together by force of will.

Aubin got to his feet. "Apologies, Lady Rose, but I did not know where in the house it would be acceptable to wait. I can return to Oberrot tonight; I need to give Thorrn his sword, and I think he would wish me to assess Lady Evyn before I depart."

Rose shook her head. "You are welcome to stay. Look, I know you two will talk, so yes, I did ask him about you." She tugged at her hair. "I know you're a good apothecarist, and it's nice to have someone onside who understands the thing she was given so we can work together."

Aubin stayed standing. "Thank you, Lady Rose. I will do everything I can."

She nodded eagerly. "What ideas do you have?"

Aubin's hands roved over his jacket. When he was an apothecary, his jerkin carried an assortment of vials and tinctures. That wasn't the case anymore; his Ranger jacket, like mine, had metal sewn into the leather over vulnerable locations, so adding glass underneath would make it bulky and liable to break. "I will think about what else I can try to give her."

"Alright. As long as you're sure it won't hurt her or make it worse."

He clasped his hands together, swaying on his feet slightly. "I will need to run tests. More tests. Samples, growing cultures. It will take time. It's harder without a medimage or mancer."

"Oh." Rose's shoulders slumped.

He looked down. "I'm merely a stopgap, the option for those who cannot afford magic or who cannot rely on them." He rubbed his chin. "There's something else. I won't be telling anyone how to make portals or about Earth, but you should know I haven't sworn to anything yet."

I stilled. *I lied to Lady Rose. Wonderful.*

Aubin shrugged. "Thorrn made a reasonable but erroneous assumption." He looked up at me. "You know I wouldn't do anything to put Lady Evyn at risk. I can swear to that, over and over again." He rubbed his forearm. He had yet to get any tattoos, representing the code that we swore etched into our bodies.

Rose put her hands on her hips. "Mm. I'll go check everything is ship-shape upstairs. Thorrn, stay near to Evyn tonight. Your being close seems to help her."

I nodded, my thoughts too unformed and full to respond. Just beyond the door was my soul companion. Our reunion should be a joyous occasion, but Aubin and I did not return covered in glory, and victory remained out of our ken and our reach.

Lifting my hand to knock on the door, I stilled. *Damn and blast, why am I afraid?* It was only Evyn. I summoned my will, smartly rapping my knuckles on the wood. When there was no response, I opened the door.

Their lounge doubled as some kind of library, shelves of books lining one wall. A small table held the moving picture box, mercifully blank but with a malevolent red eye awaiting the signal to activate. Opposite that was the couch, tattered and rather deflated.

Slumped against the armrest was Evyn, just as I had imagined her. An old bruise burnished her cheekbone, highlighted against her pale skin.

I sat slowly next to her. The cushions dipped, but she did not stir, her breathing regular and deep. My throat hurt as if a garrotte tightened around it.

Aubin hesitated before lowering himself to one knee in front of her. Taking her hands in his, he felt along her wrist. He frowned. "Her heartbeat is slower than I'd expect. It's not normal for her either."

"What does that mean?"

"Nothing yet by itself. It's a data point." He clutched her hand between his.

Our two sennights in Skien had not been fruitful and seemed to have a steep cost. "I will not leave Evyn for so long again," I vowed. "Not if she's passing out more and more frequently."

"That's if your physical presence helps at all, and we've no evidence yet to suggest whether it does." Aubin placed her hands back in her lap. "She needs a cure."

"Of course. But we don't even know what is causing this." My hand hovered over her shoulder. Was it Liara? In which case, I should hunt her down and destroy her. Or was it the bruswurt? In which case... was there anything to be done?

Evyn frowned in her sleep. "Stop. Stop!"

"Evyn?" I leant down, touching her arm.

CHAPTER 3

I FELT A SENSATION AS IF EVYN TOUCHED MY SHOULDER DESPITE HER NOT moving; Evyn Finding me. Her eyes snapped open, real fear crossing them. She shoved herself away from me. "Aubin!"

"I'm here," he said, still on his knees in front of the sofa.

She launched herself forward and he caught her, arms wrapping round her, pressing her to his chest. Trembling, she peered back over her shoulder at me.

Perhaps my heartbreak radiated from my rigid stance, for she immediately frowned, jaw dropping open. "Thorrn." She still clung to Aubin, however, sliding down slightly to rest in his lap.

He glanced at me, then away, ears flaring pink. His arms tightened around her. "What ails you?"

"Bad dreams." She shuddered.

His face darkened. "There isn't a dream mage or mancer who can affect you here."

I found my voice. "I'll help you with bad dreams." Soul companions who were close could share dreams. "Let me in there, I'll deal with them."

"I…" Aubin closed his eyes. "I will help too, if we can facilitate a link."

That would cost him much. The dream mage MasterMage Waker had nearly driven him to insanity with her false memories implanted through the dreamlands. That he would even offer at all moved me to tears.

Evyn's hands roved up to his shoulders, fingers squeezing. "Thank you. But I'll be alright." She glanced at me. "You okay?"

"Mm." I wiped my eyes.

With a quick nod to Aubin, Evyn stood. His hands slid down her arms as she rose, his head level with her solar plexus, and she stared down into his eyes. It was in my own solar plexus that I felt a surge of her feeling, the bubble of love that bloomed as she gazed down at him and his adoring face.

His gaze shuttered, and he looked away. "It's late. I suspect I'm bedding down here for the night. You two should get to your room, Lady Evyn."

"Night?" Her hand flew to her mouth, and she glared out the window. "Oh, rats."

"Where?" I paced up to the window, peering out into the darkness. All I could see clearly were our reflections overlaid over the orange-tinted night outside; Aubin still kneeling, hands limp in his lap, and Evyn now watching me.

She had a strange expression on her face, one that pierced my heart with a needle of agony. Trepidation, unease, maybe even the smallest edge of fear.

Why is she afraid of me?

I rubbed my face hard, over the prickles of a burgeoning beard, and then lowered my fists. I deliberately relaxed my hands as I turned to face them again, drawing a smile across my face even as my heart hurt.

Evyn ran up to me and hugged me around the waist. I threw my arms around her and nearly bent in half over her, locking my legs to stop them from collapsing with relief.

"Hello," she whispered.

"Well met." My voice wavered. I coughed, clearing my throat of a clasp of emotion. "I'll defeat those bad dreams." Lowering myself, I pressed her to my chest. "Let me in, I swear I will keep them from you and obliterate them." I would fight all through the night if need be, I was eager to, a roar in my blood unanswered by anything but combat, the precursor to rage. I checked it back through long practice, calling the calm of battle down to settle my limbs and heart.

Her nose wrinkled at me. "You're a bit wiffy."

"Yes. My apologies." With effort, I released her. "I'll take a bath immediately."

"I'll come hang out in the bedroom while you're doing that, if that's okay."

"Of course." I offered her my arm.

She chuckled, a distinct and welcome improvement to her disquiet earlier. "Do you have everything you need, Aubin?" she asked him.

Having spent a sennight with him camping along cramped rocky crags, I suspected he would be able to sleep directly on the floor if the couch proved too inhospitable. There was even a blanket draping off the edge; a luxury.

He smiled briefly. "Yes, thank you."

Flushing slightly, she blurted, "Well, goodnight, Aubin."

"Sleep well." He raised a hand as if to wave us off.

Evyn walked slowly but steadily up the stairs in front of me, hanging on to the rail, then pointed at the bathroom. "See you in two shakes."

I hesitated behind her. "I'll walk you to your rooms."

She sighed but did not protest, leading me into her bedroom. This was a small abode and Evyn's corner of it smallest yet, filled with a bed and then surrounded on two sides by imposing bookshelves. A chest of drawers contained the remainder of her worldly goods, including her wardrobe, stuffed and bursting at the seams. It made the soldier in me shudder. By contrast, each of her books shone with care, aligned with their fellows and categorised to her exact specifications.

She sat on the edge of her bed, bouncing slightly. "Right. Off you pop."

She seems hale, and she is in the right place if she is struck down. Still, I rushed through refreshing myself, passing hastily under the tamed waterfall Evyn called a shower rather than having a full bath. I scrubbed my hair, feeling the trip scour off me.

I re-entered the bedroom, clad in my Earthian clothes of a soft T-shirt and the thicker cloth trousers they called jeans.

Evyn looked up at me above the book she leafed through. "How was Manchester?"

"Big. Loud. We saw nothing much. One of the trains was late, and it had a knock-on effect on the journey plan you made for us."

"Yeah, that happens, sorry."

Evyn apologised for too much. "You do not command the trains, Evyn."

"Yes, I know. I guess it's a 'sorry that happened to you.' I take it you managed to cope?"

"I suppose you could call it that. We survived, anyway."

Smiling, I sat next to her to dry my feet, making the bed tip her toward me. She giggled, shoulder knocking mine, and then yawned. I reached my arms up to catch her, but she righted herself. "Last time you stopped for a visit, I felt a heck of a lot better. I think that's something to do with the soul bond."

I let my hands fall back into my lap. "Rose has made the same connection. Let's work on the soul bond." What activity could we do first to accomplish this? I hit on it immediately and steeled myself. "Let's visit the library."

She beamed. "Aw, that's sweet, but I won't subject you to that. I'm always happy to read you whatever needs reading, just sling it over."

Heartened that she knew me so well and at her instinct to protect me, I tucked her closer to me. Now how to get her to open up more to the bond, so I could push whatever I needed to toward her?

Rose had recommended talking, but all the subjects she posed were about me. How was Evyn to relax if I concerned her only with my problems?

Biting her lip, Evyn leant against my arm. "Thorrn, how are you doing? Really? I'm thinking particularly about what Liara did to you."

I looked away, hoping Evyn could not feel the surge of negative emotions that swamped me whenever I thought of that woman. Liara had used Evyn's blood to weave an enchantment around me, meaning to force me as she did it. Fortunately, Tuniel had shaken off Liara's magical shackles before she could get too far, but still I woke up shuddering at terrible nightmares.

"Working through it," I admitted quietly. *There.* I had opened up.

Evyn clucked her tongue. "I will absolutely clothesline that witch in the face."

Rolling my right shoulder, I weighed up the options. "If she's behind what is making you tired, something stronger will be warranted." Though I did not relish ever seeing her face, I would confront Liara to liberate Evyn from her clutches. My mouth filled with the taste of iron at the thought, but deep within myself I knew Liara needed to be ended swiftly and decisively.

Evyn pointed at my right shoulder, where the silvrine metal of Amare was embedded in the cap of my shoulder muscle, a small flat light green stone held in the centre. "I was thinking about this. It's Tuniel's soul jewel, but that means it's Aubin's too. The jewel lights up in response to their soul bond, right? It glows when Tuniel is near, so will it shine when Aubin is around?"

I groaned. "Yes. It will."

"Huh?" She cocked her head at my distress, puzzling it out. "Oh. Did people see you and Aubin and that light and assume you two are—"

"I am not talking about this right now. Give it a few turns." I put my head in my hands, mortified beyond words.

She cackled. "Right. But can I ask you something?"

My heart warmed. "Always."

"How does Aubin feel about you carrying her—their—soul jewel around like that?"

I frowned. "I haven't asked. Soul jewels are a recent fad, Evyn. Tuniel says the jewel industry promoted them as integral to the initiation of a marriage contract. When she was a stone mage, she did very well from this fashion."

"But they vibrate at the frequency of the bond, right?"

"Resonate, yes. Aubin can explain it better than I." I looked between the jewel and her. "You know they don't affect the bond at all, yes?"

"That we know of. But that one stores the magic to make the armour move, and it acts as a communication stone too, right? It's multifaceted. Literally." She grinned at her own joke.

"Only because Tuniel has tuned it to do so. Aubin can't sense or feel anything about this stone, Evyn, if that's what you are wondering. When we buy one of our own, you'll see."

"Oh, you just go out and buy them? From a shop? I thought you had to find them." She deflated a little.

I tapped the jewel on my shoulder. It sent a brief twinge through my arm, that bothersome pain. I shoved it back. "Tuniel tells me a great deal of jewels tune themselves to her and Aubin's bond, so she has a surfeit of them, but ordinarily a pair would need to source one, yes."

"Cool." She yawned. "I'm not sure I'm up for hitting the shops."

"Mm." I watched her closely. Her skin was sallow, her movements languid.

She shook herself. "Shall we do that first when we get back to the city?"

"Whatever is best for you."

She scowled. "I'm not an invalid just yet, Shardsson. I know you had all sorts of things you wanted to do with your soul companion when you finally met her. It would be fun to get around to some of them. And I want to join you for morning training."

"You... Are you sure?" Soul pairs joined the training together to show their commitment. It was all I had ever wanted, but now it was tempered with unease.

She tipped her head back, probably feeling my misgivings. "Should I, you mean? No one's told me not to, and I'm not going to let this weakness stand in the way of living my life, Thorrn. Soul companions of swordsmen and women are expected to be at morning training, so that's what I'm going to do." She stuck her tongue out at me.

Warmth flooded my chest. "My thanks."

"I know it's important to you." She jiggled my hand. "Talking about important to you, have you thought any more about wedding plans?"

"Yes. Something small and discreet. Tuniel wants nothing entered into the official marriage records, so I thought about asking Ellesmere to conduct it." As the MasterMage of Oberrot, Tuniel could not be seen in a relationship with anybody, and thus she pretended we were barely acquainted so I would not become the target of an ambitious mage or mancer vying for Tuniel's position. So far, that proved to be an exciting dimension to the relationship, but part of me wondered how long we could maintain such a facade.

"That's sweet; Elly would love that. So, how do weddings go over there?"

"They are simple contracts. Some words are said in front of witnesses, you enter your names in the records—we're skipping that bit—and then you get blisteringly drunk. You also have people to vouch for who you are and that you're of sound mind, and they negotiate the dowries and details. Tuniel will ask Aubin, so whoever I choose has to match wits with him."

"Good luck finding someone to do that." Evyn snorted.

I grinned down at her. "I was hoping you would do it."

"Me?"

"Yes. You." I laughed at the stunned expression on her face. "You're more than a match for him. Besides, if it gets too heated, you could expose your chest to him."

"Oh, Thorrn." Cheeks flushing, she bit her lip. "Mum has been on at me about Gerlay. She thinks she's being subtle and whatnot, but I can read her like a book. It's obvious that Gough thinks it a grand idea, because it cements relations with Dinahe while clearing the pitch for Rogan to have a shot at the Rushia princess." She sighed. "I'm not sure how we're going to put this one to bed."

"So, uh, are you going to put Gerlay in your bed?"

"Thorrn!" She blushed an even brighter pink. "I'd probably fall asleep on the poor man. No, seriously, I really don't know what to do. Look, I went from being no one on Earth to having princes propose to me." Picking at the bottom of her shirt, she murmured, "And Aubin hasn't said that he's interested anymore."

"He is."

She frowned at me. "Then he needs to say so."

I knew Aubin had been not exactly avoiding Evyn, but he was being careful around her. His feelings for her were complicated, and further muddled by Evyn's accidental promising.

"I'm going to take a manoeuvre from Teresa and speak my mind," I announced.

Evyn raised an eyebrow at me.

"He loves you."

Both eyebrows went up. "Is this his way of telling me? Through you?"

I shook my head. "You need only look at the evidence plain before you. Take the actions within a mere turn of the glass; he caught you as you leapt into his arms and held you as if he would never let you go. He even offered to go back to the dreamlands for you!"

"Yes?" Her cheeks flushed a welcome shade of pink. "I suppose you could read into that, if you wanted."

"Do you truly think that?" I eyed her.

She curled her fingers into the coverlet. "Thorrn, I need him to tell me in plain English and on his own initiative, not with you breathing down his neck or forcing him to say something at sword point."

"I would never do that," I scoffed.

Her lips twitched with mirth. "Uh-huh." She drew her knees up to her chest. "I misread things all the time. I want something I can take to the bank. Uh, something concrete." She smacked her forehead gently. "Darned idioms. What I'm trying to say is, I need something I can rely on."

I took her hand in mine. "You can rely on me," I said quietly. "I am telling you, plainly and clearly and reliably; he loves you."

Evyn sighed against my shoulder. "So did my dad. He still couldn't stay."

A gyre of complex feelings welled up within me, a mixture of hers and mine. Soul companions could sense each other's feelings if they were close, so it pleased me that I could feel her surface emotions, at least. I tried to sort through them. Sadness, yes, and a deep terrible loss at the waste I could understand from the bitter sting of losing my own father. Underneath that was a steady torrent of anger. My stomach flipped; such anger was a slow-burn of rage, insidious and poisonous, its acid eating away at everything and everyone.

"Aubin will not leave you," I said, each word ringing true to me as if I spoke a new tenet. I squeezed her hand. "You'll see. Neither he nor I will ever fail you."

The bond flexed, growing taut as if she pulled back, but then she sighed. Warmth prickled my skin as she leant into me and the connection between us renewed.

"Good!" I grinned at her. Strengthening the bond was easier than I thought it would be. "Now take some of my strength. You need it!"

She recoiled, my skin growing cool as she backed away. "Thorrn, I'm not going to take stuff from you. I don't want you to get what I have, just in case it's contagious somehow."

My heart squeezed painfully. "Even if it were, I'd gladly risk it. If I could, I would take it from you. Please, Evyn."

"No." She extricated her hand from mine. "I can cope with this. The nightmares are likely triggered by my anxiety, and I deal with that every day. And, hey, my nervousness is warranted on Oberrot, because mages and mancers could actually kill me."

My chest hurt. "I can protect you. I—"

"Thorrn, there are some things you can't fix or change. You have to accept and adapt."

The sadness in her eyes made me drop my gaze. I put my head in my hands. "I am adapting. I'm trying as hard as I can."

In the silence, fear unspooled to wind around me until she touched my shoulder. I looked up; even sitting down, I came level with her chin.

She smiled at me, a smile that lifted my heart. "Please don't think this is about you, but I know you will, because you think everything is about you." She winked, eyes glassy with tears. "I don't want you affected."

Of course I am affected. Something was eating away at her, draining her, her body was resisting something, or Liara was pulling energy from her as she had in Dinahe. As an enchantress, she had a limited reach, ten paces at most, so it had to be some kind of dark Rushia magic wrapped around her heart.

I need Tuniel to find out what magic it could be. I need Aubin to confirm whether it's the bruswurt. I need to find Liara.

I need to save Evyn. I refused to even contemplate losing her. The pain of soullessness would be too much, compounded on the long turns alone. To meet her, a brief spark to give my life meaning, and then have that ripped away...

I trembled like Rose's kettle, shivering as raw strength slammed into my muscles, rage boiling into my limbs. The edges of my vision went dark, my vision tunnelling to Evyn's face.

There is nothing to vent my anger against, no foe to defend her from! Long practice aided me in shoving those feelings down, forcing myself to open my fingers wide rather than ball them into fists. They trembled. I focused on them. *Rage is my weapon. I wield it, it doesn't wield me. I am in control, always.*

"Thorrn." Evyn's cool voice called me.

I held my voice measured and slow. "I have it under command."

She stood by the door, one hand on the doorknob, her eyes wide. "I tried staying calm myself. I'm sorry, it didn't quite work."

My jaw hurt; I released it with an effort. "I keep myself in check. I deal with it often enough." I pressed forward in my belief, for to think otherwise would invite disaster. The heartbeat I wondered if I was in control would be the heartbeat I lost control. *I am in control. I am.*

Evyn bit her lip, then slowly sat back down next to me. The scrunched covers in between us formed a small wall, one I could have reached over. Pressing my hands together, I ignored the pain in my heart.

We needed a change of subject. Clearing my throat, I asked, "How is the library?"

"Stuffy as always." She grinned at my grimace. "Just kidding, I know you're not a fan of the place, but I am loving it. Oh! While you were away, the head researcher has given me an honorary status for now." The smile slipped from her face.

"Isn't that cause for celebration?"

"Yes, absolutely, but..." Her voice lowered. "I was looking for texts on alternative histories, right? Meeting a version of myself and having tea with her on a regular basis has convinced me that there's a multiverse thing going on, which is so interesting in and of itself. It's like... for every decision we make, that causes a universe to split, where we make a different choice in a different world."

Alternative histories were not unheard of, but they were rare. Our alts, versions of us that had made different choices or had a different life experience, visited frequently, or at least they had. The alternative version of me, who let us call him Shoulders, was withdrawn and hesitant, but he would still fight to protect the people he loved. Arian, the alternative version of the woman I was promised to, seemed similar to Tunnel if a little colder; the Assassin was confident and self-assured in a way that our Aubin wasn't. Evie, though, seemed to be a complete copy of my Evyn, and I struggled to spot any differences that weren't superficial.

Evyn braided her hair down one side of her body, fingers moving quickly. "Only, well, the reading I've done here suggests there's more, and there's people who can actually change the course of history inside a timeline without causing another multiverse." Tugging her plait, she glanced up at me. "Following so far?"

"I suppose." Aubin would be better able to talk intelligibly about this. I could only nod as if I understood, too tired and wrung out to do ought else. "What do our alts say about it?"

She let out a breath. "That's the thing. We haven't seen the alts since before your... you know." Her cheeks paled, and I nodded. Before my lashing. "I asked her a lot of questions, a barrage, really, but she kept saying she was looking for answers herself. Anyway, she did a lot of research while she was here. I remember looking over once or twice, I didn't want to read over her shoulder because that's rude, but I could see the texts and I earmarked them for exploration later, but..."

"But?"

Evyn twisted her fingers in her shirt. "They're gone, Thorn. The texts have been misfiled or mislaid or... taken." Reaching over, she squeezed my hand. I was so relieved I nearly missed her words as the rest came out in a rush. "I don't want to accuse her of stealing or whatever. Maybe she put them back in a different place? If you misfile something, it's lost to the system. It's... easily done." Her gaze dropped to the floor.

"You suspect that the alternative version of you misfiled books on purpose?"

She winced, then nodded once. "I'm not sure she would be able to, it's akin to physical pain for me, and as weird as sheathing your sword hilt first would be to you, but... Thorrn, what if there was something she doesn't want us to know about the multiverse? The alternative histories, sorry."

I turned that over in my mind. The thought of the alternative versions of us—the alts—meaning harm did not sit right with me. I wouldn't be able to hurt Evyn, any version of Evyn; they were all my soul companion across all the worlds no matter where she had come from or what history she had. Shoulders felt the same way, I knew. At our core, we were not so different.

"I think she must have misfiled them," I said firmly.

Evyn nodded, tucking her hair behind her ear. "If you're sure."

Talk stuttered to a halt after that, with tiredness pulling at me and Evyn distracted. Mired in the worry for her that I hid behind a smile, I watched her carefully until she sat on the bed and then slumped backwards, asleep.

I made sure she was comfortable, then slid down to sit upright against the bed, keeping a watch throughout the night.

CHAPTER 4

I AWOKE FROM MY LIGHT SLEEP AT DAWN, AS WAS MY HABIT, EVEN THOUGH the pale sun in the sky could hardly be hailed as such. Evyn woke with me, and after her cup of tea elected to join me for morning training. She had bought me some special shoes for running in this world, but they were made of flimsy fabric that immediately let in a puddle of water when I stepped in it. My leather boots would have kept that out, but I refrained from voicing my discomfort to Evyn.

The park was partially obscured by a fine mist that made the air itself damp. It had a crisp edge to it that was pleasing to breathe in, rather than the odd bitumen taste that sometimes found its way into my mouth on this world.

As I began the push-ups, Evyn squatted next to me. "What are in these marriage contracts, so I can make sure I'm prepared?"

I caught my breath and spoke in shorter sentences. "I don't actually know. It will set out what properties or rights each brings to the marriage. From memory, Tuniel has the right to a widow's pension in the event of my death, and to be buried in our family plot. But Tuniel's family owns North Hold, so that lineage might take precedence and insist that I am buried with them." I shook my head. "Evyn, please make sure I stay in Oberrot City."

"Jeez, all this talk about burial at a wedding?"

I counted to a score, then lifted a hand. The smooth motions up and down helped me to organise my thoughts. "That's not all there is to a wedding, of course. There are the vows, the promises that we make to one another. I... I would want to compose one or two." I buried my head in my arm, wiping the sweat from it.

Evyn clapped her hands. "Aw! That's adorable!"

I mock growled at her, my face hotter from that than the exertion. "I would ask that you make sure the words all work correctly together. If you are not too busy, of course."

"I'll make time for this! What are you going to say?"

What could I say? "I'm not sure what words to use, Evyn. She's beautiful and smarter than most of the kingdom, but those are qualities anyone can see. The things that she makes are exquisite, if one is fortunate enough to afford one or have it gifted to them." I glanced again at my right shoulder, which ached only a little. "This armour is honestly incredible."

"You're going to wax lyrical about... armour?" Evyn sounded wholly disappointed.

I frowned. "I knew I wouldn't have the right words."

"No, no, keep going. Talk it out. What is it you love about her?"

I switched my arms, thinking. "She's thoughtful and practical, Evyn. She designed this armour for me, back when we were trying to attack the Palais with no hope of survival, and she keeps thinking of things to add to it. She thinks ahead and presents me with something that I never would have thought of, something practical. Rather than showering me with meals or compliments, she made me something that will keep me alive. Now, sometimes her forethought is to her detriment, such as always being worried about someone finding out about us and attacking me, but even that is for my benefit, and she leaves little clues in everything she does. Calling the armour what she did, for example."

Evyn tapped her lips. "Thoughtfulness is good. What else?"

This was deeply personal. I writhed a little inside, trying to put it into words. "She saw me at my worst, at a time when everything had been stripped away from me; you, my contingent, my sword, my friends. Aubin and you were taken. I... broke, Evyn." Even voicing it was hard; my throat closed. I had shattered at Tuniel's feet and, instead of turning away or leaving me there while she dealt with Liara, she reached with me to pick up the pieces and helped me put them into new places.

Evyn's light touch on my shoulder shocked me. I shoved the feelings back down. "I... yes. Of course, that is all behind us now, and I shouldn't bring that up. It's not good enough."

"I think it's enough," Evyn said softly.

I resumed my push-ups, determined to move the conversation to safer ground. "Back to the contract. It is important that both parties know what to expect at all times. Aubin has hinted that this contract will need to be kept secret, obviously, so there will be clauses about conduct and behaviour as well."

"Well, you're not going to run off and tell anyone, are you?"

I halted in my push-ups. "No, of course not. Perhaps... Well. We will see what the first draft looks like." I levered myself up. "Or rather, you will." I winced. "I hope this does not push back your own research on the multiverse."

"Yes, don't worry, I can multitask, and I did say I would read anything you wanted me to." She pushed her hair back from her face. Small pieces had escaped to curl and twist along her face and her snub nose was red from the cold. "Is it cheating if I ask Aubin to explain anything I don't understand?"

"I should think clarification questions are standard, and he will make allowances for you being from... here." I waved to the green grass of the park.

"Yeah. So we'll probably have to work in our dining room." She hunkered lower into her overcoat, the redness from her nose spreading across her cheeks.

A warm bubble shimmered in my solar plexus. "Mm, yes. Heads close, arguing over the meaning of any one particular word."

"Oi," she muttered, but she grinned widely.

"Perhaps it will get heated. There will be a phrase you interpret one way, and he another."

"We'll just refer to the precedents." She waved her hand.

"You'll grab his arm to lead him to one of those very important whatnots. He won't try to escape, because he won't want to. He'll let himself be led, and when you turn around, all flustered and flushed, he will gaze at you, and—"

"Ah!" Throwing her hands up to cover her eyes, Evyn giggled. "You should write a book or something. *Passion in the Precedents*." She shook her head at me, pulling her plait into her hands to worry at it. "I was thinking... He's Tuniel's soul companion, the other half of her spirit. So... are we supposed to pair off? Is it, I don't know, fated or something?"

I chuckled, pleased at her shy smile. "Well, true romantic tales have soul companions pairing off with one another. My parents did, for example. Your mother did not." I was not above admitting that the legends of true love being exemplified in your soul companion pairing off with your inamorata's soul companion delighted me. My heart swelled.

"Of course," Evyn said quietly, but her face was downcast. "I said before we loved him as a friend, and... well, maybe something more." She clapped her hands to warm them. "Whether he will accept that is another matter."

I stopped my squats. "What does that mean?"

She shook her head. "You might get frustrated with me, but... I'm thinking that even if Aubin does love me, he might still leave me. On the other hand, I'm pretty sure that Gerlay doesn't love me, not yet anyway, but... he would never leave at least, right?"

From what I understood of Prince Gerlay, he was dependable, a good soldier and followed his principles. "He's... reliable," I allowed.

"Right." Evyn shoved her hands deep into her pockets. The bubble from earlier had been dowsed, replaced by a feeling as grey as the mist surrounding us.

FINISHING OFF THE EXERCISES, we made our way home and to welcome scents of cooking from the kitchen. Rose furnished us with something called a bacon roll, then said as she wiped the surfaces, "Are we all pretty much ready to go whenever?"

"Yes, just let me grab the book I was reading." Evyn put the sandwich down on her plate. I must have eyed it hopefully, because she moved it onto mine. "There you go."

"My thanks. Is Ranger Tabreksson awake yet?" I asked.

"Yes." Aubin walked in from the wet room. He held his red leathers draped over one arm, and the T-shirt revealed more of his biceps than I saw outside of the baths. "These are dry, at least."

I grunted. They weren't fresh, and I disliked putting dirty clothes against clean skin.

Evyn stumbled back from the kitchen table. "I'll... I won't be a mo'. Bye!"

Rose frowned after her. I swallowed the mouthful of food and focused on the table; anything but Evyn's sudden embarrassment. *I can feel that as clear as orders shouted in the field.*

Aubin sat next to me. "Is there anything I can make for myself, Lady Rose?"

"I'll get you a bacon buttie. We need to use up all the food in the house, I'm not sure when we'll be back." Rose passed around mugs of restorative.

I added several little cubes of saccrine to mine and a heaping splash of milk. Aubin drank his neat, eyelids lowered. He still looked tired.

"Did you get any sleep?" I asked.

"Some, mainly thinking about the tests I could run. I will need tissue samples and to set up a space in my quarters; it'll be too risky to have something like that in our kitchen."

I snorted. "Who is going to raid a Ranger's kitchen?"

"I mean you and your elbows. You'd knock over test tubes in a heartbeat."

Rose placed a sandwich in front of Aubin, and some kind of folded yellow sponge for me. "Omelette. Dig in, I needed to use up the eggs."

"My thanks, Lady Rose."

When Evyn came down, she held the book clutched to her chest as if it were a shield. "Morning, Aubin." She sat on the edge of the seat next to me.

"Lady Evyn." Aubin inclined his head, glancing her way and then back down to his repast, barely touched.

I sighed in the middle of them both.

Once breakfast had been cleared away, Aubin and I changed back into our Ranger leathers. We had no luggage, and neither Evyn nor Rose took much to Oberrot; Evyn had what she called her "contraband" hidden in our shared room, a brace of books covered on either side by paper with a strange, flimsy veneer to it. Any person from our world finding these would recognise it as a book, but could remark on the other-worldly covering. For everyday items, they used and wore what could be provided by the castle. As the soul companion to the king, Rose could requisition a great deal, and my salary afforded Evyn a small stipend that she hardly ever used, except for more books.

I escorted Evyn, and Aubin took Lady Rose along to the secluded canal and the ping-through spot they used. "Ready?" Rose asked. "I'm still going to ask you to close your eyes, although it seems pointless now."

I nodded, but Aubin said, "A moment, please." He pulled into place a Rushia headscarf, his disguise while in Oberrot City or any place where Special Forces might recognise him. Special Forces believed him dead for attacking Gavain; while King Gough could not break the laws of the land, he had bent them for me and for Aubin in this instance, seeing the truth behind why Aubin had acted as he had.

I stepped across when Evyn tugged me forward. Crossing the worlds itself did not feel like much of anything, except the sudden change in the air from cold and misty to heat that hung like a blanket.

"Right. All the way up." Rose tugged her hair out of its bindings, smiling and sighing happily. "I'll drop you off on the way, Evyn."

"Yup." Evyn said with a dour tone, likely already imagining all the stairs up to our apartment and then the further ones her mother would take up to the royal apartments.

"We will need to report in as soon as," I informed Rose, looking down at my rather filthy leathers. "Hopefully after a quick change of uniform."

We made our way up to the apartment that Evyn, Aubin and I shared. Opening the door to a short corridor, Aubin and I pulled our boots off and hung up our coats as Evyn liked, while the ladies moved through into the kitchen. Despite having had a cup of tea less than a quarter turn of the glass ago, another was required, and Evyn started the pan we used as her kettle off to boil.

"I like what you've done to the place," Rose said, nodding at the bookshelves alongside the balcony which were filling up, and the very lifelike painting of Evyn's grandmother over our dining table.

"I'll refresh the flowers," Aubin said. "These are past gone." He fiddled about with the rather dry arrangement on the table. "I'll also inform the post station we have returned and restart our mail."

"Good. I'll change." I went upstairs where Evyn and I had moved in our belongings, both old and new, to our shared room. Mostly old on Evyn's side, as Evyn found comfort in the memories they held, but new on mine, as the army did not savour storing a soldier's possessions; as soon as I outgrew something, it went to someone else. My side looked sparse as a result, with only a single personal effect on display. Set regulation centre of my cabinet was a miniature of my father, and tucked behind that were the last few hasty words he had scrawled to me. Meanwhile, Evyn's side overflowed with a collection of books cascading to the floor, each one well-thumbed and curling along the edges.

I hunted for fresh clothes. Pressed sets of uniforms filled my side of the wardrobe, along with some off-duty togs and custom-made weapons. Evyn's contained few pieces, many of them in dark colours.

My gaze ran over the spines of her books. She talked to me about them as if they were old friends rather than possessions. It didn't smell like a library in here, thank the gods. I didn't mind her snuggling up with a book so long as she didn't get musty and dusty herself. Instead, I could pick out something that reminded me of Aubin; a crisp, lyneal kind of smell that Evyn called spearmint.

When I returned, Aubin was tidying the living room, shelving books on the wall-to-ceiling bookshelf at a height comfortable for Evyn. "You have mail," he informed me, waving a hand to the dining room table.

Evyn sat in front of a handspan's worth of letters. She opened them in a dazed way, slowly and methodically.

"Goodness." I noted the post mark. "All from Dinahe."

"And all for Evyn, from a certain prince." Rose said with delight, thumbing through the ones Evyn had already opened. "You boys go on ahead to report in, I'll just finish up here."

Evyn did not look up. Truth be told, it pleased me that her mother was with her, in case she was struck ill, but an uncomfortable churn in her chest radiated up the bond, intensifying as Aubin moved toward the table.

Ah.

Aubin's gaze stared through the letters, eyes washed pale in the bright light of the room. "We should see the king, should we not?" he asked, every word precise.

"Yes. Let's go."

We headed out and up, that feeling fading the further we went, either because I was not close enough to sense it, or because Evyn was uncomfortable having Aubin see the largesse of letters from the devoted Dinahen prince. Aubin did not speak, the soft padding of his boots the only sign that he was with me.

CHAPTER 5

Marching smartly up to the royal apartments, I flashed my identification tattoos to the Special Forces guard posted there. They squinted at the new one inscribed over the scar of my demotion from sergeant. The style did not match anything else on the rest of my tattoos as they had changed the codes since I facilitated a scare on security, but it represented a new beginning. A second chance.

"And yours?" One of the men on duty, Ferrol, asked Aubin, looking him up and down.

Aubin did not move.

"He doesn't speak a lot of Oberrotian, but I vouch for him," I said firmly. "He's the other Ranger."

"Is he?" Ferrol looked to the other man with him. "What's the protocol for this?"

"I'm glad you asked that, swordsman." The captain of Special Forces, Barlay, came up behind us. He was a head shorter than me, with muddy brown hair and an analytical gaze. The guard and I snapped into an attention stance; Aubin stayed with his arms folded.

Barlay nodded to Ferrol. "Let us in under my authorisation, but he'll get the tattoos done imminently." He fixed Aubin with a searching stare. Barlay knew about Aubin and his secret identity, and was helping to develop the Rangers from my father's idea into reality.

Aubin fell in a step behind me. I walked next to Barlay to the king's study, where the king had his head down over papers. Even with his black hair peppered with silver, the king was still a sturdy and formidable figure, shoulders wide from the turns of practice he took with his huge double-handed sword in his youth. The bits of paper he pushed around would percolate into the network of functionaries, changing their direction or speed or destination, and from there sweep wider across the city, Oberrot and indeed the world. He exuded power beyond mere physical limits, wielding a confidence and conviction honed by turns of experience.

I saluted King Gough as he looked up from his desk.

The king nodded, sitting back in his seat with a tired but warm smile. "Rangers Shardsson and Asmar, welcome back. Barlay has been keeping me apprised of your activities."

"Would you… like a report, sir?" I hedged.

He stoppered his stele. "You don't sound too happy to be giving one."

"Didn't exactly knock this one out of the park, as Evyn would say."

"Well." His fingers tapped the desk. "Let's talk about that later. First things first." He nodded to Barlay.

Barlay clicked his heels. "Rangers, the king and I have been discussing the relative rank of this new unit. I need more senior leadership that I currently have. With Sergeant Philo on review, I am under a great deal of pressure. We have determined that in an engagement, should the commander be removed, the nearest available Ranger will lead the deployment until such time as a Second or higher re-enters the field and completes a handover."

Warmth flooded my limbs, but then cold settled in my chest. "Sir, just so I'm clear. You're saying that in the event of a commander being indisposed or killed, a Ranger would lead the Regulars?"

"And Special Forces." Captain Barlay studied my face.

Lead the corps that hates me? "I cannot see that working, sir. There would be a general revolt."

Barlay grunted. "Then they had better get used to it. I'll provide you both with coaching, and you'll train with Special Forces when you are in the city."

Coaching from Barlay himself would catapult my knowledge into the realms of strategy and management. My father had valued his tactical mind and dedication; learning from him was a high honour, and it would almost be like being his Second. Part of me had longed for this, but now it felt like a burden rather than a blessing. Perhaps it was meant to; command of the lives of others was not to be taken lightly.

One word thrust out at me the hardest. "Both, sir?" I glanced at Aubin.

Gough nodded. "Both of our Rangers need to have the experience and skills to undertake this duty, should it fall to them."

I sucked in air between my teeth. Having spent the last few sennights in Aubin's back pocket, I could guess the words he would choose to respond.

"I cannot be hearing you correctly." Aubin rubbed his ears underneath the headscarf. "Say that again."

Gough smoothed another bit of paper and setting that to its destination, ignoring Aubin's theatrics. "You will both have our full support and training."

"Training. You mean—"

"Yes. It's time we introduced you to the corps as the new Ranger."

Aubin rocked back on his heel. "You would like to see me immediately eviscerated? Wonderful. Good to know the price of failure."

I waved Aubin to silence, turning to Gough. "Sir, we've kept Aubin and Special Forces apart for good reason. They believe him dead."

"I'm not suggesting he drop the alias, Ranger," Gough said gently.

"But it's a risk, sir."

Barlay tilted his head in acknowledgement. "A risk with a low probability of actualising. However, Captain Shard believed in preparing for the worst."

My heart bruised on the edges at the mention of my father, the lack of him cutting at me.

A sad smile crossed Barlay's face. "And the worst case, Ranger Shardsson, is that the corps looks to an ill-prepared Ranger for leadership."

I could see the truth in that. It would be a disaster.

Aubin shifted his weight. "Do I have a choice?"

They exchanged looks. "Could we have levels of Ranger?" Gough hazarded.

Barlay's lips twisted. "I'd prefer a to have a uniform capability." He turned to Aubin. "I want you to at least try it, while I look out for a potential sergeant. Yes, I accept that bringing you closer to Special Forces has a risk at the outset, which will lessen over time, as long as you keep vigilant."

"That's practically a core tenet for him, sir," I chipped in.

"Ah, yes, you will be developing your code. I look forward to hearing what you've got so far." Barlay put his hands behind his back.

My stomach fell.

Aubin looked away. "Nothing substantial to report, beyond the basics."

Barlay frowned.

"And Ranger manoeuvres." Gough rubbed his hands. "You'll have developed something by now, I trust?"

My cheeks heated. "Nothing... Nothing ready to be worked on by the committee, sir." My gaze fell to the floor. Why hadn't I thought of that? Working together with Aubin had to be more formalised than concocting things as we conducted ourselves.

Gough leant forward. "Thorrn, are you hale and well?" He frowned. "Is it too much?"

His words resonated inside me, a chime that rankled me. "It is a lot, sir, but I will not fail you. I will equip the Rangers so that we are equal to the challenge." I could not, would not, fail at this. With Aubin by my side, I had overcome a great deal of adversity. We would need to work to embed the partnership and continually better ourselves. The Rangers was an extra element of the corps, and of course it had to work alongside it and in partnership with the different castle forces. Moreover, I would make sure it lived up to my father's vision for it.

I saluted. "We will be worthy of the trust you've placed in us." I would just have to make sure Aubin held up his end.

He breathed low and long, deep breaths that signalled his disquiet. At least he wasn't voicing his ire at this moment, but I'd have to talk him through it later.

I kept my right fist pressed over my heart. "Sir, if that's squared away for now, I'd like to know if there has been progress in locating Liara."

Gough stood. "There has been significant progress, Ranger. Reports indicate she is indeed in Rush, as suspected. We all heard that she called out to Princess Sabatha when she was cornered, and our MasterMage has been investigating the black mist that responded to Liara and believes that it originates from Rush."

I nodded, hand tense around the hilt of my father's sword.

Gough faced us. "But the situation is extremely delicate. Oberrot does not have regular contact with Rush, and the insular country keeps to itself. There is another complication; King Gordonne of Dinahe has sent to me, saying firmly that the Dinahens have juris-diction over Liara. They want her captured alive to stand trial."

"I... am not sure that's wise, sir. That is not what I would advise to be possible at all. Ending her would be my preferred method, making sure that Liara could never use her powers over love to her own ends again."

Love. Liara twisted and tortured the sentiment, causing people to obey her every command through enchanting them to adore her. I made a conscious effort to relax my fist and breathe deeply to push back the thrum of rage whenever I thought about her and what she had done to us, to me, Evyn, Aubin and Tuniel, and nearly killing the king and his son Prince Rogan.

Gough's lips thinned. "I agree with you, but Gordonne has a point. In addition, the rather precipitous promising of Evyn to Gerlay has, shall we say, shifted relations internationally in an interesting way, moving things along substantially."

Aubin went very still beside me, almost not breathing.

My stomach fell. "I, uh, sir, that's not, well…" Evyn had found herself accidentally promised to Prince Gerlay, brother to King Gordonne of Dinahe, when she accepted what she thought was an innocuous gift of a rock. Instead, it had been Gerlay's soul jewel, a statement of intention to marry.

Gough held up a hand. "Rose has explained. I would not want anyone to marry against their will, but…" He looked up at Aubin's headscarf. "The truth is, this promising helps Oberrot a great deal."

Locking his hands behind his back, Gough moved to his window overlooking the King's Basin. "Of the five major nations, not including Hanasta, there are four unmarried princes and princesses. Prince Rogan of Oberrot and Prince Gerlay of Dinahe, of course, and princesses Sabatha of Rush and Catherine of Daron. Skien is conspicuously absent; their clan chiefs change with the moons, so I have other strategies in mind for them.

"Now, if I put the needs of our country first as I should, then I would seek to unite Rogan with Sabatha. It would finally open Rush to Oberrotian influence, and we already have family ties with Daron, so there is no advantage to Catherine."

Gough turned to face me, lips down-turned. "When I heard that Evyn and Gerlay were promised, I was quite pleased. It meant that Gerlay is no longer competing for Sabatha." He ran a hand through his hair.

"So you want this courtship to come to fruition," Aubin said slowly.

Gough flushed, for the first time I had ever seen in my life. "I also understand the decision rests between Evyn and Gerlay." Gough's brows beetled. "I haven't seen Evyn as much lately. It's an effort for her to come up to the royal apartments, and I have been remiss in visiting her. I know Rose has been worried sick. How does she fare?"

I flexed my hands, willing them to stillness. "She's getting worse. She passes out regularly. She's fallen too, sir, and she could have been walking around when it happened." Thinking of my soul companion crashing to the ground and smacking her head made me breathless. "It might happen in the baths. Or on the stairs." My heart thudded in my chest. "Sir. We need to go to Rush and find Liara. The Rangers are near certain that Liara is behind what's happening to Evyn."

Gough nodded curtly. "Then that is where I shall deploy you next, now that we have a firm lead. Find Liara and do what you must do to bring her to justice. Gordonne is sending Gerlay to assist, so you have a short period of time before he arrives. In the meantime, use whatever resources you require, and I seem to recall she did better with you close. See if improving your bond with her aids her. I hate to think of her unwell; who else will take me to task for various slights and oversights?"

I smiled in response to Gough's fond look. "Thank you, sir."

Barlay inclined his head. "There is one more thing. A report from Dinahe indicates that Gomoresson's health is improving. Once Gavain is well enough to travel, we will return him here to stand trial."

A current of rage swept through me. *How dare he live!* I held it at bay by my fingertips. In the next breath, warm relief that he hadn't died washed over me. *My oldest friend is still within my grasp, if only I knew how to reach him.*

"Thank you for the update, sir," was all I could say to that.

Aubin's headscarfed head turned away from me. *Fine, if that's how he wants to be.* I had enough to occupy me within myself, let alone him.

Barlay nodded to us both. "That's all, Ranger. For now, dismissed, and report in for morning training, where we will introduce Asmar as the new Ranger."

My stomach took a turn and curdled. "Yes, sir." Aubin was going to hate this.

As we made my way back along the corridor, I turned over the potential mission in my mind. Investigating in the isolated country of Rush would be difficult, exactly the sort of challenge I welcomed, but the circumstances were different. Beyond furthering the goals of the king and the good of the country of Oberrot, I needed to save Evyn, and to do that, Aubin and I had to start succeeding. We could not fail at this one.

Aubin gave a dark chuckle. "They cannot be serious," he said in Rushia.

"About Evyn and Gerlay?"

He looked away. "No, that I understand. I mean about me leading Special Forces."

I rubbed the callus on my right hand from a lifetime of wielding a sword. "They are serious, and I am too." I took in Aubin's stance. He held himself alert, yes, on the balls of his feet, but he did not move or think like a soldier. He was essentially a civilian, but while it had taken turns of training to bring me along, Aubin was smart. He could catch up if we tried, and tried hard. "Barlay will train us. We just need to apply ourselves fully to the task."

Aubin held up his hands. "Thorrn, I cannot order brutes around."

"They're not brutes, they are men and women. You would do well to remember that."

His voice grated. "The same contingent who tried to murder you and would kill me in a heartbeat. I would be *thrilled* to hold their lives in my hands."

"Don't talk like that. I swore to serve, alongside the contingent where I must. This is a serious undertaking, with responsibility for lives."

Aubin let out a sharp breath, as if I'd punched the air out of him. "Do not talk to me about responsibility for lives. How many times have you sat by someone's bedside knowing too much and yet not enough to help?" He broke off. "Thorrn, I am not a soldier. I'm definitely not a leader." He gestured down at himself. "I'm not sure what I am."

"You're a Ranger." I ran my hand through my hair, running through the vast sets of tasks we needed to accomplish. "Ask Evyn to help you get the manoeuvre lists out. You'll have to start with the basics, and you can do that alongside working on your code. And then let's come up with manoeuvres together."

Aubin's pace grew heavier. "That's another thing. Manoeuvres? Thorrn, we are only two men with very different fighting styles."

"Yes, but we work well together."

"Ah, yes, our stirring run of successes is testament to that." Shaking out his hands, he turned away. "I will bid you good day. It sounds like I should be locked in the library for the foreseeable."

I frowned. Usually a sentiment like that from Aubin or Evyn was expressed with pleasure, but Aubin made it sound like the cells. "Are you sure?" I asked.

"I'd better not stay up too late. Barlay wants me killed at dawn, after all."

I bit back a swearword. *Patience.* "You'll wear the headscarf, obviously."

Aubin tugged at the black fabric. "Because this will stay perfectly in place during combat training."

Now I was really hard pressed to respond without shouting. "The Rushia manage it, Aubin."

"Yes, they do, but I'm not Rushia, am I? I'm not a soldier, I'm not even an apothecary anymore."

His words rang in the corridor, louder than he had likely meant them to be.

What was he talking about? "Aubin? What is this about?"

His steps slowed. "Have you heard anyone talking about me?" he asked quietly.

"What do you mean, castle gossip? No, not a whisper about you," I reassured him. Rumours about me, however, abounded. My older sister Sylvia would diplomatically sift through these to give me the gist, but it was clear that Special Forces thought it fitting that I had been separated from them at last, and that it raised the quality of the cohort as a result. Aubin and Evyn did not need to hear about that.

Aubin's steps became quieter, barely perceptible as he walked along the edge of the long corridor carpet. Hundreds of thousands had crossed these floors, wearing deep treads in the red weave, some areas rubbed threadbare from the passage of these people.

He went on quietly. "No one has even noticed I've gone. I had to have Tuniel handle the sale of the shop, and not one of my neighbours called in." He shrank closer to me, in the shade of my shadow. "I know I... I haven't exactly encouraged interaction, but... I expected some small ripple at my apparent death. If I had really died, no one would have cared."

What was this? "Aubin, I care. Evyn cares."

He shook his head. "I don't need reminding of that, I know that."

I rolled my eyes. "Then what do you need?" I blurted.

He wrapped his arms around his chest. "Time. And low expectations. I am a civilian, Thorrn. I'm not going to match you on the field."

"No, because I'm the best. However, you'll catch up fast." He had to, and he could, if he wanted to.

When we re-entered the apartment, Aubin went to his rooms. Evyn was upstairs in ours, still leafing through the correspondence with a thoughtful look.

She glanced up at me with a brief smile. "Hi." The smile faded quicker than I would want.

"Well met. Are all of these truly from Prince Gerlay?"

"Most of them." Evyn pulled out another sheet. "You've made a really big impression, by the way. Every other sentence is about you."

I grinned. "I usually do."

"Yeah. I'd better watch out, you might steal this man from me too," she teased.

I shook my head at her.

She laughed, the sound welcome, but all too soon it trickled away. Pulling another letter free, she held it up to me. "I got another one from Dinahe."

I know that handwriting. Mastering my hands, I took it, sinking onto my bed with it held in both hands. Gavain had written to Evyn.

"I haven't opened it yet. I don't think I'm quite ready," she said.

"Nor am I," I whispered back. What words had he meant for her to have? What could words do to assuage what he had done to her, using her as a pawn in the fight against me?

"Let's leave this for today," she said. When she did not take it from me, I placed it on her dresser drawers. Gavain would have to wait.

CHAPTER 6

The next day, I was up well before dawn and rapping at Aubin's door.

"Yes?" he croaked.

"Morning training. I want to be there before Special Forces. Get out here."

The door swung open and Aubin stepped out, pulling his head-scarf tight. "Then go."

"You too. It makes for a good first impression." I shoved my feet into my boots.

I couldn't see his face, of course, except for his amber eyes. They were scrunched underneath his down-turned brows. "Thorrn, what if they recognise me?"

I waved my hand. "You had the right of it last night, you kind of faded into the background for Special Forces. But that's a good thing now!" I added when his shoulders tensed.

"Yes. Of course. All for the best." With quick movements, his boots were secured, the Battlemistress blades lying in their holsters along his forearms.

I tapped the protruding hilt above his right wrist. "Ah. Put these back. They are very noteworthy, and both Philo and Aleric saw you wielding them."

Aubin straightened up. "What am I supposed to do, then, use a sword?"

I shrugged a shoulder. "Can you?"

"No, Thorrn, no, I can't." He shoved his hand under his armpits. "Thorrn, I can't do this."

"You can. Barlay will support us. It will be fine, they'll listen to him." I reassured myself as well as him. Imagining standing shoulder-to-shoulder with men who had tried their level best to kill me, who boiled with hatred whenever they saw me, made my stomach turn. "You're not the only one finding this difficult. Dig deep and get to it."

"What if this doesn't work, Thorrn?" he pressed.

Why did I have to have the answers? I had promised the king and Barlay that we wouldn't fail, but I couldn't hold both of us up. "Stop thinking of the worst case first. Get down there, and you'll see, it won't be that bad." Grabbing his shoulder, I steered him to the door.

He set his stance. "I would reserve full right to gloat if this goes wrong, except my head will be on a pike over the city walls."

"What are you two fighting about?" Evyn yawned.

My heart lifted on seeing her, but it was tempered with anger. "We're late—"

A rush of fierce trepidation flooded over me. Gripping my father's sword, I slid into a guard stance, but just as quickly as it came over me, it was gone.

"I... Sorry." Evyn pressed herself against the corridor walls. Predawn light laid shades of grey in the corridor, and I could see the whites of her eyes.

"Are you hale and well, Evyn?" I reached out to her.

She licked her lips. "My anxiety is through the roof right now. Give me a minute."

My heart beat wildly in my chest, increasing when my hand moved close to touching her. I called calm into myself, into her, pushing it toward where I imagined the soul bond to be beside my heart.

She rubbed her chest, her eyes softening, and an accompanying lightness spread across my stomach. I sighed with relief. *If I had felt that so strongly, what must it have been like for her?*

She tucked her hair behind her ear and pulled on her boots. "Shall we away?"

"You're coming?" I smiled.

Aubin murmured, "Are you sure that's wise?"

Evyn's gaze dropped to the floor.

Scowling at Aubin for shoving her down, I took her hand. "Thank you, Evyn. I'm glad someone wants to support me in my endeavours."

I could almost hear Aubin grinding his teeth. "Fine. I will accompany you, Lady Evyn."

"Thanks, but I'm fine." Her voice was small.

"We're all fine. Let's get on." I nearly pushed them out of the door.

As we rattled down the circular staircase, I kept one ear out for Evyn, who walked with a hand along the stone wall. She became breathless within a few floors; even walking down the stairs was strenuous for her.

She stopped at the level of the baths. "Go on ahead, guys, I'll catch up."

Nerves tangled my stomach, a mixture of hers and mine. Special Forces would comment on tardiness, and if the Rangers were going to be a respected part of the army, it had to be respectable. Still, Evyn's health came first. "If you're sure?"

"I'll stay with you," Aubin said, holding out his arm.

Evyn did not take it. "I don't want you to be late. I'll be alright. I managed for weeks when you weren't here; I can manage a few steps."

I did a quick head turn, seeing no one. "Sennights, Evyn. Be careful."

Her cheeks flushed. "Of course, I'm sorry."

If anyone were to overhear Evyn using strange terms, they could have questions. They might not know immediately she was from the fabled lost realm of Earth and that it was real, but they would deduce something was different about her and start prying.

Fortunately or not, one of Evyn's traits was to fade into the background. I wanted my soul companion to stand tall and seize her power, find her voice and champion the causes she held close to her heart, but her unobtrusiveness served to protect her from prying mages and mancers.

Seeing grey light picking out the castle walls from the window, I took another few steps down. "I have to go. I cannot be late."

Evyn nodded, but Aubin did not follow me.

Shaking my head, I left them to it. Having him with her was a comfort should she fall ill, but I could not help but wonder whether he was indulging his recalcitrance.

I would not. I would face the challenge head on and defeat it.

Arriving out of breath, I smoothed my dark-red Ranger uniform just as Barlay came out of the barracks.

"Well met, Ranger," he greeted me.

Saluting, I settled into watching as all the contingents and their soul companions formed up in a loose group in the training field. The area seemed big when doing punishment laps, but really it took up only a quarter of the castle courtyard, the fence running parallel along the edge of the wall separating the castle from the city.

The day was already hot, and the leather jacket of the Rangers was thicker than I was used to. With Barlay's permission, I pulled it off, rolling down the sleeves of my dark-red shirt instead. I kept an eye on the castle door, smiling when a small shape made her way out and to the gate, another shape just after her.

When they got to the fence, Aubin vaulted it and walked between the ranks of Special Forces. They parted, turning to stare at him. His covered head stayed upright and he moved differently, a more rolling gait that put me in mind of someone who worked on the bigger boats patrolling the Serene Sea between Oberrot and Rush.

"This is Ranger Asmar," Barlay announced. "Recently relocated here from Rush. His Oberrotian is poor, so don't be surprised if he doesn't understand you to start. He's eager to learn, though."

Nothing about Aubin was eager about this. His jacket was buttoned all the way up to his rapidly working throat. He slowed his pace as he pulled up beside me, turning and locking his fingers behind his back.

"Well met," I murmured to him in Rushia.

His head twitched away from me. It struck me that walking through ranks of men and women who would kill you on sight, while being unarmed, had to be incredibly daunting, and yet he stood straight-backed.

I leant toward him. "Get through the run and the initial training, and it will be..." I trailed off as light from my right shoulder brightened, shining under my shirt to illuminate the side of our faces.

Special Forces looked at each other, then looked at me, frowning. Considering.

Damn and blast. *Not again.*

I locked my legs in place, otherwise I would have stepped smartly away from Aubin. His soul bond with Tuniel resonated with her jewel on my shoulder, causing it to burn as brightly as the sun. As my face, probably, heat radiating over my cheeks.

"He will be joining for general training from now on," Barlay went on. Even he stared at the jewel as it shone its proclamation to everyone in the dawning light.

Don't say it, I silently begged the captain.

"He and Shardsson are partners—Ranger partners." Barlay cleared his throat. "They work together."

Grey and Merrit smirked, but Aleric looked confused.

"Begin the warm-ups," Barlay barked, and Special Forces turned and broke into a run.

I glanced over at Evyn. She had her shoulders hunched, arms

wrapped around her chest and eyes closed tight as Special Forces and their soul companions thundered around her to get to the field.

Aubin moved toward her, and I grabbed his arm. "Running. Now," I said in Rushia.

"I'm going to run with Evyn." He wrenched his arm out of my hand.

"What reason would a Ranger have for worrying over my soul companion?" I asked quietly.

Aubin jerked his chin toward her. "She's the only reason I'm here, risking my life for this stupid charade. I don't care what it looks like to anyone else."

"You will if it unmasks you."

Aubin flicked his hand at me. "You do what you think you need to do, and I will do what I need to do."

Shaking my head, I took off after Special Forces.

We completed three laps before Evyn had finished one. I tried to ignore the comments the others made about her pace, but I was sensitive to them. I had thought that way myself, once, but couldn't they see her enduring nature?

We moved on to other warm-up exercises while Evyn stood near Barlay, panting, her hands on her thighs. Aubin hovered close, openly watching her. I signalled to him to join in; he stayed apart but started doing balance work. Evyn copied him, slowly moving into her own exercises.

When we partnered off, I went for Evyn, but Aubin intercepted me. "I don't want to practise with anyone who might realise the truth," he hissed in Rushia.

"You partner with Evyn for the warm-ups, then."

"This is a terrible idea. She's straining herself because she thinks this is important to you, and I'm far too close to people who know how I fight." His eyes darted in the shadows of the headscarf.

"We have to let her live her life, Au—Asmar." I harangued myself for my near misstep.

His clenched fist wavered, then he stalked over to Evyn.

Turning away from them, I settled to wait with bile churning in my stomach for whoever would be left without a partner and forced to spar with me, but behind me stood Aleric.

My former friend and confidant had a new line to his jaw, holding his mouth tight. "Thorrn, you're back. How was the mission?"

None of your concern. "The exercise we have to do is the overhand swing. Do you want to go first, or shall I?" I kept my feelings from my face with great effort.

Aleric's brows drooped. "You go first."

I raised the practice sword and swung down hard.

He caught the blade and spun it away. "Well?" he asked.

"Your turn." I raised my sword in a guard.

He thwacked his blade down, but off to one side, nowhere near my head, so I didn't move. His eyes cut away. "Thorrn, I want to talk."

"We're not here to talk. We're here to train." I hammered my blade toward him.

He parried it, pushing the wood away. "Later, then. In the mess hall." His jaw ticked.

"I'm not ready to talk about it, Al. Focus on your work. The move is an overhead swing."

Aleric's arms dropped, leaving his guard wide open.

I lowered my sword in response. "It's morning training. I know it's the warm-ups, but we have orders to train."

"Thorrn, please. We need to talk." He threw his practice blade down.

"Pick that up," I barked.

His hands hung limp at his sides. "Please, I need to talk. Just listen."

"I don't want to listen," I said, realising that sounded petty. But he *had* tried to kill me.

He ran his hands through his hair, the gesture familiar and sending a pang through me. "What happened? Where did it go so wrong? You, me and Gav all together and I thought nothing would ever drive us apart, but then you found your soul companion and then Torgund appeared, and it all went badly from there. I thought that was terrible, but then you came back and restored Gough... and then that went wrong."

"Things happen and create change," I said. "It's how we react to them that matters." My lips twisted. Aleric had reacted poorly to them as far as I was concerned, taking Gavain's side despite being tortured by him... although Gavain *had* rescued him.

"You've changed, Thorrn." Aleric swallowed hard. "And not for the better."

That spiked deep inside me. "So have you. You thought nothing would drive us apart? How about when you abandoned our friendship, turning on me just like the others?"

Aleric's eyes were pinched. "You turned on me first. And Gavain might have undertaken his orders to torture me, but he also disobeyed them to save my life." His chest heaved. "Do you even care that he could have died?"

I flinched. Aubin's attack against Gavain was still unsettled in my mind. *He deserved it*, one part of me raged with righteous anger. *He is lost, and he can be found*, another part whispered. The part that remembered my friends as they were.

Aleric dropped his head. "We couldn't break the tenets, Thorrn, Torgund would have killed us. He did kill many of us, and he was about to kill me because of something you said."

I let that sink into me, the unjust accusation sticking in my throat. "That was an accident, but you must have been scared." I raised my chin. "I was scared."

He looked up at my admission, eyes shining.

I gripped the hilt of my practice weapon, feeling the heavy weight of my father's sword on my hip. "But I never let that stop me from following what I knew to be the right and only thing to do."

Aleric's face darkened. He swiped a hand across his eyes. "So you'd prefer it if I were dead, then? A noble sacrifice, with an ignoble death." He thrust his fist toward the gates of the city. "There was a line, Thorrn, a line of men and women in red waiting to be executed. Hanged, then cut down immediately for the next to be strung up. It took all day."

He fell to his knees, head in his hands, and the men and women around us slowed and stopped, staring at him. "You don't understand." His voice came out choked.

My heart pounded, imagining what it must have been like. The captain killed, and then I ran away with my soul companion, leaving my contingent to their fate. Torgund had systematically gutted our ranks, consolidating his hold on castle forces through fear, and any inkling of treason or disobedience was swiftly punished.

It would have seemed like I fled, except that I returned, restoring the rightful ruler of Oberrot to the throne, then swaggered around, not realising how shaken the corps was.

"Al..." Hunkering down next to him, I put a hand on his shoulder.

He shrugged me off. "It's all your fault!"

This again. My stomach soured. He was looking for someone to blame.

Who was to blame, if anyone? Or had events magnified our differences and flaws, and accelerated what would have happened anyway?

"Aleric?" Barlay shoved through the ranks. "Aleric, what ails you?" He raised a questioning eyebrow at me.

"He's struggling, sir," I said quietly. "He made some choices he regrets that did not align with his core tenets."

Aleric gasped. "No, I'm fine! I didn't, I'm not struggling. I'm strong, I can do this!"

Barlay pulled him to his feet. "Lad, take a breath," he said in a low voice. "You're not in any trouble, but go back to your bunk and calm yourself."

My hand tightened on the hilt of my father's sword, my eyes passing over the men and women moving back to their exercises, giving Aleric space. A smaller shape sped through the sparring matches toward us, Aleric's small, dark-haired soul companion Alyssa, and she darted to Aleric's side.

"Go away, Lys, I don't need you hanging over me," Aleric snapped at her.

Her eyes widened slightly, hands making shapes in the air. A mute, she could only communicate through her hands and the written word. I watched her fingers flickering, but Aleric turned his face away. She froze, silenced.

"I know I Called you," he muttered. "Leave me be. I don't need help." Shoulders shaking, Aleric saluted and quit the field.

Watching him leave, I wondered at the mental state of all of Special Forces. They might be similarly struggling. They all could be.

My stomach hardened, my heart hurting. They had turned on me given the opportunity. And after I'd saved them too!

Gavain had needed help.

I pushed that intrusive thought away. Gavain had poisoned my soul companion and nearly killed her. Anger curdled my stomach, and I deliberately turned away from Aleric's retreating form.

Alyssa stared after him, tears in her eyes.

I opened and closed my fists. "Alyssa, I think he needs you, whatever he might say."

She turned her pale face toward me, her lip trembling.

I shook my head. "I don't know what to do either," I said gruffly. *Why is everyone turning to me for answers?* I rolled my right shoulder; it ached fiercely.

Barlay stared after Aleric, his eyes pinched at the edges. Every single member of the contingent turned to him and counted on him. The captain had to be everywhere at once, answering to Gough as well as providing us with guidance.

He probably felt ten times what I was feeling. I had to help the captain by not being a burden on him or anyone else. I was trained, so I could help Aubin step up. I'd have to show him what to do. It solidified in me, something that felt like a new tenet. *Yes.* I would give it time to firm up, but something about making sure the Rangers could shoulder the burden made me excited. We couldn't break down like Aleric, or fail like Gavain.

We went through three more rounds of warm-up exercises, which I went to with a will even with no partner facing me. When Barlay called for soul companions to quit the field, I ran up to give Evyn a hug. "How are you feeling?" I asked her.

"Good. Getting better every time." She pushed her hair behind her ears, smiling. "It was nice of your partner to spar with me. It's really good to get to know him."

Clever girl.

She squeezed my arm. "I need to take a breather at the fence, but don't worry about me. I'm better in the mornings." With a wave, she made her way toward the gate.

My heart went after her. Approaching Barlay, I saluted. "Thanks for letting my soul companion participate today, sir."

"Today?" He raised his eyebrow. "She's here every day when she's at the castle, Ranger. She does what she can."

I stared after Evyn. She really was the stronger one. "Has she ever fallen ill, sir?"

"Once or twice." He grimaced. "She comes to quickly and rests after that. I keep the others occupied so they don't fuss."

My stomach twisted. I could well imagine what kind of comments Special Forces would make about her. It did not endear them to me. The idea of working alongside them was more and more abhorrent. The Rangers would stand apart, and the quicker Aubin and I were deployed to Rush, the better.

We had to move forward. "Captain, I have a request. Do you have any Dinahen staffs lying around? I'll take the new Ranger through them."

Barlay cocked his head. "Perhaps in the armoury, Ranger. You're welcome to search there. I look forward to seeing what you come up with."

I led Aubin to the armoury behind the barracks. The room was chilly, thick stone sheltering the spare armaments from the heat. I had to hunt, but eventually found my quarry, blowing dust off the purloined Dinahen war-era staffs. "Staffs are basic, or at least I thought they were, but I liked how Gerlay was able to put his to good use in a non-lethal but highly effective way." I grinned down at Aubin. "We're going to get the benefit of training with Gerlay. I'm really looking forward to it."

"Of course you are," Aubin grumbled. He looked quickly down-cast again at the mention of the Dinahen Prince, although it was hard to tell behind the headscarf. "What's your bright idea?" he asked in Rushia as I sidled back past the hard-won trophies of bygone wars, at least the ones too battered for a formal display in the castle.

"You gave me the idea, actually. You have a certain style, and we shouldn't wave that around while we're in the castle. At the same time, I'm not limited to swords anymore. So, we're going to do a world tour of weapons training and pick out the things that work for us. We'll put it all together in a new style." I grinned at him. "The Ranger style of fighting."

Instead of looking impressed, he tapped his foot. "That sounds like a lot of work."

"Never fear, there will be books involved, as we'll have to do research. It's not as if we can ask a Rushia dagger thrower to train us." I wiped down the staffs. "In fact, how do you know Skienien Battlemistress blades?"

Aubin kept his arms tightly folded. "My soul companion had a retired Battlemistress as a nursemaid."

"That seems excessive for a toddler."

"A toddler that can level the nursery?"

"Ah. Yes." I passed him a staff. "For now, no Battlemistress blades near Special Forces. Later on, we can explain your proficiency with them as part of this tour we're doing."

We made our way back to the practice field, where Barlay was taking the men and women through an attack formation.

I spun the staff. Dust drifted off it. "Want to see what baseline you have with these?"

"You mean fight using them for the first time? Against that?" He stared at the six-man formation. "It would damage my credibility with the troops beyond repair."

"You need a confidence boost. You're much more able than you think you are."

"Thorrn, I am a hobbyist."

"A hobbyist who has fought by my side several times and never let me down during an engagement." I threw the staff in the air and caught it. "You do well under pressure."

He took a step back. "No, I don't. When Evyn lay dying on that table, I couldn't think at all."

I stilled. Recalling her slack face and yellow tone, knowing I had done that to her, made a searing pain well up inside my throat. "There was nothing to think about. There wasn't a combination of herbs that would reverse what I did to her. It needed magic, and neither of us have it. We just fight it." I touched his shoulder.

"It won't happen again. I've been studying her physiology."

I grinned at him. "Yes, I caught you looking. Looking is fine."

"No, argh, no, I mean... argh." He spun the staff in his hands, fingers flickering as the staff blurred with speed. "You are really annoying."

"So I've been told. I think I'm charming and astute."

With a grunt, he swept the staff down at my legs.

Jumping, I lunged, slamming my staff down at his head. He had already brought his up to block, but my staff slid down the length and smashed into his hand.

He dropped the staff, swearing and shaking out his fingers.

"Hm. Maybe we *should* practise," I said.

"Yes," he snapped. "I haven't lived and breathed fighting, Thorrn! I am not a disciplined swordsman. I'm not going to do well at planning, or deploying, or any of those things! I only fight when I need to, and that's only if every other avenue has been exhausted." He took hold of the headscarf. "I'm not even sure what Gough chose me for. Oh, I can kill people in cold blood. Is that what Gough found the most interesting?"

I frowned. "You just need to—"

He rounded on me. "Change, to better suit the ends? And have we actually achieved them? How many of our missions have ended in success again?"

"Aubin, we have only been on two." Still, his disquiet chimed with my own.

"Two with two failures. How many more international incidents will Gough send us on to muck up further before he decides this isn't working? And then what happens to me? I'm dead, after all."

I set down my staff, raising my hands to placate him. "Some initial issues are to be expected. I haven't exactly been thinking strategically about this. Barlay's right, we need to train together, and this is a start."

"But what if this doesn't work, Thorrn?" His chest heaved, breath choked behind his disguise. "What if I fail? What happens to you? What happens to me?"

"It will work. Don't worry—"

A shout went up from Special Forces. "It's him!" "How is he still alive?" "Get him!"

CHAPTER 7

My stomach fell as I drew my sword, moving between Aubin and the rest of Special Forces. *How had they realised?*

Their attention wasn't focused on us; it was on Evyn at the rail. Next to her stood another Evyn, and beside them lounged the Assassin. Our alternative versions had come to visit, without forewarning.

I swore and bolted toward them, my Aubin right on my heels, to intercept Special Forces as they formed up against the small group at the rail.

The Assassin immediately saw that he'd caused a stir and held up his hands. My Evyn explained something quickly and Evie nodded, shouting to them, "We're alternative versions. We aren't from your history!"

"Special Forces, stand down!" I roared. "That's an order!"

Some stopped, but enough pushed on in a determined line to cause me to put on a burst of speed.

"Special Forces, get back over here," Barlay snapped.

The men halted, angry and confused, but an order from the captain was incontrovertible, and they went back to their places grumbling.

Panting as I drew up to the group at the fence, I sheathed my father's sword. *That was close.*

"Well, at least I know what they will do if they find out our little secret," Aubin said in Rushia, echoing my thoughts.

I hated that he was right.

We paced up to the fence line. Evyn gave me a timid wave, high spots of colour in her cheeks from the scare. Having a line of armed men and women charge at you was not a pleasant experience by any means. I put my arm around her shoulders, trying to exude calm to help us both.

The exact double of Evyn waved to me. Evie looked a little more composed, hands curled around the top of the rail.

"Are you hale and well, Lady Evie?" I asked.

"Well, that was exciting." She patted her chest. "I'm not a lady anything though, so just call me Evie."

"Gran calls me Evie," my Evyn said.

Evie smiled. "Mine too."

Raising an eyebrow at his counterpart, the Assassin sneered. "You're in uniform. Don't tell me you got roped into their little game of soldiers."

"Assassin, this is Ranger Asmar," I said firmly.

The Assassin snorted in clear disbelief.

"Where's Shoulders?" I looked around, as if I ever had a hope of hiding behind Evie and the Assassin.

Evie tucked her hair behind her ear. "He didn't want to come in case he caused an issue, but I can see he's not flavour of the month anymore."

"Yes. Well." I tapped the hilt of my father's sword at my hip. "If you would help Evyn up to our apartments, we will just finish up here and see you there."

"What are you here for?" Aubin asked his counterpart bluntly in Rushia.

"You asked me to help you," the Assassin snapped back in the same language. He jerked his head at the retreating Special Forces, who were shooting angry looks over their shoulders at him. "Some warning about that would have been nice."

Evie patted her husband's arm. "We're time-jumping a bit. We'll explain when we see you up there." Beckoning, she held out her arm for my Evyn.

The Assassin sighed. "I take it I'm not to enter the castle?"

"Probably best not to, unless you want to end up in the cells," I said.

He sighed. "Which apartment is it?" I described it, and he nodded. "Easy enough. Evyns, I'll see you there." He sauntered back out toward the city.

"Are you going to climb the castle?" I called after him.

He waved a hand. "Yes. It's not that hard."

"Exactly like an Assassin."

Evie's gaze slid away from mine. "A bit close to home."

Cold settled along my spine. "Ah."

Aubin and I excused ourselves to put the staffs away, and left training early to rejoin everyone in the apartment.

Evyn lay on the sofa. "Is she well? Did she fall?" I asked Evie.

Evie nodded, putting water on to heat. She and my Evyn were the same in their insatiable thirst for Earthian tea. "She managed to make her way to the sofa before she collapsed." She tucked her hair behind her ear in a motion I knew well from my Evyn. "It's... not good news, I'm afraid."

"What isn't?" I looked between them.

"What's wrong with your Evyn. I'm sorry."

Aubin pulled off his headscarf. "What are you talking about? How do you know what's going on here?"

She rubbed her face. "Right, yes, sorry. So, I'm what you call a travelling mage, I think, in this timeline, anyway. They study alt-histories and let the rulers know what policies work out and such, right?"

Aubin nodded warily, as if reticent to agree.

Evie smiled. "Well, the way they do that is to jump around in time." She held up her hands. "Yes, yes, I know. It is very dangerous and I have to be really careful. I'm not going to tell you how I do it, for your own safety, because I know you," she pointed at me, "would want to have a go."

"I will not put Evyn at risk ever again," I told her.

"Hold on to that thought."

A rat-a-tat rap rang out on the window, and Evie jumped to answer it. Waving at her from the balcony was the Assassin, and she opened the balcony door to let him in. "I've explained the time-jumping bit," she told him.

The Assassin was barely winded. "Wonderful. Evie called in a few sennights from now and you had left her a note here in these apartments, describing what happened to your Evyn and asking me for help."

"How did we know to do that?" Aubin asked.

"Because we're telling you now."

"My head hurts," I said.

"I can follow it, carry on." Aubin glared at his alt. "Why you, specifically?"

"Because I'm amazing." The Assassin put his hands on his hips, teeth flashing in a wide smile.

He was incredibly confident, more so than my Aubin. I wondered what life chances and choices had resulted in Aubin's self-belief being so low here in this version of reality.

The Aubin from my timeline paced. "Moving on. You're me, but with a colossal head. What do you know that I don't?"

"It isn't necessarily what I know, but the advantages of time. I have spent the last two turns working on your problem for you. You're welcome, by the way. Next time, warn me we are persona non grata."

"What problem?"

"The problem of what's wrong with Evyn." Evie took her tea and sat on the sofa. "It's not good news. I'd... rather she was awake to tell you all together."

Dread uncurled in my stomach, and my limbs were suddenly heavy. I sank slowly to the floor. "No. Please. There must be something."

Evie gave me a sad look.

I took my Evyn's hand, closing my eyes as I felt the low tremble that seemed to be part of her now.

"While we're waiting, what's been going on here?" Evie asked, sipping her tea exactly as my Evyn did, in little slurps, waiting for it to get cold enough so she could take deeper draughts. The similarity underlined the condition that my Evyn had been subjected to; she should be awake and full of health and vigour, not sleeping her life away.

I fell back into the cadence of reporting to bring them up to speed with the formation of the Rangers, what that meant for Aubin Tabreksson, and Liara's role in the plot against the king and Tuniel in revenge for Waker's demise.

The Assassin cocked his head. "Ah. Liara is a little different on our world. Instead, she—" He closed his mouth as Evie glared at him. "Sorry, I've been given the universal spouse signal for 'stop talking'."

"Different timelines, different people. Like Luc," Evie pressed.

Luc was a rogue mancer we had met who had fallen into Earth, and now styled himself as the protector of that dimension to protect his home with his soul companion, James. On their world, he had been the MasterMancer instead. It seemed that there were key moments in our histories where events diverged, causing different situations to play out, resulting in these odd mirror images where either very little or quite a lot could be different. The alts were the only alternative history versions of ourselves that we had ever seen, and only they seemed to have the ability to cross into different timelines.

Evyn stirred, and I attended to her, relieved to see that her eyes focused on me quickly.

She used me to lever herself upright. "Sorry. Hi everyone. Help yourselves to tea and coffee."

"We have, thank you." Evie pulled a packet from her bag. "I brought Rich Tea."

"Oh, you're a star, thanks."

Evie set the biscuits to one side. "When you're ready, we've got the answer to the problem you set us."

A small, scared smile crossed Evyn's face. "Is it forty-two?"

Evie smiled. "No, hah."

Evyn winked at her, but she clung onto my hand, trembling lightly.

Putting my arm around her shoulder, I sat next to her, waiting to hear the tidings. Fear churned my stomach, twisting and multiplying, but there was nothing else to do but breathe through it. There was no calming this. Aubin paced behind the sofa, turning silently on his heel at each pass.

The Assassin began. "For the last two turns, my Evyn and I have been running experiments—"

"You didn't give it to Evie, did you?" Aubin interrupted.

The Assassin gave him a flat look. "Yes, I thought it would add something to our marriage, as well as a sense of urgency to the task at hand."

"Aubin, don't," Evie chided her husband. She smiled at my Aubin. "Thank you for the concern, though."

Aubin scowled.

The Assassin rolled his eyes. "As I was saying, I've completed long-term experiments on tissue samples, scoured the library, visited with so-called experts and actual experts, and now I know everything there is to know about bruswurt and what it does to off-worlders and especially Evyn. Here are my detailed notes." With a flourish, he pulled out three thick volumes from his bag and thumped them onto the table. "Ta da."

Taking one, Aubin flicked through it, eyes widening.

The Assassin studied his nails. "I'll save you the time. It's not the bruswurt that is causing the chronic tiredness and sudden sleep issues. Once it is out of your system, Evyn, it doesn't do anything else."

Evie patted her hand. "I'm so sorry," she whispered.

"It's okay. Thank you," Evyn replied quietly.

I looked between them. "Wait. That's the bad news?"

The Assassin frowned. "Yes?"

"Why is that bad news?"

"Because if it's not the bruswurt, then it's Liara and whatever the hell she called on," Aubin snapped, leafing furiously through the copious notes.

I straightened up, hand on my father's sword. "Capital! Let's go to Rush and kill it, job done."

"Oh, Thorrn," Evie sighed.

"You are not going to go slap some weird magic's wrist, Thorrn," my Evyn said firmly.

"I think you'll find I am! This is wonderful news, thank you."

"What is wrong with you?" both the Aubins muttered at the same time.

Evyn snatched her hand from me. "I can't believe you sometimes!"

My arms fell to my sides. "What's wrong?"

Eyelashes heavy with tears and cheeks reddening, she stormed, "What's wrong is you're happy I have some kind of parasite leeching away at me!"

"I'm not happy about that. No." I went to one knee. "Evyn, I only meant that we have a chance to fix it. If it was some long-term effect of the bruswurt, there's no telling whether or not there would be some way to cure it or reverse it or manage it, right?" I asked the Aubins.

"I suppose that's right," the Assassin mused. "If it was some sort of effect, I'd need to borrow your Evyn anyway to develop the cure. Or at least keep coming back and forth."

"There." I looked into her pale face. "I kill this thing, it's over. You're cured."

"Thorrn." Her shaking hand attempted to push her hair behind one ear, failing to get all the strands. I helped her, smoothing back her long hair. She looked away. "I don't want you trying to attack some kind of big, scary magic."

"I'm getting immune to magic, though. I might be the only one who can attack it. Liara dared to attack the king, so I will have to deal with her and that magic anyway." I looked at the alts. "You are well-travelled. Do you have any idea what it is?"

Evie shook her head. "Only suspicions, and I can't jump ahead and see," she said. "Well, I can, but that involves you committing to a course of action and seeing it through in this timeline. When I come to visit you, I'm actually jumping to a new timeline with... I suppose you could call them copies."

I stared at her. "Pardon?"

"You wouldn't benefit from us doing that. You'd still have to figure out what this is and kill it," the Assassin said.

I stared at him. "Pardon?"

"Timelines are complicated, Thorrn." Aubin sighed. "But I understand what they are explaining and I assure you, it can't be done."

I shook my head. "Very well."

"Sorry. I misunderstood." Evyn reached out to put her hand in mine again.

I squeezed it in forgiveness. "You said you had suspicions," I asked the alts.

"Mm." Evie hugged herself. "We really don't like to tell other histories about anything that might upset their timeline."

"But you're perfectly content to give us all this information?" Aubin hefted the tomes containing their research.

The Assassin's eyebrows twitched. "You asked for help."

"Did I? Only because you've said so. How do I know you aren't creating a new timeline as we speak? One where instead of taking the time to figure out whether it's the bruswurt causing this, we rush off down to Rush?" Standing slowly, Aubin faced Evie.

She met his hard gaze unflinchingly.

"Aubin." I caught his sleeve. "They're versions of us. Of course we'd help if asked."

Aubin glared down at me, Evie, and lastly the Assassin.

Smirking, the Assassin leant back, hands behind his head. "Can't contemplate what a decent version of you is like? Hardly a surprise. If it makes you feel better, then you can owe me a favour."

"Decent?" Pulling his arm free, Aubin crossed his arms over his chest, then unfolded them quickly. Heaving the books up, he went into his room, shaking his head.

"Sorry about that," I said. "He's... not at his best."

The Assassin shrugged, but Evie stared after Aubin's retreating back, biting her lip.

CHAPTER 8

WE CHATTED WITH THE ALTS, BUT AFTER A HALF TURN OF THE GLASS, I wondered if Aubin was going to return. We were of one mind; Evyn gave me a little frown and nodded her head toward Aubin's room, and that decided it for me. Saluting, I made out that I was going to get some water, then knocked on his door.

Aubin sat forward at his desk, reading through the reams of information the Assassin had provided. Something steeped in the dark corners of the room giving off a mulchy, alcoholic smell. It didn't exactly put me in mind of the infirmary, but it was in that direction; nor did it exactly ring for his old shop, as there was too much of a bitter edge for that.

Next to him glowed the dark green al athmadi soul jewel, the one Evyn had called an emerald. Putting it in his pocket, he looked up at me, then away.

"Are you hale and well?" I asked.

"Yes, just... not really able to look myself in the eye. I don't know how you do it."

"Because I'm adorable. Shoulders is really a big softie. Kind of like me." I perched on the end of his meticulously made-up bed.

"You've been more pessimistic than usual these last few days. What's wrong?"

"What's wrong?" He pinched the bridge of his nose. "I don't belong here. Gough should never have chosen me."

That hit me like a sideways blow. "What? What are you talking about? Where has this come from?"

He studied my face, amber eyes piercing. "What is it I do that you or someone else can't? You're picking up other weapons at pace. I just need to teach you the blades and you'll get it, I know you will. I can't do that. I can't get used to the staff; it's far too different to the blades. On top of that, I'm not a soldier. I can't think like one, so I can't be ordering men around to their deaths."

I opened my mouth, but he held up a hand to forestall me, waving at the corners of the room. "Knowledge of herbs and apothecary. Well, that Assassin version of me just concluded a detailed investigation that put me to shame. I didn't even think of running the experiments he did. I can only ease pain, I can't heal people with anything major or internal injuries; they need a medimancer or mage for that. I'm a stop-gap. I limited my thinking to that, and it shows.

"I'm piecing together a code to swear to and live by, but there's too many situations where I can see something will need to get bent or broken. I can't swear to anything, I can't be sure I won't need to do something someday. Gough said I would teach you flexibility, but that's not flexibility, that's being unable to commit. Paralysed by analysis."

Standing, he paced in the small room, the ghoulish green glow of the jewel flickering on his desk as he moved. "I can ping between the worlds, yes, but slowly. I don't think I'll ever be able to do what you and Evyn did. I can't anticipate you as well as she did, and she's better at pinging in general.

"And really, the last two major confrontations we had, I was fighting on the wrong side. During the Waker campaign, I actively worked against you half of the time. In the fight against Liara, I became a weapon against you. Both times brought Evyn very close to an awful end. You would have been better off without me, and our missions together really have not worked as any of us hoped. I don't know that—"

"Aubin." I waited for him to collect himself, gathering my own thoughts.

He smoothed his shirt and adjusted the cuffs, folding his arms and looking up at me.

I folded my arms to match. "You're right, we're disparate fighters, but we are each capable. We need a little practice together, to plan and develop some manoeuvres, and we'll be able to work more as a team. Barlay is correct. And the rest of it, well, now you know what else you can do with your knowledge, you can probably match or surpass the Assassin. He had the luxury of time, remember? It took him two turns to come to his conclusions."

Standing, I put my hand on his shoulder. "You helped me keep a clear head to rescue Evyn from Torgund. You came with me. Without you, I'd be dead, and she'd be in that Tower. You gave yourself up to save us all. Without you, we'd be trapped in the dreamlands or I would be Waker's plaything. You helped me recover, and without you, I'd be no swordsman at all, retired before I was even a score of turns old. Without you, Evyn wouldn't be alive. It was you who came back for me in Dinahe. Without you, we would be dead."

His eyes studied mine, then cut away. "Luck. None of those were planned," he murmured.

I chuckled. "This formal partnership is still new, but we've done great things and I know we will do so again. Keep trying, Aubin, I know that you're more than a match for me. Honestly. Mentally, physically, all of it, and you're not even trained. Think of how much potential it shows! A bit of training and we'll be amazing. But I'll be training too, to make sure I don't fall behind." I squeezed his shoulder.

His gaze fell to the floor. "I can't fail at this," he said quietly. "If I fail, other people... you... might die. And that scares me."

His admission warmed me, a chime in line with my own

thoughts on the burden of responsibility. "It's good that it does. It should, and I'm glad you're taking it seriously." I lowered my voice. "I will tell only you this, but sometimes, I cover that feeling with jokes."

He rolled his eyes. "Thorrn, everyone knows that you're doing it to cover insecurity." Shrugging my hand off, he nodded to me. "I don't make jokes. I make cutting, insightful remarks meant to unsettle and disarm."

"And they're really funny as long as you aren't the brunt of them. Good. So we both have our thing."

He looked toward the ledgers bursting out of the shelves above the desk. "You seem to be coping admirably."

"Hm? With what?"

"I am referring to Liara's mistreatment of you."

I stilled. This was one conversation I was not sufficiently armed for. "She mistreated you as well. And Tuniel."

"Tuniel says she does not remember, and I believe her. I recall little between ministering to Evyn, waiting for you to come back with word that Tuniel would convince Liara to let her go, to suddenly bleeding copiously at your feet and wearing something utterly disgraceful." He shook his head angrily. "Magic."

"Indeed. Nasty stuff. Good job we know how to fight it. Come on, let's practise."

"Thorrn..." Aubin put his hands flat on his desk, staring at the shelves. "You no doubt have others you confide in, others more qualified than me to help you. I hear you call out in the night. I can give you something to help with that, but it masks the root of the infection only. I will destroy her for what she did to you, and what she is doing to Evyn."

His face was hard, hiding all the insecurity he had bared and leaving only dire determination. He did not look like the Aubin I knew. I might have thought him an alternative version.

I felt a trickle of cold slide up my spine, as if Amare had chilled. "Thanks, but not if I get there first. My code is clear. I'm ending her when I get the chance." I gestured to the door. "How about we work together to do it? Let's try to develop some Ranger manoeuvres."

He smiled slowly, a small but heartening thing, and my chest warmed, banishing the cold.

"We're going to the practice field," I told the others, pulling on my jacket.

Evie brushed biscuit crumbs from her lap. "My Aubin and I will head off shortly. Just wanted to say good luck."

"Oh." A brief visit indeed. Disappointment coated my tongue. "I was hoping to have more time with you. When will you be back?"

The Assassin shrugged.

Aubin murmured, "An earlier version of them will come in less than a sennight, I think, to find the note that we will leave."

"But we won't be here to see them," Evyn mused. "Which means... I go somewhere too?"

Evie flushed. "Oh, come on. Please stop trying to guess the future."

Evyn hugged her knees. "Sorry, but it's interesting. You must have so much to think through all the time."

Evie nodded slowly. "I know this is... not normal. I'd love to be open and just gossip with you about everything, but... that's how things go wrong. What I will say is, never underestimate the power of now. You have the power right now to take strides and shape your futures, and it's the greatest power in the universe. Choices are hard to unmake."

"For most people." The Assassin patted Evie's head.

"Wait till I get you home." Evie sighed, snagging his hand.

"Don't threaten me with a good time." He winked at her.

My Evyn looked between them, and then toward Aubin. He was staring out of the window, amber eyes translucent in the bright light.

Collaring him, I led him out. As we left the corridor, I leant down. "I take it you aren't so highly suspicious of the alts after all. You've left Evyn alone with them without a murmur of protest."

His voice was quiet but clear behind the headscarf. "I don't believe they mean immediate harm. That they have given us the information on bruswurt attests to that. But I reserve the right to be suspicious of their motives, and you should as well. They are from a different alt-history with the coveted ability to travel between them. Alt-historians are infamous for experimenting and trialling on other timelines, Thorrn. The fact that they are us should not lull you. In fact, because they have a me, I'm even more suspicious."

Taking the stairs down two at a time, I wondered about that. Aubin was naturally pessimistic, but Evyn also had concerns. I trusted their instincts.

On the other hand, it came easily to me to trust the alts. They had helped us in the campaign against MasterMage Waker, even though it went against their credence not to interfere with other timelines. Evyn might have been killed. That Aubin had refused to give her up in the end had not mattered; by then, Evyn was in Waker's Palais and in her power. The alts had turned it for us.

I would have found myself unable to do nothing, were I in the same situation. Thinking of my double's shy strength, I was content. He wouldn't ever hurt Evyn, any Evyn. I was sure of it.

CHAPTER 9

He lowered his arms. "Why do I need to know how to turn in formation, Thorrn?"

I scrubbed my face. "It's not that exactly. Each manoeuvre builds on or takes from others before it. Like your balancing exercises have sub-exercises that help lay the foundations."

"So you've said before, but why do I need these, Thorrn? We are not going to be marching in a contingent."

"We might. You never know."

Evyn wiped her forehead. "Well, I'm getting a workout."

I grinned at her. She was doing some of Aubin's balancing exercises beside us.

Aubin put his hands on his hips. "Thorrn, I don't think this is helping."

"We don't know yet until we try. Some discipline is useful, it's helpful to fall back on expected behaviours in a heated situation. We can bed some of those instincts in you at least."

He gave a curt nod, then essayed the turns perfectly.

"Aha! See! When you apply yourself, you can do it."

"I can do it here and now, but in terms of instincts, Thorrn, I am just an untrained fighter."

I secured my patience. "For now, but we're working on that. Starting right now."

"Right now, I need a break." Aubin sat on his haunches, pulling at the headscarf.

"I suppose we can take a short breather." I grabbed the water jug, pouring out three glasses. My right shoulder was hurting; I winced as it twinged at me again.

Evyn looked between us, drying her hands on a towel. "Um. I had something I wanted to discuss."

"Yes?" I passed her the water.

She touched my hand as she took her cup. "I think I should come to Rush with you."

Warmth flooded my chest, but coldness twisted my stomach. "I would love to take you along with me wherever I go, but Rush is very dangerous, and for you in particular."

"Oh yeah?"

Aubin nodded. "I think out of the two of us, I know more about Rush. I learnt from a Rushia lady of the apothecary shop in the Academy. She's the reason I have the shop in the first place; she left it to me when she died." He leant forward. "A lot of Rushia flee Rush. She was one of them. That's why this disguise works so well for our purposes, I suppose." He fingered the headscarf. "The Rushia believe everything comes at a cost, that everything good has to be counterbalanced by something else, otherwise the balance will overspill and something bad will happen. They leave lots of offerings to their gods, and most of the time it's small things. But on a national scale, things get a bit more magnified.

"They apparently sacrifice people, offering their lives in order to guarantee prosperity for the country. It's supposed to be only the willing; the sick, the old, the terminally ill, and the soul companions of mages and mancers. Magic users have to give up their soul companions for their gift of magic, or else the gods will visit terrible things on them." He shrugged. "Yes. Life is going so poorly for Tuniel as a result of keeping me."

Evyn's eyes were wide. "That's awful."

"There's more," Aubin said. "There are unwilling sacrifices. Condemned criminals and prisoners of war. But the best sacrifice of all is an Earthian heart."

I gritted my teeth. I would not have said it like that. Evyn went white, and I squeezed her hand, feeling her sudden leap in fear.

"Or the soul companion of an Earthian," Aubin mused. "Think about it. The pair of you upset the balance a lot—"

"Yes, thank you," I snapped.

He flushed. "It is too perilous."

"Right, but I can be useful." Evyn picked at the ends of her hair. "I'm immune to magic too, aren't I? Might be you need me."

Evyn's ability to ping could be invaluable, even Aubin recognised that. "And you do better with me around."

"Out of the question," Aubin said firmly.

"Last time I checked, it wasn't up to you." Curling her hands into the grey grass, she grimaced. "Sorry, but it's getting to me. Randomly falling asleep all the time sucks massively. I have stuff I want to do, and I know it's just sitting in the library most of the time, but..." Her head drooped, long curtains of hair hiding her face. "I'm sorry, I shouldn't take it out on you." Blowing hair out of her face, she looked up at me, eyes welling with tears.

"I'll either stay with you, or you will come with us," I promised. "You are improving around me, and that must be an effect of our bond, our spirit shoring you up."

Aubin cleared his throat. "Physical closeness is one way to strengthen a bond, but you can have a strong bond with physical separation." He shrugged. "Look at myself and Tuniel. We live utterly separate lives and hardly speak to one another, but we are aligned with intent and purpose. We both determined to make it appear Tuniel cares little for me, to protect me, and we are both resolute on that course of action."

I had heard of bonds like that, but that scenario was not what I wanted from ours. A frisson of nerves trembled in my stomach. What did Evyn prefer?

Evyn glanced at me. "We would probably have to work up to that, though. And this is helping right now."

Not the resounding reassurance I wanted, but it would have to do. "And we will be deployed within the sennight, Gough indicated, pretty much as soon as Gerlay arrives. Of course I'm eager to deepen our bond, Evyn, I'm... just not sure how," I admitted.

"Mental and emotional closeness, Mum said." Evyn bit her lip and looked down. "Thorrn, now that I think about it, your shoulder is really hurting you, isn't it?"

Aubin beckoned me closer. "What's wrong with your shoulder?"

"I don't know. It's hot, and it hurts sometimes." Pulling down my shirt, I exposed the spot where Amare lay embedded in my right shoulder along with Tuniel's soul jewel. Flickering to life, it flared brightly as Aubin came close, responding to the resonance of their soul bond.

As it did in Skien. I shoved away that memory.

Aubin smirked as if he'd read my mind, and my heart lifted at the sign of his usual humour, but then his face fell, frowning at the red, inflamed skin around the metal. "This is an immune reaction. Your body is fighting a foreign object. I wondered if that would happen. The armour is metal, so it should be unreactive but..." He rubbed his chin. "We need to talk to Tuniel."

He tapped the soul jewel. With his hand on it, I could hear their conversation but not participate, which was strange, to say the least.

"Tuniel. It's Aubin by way of Amare."

Tuniel's voice rang out, somehow reverberating through my chest, her clipped northern tones preoccupied. *"I know, I can tell. Does Thorrn need the armour put away?"*

"No, something else. Thorrn's body is starting to reject it. It's metal, but it's also magical. As he becomes more immune to magic, he's fighting it."

"Accidentally," I said out loud.

"Hm. Didn't Queen Ellesmere say something to the effect that Gough isn't immune to magic when his soul companion is near him? Could Evyn, I don't know, touch him on the shoulder and have that settle things down?"

Aubin's lips twisted. *"Good idea. I should have thought of that. My thanks."*

I gritted my teeth at his self-deprecation, wondering how to combat it for him, as Aubin lifted his hand from the jewel.

We relayed the conversation to Evyn. "Am I going to get prescribed hugs?" I asked Aubin.

Picking his lip, he said, "Yes, I suppose. Let's see what that does to slow this rejection reaction. I don't think it will work forever, however. We'll have to think about what to do with it when your body really rejects it—"

"Aubin, you're borrowing trouble!" I buttoned my shirt back up, using one of Evyn's phrases. "Don't always go for the worst case. We haven't even tried Evyn touching it yet, and you've already written it off."

He knuckled his eyelids. "I always anticipate the worst. That way I am prepared, and pleasantly surprised when it turns out differently."

Evyn touched my hand. I tried to feel if I could notice a difference, perhaps an easing of the discomfort in the shoulder, apart from the usual contentedness I experienced around her. I did feel lighter. I moved her hand to my neck, and coolness spread across the ache. "Oh, yes. That's better."

Evyn smiled, then took a deep breath. "Speaking of the worst, boys... I think I should come with. Evie hinted as much."

I nodded slowly. Maybe our spirit was aligning on the issue. "We will all have to be careful. We will not treat this lightly."

Aubin clucked his tongue. "That aside, how are we going to solve the practical problem of how to move around?"

"Gough said he was procuring a travel mage or mancer to get us close enough. Then we will cross the sea and get a caravan across the desert to the capital." Roads did not last in the Rushia sands, and water from any attempt to construct canals quickly soaked into the parched ground.

"And in a battle, we'll...?"

My jaw felt tight. I deliberately relaxed it. "She can ping. You can ping. We will work around it."

Aubin shook his head. "What's the formation and procedure for this again?"

I scowled. "Yes, it's not ideal, but we have to work with it."

"Oh, I can see multiple ways that this can go horribly, terribly wrong."

"You always do."

Evyn sighed. "Just think of me as a logistical problem that can get out of the way. I'll ask Mum where the ping-through spots are likely to be." She hugged her knees. "Asmar, can I talk to you later?"

"Of course." Aubin laced his fingers together. "I have the draft contract for us to discuss. I can find you in the library after this, and escort you to our apartment?"

Her cheeks glowed pink. "Great. Yes please."

I wondered what that was about, looking between them with a grin on my face. Evyn kept her eyes on the floor, and a bubble of nervous energy sparked in my solar plexus. I rubbed my hands.

Uncurling her legs, Evyn rose to her feet slowly and stiffly. Holding out my arm for her, I could feel something of her pain, an unpleasant tingle that radiated from the base of my skull. She used my arm to climb up, but then I felt her deliberately draw away. "Thanks."

"You can lean into me," I told her.

"I don't want you feeling this. It's not nice," she whispered.

I clasped her hands. "You are not alone."

She pulled hers free, a sad smile on her face. "I know. But I don't want you affected." With a wink at me and a wave to Aubin, she made her way inside.

Aubin watched after her.

"Ready to get back into it?" I asked.

"Not back to learning how to walk like a soldier, Thorrn. That's not why Gough asked me to do this. If he wanted a soldier, he's got a slew of them."

"Yes. Men like Aleric and Gavain. We're a cut above, and we have to act it."

His headscarfed head turned away from me. "I'm not going to be a leader, Thorrn. That's just not who I am."

"I'll lead, you follow. Sounds good. So, you have to follow my directions."

He sighed.

I snatched at my rapidly disappearing patience and missed. "I'm not asking you to do something I wouldn't! These are important, *Asmar*."

"Being a leader is about more than demanding things of yourself and the people under your command. It's bringing out the best in people. You have... a spark of that, I'll admit, but this isn't the way you draw others out. However..." He let his arms drop. "I trust you, and I suppose I'll have to trust that you have a plan, which includes these ridiculous actions for some reason I cannot see yet."

A plan. I did not tend to plan too far ahead, instead trusting in my skills and my friends to win through. But maybe I needed to have something more, something greater than the amorphous vision of what I wanted the Rangers to be, and something more substantial than just blasting through each encounter.

Aubin climbed to his feet and essayed the turns perfectly, but now that he said it, I wondered what habits I was drilling into him with these movements. Were they ones that would stand us in good stead in the field? I'd need to think about it.

"That's enough." I handed him the water bottle. "You're going to meet Evyn?" I grinned at him. "I'll stay out of your way, get some training of my own in."

"Yes," he murmured. "I expect she wants some advice on herbs to help her condition. I want to formally present the contract and go through it with her, and she'll no doubt have questions."

"Or maybe," I said slowly, "she wants to kiss you all over in between the stacks."

His hands roved over his pockets. He likely kept his soul jewel in one of them. "You can feel that?"

"I can feel what she feels about you, yes."

His head dropped, movements stilling.

"Well, then, I'll see you later." I lifted my hand to slap him on the back, as I would have Gavain or Aleric, but his slender form was already heading toward the castle.

I ran through a few exercises, trying to pull my mind toward turning over what I wanted to instil in the Rangers, but another related thought surfaced. Special Forces had been my life for so long. Gavain and Aleric were part of that, part of me. Learning together, we had pushed and challenged each other, and that had inspired growth. My father had been strict on me, but it was competing with Gav and Al that had spurred me on in later turns.

Lowering my arms, I let myself recover, waiting for my heart rate to slow to a resting state. It hurt, a radiating pain that I associated with thinking about my father.

Grief, for a time that I could never return to. A time and a place that didn't exist anymore.

Quitting the field, I headed toward the city. As I walked through the city gates, I touched the plaque erected in honour of my father.

I knew a cut-through to my destination through the upper levels. The district immediately outside the gates separating the castle grounds from the city belonged to the lords and ladies of Oberrot, their city houses crowded close to one another, subtly competing for attention. Bright golds and greens sat next to pinks and yellows, metal decorations and mosaic patterns drawing the eye. The canals here were mainly for pleasure, thin watercourses that allowed lords to serenade their next conquest, or expensive restaurants to seat their clientele by the waterside.

I marched on, ignoring the questioning looks from patrolling Regulars. The main gates to the upper levels of the cemetery stood open, candied apple sellers standing outside but not daring to desecrate the hallowed hills of the dead with sales.

Family tombs and mausoleums in gleaming marble were laid along the well-maintained path. I saluted our family tomb, the place where my father's body had been sequestered, and where, one day, I too would rest, my body eschewed and the half-spirit I harboured finally fusing with Evyn's to restore our whole.

I made my way down the quiet hill. The merchant class could not afford large family plots on the sloping tops, and so as the aspect turned steep, burial plots made up the side of the mountain here. Glass panes sparkled in the light, each colour chosen to represent the soul jewel that had resonated with his or her bond. Further down, towering columns of stone represented the poor, family members doing what they could to scratch the names of their loved ones into them. I surveyed the forest of stone below, the deeper scrawls, etched with loss, visible even to here.

A set of special rows of interment had been laid out for the fallen of Torgund's reign of terror. Captain Barlay stood among them, hands clasped behind his back, surveying the twinkling glass frontages of the graves.

I walked up to him. "Sir. I don't mean to disturb. Do you mind if I join you?"

"At ease, Ranger," he murmured. Glancing at me, he waved toward the rows. "I haven't seen you here before."

"No, sir." I scanned the colours, looking for any I recognised. A sprig of some kind of pink flowering plant had been laid along the edge of one; I stared at it.

I had definitely seen that plant before.

Barlay nodded. "I see the other Ranger here most evenings. We have had some interesting talks." Barlay peered up at me. "He's struggling, Thorrn."

Gavain struggled too, and I failed to help him. "I don't know how to help him. I don't know what to do to get him up to the level I know he can be at. It's frustrating, sir. There is genuine talent in him. He's a fantastic Battlemistress blade fighter. He is incredibly intelligent—just look at all the languages he speaks! He's self-disciplined and dedicated to certain things, and he's great at teaching himself and picking up new skills. I only wish he could see it!"

Barlay nodded. "You've told him this, I take it?"

"Repeatedly."

His lips turned down. "And you'll be modelling the behaviours." Not quite a question.

"Yessir, by the book, sir."

Barlay waved me down. "I know you are. You tend to, and you lead by example." He was quiet for a moment, searching for the right words. "There's a lot of pressure on Special Forces; the swordsmen and women have been slowly built up to uphold under it, but even their faith has been shaken. We need to focus on restoring it." He knuckled his eyes. "That's my problem, not yours. With regards to Asmar, we recognise he has enormous potential, but he's not something we've carefully curated. He's a new type of resource, Ranger. We're not sure how to bring him along either, but we—the king and I—feel that the partnership between you is the key ingredient. We trust that the two of you together will work it out.

"You have time to do so, Ranger. Don't feel that it has to be perfect from the get-go."

But perfect was what we needed *now*. "We cannot fail on this next mission, sir. Evyn is... is too impacted. We're both committed to that. That will have to be enough of a foundation to go on."

The colours of the graves and the sprig of bitter bruswurt set in front of it filled my vision. "I miss Gavain, sir. Even though he did something that infuriates me still."

I closed my eyes. Gavain was calculating, intelligent, and committed. He had also been forced to do things that went against his nature, pushed by Torgund and the unrelenting tenets of Special Forces that rewarded failure with death.

Gavain made a mistake. He took it too far.

Barlay nodded slowly. "Events twisted him, but I feel like, given a second chance with the right person showing him an alternative path, he could fulfil his potential."

That set my thoughts off in a different direction. Perhaps seeing the effect of the poison on Evyn and realising he had gone too far would be the turning point for Gavain. I had pushed it too far once; it was only Evyn's forgiveness and understanding nature that allowed us to still be soul companions, for she would have had every reason to cut herself free of me. Evie's words excited me: that we held the power of now and all the possibilities therein. Gavain had the chance to change.

And maybe we did exist in some alternative history, and there, we carried on as we were. There were no betrayals, no tests against our friendship. Then again, there would be no room for Aubin, and I wasn't sure I would trade any friendship for him.

A spike of pain lanced my heart, enough to stagger me. "Evyn?"

Barlay looked at me sharply. "Go to, Ranger."

CHAPTER 10

Saluting, I bolted, running through the cemetery with no regard for decorum. As I thundered along the thoroughfares, lords and ladies leering away, I tried to stay above the rising curtain of red. Rage wouldn't help me, I had to control myself.

Sprinting through the grounds and into the castle courtyard, I took the main stairway two at a time and hung a quick right to get up the spiral stairs. She and Aubin were in our apartments, so I headed there at pace. Servants scattered and soldiers tensed, as if listening for the bell for alarm and to arms, but all moved out of my way. The pain was intense, driving me upward faster and faster. What if she had fallen and landed badly? Was this what it felt like when my soul companion broke a bone? Or worse?

She's safe with Aubin. Even so, I needed to be there, now, every instinct screaming at me that she needed me.

I burst through the door and it banged against the back wall, coats dropping from the rack as I raced to the main room. Papers were spread across the dining table, and Aubin and Evyn faced each other across the length of it.

Evyn's chest heaved, and Aubin had his hands flat on the table.

"What's happening?" I asked, my voice ringing to the high ceiling, heart thumping in my throat.

Evyn did not look my way. "Thorrn, please go. I don't need an emotional barometer right now." She was calm, detached.

I looked between them, dragging in breath. Sweat coated me, cold against my skin. "You're hurt."

Evyn winced. "Sorry. I suppose I spilt over to you."

Aubin picked up his headscarf, winding it around his face. "I will report to the practice yard."

"We're not done here." Evyn moved in his way.

"We are," he said quietly. "I have made my position clear."

She balled her little fists. "It's obvious to *me* you're lying."

"I need more time."

"I feel like I'm running out of time!" She wrapped her arms around her chest. "How long have I got to give you, and how long do I have left?"

I came up behind her, putting my hand on her shoulder. A tremble of fear flashed across to me, but then she drew away, pulling back from the bond.

Aubin finished winding his disguise. "I will make sure you are hale and well, Evyn. You do not need to worry about that. I will not let anything happen to you, and will fight to make sure you are safe."

Evyn's lips trembled. "I don't need you to promise me that, or fight for me, or any of that. I want you to be honest with me."

She reached for his hand.

He snatched it away from her. "I am. I have asked for more time. You should take what you need from the man offering it with both hands and a slew of letters conveying his honest intent." He gestured to the table, arm stiff. "A stable, comfortable life awaits you."

Evyn's gaze turned pitying. "I changed my mind. I want you to be honest with yourself, if not with me."

"I am honest with myself, and about myself." Sketching a bow, he walked toward the door, pressing one hand along the wall.

Perhaps he thought he could hold himself up with the stone, as if he were the stone mancer and not Tuniel.

As the door closed, I spoke. "Evyn?" My throat was clogged with unshed tears.

She lifted her arms toward me, biting her lip. Fresh tears glistened in her eyes.

I put my hand over hers, pressing her arm to my torso. "What —?" My voice cracked. I mastered it. "What happened?"

Evyn clung onto me. "He got this stupid contract out. We were leafing through it, and I sort of sidled up to him, but then I started reading. It's horrible, Thorrn. Tuniel has all these restrictions on your behaviour and what you can expect, and it's barely anything!"

My heart stuttered. "What do you mean, restrictions?"

She scowled, picking up a sheet. "This says here you aren't to approach her, under any circumstances, ever. You must wait to be called. The only time you can speak openly to her is in her bedchambers. It was hers and yours, but yours is crossed out here." She scowled. "She's compartmentalising you to be her husband in her bedroom only."

I glanced at the sheet, but the words were far too small for me to get a sense of. I trusted Evyn's summary. "Is there more?"

"There's loads more. There's all this about whether you should attend her funeral, and that she won't be attending yours or observing a mourning period." Evyn screwed the paper in her fist. "I told him that's horrible, that a wedding should be a joyous thing, but he said this was for your protection. Then I found something really awful." She waved a sheet in my face. "Partway down here is a clause that basically says if you get into trouble on a mission, you cannot call on her. She won't come sweeping in to rescue you, and she's bloody written that down in black and white."

Tuniel would not aid me? My throat closed. We had worked together to defeat our enemies and save Gough twice now. Why did she feel the need to cut that off?

"So then, yes, it got heated, but not in the way you envisaged." Evyn blew her hair out of her face. "He can't say it's to help you when there's something here in front of me that says she won't be doing anything of the sort." She looked up at me. "Is this really what you want? To be Tuniel's... plaything?" Her face scrunched at the word. "Not really having any say in her life at all, not meaning anything to her in public?"

"I... need to think about this. It is what Tuniel had set out from the start. She fears that someone could use me against her, could hurt me to have an advantage over her, and she insisted no one could find out about our relationship."

"But is that to protect you, or them? They're both doing it, Thorrn, keeping their feelings close to their chests and not daring to admit to loving someone." She sighed.

I wrapped my arms around her. "I caught the tail end of a different argument, I feel."

"Yes." She closed her eyes. "I told him I intended to give Gerlay his soul jewel back when he arrived, explaining that I had not meant to enter any agreement or extend a promise to marry." She spoke calmly.

This was new intel to me, and my chest swelled.

"He said he couldn't see a future with me, that I shouldn't call it off with Gerlay, that I should at least spend time with the prince to see if we were a match before I did anything 'ill-advised', as he put it." She took a deep, shuddering breath. "When I pushed him, he said he still struggles with the things Waker put in his head, but... It feels like an excuse, Thorrn, a smoke-screen he puts up to make me stop pushing him. And, well, maybe I am taking some energy from you because I felt like pushing. I want him to... want me." She flushed again. "I want him to say so. I want to matter to someone, Thorrn, and I know I matter to you, but it's not the same. Oh, Gerlay's nice enough, but he doesn't love me, not yet. But he won't up and leave, either. On the other hand, Aubin does love me, but he might leave because he thinks it's best or he can't handle it or something."

Cold calculation would cause me to agree but the lies layered onto it rankled me. I knew he was lying, that he loved Evyn, and that he thought doing this to her was a kindness. It was foolish, stupid and untrue. *He isn't being honest with himself. He isn't following his heart.* "He's not pursuing his truth. He isn't fighting for what he wants!"

Evyn's head drooped. "Maybe this is what he wants, Thorrn. We have to respect what he asks for."

Anger burnt the edges of my lungs. "I judge a man by what he does, by his actions, what he shows himself to be!"

A small smile crossed her pale face. "Ah, so all your actions stand for all time, like some kind of monument? You haven't made a single mistake?"

I scoffed. "Not always, not like... I make up for my errors, I hope, and..." I stopped in my tracks.

Evyn laughed, the sound halting but heartening to me, and patted my arm.

Aubin was trying to help her, in a twisted way. On paper, which would I rather for my soul companion; a prince with firm principles, or a would-be murderer who had to hide his identity?

I knew exactly who I wanted for her. The man who broke through enchantments, Waker's false dreams and Liara's twisted love, to return to her and keep her safe. The man who would do anything for her happiness.

As he was doing right now.

Evyn sighed, rubbing her eyes and sitting at the table. Despite all the sleep she was subjected to, she looked tired as she moved the slips of paper around. Her skin, pale in any case, was yellowing and sallow. Fear wrapped around my chest. *I have to strengthen the bond. That will help shore her up for now until I get to the root of it.*

Pushing back my anger at Liara for doing this to her and at Aubin for hurting her further while she was ill, I tried to remain open. "How are you, Evyn? Really?"

"I'm fine," she said automatically, putting the papers in order.

I put my hand up on the table. She touched my palm, her fingers soft and cold. Too cold.

"I'm tired," she admitted quietly. "Tired of what feels like fighting uphill all the time. It's a sucking kind of feeling, where everything I do requires far too much of me. I've tried rationing my resources—we call them spoons on Earth." She chuckled lightly, but I could feel no mirth in her. I could hardly feel anything.

"You can take from me. I've got enough to spare." I put my other hand over hers. "Similar to Finders and Callers, you can have Takers and Givers. I'll happily Give you anything you need, Evyn."

"How does that work?" she asked our hands quietly.

"I'll find out and I'll do it. It probably needs a stronger bond, which we're working on anyway."

With a sad smile, she extracted her hand from the fortress I had created. "I don't know that that's a good idea, feeding whatever this is with your energy as well as mine. I don't want you anywhere near the thing that's inside me. One of us needs to function."

It hurt, the pain and the fact that Evyn tried to stand in between it and me like a shield. "What do you mean, the thing that's inside you?"

She frowned. "Oh. Nothing. Forget I said anything."

"Evyn," I admonished softly.

Putting her knuckles to her eyes, she whispered, "I've been having bad visions whenever I fall asleep. Bad visions about... you." She dropped her hands. "That's why I didn't want to tell you, I didn't want you to think I was really afraid of you or anything like that."

"The nightmares? Evyn, I can help you with those! We can beat the dreamlands." Finally, something I could do to help!

But she shook her head. "These aren't like that. I'm calling them visions rather than dreams. I think it's this whatever it is trying to scare me maybe. Turn me away from you, separate us. I'm trying to fight it, but it's so hard, and I'm getting tired."

"What are the visions about?"

She turned her head away. "You are... a version of you is going to kill me. I'm stuck flat out on a bed, I can't move, and you've got a knife." She shrugged, but her eyes filled with tears. "It's not very imaginative. But... it is scary."

The wood of the table creaked in my grip. "Let me in there. I'll fight it." I would destroy it a hundred times over.

She shook her head. "I don't want you anywhere near this, and I need to sort through my feelings for Aubin." She squinted up at my shoulder. "How's the armour doing?"

Getting up, I squeezed her in my arms, my heart easing as she squealed. Coolness spread across the soreness in my shoulder from her hand on my neck. Letting her go, I said, "That's fast-acting stuff."

She winked at me, red-rimmed eyes dancing with mirth. "Yep. Instant magic-immunity removal, that's me."

She jumped at a rap from the door, and a spike of shock went down the soul bond, putting me on the defensive. Our bond must be getting stronger. I calmed myself, taking a steadying breath before answering the door.

It was a messenger boy. "Captain Barlay wants to see you."

CHAPTER II

Gerlay had arrived on his own with no entourage or fanfare and had called in at the barracks looking for us. Captain Barlay sent messengers to retrieve us, and Aubin got there first.

"Well met, Ranger," Gerlay greeted me, slapping me on the back. He looked well-travelled but rested, worn by sun and wind in the right places, with a black beard covering his jaw and cheeks.

"Well met indeed. I like the beard. Very rugged." I grinned.

His hand flew up to touch it. "Will your soul companion like it as much? And your command of Dinahen is much improved." He glanced down at Aubin. "I've met your Ranger partner. I am sorry, but my Rushia is poor. Do let him know I look forward to working together."

"Oh, I'm sure he'll say the same thing. He can speak Dinahen, you know."

"He can? I tried it on him and did not receive a response."

"No?" I glared at Aubin.

He turned his face away.

Gerlay drew close to me, dark eyes full of sympathy. "I am very saddened to hear of the passing of your friend, Aubin. I know you

114

thought highly of him and held him as a close confidant. You have my condolences."

That rocked me back a little, a twist of unease about lying to the prince, even by omission. He had a good, compassionate heart. "I ... Indeed, thanks. We'll talk more later." I waved Gerlay toward the castle courtyard.

He walked next to me, matching my long strides up the main stairs toward the living areas of the castle. "I wish to see Lady Evyn as soon as is convenient. Her letters have come infrequently. Does she fare well?"

"She's not completely hale or well, but she fares better now I'm with her every day. We'll explain more upstairs." Leading Gerlay to our rooms, I prodded and cajoled the prince to talk about his journey here. He had taken various barges, preferring to make his own way rather than commandeer public resources. Aubin lagged behind us, a silent smaller shadow.

"Sleeping under the stars and bartering meals along the way sounds like great fun. Do you have any dramatic stories about bandits?" I asked Gerlay.

"I had to dissuade a few from thinking me an easy mark. Truly, it was nothing." The prince cleared his throat.

"Good job. I look forward to hearing more on our journey to Rush. Here we are." Gesturing Gerlay to enter, I called out to Evyn, "We're here."

Pacing toward the window, I found her sitting very still, leaning on the side of the sofa. I thought she was asleep, but she closed the large book in her lap and stood to face us.

"Hi boys... oh! Hi, Gerlay," Evyn said shyly.

"Lady Evyn." Gerlay bowed low. "I hope I do not disturb you. You have heard words of my come?" he asked in halting Oberrotian.

Aubin slunk off to his room without so much as a by-your-leave. Evyn's gaze followed after him, but then she refocused on Gerlay. "Pardon? Oh, yes, I did, thanks. All those letters. Did you have a nice trip?" she asked in Dinahen.

The prince beamed widely. "A pleasant one, with a wonderful end. Your accent is darling."

A small sad smile crossed her face, her gaze wandering to Aubin's tightly closed door. I tried to turn my thoughts away from him. He was making his choice, to go against his heart, and Evyn would have to decide what to do in response. All I could do was support her and, to some extent, him.

Gerlay leant his staff against the wall to unsling his pack from his back, carefully minding the painting of Evyn's Gran. He held his pack to his chest. "I hope you do not mind, I brought you a gift." He looked at me. "May I approach?"

I cocked my head. "You're asking me? She won't bite."

Gerlay flushed. "Of course not. I would not wish to be improper."

Glancing at Evyn, she seemed uncomfortable, but nodded to me.

"Go to. Can I have a spin with this?" I pointed to his weapon.

"Indeed, but perhaps later."

"Of course. We will all need to practise with each other on the trip. The Rangers are pulling together the best of all styles of fighting, and I thought of you as the expert in the staff."

"Hardly an expert." Gerlay held out a thick tome. "Lady Evyn, I would ask that you accept this."

"Um, thanks, Gerlay, you really didn't have to... oh wow, what is this?" She took the heavy book, immediately flicking through it. "This is really heavy. You carried that all the way here? Oh! It's Oberrotian this side and Dinahen this side?"

"It is more subtle than that. It starts in Oberrotian and the script introduces more and more Dinahen characters in context until, by the end, it is in Dinahen." He took another step toward her, leaning in to point it out. "There are even some of the hand signals, the High Dinahen language of signs."

High Dinahen was what Alyssa used to communicate. Special Forces had signals and signs for use when speaking aloud was ill-advised, but the idea of carrying conversations with them was interesting to me. Aubin knew High Dinahen, I'd seen him using some signs, and that way we could communicate with Gerlay in the field.

Another thing added to the Ranger list of competencies.

Gerlay gazed at the words under Evyn's fingers. "I have been told it helps immensely with learning to read our script, although I know you are intelligent enough to learn by yourself."

I watched Evyn, trying to sense what she was feeling. There was a small warmth in my solar plexus, the place where I usually felt Evyn's emotions, but nothing like what I had felt from her when she was close to Aubin. Usually. I wondered how that would change now.

She was intent, her attention fixed on the book. "This is really cool, thank you."

"It is cold? I had it on top of my pack, excuse me." Gerlay took it back and chafed the cover to warm it.

Evyn covered a smile with her hand. "I didn't mean—"

"My apologies."

He held it back out to her, and Evyn blinked slowly, my only warning before her knees buckled. The book thudded to the floor.

I darted for her, but Gerlay swept her into his arms first.

"Shardsson, I apologise, but she fainted." Gerlay held her out to me.

"Au—Asmar, get in here!" I bellowed.

Aubin came out as I took Evyn from Gerlay, following at my heels while I laid her on the sofa. He checked her over, still wearing the headscarf.

Gerlay hovered at her side. "How is she?"

My voice was strained. "She's being drained by whatever Liara is doing to her."

He put a hand to his mouth, then balled his fists. "I swear, my friend: I will endeavour to free Lady Evyn from this curse if it costs me my life." He bowed again. "May I help in any way for now?"

"No, she's just sleeping." I sat on the sofa near her feet. "She will recover shortly and be embarrassed she collapsed in front of you."

"All right." Picking up the dropped book, Gerlay set it on the table. "Then I will not make a thing of it."

Glancing at Aubin, I said, "There's... something else we need you to not make a thing of."

With a sigh, Aubin pulled off his headscarf, and Gerlay startled with an oath.

I rubbed the back of my neck. "Indeed. This is Ranger Asmar, otherwise known as Aubin Tabreksson."

Gerlay's eyes were wide. "You... you were executed..."

"It didn't take," Aubin said dryly in Dinahen.

"Gough knows, he arranged it," I told Gerlay. "You can confirm that if you need to."

The prince scratched his beard. "Well. I am surprised, but I do not hold with execution of wrong-doers. Much better for the criminal to rescind their ways and learn a better path." Nodding to Aubin, he said, "I welcome you on your journey of rehabilitation, and if Shardsson trusts you, then I, too, will trust you."

Aubin's face went flat as he turned back to Evyn.

"Thanks," I said to Gerlay. "It's a secret, in case you can't tell."

"My thanks for bringing me into your confidence. I will not let you down."

I showed Gerlay where our baths were while Aubin stayed with Evyn. He was holding her hands when I came back down.

I sighed, sinking to sit next to Evyn. "I know what you're doing, and why you're doing it."

"Then you'll thank me." He nodded to the book on the table. "He will do well for her. He's ruggedly handsome, he gives the perfect gifts, having fought his way here, he's good friends to all and sundry, and, well, probably wealthy beyond all reason. Good."

Frustration bubbled in me. "Aubin, you're selling yourself short. With her and in the Rangers."

"I'm the only one able to see clearly, it seems. Whatever romanticised notion you have of me in your heads, my actions will soon disabuse you of it. She deserves the prince who can forgive the black-hearted would-be murderer in a heartbeat, not the incompetent murderer."

I bunched my fists, but what he said made sense. My heart squeezed painfully. "You're meant to be together," I finished.

"What, destined to be together because you and Tuniel are? Or because the alternative versions of us are? Destiny is rubbish, Thorrn. I'm happy for them, I am, but it doesn't mean it's best that Evyn and I are together. It's not best for her." He lowered Evyn's trembling hands. "Her pulse is weaker. Whatever this is, we have to stop it fast."

I focused on the more pressing problem. "And we will. Our chances went up with help like Gerlay's. He's good in a fight, and we have you for—"

"Killing Liara." Aubin looked up at me, amber eyes flat and cold. "Someone has to do it."

My chest tightened thinking of that woman. "I will. If I see her again, I'll end her."

"Would Gerlay support that or obstruct it? Important to get that straight before we set off."

Gerlay held to a core belief of many Dinahens that taking life was inexcusable in all circumstances. "You're right," I said. "I'll confirm with him."

Aubin faced the windows, the bright light searing his face and making his eyes even paler. "I'm doing it, in any case," he said, his voice low. "One of us has to do what needs to be done, and I promised I would kill her."

The back of my neck went cold, not from the sentiment, but the coldness of his voice.

"Kill who?" Gerlay's words rang with authority. He had washed but kept the beard and wore a crisp set of Dinahen blues that he straightened as he looked from Aubin to Evyn.

"Liara. We'll need to end her quickly," Aubin said.

Gerlay frowned. "She is our mistake. It embarrasses my brother that she affects other nations, and I am here to see to it that she comes to justice."

Aubin bristled. "Do you have a quiescent collar or something in that pack of yours? No? That's the only way you're getting Liara anywhere she doesn't want to go. If she lets you get that close, of course."

"Wha... Where?' Evyn yawned. "Oh, drat. What time is it?"

"Only a quarter turn of the glass since you left us," I reassured her.

She knuckled her eyes. "Where... Did I dream Gerlay arriving, or did he actually get here?"

"No, he's real," Aubin murmured in Rushia.

I glared at him.

Aubin swallowed hard and looked away.

Gerlay looked between us with a frown, then bowed to Evyn. "I did arrive, Lady Evyn. I promised the Rangers but I will swear to you as well; I will give everything I have to see you well again, even if it takes my life."

She flushed. "Uh, thanks. But don't, actually. As I keep telling the boys, this isn't worth losing important bits over."

Aubin shook his head, his face hardening. I felt my own resolve tight and firm within me, but Aubin's looked to be something else again. Something with a sharp cutting edge to it.

CHAPTER 12

THE NEXT MORNING AT MID-SUN, GOUGH CALLED US UP TO THE ROYAL apartments; Aubin and myself as the official Rangers, Gerlay as an honorary Ranger, and Evyn.

Sitting in the living room sipping a rich red wine rather than the bitter welcoming brew for mages and mancer was the MasterMage. I smiled at her and searched her face for signs that she was as pleased to see me as I was her. Wearing her pale green travelling dress, Tuniel barely lifted her eyebrows as we entered, her gaze sweeping over us and immediately going back to Gough, her face composed.

Gough sat across from her, one ankle on his opposite knee and a half-full wine glass in hand. He inclined his head as Aubin and I saluted. "I can leave you to discuss a course of action and come back for the summation. I would like to speak with the prince of Dinahe in the meantime."

"Very good, sir." My chest swelled at his thoughtfulness. He knew that Tuniel and I were promised to one another, and that Tuniel was Aubin's soul companion, but we were rarely able to speak freely to one another.

Standing, Gough motioned for Gerlay to proceed him back into the corridor to go to his office.

Tuniel watched the door close, and only then did her eyes come alive, alighting on each of us in turn. Her cheeks flushed as she met my gaze, her eyes crinkled at Aubin, and then her eyebrows dipped down looking at Evyn.

"Hi, Tuniel. Been ages since we caught up." Evyn folded her arms tight, making no move toward her.

Tuniel remained calm and unruffled. "Well met, Evyn. Aubin. Thorrn." She let her gaze linger on me from under her lashes, and Amare gave a gentle squeeze. Unfortunately that sent a spike of pain in my chest, and I winced.

Frowning, Tuniel looked away from me. "Shall we get started?"

I shrugged off the pain. "We need to talk about what we might be up against in Rush. Rush uses... dead magic, correct? Necromantic energy?"

Tuniel shook her head. "*Death* magic."

Evyn glanced up at me.

I raised my hands. "I don't actually know what makes it different from other magic."

Tuniel tilted her head, her silvrine hair sliding across her shoulders. "Are you not trained in identifying different types of magic?"

"Not to a great degree. We—Special Forces, that is—need to know the effects more than what to call it. Is it area wide or individual targets, and what is needed to achieve that, such as line of sight? The most dangerous rogue mancers and mages wield wide area effects without the need to see their targets." I inclined my head to Tuniel. "But they seem to tire quicker, so pressing forward works well against them. That's why we prize endurance above all else."

Tuniel stroked a strand of her hair. "Or you arrive in packs. The contingent, I mean."

"Unless you're a Ranger." I grinned at her. "And have spectacular stamina."

She shook her head with a small smile.

Evyn looked between us. "If we're done with this strange 'I could totally kill you' flirting, let's get back on topic. What is death magic, Tuniel?"

Tuniel's face went flat at Evyn's comment about flirting, and she dropped her hands to her sides. "Death magic and the country of Rush are intertwined and as mysterious as each other. Death magic has a reputation for acting in unpredictable ways, but I'm sure that is only because the magical community isn't sure how it operates and what rules it follows, a situation I am seeking to address. It is second in strangeness only to the so-called magic of the dead, necromantic energy, which is my personal project to understand. In any case, with regard to death magic, the Rushia used to form together large collectives from spirits."

Evyn frowned. "Spirits as in... can you translate for me? Because spirits means dead people where I'm from."

"They do here too," I said. "Recall that we share a single spirit, Evyn. That's because then it can experience different things at once. When we pass on, it will fuse together in the Labyrinth to become our whole, as long as our bond is strong and we are in accord, that we balance and harmonise on the issues that were important to us." I smiled to cover a trickle of uncertainty. Everything depended on our bond being strengthened in life.

Tuniel lowered her voice. "Spirits can affect living people. We call it a spiritsight, where a person is taken over by the spirit. We are only halves while we live, and that can attract another spirit to attempt to coexist with us. They are usually fatal to experience."

"I've seen one," I said. "It happened on Spiritshere mountain. Shard had us go up and down it for training one summer. We could see the canal carved into the mountain, but we weren't allowed to use the slave-ladders to traverse it. We had to pick up supplies from it a couple of times.

"One day, a slave just... attacked. He killed a few of the others, shouting and screaming enough that the entire mountain could hear him."

"And that's just not a sign this system is bad for everyone involved why?" Evyn's voice had gone steely. She heavily disapproved of slavery.

I raised my hands. "That aside, the slave died quickly, within a half turn of the glass. A spirit had taken over his body, desperate to live again, but it always goes horribly wrong like that. It's as if the body rejects both spirits, or there isn't enough room to manoeuvre." I looked at Tuniel to confirm.

Evyn clucked her tongue. "Are you sure that it was a ghost and not just some poor guy at the end of his tether?"

I shook my head. "No, Evyn. You see, he spoke old Oberrotian. No slave would know it."

Tuniel nodded. "That does sound like a spiritsight. And Thorrn is right; no one knows why they happen. My personal theory is just as Thorrn said, though, because of how we react to one another and observations after death. What else can the soul bond be but one spirit, two bodies? It's the best theory we have, and it leads us to concluding that we are vulnerable to another half a spirit trying to fuse with us."

Evyn sat forward, hands in fists at her sides. "So it's not bad dreams or feelings or whatever. It's a physical takeover thing?"

Tuniel cocked her head. "Indeed." Something passed between the women, a look, Evyn biting her lip and Tuniel nodding once. "Let's speak later, Evyn. For now, having done further reading and research on the phenomenon we witnessed, I can confirm that the experience aligns with descriptions in texts of a manifestation of spirits such as those the Rushia are said to enlist. While it can be directed, it cannot be entirely controlled, so it is extremely dangerous. They can be spectacularly destructive while they last. But to uncover more, we need to go to Rush."

I nodded firmly. "MasterMage, might I have a word in private?"

Her eyes narrowed. "You may as well."

Evyn glanced at Aubin. "I guess we'll just sit here in angry silence."

Wonderful. Grimacing, I led Tuniel to the corner of the room. "Well met," I began, touching her hand.

She pulled it away from me. "I dropped my guard earlier during the discussion, but we cannot be stupid, Thorrn. Haven't you read the contract yet?"

A churn of unease roiled through me. "Evyn has read the most... restrictive parts, yes. It's only us present, Tuniel." I gestured back to Evyn and Aubin, sat on opposite sides of the sofa and resolutely not looking at each other or us.

"Gough and Gerlay could come back at any minute. A servant could walk in. Special Forces could enter. This is why Aubin never takes off his disguise, Thorrn. Nowhere is safe." Her lips twisted. "We have to keep this secret from as many people as we can. That means being vigilant, always."

"Are you really worried about mages and mancers? I train to defeat them, Tuniel. It's my life's work." I tapped the hilt of my father's sword. "Anyone who attacks me will feel the wrath of the Crown."

Tuniel rolled her eyes. "It's easier to stop something before it happens. Yes, Gough might seek retribution for you, but you will still be lost. I can prevent you from being attacked because of me simply by being careful in how I interact with you. You know from Aubin that unobtrusive actions work to conceal a person from interest. I refuse to be careless with your safety, not when mages and mancers are constantly looking for leverage over me."

I opened my mouth to argue that I could protect myself, but she held up her hand. "Enough. I will brook no discussion on this matter."

Rocking back on my heels, I grasped the hilt of my father's sword hard enough that my tendons creaked.

Pulling her hair over one shoulder, she nibbled one side of her mouth. "I could speak to you tonight. I am in the Hunter's Suite again." She afforded me the smallest and briefest of smiles. Her face grew stony when I did not respond. "You can get to the Hunter's

Suite easily enough without detection. You've done it multiple times."

Expecting me to wait until the dead of night to slip out and infiltrate my own castle seemed rather presumptuous now. She would also expect me to return to my apartment shortly after; I had never stayed a night in her rooms.

I opened my mouth to tell her I would never demand that of an inamorata when the door opened and Gough and Gerlay returned.

The king nodded to us, gesturing for us to take seats. Leaving Tuniel, I sat next to Evyn, straight-backed and pushing aside my misgivings for now. I had to focus on the king.

Tuniel circled and stood next to Aubin, who remained sitting, arms folded tightly around his chest.

Gerlay looked toward Gough and then Evyn. Gough gestured grandly toward the sofa we sat on. "Please, Prince Gerlay, take a seat next to Lady Evyn."

Aubin stood up to accommodate him, sliding behind the seat. Evyn scrunched closer to me, and Gerlay perched right on the edge, attention firmly fixed on Gough.

Tuniel spoke first, voice calm and clear. "I have concluded that I will need to investigate Rush," she summarised for Gough. "However, as the MasterMage, I cannot simply travel into the capital. I do not have an existing relationship with the Sultanate." For Evyn's benefit, she explained, "The sultan and his heirs are the rulers over magical matters as well as mundane lives. I will need some form of introduction."

Gough tapped his lip. "Of course, the Crown would be delighted to offer such an introduction, however..." He looked between Gerlay and Evyn. "Relations have become a little uncertain recently, and our missives go unanswered."

"I cannot arrive at the capital unannounced. That could have unintended consequences," Tuniel mused.

Like the Rushia deciding they were being invaded by Oberrotian magic users.

"But I do want Rush opened," Gough said. He turned toward me, and I straightened in my seat. "Ranger Shardsson, you and the Rangers are to make the initial inroads into Rush. Make your way to the capital with a letter of intent that I will provide you, facilitate the necessary arrangements, and then call myself and the MasterMage to attend."

"Yourself as well, sir?" I asked, surprised.

His brown eyes studied mine. "I too would like to get to the bottom of this mystery, and it's too delicate to leave with Rogan or any functionary. I trust you will secure some sort of accommodation and provide a basic protection service."

"Of course, sir." I saluted, my heart jumping under my fist. Having the king under our sole protection in a potentially hostile country would be a challenge and then some, one that I knew I was more than up to the task for.

Aubin had gone very still. I could well imagine the complaints I would be subjected to later. I'd need to ensure he was fully engaged; any weakness in the Rangers could compromise the king's safety, and I would not allow that.

Tuniel studied her nails. "The magical community will be able to provide some assistance to this endeavour. I can recommend an experienced travel mage for the first leg of the journey, to transport the Rangers to southern Oberrot. You'll need to secure passage on a barge to the Oberrotian border city of Al Shur, and then you will need to proceed on your own. In a caravan, I would suggest."

Recalling Aubin's misgivings, I glanced over at him again. His face was clouded, jaw tight.

"Do you have something to add, Ranger?" I asked.

When everyone turned toward him, he shook his head once, then he pulled his shoulders upright. "It's too dangerous for us to take Lady Evyn."

"With you three directly nearby, the enterprise is as safe as we can make it," Gough pointed out.

"I am doing a bit better near Thorrn," Evyn said. "And I'm not completely helpless. I could even be useful."

"You aren't helpless, and you are useful, you have nothing to prove." Aubin dug his fingernails into his palms, the tendons in the back of his hands standing stark. "But there are far too many unknowns with this Rushia magic."

Tuniel folded her hands in her lap. "Which is why we have to investigate it."

Aubin's eyes narrowed. "Are you using her as bait?"

Anger turned my stomach. "Ranger, how dare you accuse the MasterMage of anything like that?"

Two spots of colour signalled Tuniel's disquiet, even though her face and voice were composed. "Of course not."

He shook his head. "I wish I could trust in that, but it seems like I have no choice." Eyeing the people arrayed around him, staring at him, his head dropped.

Securing my patience, I ran through a few of the phrases that my father might have used. *The contingent is only as strong as its weakest member. Excuses are failure, and failure is not tolerated.* But while that kind of thing lit a fire in my belly to shove myself onwards, Aubin would need more careful handling, and we didn't have time for it. *Why can't he just step up?*

I was annoyed with them both, hiding their true feelings from me and from Evyn, both for different reasons but strongly believing they were in the right of it. What about our feelings or opinions? Did they not matter?

Gough cleared his throat. "I'll give you the rubles to procure passage and the letter of introduction. How soon can you be ready?"

"Tomorrow at dawn," I asserted.

Aubin rolled his eyes, but Gerlay nodded thoughtfully.

"I am sure to make that work for my travel mage, who will take you to the port." Tuniel looked at me, one eyebrow arched.

I looked away from her. If she expected me to visit with her tonight, then she would be as disappointed as I was by her conduct at this meeting.

Gough nodded. "If that's all, then you are dismissed to your preparations, Rangers. Lady Evyn, you are welcome to stay, of course, as are you, Prince Gerlay."

"I'd like to catch up with Tuniel, if you've got some time," Evyn said, voice cool.

"Of course," she murmured back.

Gerlay stood. "If it favours, I am being helpful to the Rangers," he said in halting Oberrotian.

My heart lifted. He would be a big help in organising the equipment and thinking through what we might need. Saluting, we left, and I hustled him down toward our apartment.

"Why tomorrow at dawn?" Aubin asked in Rushia, trailing behind us.

"Why not tomorrow? We need to get going," I responded in Dinahen, for Gerlay's benefit.

"But that will be far too early to catch the mid-sun tide. We'll all be waiting around in the heat."

"Then we'll have ample time to train. And speak Dinahen, please."

Aubin made a show of looking around.

I scowled. "There's no one here."

Aubin pointed in front of us. Around the corner came a steward, flicking through a sheaf of papers.

I scoffed.

Three men from Special Forces rounded the bend, talking loudly to each other.

Aubin folded his arms, and somehow his headscarfed head managed to radiate smugness.

I growled under my breath. "Fine."

When we got to the apartment, I was dismayed to find a pile of papers in the arms of a messenger just outside. "What is this?"

Aubin hefted them. "Immigration information and the latest intelligence from Rush," he said in Rushia.

"Great." I eyed the stack of sheets. "You read that, answer anything that needs answering, and Gerlay and I will see to stores."

Aubin frowned. "We won't be able to take much in a caravan."

"All the more reason why we should have two experienced soldiers go through what we need." I held up my hand, forestalling his opening mouth. "We've got a lot to do and not much time to do it in. Get to it."

"Very well." Turning, Aubin slammed the door shut behind him.

I balled my fists, red rage rearing up at the edges of my vision.

"He seems... nice?" Gerlay tried.

Pacing away, I growled, "He's frustrating, is what he is. And perhaps a liability. He isn't used to working as part of a team." That concerned me. We couldn't go into Rush and protect the king and Evyn if we couldn't work as a team. Rage prickled under my skin, searching for an outlet. I shoved it back through long practice, calling the calm of battle down and trying to think objectively. "Maybe we need to spend a few days working together before embarking on the mission. I snatched at the earliest opportunity rather than the most sensible, because Evyn is running out of time."

Gerlay nodded slowly, fingers tapping the staff in his hands. "Then all haste is called for, and we will be ready for it."

That was the sort of sentiment I wanted at my side. I slapped Gerlay on the back, grinning, and it felt like old times even though he was a newer friend.

This feels like it did before all this happened. This chimes for Gavain and Aleric.

We were able to sort basic provisions and cooler clothes for the desert country of Rush. Having been on the road recently, Gerlay selected what we needed and counsel against what he hadn't ended up using.

"As long as Evyn packs light, we're done," I said, pleased. That was completed in record time, and I was comfortable with Gerlay's choices. We even had time for a sparring match, which helped to burn off more of my uncertainty.

When we returned to the apartment, the table was covered with papers. Aubin leafed through it and didn't even bother to look up at us. "Evyn returned but fell asleep. I took her to her bed."

Gerlay tensed beside me. Unmarried ladies were chaperoned in Dinahe, as in Oberrot. Gerlay could issue a challenge over such an admission.

"Aubin used to be an apothecarist," I explained quickly.

Gerlay looked between us, then grunted, laying his staff along the table and pinning some documents underneath.

Aubin raised his eyes slowly. "Are you all packed and ready, then?"

I pulled off my Ranger jacket. "Apart from uniforms and weapons, yes. Gerlay is already ready."

A flash of fear raced through me, strong enough that I reeled. "Evyn. Something's wrong." Racing upstairs, I approached her bed.

She moaned softly, sweat standing out on her forehead.

"Evyn?" I whispered, my throat tight.

"Don't. Please... don't." Her soft moans tore at my heart.

I took her shoulders. "Evyn, wake up. Evyn."

But of course she didn't, she couldn't, and I could only stand sentinel while whatever she dreamt terrorised her. Rage lit, curdling in my stomach. *Is this something Liara is doing?*

"Is she hale and well?" Aubin approached, hands flexing.

I whirled around to him. "I need to get in there, she's having nightmares. Put me out or something." Red curled across my vision. She was frightened, aftershocks of fear twanging through the bond. I had to do something!

Aubin grimaced. "It won't work like that."

"I will make it work!" I shouted.

"Thorrn, really—"

I grabbed his shirt, my hands flexing and curling into claws.

"Stop it," he hissed.

"Please," Evyn whined.

I shook him. "We have to help her!"

Aubin broke my hold, pain lancing up my forearms. "Get out of the way and calm down."

I raised my arm to strike him, a punch that would knock him down. My vision centred on exactly where I would hit him. *Aubin will help Evyn.* Pushing my fingers outstretched so they would not form a fist, I went to the other side of the bed, breathing deeply. My shadow fell on her face, blocking the light from her bedside glowstone.

Her eyelids flickered open, then opened wide. She screamed.

I grabbed her. She screamed harder.

Her fear was surging through me now, and it took everything I had to stay present, fighting off the waves of rage. "Evyn," I choked out.

"Get off me!" She kicked me.

"Thorrn, get back, give her some room. Evyn, it's alright, you're awake now. Calm down, both of you." Aubin kept his voice low and measured.

Evyn reached out for him. "Am I definitely awake?"

"Yes."

With a shudder, she dropped her head into her hands. The fear receded, leaving only cold sweat on her skin and the last of the tension as an upwelling of bile. I lowered my arms.

Evyn is afraid of me.

"Sorry, Thorrn, but when I saw you there..." Evyn shuddered. "Just don't be looming right now, okay? Jeez."

Aubin took another step toward the bed. "Are you ready to talk about these bad dreams?"

She sniffed. "I talked to Thorrn and now Tuniel about it. Tuniel is having a think about what it means." The air whistled in her throat. "I just need a minute, guys, please."

"I... I'm here for you." My voice cracked.

She did not raise her head, nor look my way. "Thank you, but can you go just for now? I need to sort myself out."

She wanted to be alone. She did not want me near her. Everything in me screamed to reach out and reassure her, but she had asked me to leave. Why? What had I done?

"Is everything alright?" Gerlay said from the stairs.

Evyn threw her hands up. "Everyone, bugger off!"

"At once." Aubin turned on his heel, grabbing my arm on the way to tug me down the stairs.

Evyn did not meet my gaze.

CHAPTER 13

I TOSSED AND TURNED MOST OF THE NIGHT, THE ABILITY TO REST BEFORE AN engagement disturbed by thoughts of Evyn, Tuniel and Aubin all hiding what they truly felt from me. I would have a chance to speak to Evyn and Aubin, but Tuniel would not be coming with us on this first leg. I debated with myself as night waxed full and the castle slept around me; she was a few floors down and a few words might be spoken. What kept me back was renewing my focus on Evyn; I had to strengthen our bond and concentrate on that, as well as succeeding on this mission.

We met our bleary-eyed Journey Mage at dawn as arranged, and the mage set about sizing us and our gear. She looked me up and down a few times. Aubin and I would be on guard against magic users feeling the power in Evyn's blood, but this mage seemed more interested in me than Evyn.

Evyn was wide-eyed with excitement, the colour to her cheeks heartening. She did not mention the nightmares from last night, and I did not want to remind her of them. I took her hand, and she squeezed mine back as she asked the Journey Mage lots of questions.

Gerlay shouldered his pack easily, staff in both hands. Aubin had a fair share of the load, but on him it looked oversized. He kept adjusting and readjusting his Battlemistress blade holsters.

When the mage declared she was ready, we held hands in a circle. I put myself between Evyn and the mage, and Aubin took the mage's other hand with firm resolve. Gerlay took Evyn's arm and then extended his hand toward Aubin.

Aubin's lip curled, but he took it.

Wind whipped up around us, and I tightened my grip as my feet left the ground. Evyn and the mage squeaked in protest, and I let up slightly. Magic travel was disorientating and dizzying, a whirl of sensation with no direction; I felt I moved forwards or to either side, and sometimes backwards, the world in front a blur of greys and reds and then gold.

"There." The spell ended, and the mage spoke with satisfaction. "Southern-most Lightreach. The harbour is half a mile in that direction." She squinted and pointed. "Anything else, Ranger?" she asked me, with a light note in her voice.

"My thanks, Journey Mage." I saluted, flexing my bicep for good measure. She simpered and handed me a lodestone, so I could contact her whenever I wished. *I haven't lost my touch.*

Aubin rolled his eyes, then pulled off his headscarf once the mage had left in a rush of wind. "I thought she was going to volunteer to come with us."

"This is as far as Tuniel said the mage would take us." Shoving back the uneasy thoughts of her stirred, I surveyed the boggy ground, the sluggish brown canal and the hard-packed path running in the direction the mage had pointed. We were on a mission, and I had to focus.

We started to walk, and I kept my hand on the hilt of my father's sword. "I suppose the mages and mancers of Oberrot cannot use their magic to enter Rush?"

"Not without invitation," Aubin said.

"And why is that?" Evyn asked him.

"Recall that the Rushia believe in balance. Use of magic is as subject to the balance as everything else, but other cultures do not share the same views. As a result, a magic user can upset a great deal of people there, and that's usually fatal."

The walk was short, but we passed many slaves tending to the paddy fields of rice on either side. Evyn stared but did not seem overly concerned, even though I knew she opposed the idea of slavery. These perhaps did not look like slaves, with shirts and broad hats to protect them from the merciless sun, but I knew that anyone working the fields were indentured to some degree.

Gerlay's lip curled. "A barbaric practice," he muttered in Dinahen.

"What is?" Evyn asked.

"Oh, my apologies. I would not want to trouble or upset you with the subject."

Evyn frowned, and I grinned. That was exactly the way to get Evyn to engage with a topic; tell her it wasn't for her to know.

But then she stumbled, and I lunged for her. She passed out in my arms.

"First obstacle reached," Aubin murmured.

"Shut up and help. Take my pack, I'll carry her for a while."

We moved slower, me carrying Evyn and Aubin staggering under both my pack and his. Gerlay led the way, on guard against bandits. The path widened and grew busier as we got closer to the shoreline, with merchants on their way to buy the wares that came from Rush —spices, fabrics and medicines, all from the tropical forests beyond the great desert—or sellers' slaves overburdened with Oberrot's food goods, metals, precious gems and furs to try to trade.

Shading my eyes against the bright glitter of the rising sun on the Mid-Ete sea, I could just about make out the blurry grey headland of our town, Al Shur, on the Rushia side of the wide estuary. Gough maintained a toehold on Rushia soil, and our merchant class made use of it to attempt to sell into Rush. But no matter what goods they brought, Rush proved hard to break into, declining to buy anything in the bulk required to sustain relations indefinitely.

We made our way to the docks, where boats listed in the mudflats. The tide had gone out, and they would be lifted and mobile again when the tide returned at mid-sun.

"Looks like we're just hanging around, then," Aubin grumbled. "Gosh, I wish someone would have pointed out we would have to wait here for turns of the glass."

"At least we got here. We can gather some intelligence on the current situation," I snapped back.

By the time we had secured passage on a boat and the tide came in to lift it, Evyn had woken up. She stood at the rail, the wind tossing her hair. Aubin and Gerlay both hovered nearby, but Gerlay made a point of standing between Aubin and Evyn. He pointed out the features to the east, where the Serene Sea became the Mid-Ete, the largest tidal river in the known world and whose origins lay in Dinahe. A flicker of something in my solar plexus whenever Gerlay's arm brushed hers gave me pause. That small bubble of love did not exactly sing out when Evyn was with Gerlay, but she clearly enjoyed talking to him and practising her Dinahen.

But fairly soon I felt queasy, and then Evyn was leaning over the rail. Gerlay hovered his hand over her back, but Aubin took charge, patting her back and offering her something to chew on. She clung onto his shirt, the knuckles white, and in an unguarded moment, Aubin's amber eyes softened. He steadied her waist with his hands as she tottered.

Gerlay frowned, watching them.

THE DOCK at Al Shur was little more than a long pontoon out across the tidemark. By the time we unloaded, the tide had turned and our boat was marooned on the mud until the eventide. The wooden structure bounced and bucked as we made our way up it, and I was relieved to finally hit the stone part of the quayside wall.

"It's a bit on the warm side." Evyn pulled off her blouse,

revealing a vest, and Gerlay looked away from her bare arms as if repulsed.

I frowned. He was extremely principled so I could explain his actions away, but he had not even tried a chaste kiss on the cheek. I highly suspected he would never circumvent my chaperoning in any way, which I was pleased about but also slightly suspicious of. Was this a marriage of politics for him as well, or was he really interested in my soul companion for herself?

The Oberrotian barracks in this town sat on the very edge of the boundary between Oberrot and Rush. The design was ours, and the grey stone must have cost a fortune to ferry, enough to withstand the frightful sandstorms that plagued the region. Surrounded by the Rushia's cheerful bright tents that could be dismantled and stowed at the first sign of a storm, the squat building reminded me of a bull-headed Skienien refusing to back down from any fight, however ill-advised. A short road led from the docks to the barracks, lined by caravan traders setting up temporary awnings to load and unload their wares.

We were hustled into a small building near the harbour where a tired-looking Oberrotian took Gough's letter and our papers and read through them with meticulous slowness, pausing when he got to Gerlay's. Finally, we were stamped and let through.

Aubin stood to one side. "I suggest we check the border records to see if anyone matching Liara's description has been through here."

I nodded to him. "You get on that, since you enjoy paperwork—" I slapped my forehead. "I forgot to leave that note for Evie. You know, the one she finds."

"I did it," Aubin said.

Relief tempered with irritation spiked in me. "You placed the note, then, despite your reservations about them."

"I have no desire to facilitate a paradox. In it, I ask for the Assassin's help because I'm an incompetent ninny."

"You are not," I said, resisting the urge to scream. "Did you add the warning about him being a bit controversial right now?"

"No. I deliberately left it out."

I glared at him. "That's shockingly mean. He survived it, obviously, but he asked to be told."

"Then we would be in a different timeline. I did not warn him, he was not warned, therefore I cannot warn him now."

"I really don't get it."

Jaw clenched, he looked up and down the street. "You don't have to. It's done. Forget about it."

"Fine." My patience with him had run out. "I'll look around for a caravan to take us to Rush. But I want us to stay in pairs at the very least."

Evyn straightened up. "I can look through border records! I'm useful at last!"

"You're always useful. Very well, Aubin and Ev—"

Gerlay cleared his throat. "I would prefer not." His dark eyes studied Aubin. "Liara is Dinahe's doing, our stain to correct."

Aubin's jaw worked, looking like he was trying not to grind his teeth into dust as fine and biting as the Rushia sands. "Very well."

I held out my arm for Evyn. "Let's forward scout the caravan parties, Evyn."

She nodded, looking back over her shoulder as Aubin and Gerlay went back to the border office, then letting out a loud sigh.

"He's getting to you too?" I asked her.

"Who, Gerlay?"

"No, Aubin. There's something wrong with him lately. I don't know what he's hoping to achieve or what he wants to get out of it. If it's 'drive away my friends', he's getting a pretty good crack at it."

She smiled sadly. "Depression is weird, Thorrn. It tells you that you can't do stuff, that you're not worthy, that it's too much effort, that you'll never manage it. The more people respond poorly to you, the more it reinforces that self-belief, or rather lack of it. So you don't want to see people anymore, and driving them away with the things you believe yourself to be is like a self-fulfilling prophecy."

"I cannot fathom it. Why do it at all? That just sounds—"

"Awful?" Evyn gave me a rueful smile, her gaze sliding past me. "He's not well, Thorrn. Think of it like he's got a broken arm. It hurts, and it needs time to heal, but as long as he has our support, he will find his way back to us."

I shook my head. "But I know he's better than this! Why can't he be the man I know he is?"

Evyn touched my hand. "He needs time to find that man. He's figuring everything out, and meanwhile, everything is moving at pace. He'll get there, Thorrn. We just need to shine a light for him so he can find us when he's ready." She shaded her eyes. "He's getting overwhelmed. He might be having an attack of confidence. They say fake it till you make it, and maybe he's been faking it all this time."

My hand tightened around the pommel of my father's sword at my hip. "We don't have time for this. There is real talent in him, and he needs to use it. We are in Rush. The danger could start now, today." I eased my hands open, trying to rein in my frustration.

I had decent Rushia conversation skills from Aubin, enough to enquire with the caravan master about some likely candidates. The headscarfed man jerked his head toward the Oberrotian barracks. "There is a caravan setting out by nightfall. She said she had business in the town and would be coming back soon."

"My thanks. Do you mind if we wait here for her?"

The man's eyes, wrinkled from squinting against desert sand-storms, narrowed even further. "I do mind. You are too big for my tent. There are plenty of places for you to find food, peche and meats that are not too spicy for you. You will not miss the caravan mistress, she is distinctive."

"Oh? What should I look out for?"

The man hesitated, but then a lackey came in shouting something, and they argued.

Turning to Evyn, I shrugged one shoulder. "Peche?"

"Please." Evyn tucked her hair behind her ear. "I wish I could have brought my sunshades, I'm getting a killer headache. Oh, don't worry," she smiled when I tensed. "I'm just not a hothouse flower. It barely gets above mild where I'm from." She pulled her blouse out and back, creating a small breeze for her flushed face. "This is far too hot."

We wandered up and down the dusty main street, searching out a shaded alcove where the food traders had pitched their tents. "I wonder how long Aubin and Gerlay are going to be, but at least we have found the next leg of our journey—"

"Well met, Thorrn Shardsson," Liara said from behind me, stepping into the street. "The caravan master said you were looking for me?"

CHAPTER 14

Panic doused me, hot and cold chasing over my skin, my limbs fouled and frozen. I was a well-trained swordsman. The sound of her voice would not unman me, I refused to let it. Yanking Evyn behind me, I drew my father's blade to fend against Liara. The tip trembled in the air between us.

A Rushia couple scattered, shrieking, and shopkeepers peered over.

Curls cascaded over her bare shoulders. She smirked, her cruel smile cutting into me. "Aren't you going to greet me? How rude." She made a fist, and her gaze moved to Evyn behind me.

Evyn sagged, and I had to catch her before she fell. I scrabbled to put my shaking arms around her and raise my sword. "You are under arrest, Liara. Desist or be disabled." The words barely left my lips. Clutching onto Evyn was the only thing keeping my knees locked upright, but my hands were encumbered and I'd never tried to fight while holding a person in front of me before. I tucked her head into my shoulder, and her cheek touched my neck.

Liara's smile widened, ripping a trench through my self-mastery.

Panic wrapped like a rope around my throat, shutting off my air as effectively and painfully as a noose.

A strange urge came over me to take a step forward. Liara crooked a finger at me, and that urge became overpowering.

I snatched at my scattered wits. *No! How could she enchant me?* Fear flared, threatening to shove my reasoning aside in a blast of rage against her.

Wide-eyed, I glanced down at Evyn in my arms. When Evyn touched me, my immunity to magic was negated. I had to think, I had to hold onto myself and not panic, not slip into a rage!

Liara sneered at Evyn. "I'm surprised she's still alive. I suppose she won't be for much longer."

Red flickered at the edges of my vision. "Get your foul magic out of her now!"

"This isn't solely *my* magic. A spirit has nestled within her, part of a larger whole."

My heart stuttered, but she could be lying. She had to be. *A spirit-sight is fatal.* Anger, hot and choking, filled my mind with a screaming desire to see Liara dead.

Liara continued talking. "A larger whole I will bring to bear against you, for it seems you aren't immune to death magic. These spirits affect you as much as they affect anyone."

She pulled a ring off her finger and dropped it to the floor, stamping on it. Black mist rippled and boiled from the bottom of her foot.

The remaining Rushia yelled, running for cover in the alleyways, and that was enough warning for me. I grabbed Evyn and turned to run.

"Oh, a mistake," Liara hissed, pointing at me. My feet turned and I fell, landing on my elbows to keep from crushing Evyn underneath me. I pulled my body over hers, covering our heads as the black mist boiled over us from all sides.

No! Whatever this was, I would not let it harm her, it would not get to her! Blistering rage boiled under my skin, and it slipped out of my control, unleashed fully and finally.

The mist thrust into my nose and mouth and down my throat. Coughing, I tried to spit it out, to bite it, my lungs burning with every breath.

"Ah. A berserker. The easiest to control." An unfamiliar voice, one I had never heard before but occupying the same space that Queen Ellesmere's words would in my mind. Pain flashed across my whole body, and I screamed as something deep inside twisted.

"With an Earthian soul companion." The voice turned excited. *"What a wonderful offering for the gods."*

No! I roared as the rage seized my limbs, lending me tireless strength. The black mist was fading from my vision to be replaced with red.

My body turned toward Liara. She watched me warily, fanning her hands through the receding mist. Her eyes flashed green.

Something stirred in me regarding her. *"I was part of an agreement made with the princess. I am to serve this foreign wench, to protect her and give her everything she wants, as it is the princess's wish."* Her smile widened, and my heart swelled. *"Yes. Serving the royal family is my honour."*

Of its own accord, my body moved to my knees, pressing my head to the floor. "Mistress, I live again to serve you." I spoke fluent Rushia, the syllables unfamiliar but wielded with confidence. My hand gestured to Evyn, lying flat on her back on the ground. "We have the Earthian. She will make a fine sacrifice to the gods." Thinking about it caused extreme pain.

"Good. The gods will be delighted."

How was my body moving without my say-so? What was this voice in my head, and why was it spewing out such horrific nonsense? I tried to scream, to move, anything. My body did not even twitch to my commands.

Liara reached out slowly to touch my arm. The slide of her fingertips against my shoulder made me scream even louder, but no sound came from my mouth. I was locked in a cycle of anger; Evyn was at my feet and the woman who meant her harm was right there!

The mage frowned. "This is an interesting effect. Are you in complete command of him, spirit?"

My forehead pressed against the sandy floor. "Yes. He is a berserker, and has lost control of himself." My own lips tugged up in a smile.

My own damn lips mocked me! I wanted to throttle him —me—it.

Liara tapped my sore shoulder. The pain that shot through my arm made me gasp, but a pleased chuckle sounded in my mind. *"Yes. Good."*

"Sit up. I have questions."

Sitting upright, my hands composed themselves in my lap. I tried to reach out my fists to grasp around her throat, but nothing happened.

Nothing except another mocking laugh, ringing around my mind.

"What is your name?" Liara asked in halting Rushia.

"Aglo was my name in my life before serving the gods through the royal family in this one, Mistress."

Aglo. My enemy had a name. I screamed at him.

Liara's green eyes searched mine. "And you definitely have complete control over that... vessel?"

Aglo lifted my arm. Making a fist, he punched it into my chest in a parody of a salute. "Yes, Mistress." Aglo smiled. "He is loud, but he is a prisoner of his own anger." He pointed to Evyn. "I need only think about threatening her, and he ties himself up in ropes of rage."

I have to fight this! Straining as hard as I could, I tried to ball my other fist. *This is my body! Get out!*

Evyn lay helpless. *"I could kill her with your own hands,"* Aglo taunted.

No! No, don't you dare! I'll kill you!

He chuckled. *"That has already come to pass and not slowed me, berserker."*

My legs straightened, lifting me to standing. Liara took a step back, the ragged ends of her skirts catching on the stones, and she watched me warily.

Aglo bowed my head. "You do not need to be concerned about him, but he may not be alone." A blast of pain radiated through my head, rattling my teeth. "Mistress, there are others here," he informed her.

"How many? A full contingent?"

He shook my head. "Just two others."

Her face fell. "Mm. Only two? A disappointment. Bring me their heads."

"At once." Shaking out my shoulders, he hefted my sword and headed toward the border control.

I was nothing but a passenger, travelling inside my own body as I would in a train beast, forced to ride along as he menaced anyone who dared get in the way.

"It's good to have a body again. A big, hulking brute of a body, one with interesting skills for me to use." Another shock of agony blasted from one temple to another.

Get out! I screamed at him.

He used my voice to laugh aloud.

The stone corridors of the border guard were empty of people. The screams of the populace would have alerted them to something happening.

"Now, then, what are your allies called?"

I'll never tell you!

"You have no choice. The information erupts from your enraged mind like a volcano." A squeeze like a vice ratcheted tight on my skull. *"Aubin, an Oberrotian. Gerlay, the Dinahen Prince. Royal blood would be a rare offering to the gods."*

"Aubin?" my voice called aloud. "Gerlay? Where are you? We need to regroup."

"Thorrn?" Aubin rounded the corner, blades drawn. "What's happening? Where's Evyn?"

"Now to get close." Aglo grabbed me again. *"How do you greet one another? Are you on friendly terms?"*

A jumble of memories about Aubin crossed my mind. I shoved one at Aglo. *Choke on it.*

It was a memory from Skien. Aglo seized it. *"Ah, so this will be a significant betrayal. Offer your pain to the gods, weakling, and weep as I claim his death in their name."*

You'll have to trick Aubin first. You'll need all your gods' help with that. I tried again to wrest control of my own limbs, to stop my legs from pacing toward Aubin, my hand from reaching out toward him.

Aglo took Aubin's shoulder, squeezing hard. "Come quickly, I need your help."

"What is it? The townspeople are..." Aubin trailed off as my hand roved down his arm.

Taking a smart step back, he raised his blades. "Thorrn?" His gaze flicked between my eyes. He swore. "What happened to you?"

Aglo seethed. Now it was my turn to laugh.

Lunging, Aglo grabbed Aubin by the throat. He slashed at me with his blades, and Aglo dropped him. Laughing, he brought up my sword in a powerful swing, knocking Aubin's blades clear out of his hands.

Aubin backed away. "Who are you?"

Aglo grinned. "Your friend has never hit you that hard, has he? You weren't ready for it."

"Amare prohibere!" Aubin said.

My upper body locked into place. The armour had deployed but instead of moving fluidly with my movements, it was rigid and unyielding.

I was as shocked as Aglo. *A failsafe? Tuniel put this into the armour? Why?*

"Tuniel?" Aglo grunted, wading through another tumult of memories. *"Ah. Your true inamorata. That is, if you can trust her."*

Of course I can trust her! A wave of anger dimmed my vision, but the fact that Amare had trapped me collided with the contract, both to keep me in my place.

Aglo could still wave my forearms, and my hips and legs were free. Dropping my sword, he tackled Aubin, taking us both to the ground. Heaving our body up, he knelt on Aubin's chest, grinding him into the floor with my weight, and stomped on his shoulders and arms a few times.

Aglo panted. "Now then. I want you to contact your soul companion on the lodestone."

"What? Why?" He coughed. He would have more than a few bruises, maybe broken bones.

"What harm can I do to her through a lodestone, mm?" Aglo waited for him to get a stone out of his breast pocket with a shaking hand. "Toss it up here." Catching it one-handed, he put my foot on his throat.

Aubin thrashed underneath me. I hurled my effort toward raising my foot, lifting my weight off him, even just leaning back, but Aglo's control of my body was absolute.

"*Tuniel MasterMage,*" he called through the stone.

Her voice rang out in my mind. "*Thorrn? Thorrn, what's going on, what's happening to Aubin?*"

Tuniel! It's not me!

"*What's happening is that you're going to take this armour off me, or he's going to die.*"

"*What are you—*" Tuniel gasped. "*Who are you? What have you done with Thorrn?*"

Grim relief at the situation being recognised was outweighed by my mounting panic, as Aubin shoved and heaved at my foot on his neck.

"*Don't change the subject, Tuniel.*" Aglo ground my heel. Aubin gargled.

Tuniel's voice cut into us. "*We can't take it off, it's bonded to him!*"

Aglo seethed. "*From his memories, it seems you didn't exactly try very hard, and now you have the correct motivation."* Aglo stomped on Aubin's chest with my other foot. *"That was a very satisfying crack."*

Tuniel gasped. *"Stop this right now. Return the Ranger at once."*

The Ranger. Not Thorrn.

Aglo shook my head. *"Wrong answer. I want to hear, Yes, at once, and then I want this foul metal off me. Quickly now, he's turning purple."*

Tuniel swore. I felt the metal give again, sliding back into position on my shoulder. *"Eh, not exactly what I asked for. I suppose it will do."* Aglo threw the lodestone to crash into pieces against the wall.

Aglo jumped off Aubin and retrieved my sword. Aubin rolled onto his side, clawing at his throat. Had my weight crushed his windpipe? Screaming, I tried to stop myself from moving, shoving and pushing against my own limbs, having as little impact as howling into the wind would stop a hurricane.

Aglo shook me off. *"Give it up, berserker. Now watch your friend die, and offer your pain up to the gods."*

No! Aglo lifted my blade above my head for the downward swing to sever Aubin's unguarded neck. *Stop!*

Smash! We were knocked sideways, my head smacking the floor. My ears rang, and Aglo swore in Rushia. Shaking my head, he got up and staggered, dizzy.

We looked up at Gerlay, helping Aubin to his feet. "Shardsson, you are not yourself," Gerlay said, voice grave. "Collect and regroup."

Aglo flexed my hands. *Damn and blast, he is still in control.*

Rubbing the back of my head, eyes swimming back into focus, Aglo grunted. "Yes, that blow to the head set me right."

Gerlay lowered his staff.

"Stupid man," Aglo scoffed.

Part of me agreed. *Gerlay, keep attacking, don't let up!*

"Where is Evyn?" Gerlay looked under one of the desks, as if she might be hiding there.

"In the street. Quick, someone has her." Aglo waited for Gerlay to pass me and swung my sword at his unprotected back.

Aubin darted inside my guard and slashed at my chest and arms.

Aglo had to dodge back and bring my sword close to block, missing the chance to end Gerlay.

Despite my predicament, I was impressed. *Where has* this *been the past mooncycle?* This was what I wanted to see! I had to hope he did not tire.

Aglo must have caught that thought. "Don't get exhausted now, it's difficult to keep up this kind of sustained attack," he said, Rushia syllables guttural.

Aubin's eyes bulged and he wheezed.

"Tired already? I suppose I did break a few ribs. Here, let me open your throat, get some air in." Aglo went on the offence. *"He can't stand against your body at your full strength."*

Aubin's fists opened as Aglo pushed the blades back, unable to hold against the pressure he applied.

Aubin! Stand firm!

"You'll never best me in this body or in any other," Aglo panted. "You know why? He says you defeat yourself before you even begin." Shoving him back, Aglo turned my blade for a stabbing thrust.

Smack! Another blow from Gerlay's staff, this time on the back of the head. Aglo swore in Rushia, muttering. "Why do I keep forgetting that prince is here?" Pushing up against the floor, Aglo rubbed my head, my hand coming away streaked with blood.

Gerlay and Aubin spoke to each other rapidly in Dinahen.

Aglo tutted. "I can't follow along that fast, the berserker isn't fluent in Dinahen... ah, I heard that, shock and blood loss." A welter of memories flooded from me, and Aglo smiled. "Going to cut his hand off, Gerlay?" He waved my bloody hand at him. "Go ahead. It won't work."

Taking a short knife out of my belt, he slid it down my forearm across my identification tattoos. The sting lanced across me. He pulled down my collar to put a big cross through the one there, blood blooming and trickling down my skin. "Need any more proof?" He shook out my hands. "The cutting has awakened all my senses. Now I felt truly on edge and alive."

You're a fanatic, man!

"You cannot even begin to understand the sacrifices I have made for my gods." Aglo laughed aloud.

"Rushia death magic." Aubin shifted backwards, sinking into his stance.

Aglo stood up straight. "It feels superb. Would you like to try some?"

Aubin raised his blades into a guard position. "Thorrn, if you're in there, you have to fight this enchantment. Liara is in Rush and Evyn is in danger here."

"Yes. Good." Aglo wiped my mouth. The iron taste of blood added to the red rage swirling within me. *Liara already has Evyn, and I cannot help her!*

"She's your soul companion! Fight it!" Aubin ordered.

I am trying! Aubin, save her!

"We are done talking with you." Aglo attacked.

I screamed in frustrated fury, but they couldn't hope to win against my skills. Gerlay was good with the staff, but he wounded rather than killed, and as much as it galled me to admit it, Aglo was right; Aubin had a tendency to defeat himself.

Gerlay engaged first. He blocked and swung, but Aglo anticipated his moves. Aubin circled, limping. He would be the first to go down. Aglo focused on Gerlay, but then Aubin rapidly told him something in Dinahen. Gerlay nodded.

Aglo went for a downswing, but Gerlay did something I'd never seen before, lifting his staff crosswise into the path of my blade. As the sword bit in, he twisted the staff, ripping the sword out of my hands.

Yes! I cheered. *Adding that to the Ranger manoeuvres.* Maybe working together they would defeat me. Maybe they—

Aglo leapt over the staff and smashed my boots into Gerlay's chest. Turning, Aglo plunged my knife into Gerlay's shoulder.

Gerlay howled and went down onto his knee, and Aglo pulled the knife free, ready to slash across his throat.

No!

Aubin blocked and shoved us back, kicking my knee out from under me. Aglo managed to keep upright, and Gerlay rolled away.

Aglo spat to one side. "You are really annoying."

"Good." Aubin slashed at me again and again.

Aglo put my forearms up to block, laughing as the Battlemistress blades came away bloody, my forearms sliced. "I told you, that's not going to... work..."

"Somnus root, applied directly into the bloodstream," Aubin snarled, as everything went black.

CHAPTER 15

I woke up slowly to voices. I could hear Aubin, Gerlay, Gough and Tuniel. Gough and Tuniel's voices were tinny, far off. They had to be broadcasting from lodestones.

Snatches of a weird dream came back to me. My body moving of its own accord, and...

I jerked to full alertness, anger flaring. *Evyn! Liara has Evyn!*

My body did not respond when I tried to stand. *"Welcome back, berserker."* Aglo's smug voice.

I was being held upright on a chair, thin cord binding my wrists behind my back and each ankle tied to a chair leg. Something dug into my collarbone. A quiescent collar, a magical artefact meant to subdue me, except that since it was magical, it was unlikely to work on me.

Listening carefully, I could hear men going about their daily lives downstairs in the pattern of soldiers, a familiar and comforting refrain throughout my life. Barracks.

"He's awake." Aubin's voice was accusing.

"Indeed." Aglo lifted my head. We were at the back wall of a small stone-lined room, right underneath the grated window. A cell in the barracks, most likely. Aubin and Gerlay stood next to the door, Gerlay with his staff raised warily, Aubin holding glowing lodestones.

Aglo twisted my lips in a sneer. "It is terrible manners to talk about someone as if they aren't there in the room with you."

"Where is he? Is he there?" Aubin's hands tensed around the stones, one side lit red, the other green. "What have you done with him?"

Aglo licked my dry lips. "The previous incumbent of this body is cowering in the back somewhere."

I screamed curses at him.

Aubin searched my eyes. "I very much doubt that. If he's there, he will be fighting you."

Aglo shrugged one shoulder. "I can keep him contained. All I need to do is promise dire things against his soul companion and he degenerates into profanity, locking himself in a cage of rage."

The green stone flared. "You're telling us this far too easily. Thorrn, you need to calm down, and that will help you get back in control of your body."

Calm. *Calm, Tuniel says, when this monster is piloting me around and Evyn is out there, Liara has her and is doing who knows what to her, and all my allies are here with me rather than out there looking for her!*

Aglo smiled. "He's not open to listening to you. Perhaps you in particular. You claim to be his inamorata, yet the armour he wears from you can immobilise him with a word. Don't you trust him?"

"What's this?" The king's red lodestone glowed. "MasterMage, there's something in Thorrn's armour that can be used against him?"

Aubin huffed. "Let's not discuss this now in front of an enemy who can use the intelligence." He took a step toward me, us, the red and green light playing on his face. His eyes never left mine. "Where is Evyn?"

"On her way to being sacrificed, I should imagine," Aglo replied. "It's going to be wonderful." Fear and delight mingled in my breast.

Gerlay blanched. "She is your soul companion!"

"I know. It will be my honour." That tingled the way lies did on my tongue, exciting and wrong at the same time. "It is what the gods demand, and I will obey."

Aubin shook his head. "Prince Gerlay, this isn't Thorrn. It's his body, but he has been taken over by a spiritsight. A Rushia fanatic, from the sounds of it." He jerked his head. "What's your name, spirit?"

"I will not tell you." Aglo smiled at him. "Do you want to torture it out of me? I might enjoy that."

Aubin scowled. "I'm getting a strong sense that there is Rushia death magic flying around."

"Yes, can't imagine why you came to that conclusion." Aglo gave an experimental tug against the ties. My wrists hurt, a sharp pain that radiated up my forearms.

"Did you meet Liara?" Gerlay asked. "Have you seen her? She was in Al Shur, there are records of a woman but no identifying information, which was her enchanting her way past."

Aglo gave another tug. "Let me go, and I'll go to Liara. I'll kill you first, then I'll find her."

Gough muttered, confused. "Has he been replaced by something else? Is he actually in there screaming for help?"

Yes! Help me!

"*They cannot. Your mortal remains are mine to command.*" Aglo batted me away,

Aubin's jaw ticked. "Some of the phrases are him, but his Rushia is as flawless as a native's. The spirits are merging, fusing to create a new entity, with a changed heart."

That sounds bad.

Aglo laughed. "Oh, yes, you'd know all about his heart."

Aubin barely twitched, but I knew him well. He was too still, holding himself tight to hide his pain. "Yes, I do. This is a travesty." He spoke quietly, but his words rang around the cell.

Aglo smirked. "Well, come and kiss him again. See if you really can tell the difference."

Aubin shifted his stance.

"Your pardon?" Tuniel asked into the silence.

"It was necessary for the subterfuge." Aubin's ears flamed pink.

Aglo snorted. "Yes, very necessary."

"Was this in Skien?" Gerlay asked. "We have a saying."

Aglo laughed again. "What goes on in Skien—"

"—stays in Skien, yes." Gerlay cleared his throat.

Leaning back, Aglo smirked at Aubin. "At least you were useful for something in Skien. You're more hindrance than help to him, you know."

I froze, anger lashing out at him, at the cavalier revelation of something I held close to my heart and would never voice to Aubin.

Aglo smirked. "Ah. He says it feels wonderful to unburden himself of that."

No, Aubin!

"Some truth at last," Aubin said absently, tapping the lodestones.

That threw Aglo. *"I need him angry, so his thinking will be occluded."* That slipped out to me.

So the information could flow two ways.

He regrouped and tried again. "You could have had a great partnership, but instead, you refused to train. You seemed determined to show yourself up as incompetent from the get-go. You failed him, Aubin."

Aubin nodded in agreement.

"He is refusing to react." Aglo seemed impressed.

He is impressive, and he won't fail me or Evyn. I shoved my certainty toward the invader.

"Ah. This might work." Aglo shook my head at him. "All that aside, I think Aubin the pessimist is rapidly coming to the only conclusion there is. Am I right, Ranger?"

Aubin's eyes had gone flat and blank, the edges I'd seen in his resolve sharp and hard. The pink drained, leaving a sallow sick certainty in his face.

"*Perfect.*" Aglo hissed. "Yesss. All the rest of you northerners are too soft. You won't have come to that place yet but Aubin, oh, Aubin, he always thinks of the worst case first. Don't you?"

He wasn't breathing.

What are you talking about?

Aglo smirked. "He might also be the only one who can bear to do it, too. Well, come here then. All it will take is a blade against his throat. Or maybe through his ribs into his heart. But you better do it, you had better take this chance, because the heartbeat I get out of this, I'm coming to kill you first."

Shock swept me to one side. Was killing me the only thing Aubin could do?

"He's goading you for some reason," Tuniel cautioned.

Aubin's fists opened and closed around the lodestones. His voice, when he spoke, was calm. "I'm not going to kill you. That would kill Thorrn."

"Oh, but you have to. The best offerings are brother to brother, so it's either me killing you or you killing me."

"Lots of Rushia death magic," Aubin muttered. His gaze flicked between my eyes. "Thorrn, if you can, get a message to us. Where is Evyn?"

Aglo gritted my teeth.

Liara has taken her! I tried to think toward the lodestone embedded in my shoulder, but only Aubin had been able to use that to communicate with Tuniel.

He stared down at me, waiting patiently. "Try, Thorrn. Try to stay calm."

I concentrated hard on directing my rage toward my hands. They were locked in fists, blood dribbling down from the deep ruts Aglo had dug into my wrists. *Open! Open, damn you!*

"*Give it up, berserker. Your madness makes you mine.*" Aglo feigned a yawn. "This is a pretty poor attempt at an interrogation, I'm not even in any pain yet." He leant back, searching my memories. He snorted at one. "This is worse than James and Luc."

Gough gasped. "Luc. Luc might be able to help."

Aglo shivered in pleasure as my thoughts turned traitor to me and revealed what I knew of the man. "Mm, a pain mancer. Yes, please."

"My gods," Tuniel swore, the green lodestone flaring.

Aglo shuffled, the movement hiding a sharp tug that he gave the cords. *"There,"* he thought in triumph as the cords loosened.

He's free! No!

Aglo turned toward the green lodestone. "Do you want to try, Tuniel? I'd wager you could put something nasty into the shoulder here. Or whatever this metal thing is around my neck."

"It's a quiescent collar, which is clearly not working." Aubin frowned toward my back, but Aglo kept my arms straight behind the chair, pretending to still be tied.

Aubin! Run!

"It means magic won't work on him until we can get Evyn," Gough said.

"There is no cure for a spiritsight." Aubin put the lodestones into his pocket. "We've lost him."

If that is true, if there really is no coming back, then they had better kill me now. This was too painfully similar to a bout of rage, where my body acted without my direction and against my wishes, but worse; I was conscious for all the acts it would perpetrate. Blood would cover my hands, Aglo would use my voice to goad and decry, and there would be nothing I could do.

Aubin stepped closer to me. Inside his jacket the lodestones were muffled, Gough calling orders for Aubin to stop, Tuniel silent.

Aglo smiled up at Aubin. "He begs for death. For me, it would be a blessed release of my service, and this final offering would buy me a seat next to my gods."

"Well." Aubin's blades glittered in the light from the window as he drew them. Curved, with flowing designs in the metal. Bloodletting lines.

"Yes." Aglo's delight washed over me. He tipped my chin back, baring my throat.

Cold metal pressed against my lifebeat, jumping against the edge, sharpening both Aglo's and my awareness to a needlepoint where that knife touched us. My awareness, red and dim, focused only on that knife.

Aubin jerked away. Gerlay had pulled him back. "Stop! You would kill him, an ally, and tied to a chair?"

"You would prefer we duelled him to death?"

"No! I would prefer that we did not kill him!"

Aubin shrugged Gerlay off. "I might prefer that too, but our options are rather limited," he snapped. He cocked his head. "What is that noise?"

Aglo's disappointment at death being snatched away coated my stomach with a sour fire. *Good*, I snarled at him, straining to turn my senses toward the window. We could hear a faint beat outside. A chant. A roar.

A mob!

Aglo grinned. "Lady Liara comes for me after all. I suppose I had better go meet her."

Downstairs, the barracks scrambled into action, but it would not matter. Once the crowd reached them, they would be through.

"You idiots have been wasting time, and Liara's got all the Earthian blood she needs." Aglo pulled my wrists one last time, snapping the cord. My wrists hurt badly, but they were free.

Pulling my arms in front of me, he stood up, picking up the chair to release my ankles from the chair legs, if not getting the cord off my legs just yet.

"Aubin, get yourself and Gerlay out away from that mob immediately!" Tuniel cried. "The travel mancer left you a lodestone."

"She left the berserker the lodestone," Aglo said, patting my leathers. "It's right—"

Aubin held it up in his hand.

"Excuse me, she left that for him, not you! Stealing women because you can't get your own, that's low." He rolled my shoulders. "And even if she can get here in the next two heartbeats, you'll still be dead. Liara has been busy while you've been here talking." He snapped the chair leg off, testing the end, the calm and clarity of battle rising in us both. "Mm. Pointy."

Using my senses, my reactions, he ducked as Gerlay's staff swung at my head. Rolling to one side he jumped up, stabbing with my makeshift stake, but Gerlay landed a solid hit in my ribs.

"That hurts," he said, gasping, my voice hoarse. "It's wonderful. Do it some more."

"Fine by me." Gerlay rapped me in the chest and back.

Through the pain, I fought to keep my knowledge mine. Aglo wasn't a swordsman, that much I could discern. Instead, he used small knives, the memory of them held loose in his hand ready to throw dropping into my mind. His memory, now mine, of knife-throwing. No, not knife-throwing. *The Rushia Art.*

Rolling away from Gerlay, Aglo got back onto my feet next to the broken chair. *"Stay out of my memories, berserker, or I'll make their deaths more painful than they need to be."*

"This is more than two heartbeats, spirit." Aubin held up his blades to ward me away. "You're getting cocky, like he is."

"Yes, well, sometimes he overreaches himself." Aglo locked onto him.

Aubin adjusted his stance and drew a small knife.

It was not the blade of an Artist. "What's that going to do?" Aglo snorted.

Aubin paced backwards, waving Gerlay behind him, making for the door. "More somnus root."

"Ah, yes, it's kind of your signature. But I don't think you brought all that much with you."

He shifted his grip on his blades. "I resupplied here."

"Really now." Aglo took a pace toward the edge of the small cell. "And yet you look travel-stained and weary. I don't think you've been anywhere near your supplies, you would have at least changed your shirt."

"Why would I do that when I knew I'd get blood on it again?"

"Yours, or his?"

"Probably both, if I'm honest."

"Being a pessimist again, Aubin. Tell me again how you're going to get his blood all over you. It's delicious. Ah!" Aglo dodged out of the way of Gerlay's smack. "You are really taking advantage of me when I'm in the middle of a conversation!"

"Try and secure him, but if you can't, just go!" Gough's muffled voice called through the lodestone in Aubin's pocket.

"I don't think there's any securing here." Aglo panted, blood leaking from my wrists. They ached and hurt, but while I mastered the pain, Aglo offered it up to his gods.

"He's weakening. We can secure him," Aubin said.

"The travel mage is there! Get to her, get out!" Tuniel shouted through the stone.

"Are you going to be able to drag his limp body through that?" Aglo nodded to the window.

Shouts and screams rang outside. The enchanted mob had reached me.

"Gods' luck," he sneered, raising the stake, pretending to look ready for a battle. "Well then. Which one is it?"

Aubin's eyes narrowed at me. "Evyn needs him to be near her." A cold look settled in his face, signalling his resolve.

Fear surged through me, and Aglo must have felt it. Aglo darted for him, but Gerlay swung his staff. Dodging around it, he slipped and slammed into the wall by accident.

Did I do that? Had I wrested control for a heartbeat?

"*No,*" Aglo said. "*I merely let my attention slip.*" Underneath his calm was a current of uncertainty.

You cannot hide anything from me. I'm in your head, same as you're in mine!

Aubin opened the door. "Gerlay, let's go!"

The prince hesitated for a heartbeat, and Aglo got to his feet. Gerlay fled, Aubin slamming the door shut in my face.

The key snicked in the lock as Aglo slammed my shoulder into it.

He rattled the knob, swearing in Rushia.

Good to know you can be tricked and bested in battle, I shot at him. *It's a disgrace you're piloting my body.*

To that he answered with a memory of Evyn lying in the street. *"I'll be piloting your body when you choke the life out of her. Tell me then how much your prowess in battle matters."*

I tried to reach him, to grab something, to tear him apart, but all I felt were spikes of pain. I could not affect how my body moved, a terrifying lack of control.

Aglo sat against the door. *"Well. There is nothing else to do but wait."* Pulling off my shirt, he ripped it up and bandaged my aching wrists. *"Tell me more about Mistress Liara."*

As much as I didn't want to, I could not prevent the upswell of disgust and cloying fear that rose in me when I thought of Liara and what she did to me, to Tuniel, to Aubin and now to Evyn. Aglo caught that, riffling through my memories, pressing the worst ones in front of me so I could not avoid them. Whatever I was, trapped inside my body, I had no eyes to close, nowhere to escape to or hide from the feelings that bubbled up inside me, surging through me as a fresh wave of rage.

"That bad, eh?" The Rushia chuckled. *"Let's see..."*

Over the next four turns of the glass, he pulled and pried my memories from me, pawing through them and turning them over this way and that. *"Interesting life, berserker. If only you knew the way to Earth. I would be celebrated if I brought several victims for the athame rather than just the one."*

Don't you dare hurt her! I'll fight you every step of the way!

"And how is that turning out so far?" Aglo stood as the door opened.

Liara grimaced at me, her face flushed and a curl stuck to the sheen of sweat on her forehead. My stomach turned. "There you are," she said.

Aglo bowed. "Mistress, I'm sorry to report they got away."

"Mm. So I see. You did not do enough."

"No, Mistress." He bowed my head.

"You have sustained injury. Were they really that formidable that you couldn't overcome them easily?"

Aglo fell to my knees, bashing them painfully on the stone floor. "I'm sorry to displease you, Mistress, but perhaps the knowledge I have wrung out of this wretch will assuage your rightful disappointment in me?"

Liara smoothed back her hair. "The only thing I am interested in is who took my Waker from me, and I know that already."

Aglo pulled my lips up in a smile. "I can see his memories. It was he who took her life, Mistress, with this very sword." Drawing it, he placed it across my palms and lifted it up before her.

Oh, damn and blast.

Liara trembled. "This is the truth? You would not lie to me, spirit?"

"Mistress, I cannot. I serve you," Aglo wheedled. "And I serve the gods. Where I offer my agony to their attention, I serve them well." Aglo stood. "I suspect you have a great deal of pain you wish to administer to the brute now."

"Is he still in there?"

Aglo nodded. "Still ensnared in his own anger. He feels everything as I do."

Liara stared into my eyes, clenching her jaw. She slapped me across the face.

Aglo pressed my hand into my throbbing cheek, purring.

I reeled, physical pain spiking alongside emotional pain. Rage rose around me, the only response remaining when the situation was so dire.

"Follow me," she said, green eyes flashing.

CHAPTER 16

My body helped load the wagons with the caravan guard, who were hardened men from the sand-blasted hells of the desert. None of them seemed slow-witted and thus enchanted, just well paid for the task of escorting a woman and her two slaves across the sands to the capital. Aglo was not permitted to go anywhere near Evyn as they threw her into her wagon, drained into a sleep as deep as death, and we left the town in flames.

A few miles out, Liara called a halt for the night. She had Aglo kneel my body in the cold, shifting sands. "That infection needs to be cut out."

He glanced at my shoulder, at the shining silvrine metal surrounded by painful red swelling.

No. No, no, no!

Men heated their knives in the campfire and stepped toward me. "He will object strongly," they said. It was rapid and I would not have been able to understand it before, but Aglo's native speech came easily to me now.

"He won't move. Not even to breathe," Liara promised them, her eyes glittering red in the firelight. Fear turned my stomach over.

Aglo sighed. "No. I will not." Lifting his head to the star-strewn sky, he started murmuring a prayer in a low, soft voice.

Are you insane? Don't answer that! I stared at the men approaching me, awaiting the agony. When the first bite of the heated knife sliced into me, I screamed.

He managed to stay immobile while they gouged at my shoulder for what felt like forty turns, but I surged and fought, desperate to take back control. Liara watched with deadly intent at first, but even she turned her face away, swallowing hard. Eventually, the men concluded they couldn't remove the metal without permanently damaging my arm, and Aglo haltingly agreed that he still had use for my arm yet.

He laid us down, the cold sand gritting into the open wound seeping on my shoulder. *"What a good largesse for the gods."*

I could barely think. Black tendrils of pain snagged and slowed my thoughts.

"Here." One of the men passed Liara the stone they chipped from the armour.

Smoothing Tuniel's soul jewel in her hand, Liara turned a tear-stained face to me. "I wish I could take your love from you, so you could feel as I do. I thought Tuniel had killed Waker, so I was going to make *her* suffer for it, pitching Oberrot into turmoil by making it seem like she wilfully broke the Accords."

My stomach turned, recalling Tuniel in Liara's bedchambers, the subservient way she acted while she was under Liara's enchantment.

"But it was you, this whole time..." She turned and flung the stone into the desert. Her chest heaved.

She pushed her hair behind her ear. "Death awaits you both when I get you back to the princess. I'll keep you alive until then, but I'll make sure you realise that it is not a mercy."

Aglo grunted, satisfied, and darkness dragged us down into oblivion.

We travelled on at grey daybreak, but my body was unable to move. Aglo and I were delirious with pain, lying in the back of an overheated wagon alone, trying to drink sips of water and failing. It was like that for what felt like days.

Aglo's thoughts were as blurry as mine, weaving together in a litany of pain so I could not tell where he ended and I began. Would our spirits merge? I tried to pull apart, to lean toward Evyn. Evyn and I were supposed to merge at the end of our lives, not me and some fanatic!

Evyn, I called out. *Please be hale and well!* Liara must have drained her to the edge of death, enchanting as many people as she had to turn against the town.

"Ellen," Aglo whispered. The yearning was the same as mine, our feelings aligning. *"My soul companion."* A deluge of memories swamped me, of a woman with black hair and dressed like an Oberrotian baker with a pinafore. She smiled at Aglo – at us – and our heart lifted, exactly when it did when Evyn smiled at me.

What happened to her?

Aglo shuddered. Another memory, of shadows on stone, the iron tang of blood. Our arms raised up, a prayer to the gods on our lips, and Ellen's scream cut short.

"I gave up much for my gods."

Fear seized me. *You didn't!*

"I did. And I will do so again. The gods demand it."

What are you? Horror mixed with fascination.

"I am a soldier, of sorts. I pledged my life to the royal family of Rush, to always answer their call. They had me place my life in their hands, and they chose me to serve them for eternity as a tangle."

A tangle?

He shoved me away. *"You can understand orders at least, brute, when you aren't out of your mind with anger. These are my orders."* He kept fast to his course, stubbornly clinging onto his doctrine. *"The pain will all be worth it."*

Gradually my shoulder eased a little, burning and aching whenever Aglo moved it. He dragged my body up and out to survey the wagons.

We made a solitary snake wending its way through the harsh desert. Aglo staggered along the line, looking into each wagon. Mine, Liara's, the guides and our guards, and...

He approached the final wagon. This one had bars on the windows and doors, and all that was inside was Evyn.

Evyn! She was asleep, sprawled in a heap, her hair over her face. *See to her, make sure she's alright!*

My body took a step toward the wagon. Had I done that? I tried again, harder, shoving as much as I could to make my damned legs move.

Hissing, Aglo skidded to a halt and turned about-turn. *"She is for the princess. When we get to the city..."* His thought trailed off, the pain of soullessness rising up like bile in his throat.

We cannot hurt her, I snapped. *I will never let you. I will fight you!*

Far from dissuading him, that seemed to invigorate him. *"Fight me, then, berserker. I'm waiting."*

No matter how much I tried, it was like flailing against a shadow. I couldn't form any blows, let alone land any. How could I fight a spirit? I had to think of something, but the red rage that descended every time Aglo taunted me fogged my thinking.

We were running out of time. Each day the wagons made progress through the desert, wending our way across the shifting sands toward the capital city. Where were Aubin and Gerlay? Why hadn't they intercepted us yet? The sunrises and sunsets brought Evyn closer and closer to the Rushia princess and whatever she wanted her for. I did not have to imagine her fate; Aglo recounted it for me multiple times over to drive me into a towering rage. *"It will be splendid,"* Aglo repeated, laughing at me.

He refused to eat and drank only sparingly, forcing me to walk all day in the blistering heat, so my body was throbbing with exhaustion and my skin cracking with burns at the end of each day. Any time I fell, Liara would laugh, but quietly. She had retreated into herself, a smouldering coal of anger, her green eyes following my every move with the grim promise of pain.

This was the pattern of days for the sennight. And then, we arrived.

RUSH, the capital city of Rush the country, glimmered on the horizon like a mirage in the flat, hot desert. White stone spires pierced the grey dawn of the sky. Watching it come into focus from the heat haze as we approached, the bright colours of the tents and the looming palace in the middle made of white stone brought to mind a rock tossed amongst fragile blooms.

Aglo breathed in deeply. "The palace is complete at last."

A memory drifted out to me, of the city half-built. Heaps of slaves died dragging all that material across the desert, mined or cut from who knows where and shoved across the sands to here. *"I gave up my mortal form before its glory could be realised."*

It is highly impractical and wasteful, I scorned.

"So is building a city on the side of a mountain," he sneered, flicking a memory of Oberrot City at me.

Before I could retort, a sound behind me grabbed all my attention.

"Thorrn?" Evyn was awake in her cell. "Shoulders, is that you?" she called out, voice wavering.

Evyn! I strained to move my body, to turn my head.

Gritting my teeth, Aglo refused to give ground. "Liara, she awakens," he called.

Liara, riding in one of the fore wagons, was travel-worn, the lines along her mouth deeper and hardening her face. She turned to smirk at Evyn, eyes weary. "Good. Just in time to see Sabatha." She beckoned to me.

Aglo vaulted to sit next to her on the bench, and she laid a hand on my bare chest, looking back behind me at Evyn.

Beside the sheer fury at having her hand on me, I felt something like a gentle caress on my sore shoulder.

"Thorrn! Thorrn, it is you, what has she done to you..." Evyn stood, wavering on her feet and clutching her bars. My heart ached.

"Are you sure you have control of him?" Liara murmured in my ear.

"Has this past sennight not convinced you, Mistress?" A spike of annoyance at being asked this question yet again darted through Aglo. "I could run her through right now, he is powerless to resist."

A fleeting thought nearly escaped past me before I snatched it: *to question control is to lose control.* That chimed with what I leant into when controlling my rage. Could he have been *bluffing* this whole time?

No, I couldn't break through his control no matter how much I struggled and fought. I would never stop trying, though.

"Thorrn, what's going on? Talk to me." Evyn's confusion fuelled my rage. I needed to free her, and do it now!

The wagons rattled and bounced along the paved pathways to the central palace. The sultan's seat of power was a frightful size, columns like something a god had to have stood on their ends. The harsh white of the stones concentrated the blazing sun, and I could feel the heat on the burns on my bare skin. It was not the only stone structure in the city, but certainly the biggest.

Guides took us around the back and into a dusty courtyard, mercifully tacked overhead with tatters of tents. Aglo peered into the entrance ahead of us – some kind of loading bay – and let us be disarmed, my sword flung back into the wagon.

"Thorrn, I need you to help me." Evyn's plaintive cry speared my heart, and I redoubled my efforts, straining against Aglo.

He rapped her bars loudly. "Desist, woman."

She sat on her haunches, reaching out between the bars, her lips trembling. I could not even reach out to take her hand! I screamed helplessly.

"Thorrn, something really bad has happened to you. Where are we, what's happening? I really don't feel well. Can you help me?"

She hasn't realised yet that it isn't me!

Aglo grunted. "What do you need?"

Perhaps I was getting somewhere!

Evyn shivered despite the heat, rubbing her cracked lips. "Water. Water to start."

Grabbing a waterskin from the guard, Aglo opened it, splashing it across her bars. "There. Water. Lick it off." Throwing the waterskin to the ground, he stalked up to the entrance, me screaming obscenities at him.

The courtyard fed into a shadowed corridor into the palace, tall walls encouraging breezes to flap the bright fabrics. *"It looks like something I can get lost in, swallowed up never to see daylight again,"* he mused, pleased. *"Inside waits Sabatha, the current Rushia princess of the proud line that I serve, and the destiny of the little Earthian in the wagon."*

A pang raced through him at that thought, but he quickly shook my head. *"It is necessary."*

The hell it is! Don't even think about hurting her, I'll... I'll... But I knew as well as he my threats could only come to naught.

"Psst."

Aglo looked down. Evyn stood beside me, watery grey eyes adjusting to the shade.

Swearing, he raised my hand. She flinched back and my heart cried out a single word – *No!*

My fist froze in the air. Aglo lowered it. "How did you get out?"

She pinged out of the wagon! Evyn, run!

She wrung her hands, blinking away her tears. A single stray one slid down her cheek. "You are really not well. What's happened?"

Aglo took a step back. "Stay away from me, witch." His thoughts whirled. This close, the bond between me and Evyn warmed, comforting and calming me. A gentle, quiet peace beckoned to me beyond the desperate heat of the fiery fury that fuelled me.

I shook it away. *I cannot rest yet. I have to fight to get us free!* I could not give up!

She spoke directly to me, her eyes searching mine. "I promise you, everything is going to be okay. Take my hand." She held it outstretched.

Aglo focused on it, as if she had spoken to him, not me.

She's mine! You killed yours! You don't deserve her, I raged at him.

His thoughts were murky, half-formed. "Ellen," he murmured aloud.

Evyn's eyes widened. "What? Where did you hear that name?" Her hand wavered, but it remained, shaking slightly. "Nevermind that for now, I guess. Let's get out of here, and we will figure it out together."

I tried, oh, how I tried, wrenching at some way to control my own body, to shove Aglo aside, to take her hand. *Take it,* I screamed. *Take it and take her far away from here!*

He wavered. *"I have to keep to orders."*

What does your heart say?

Aglo shoved me away. "No." Aglo's voice was firm. *"This pain is exactly what the gods demand."* As he took her hand, he steeled himself, pulling her into a hold and starting another prayer, drowning out my voice.

Evyn wrapped her arms around me, embracing me, and my heart bled. *Run, Evyn!*

"Liara!" Aglo shouted. "She escaped!"

Evyn tensed. "Thorrn, no! She's not our friend, she—"

"Liara!" Aglo bellowed.

Evyn, run!

Evyn struggled against me, but Aglo held her wrists locked in my grasp. She was small and easy to contain. I flung everything I could at him, to no avail.

Liara stepped from the shadows of the corridor surrounding the palace. "Ah, well done. I should have taken steps when she regained consciousness."

"Thorrn, get out of here!" Evyn cried.

Liara jerked her hand, and Evyn collapsed, dangling from my arms.

No!

Aglo heaved her up and passed her to a guard. "Sorry, Mistress. I did not realise she could escape through bars."

Liara touched my sore shoulder, sending a shock of pain through my right arm. "The crisis was averted. Let's go see Princess Sabatha, shall we?"

"Yes. The time of sacrifice is at hand." Aglo's resolve settled, composed and serene.

No, stop! Not Evyn! I fought wildly, raging against whatever it was holding me back.

Aglo sneered at me. "Let's."

We walked along a cool corridor, headscarfed men and women wearing long white robes passing back and forth. They stared at me and at Evyn over the man's shoulder, averting their eyes when Aglo glared at them. *"Times have changed. Servants would never dare to meet the eyes of their betters before."*

Liara paused at a door to speak to a functionary. She hissed through her teeth. "The Oberrotian king is here," she muttered to herself.

My heart leapt. *If Gough is here, then maybe...*

"They dare not interfere with our commune with the gods," Aglo spat. *"They will be struck down."* He nodded for the guard holding Evyn to go through.

The man let her head fall back, her long hair nearly sweeping the floor as we entered a large hall with dozens of rows of empty stalls facing a dais. Our steps rang down the long aisle, my skin prickling from the sudden cold.

Watching us approach was a girl with deep black hair and dark eyes, seated in front of a large stone slab. Her throat and chest glittered with jewels, heavy rings adorning her tapping fingers. No older than sixteen turns, the sight of the princess of Rushia sent a dart of terror into my heart.

Aglo felt a glow of warmth. *"My princess."* Behind her bristled an array of weather-beaten men, belts of small knives crisscrossing their chests. *"Artists."* Aglo nodded to them.

"Thorrn!" My king and the MasterMage herself were seated in a dock to the right, along with Aubin and Prince Gerlay. A high, wrought-metal railing separated us.

Relief doused me at seeing Aubin and Gerlay. They seemed travel-scuffed but whole and unharmed. Aubin tapped the bars in front of him, watching the man holding Evyn before turning his attention to me.

Aglo halted us. "You survived the mob, then?" he called cheerily.

"No problem," Aubin murmured. His gaze slid back to Evyn. "Is she well? How has she been?"

"None of my concern." Aglo moved to stay with Liara.

"Oh! What has she done to Amare?" Tuniel gasped.

Yes, Amare has taken damage, but so have I. The armour was surrounded by red, inflamed tissue and raw wounds where the men had tried to dig it out of me.

Aglo chuckled at me. *"It seems as though she was only interested in you for one thing. An experiment, kept on a leash and tightly controlled."*

I could vehemently deny it but he saw my experience as much as I had lived through it. I said nothing to him, opting for a bitter silence.

We approached the dais alongside Liara. The guard laid Evyn on a stone table. Shackles gaped open either end of it, but as she lay unconscious no one moved to restrain her.

Princess Sabatha's dark eyes studied her intently. Her gaze flicked up to Liara. "Are you sure this is she? There are tales that Earthians are so beautiful you fall in love with them instantly."

Gough's voice raised in alarm. "Princess Sabatha, the girl before you is the daughter of my soul companion. She is being held against her will."

The princess lifted her hand. "Oberrot will be silent."

Gough's face reddened. "Princess, if you move to harm that girl, it will be considered an act of war."

"Oberrot will be silent, or they will leave the hall. Do not interfere." She was young but held her power with confidence, her voice ringing with authority. "This is my hall, in my father's lands. You have no jurisdiction here whatsoever, and so you will keep that in consideration." She nodded to Liara.

"It is her. I can feel the power in her blood," Liara said in Rushia.

The princess turned her sceptical eyes up to me. "And you? Are you immune to magic?"

"Yes, Your Highness." Aglo went to my hands and knees, pressing my forehead to the cold floor briefly before sitting back on my heels.

Her eyes widened slightly. "Your Rushia is... old." Frowning, she stood from her throne, making her way over to the stone table with steady steps, seeming unable to take her eyes off Evyn.

Nodding to herself, the princess set a hand next to the Evyn's head. "I wish to speak with her."

"Speak?"

The princess frowned. "Yes, Liara, the act that allows minds to meet." She called her guards over. "Bring her to the rest hall. Give her attention so that she recovers and treat her well."

One came forward to take Evyn from the stone table.

Aglo frowned. *"This isn't right."*

Good. Anything that makes you uncomfortable, I'm all for it. Aglo's confusion could only be to the good. Evyn wasn't immediately being eviscerated as he had expected. *Maybe times have changed since you threw your life away.*

"Princess, are you going to kill her?" he asked as the guards took Evyn into their arms.

Indignant spots of colour rose in the princess's cheeks. "Of course I'm not going to kill her," she said, nose wrinkling in disgust. "You foreigners and your wild notions."

Aglo's hot disappointment was matched against the surge of hope blasting through me.

The princess looked me up and down. "Are you in distress? Do you need rescue?"

Yes! Help me!

Aglo bent my body down to the floor. "I am exactly where I need to be, Your Highness." He stood slowly, my legs shaking as what he expected to happen clashed against reality. *"Is she truly a princess of the old line, if she holds to these... soft ways?"*

Studying me for a moment more, Sabatha nodded. "Very well." The princess turned her piercing gaze to Liara. "Your gift is well received. You will be rewarded in time."

"But... you said you would give me the tangle immediately in exchange for the Earthian," Liara said, her eyes hot.

The princess's lips thinned.

Liara dug her chipped fingernails into my forearm. Aglo kept my face stoic, offering up the pinpricks of pain.

The princess's expression darkened, her gaze flicking to Liara's hand clenched around my arm. "We will discuss your reward later. In the meantime, you will enjoy the protection of the palace." She raised her voice toward the king's party. "You Oberrotians and Dinahens are not to continue your little fights here. I will consider it an act of grave discourtesy."

"What about if we take it outside?" Aubin asked, voice deadly serious.

Gough shushed him with a sharp jerk of his hand, frustration in his tight lips.

The princess shook her head in disgust and left along with Evyn and her guards. My heart went with her. What would happen to Evyn now?

"Ranger Shardsson," Gough growled. "I am your ultimate authority. Desist what you are doing and return to me, now."

"He's not himself." Aubin pressed himself against the dock sides. "Come here. I need a word with you, spirit."

To my shock, Aglo swaggered up. *I'll place bets hands down that he'll get the best of you.*

"I have the upper hand, fool. I hold your life in my hands, and he will not want to cause an international incident on Rushia lands."

I cannot wait to see this.

Stalking up, Aglo kept a wary guard against trickery, stopping out of range. "Well? I'll let you go first."

Aubin's lips thinned, taking in my sunburnt skin baking me browns and reds, and the prominent swelling of my right shoulder. "Amare prohibere."

Agony lanced across my chest and arm as the armour deployed, flowing from my savaged shoulder. Even so, I laughed at Aubin cornering Aglo.

"You rat," Aglo shouted as the armour froze my arms to my sides.

Aubin's gaze was cold. "Now you'll have to come see us if you want to wipe your own arse tonight."

Aglo boiled with hot shame. "Fine," he snapped. Under the simmer of his anger, I felt a hideous resolve.

What can you possibly do now to escape this?

He made an about-turn and marched back to Liara. "Mistress, this body has been compromised. I suggest we dispose of it."

Uh oh.

Her far-away gaze swept onto me, disgust curling her lip. Wiping her eyes, she let out a low, slow breath. "I am this close to breaking point," she mumbled. She looked it, clothes travel-stained, her shoulders trembling with exhaustion.

"Vent some of your anger. Kill me."

Shock lanced through my chest.

Liara's fingers parted to peer at me through them. "Your pardon?"

"Kill the swordsman. Spill his blood here, in homage to my gods, and release me from my service. I have fulfilled the task you asked of me."

Oh, hells.

Liara mouth fixed into a hard line. "Kneel facing the Oberrotians and give me your knife."

He obeyed, and my field of view was straight ahead at the party leaving opposite, Gough giving his arm to Tuniel. Aubin saw and frowned, halting the others.

Liara laid the knife across my throat. "Well, Tuniel," she called. Her voice trilled, too high and bright. "It looks like this pawn is useless to me now."

CHAPTER 17

Aubin touched her elbow, then stepped forward. "He's useless to us as well. Spiritsights are fatal. He's just a danger to us." He leant against the bars separating us, arms folded. "I gave him up for dead, and when we tracked the soul jewel and saw it unmoving in the desert, I mourned him then."

Part of me hoped this was a bluff, because if not, it meant he wouldn't attempt to save me from this utter hell of an existence, trapped in a body I couldn't influence committing atrocities with my skills. I tried to guard my thoughts from Aglo, but as in a lodestone, they slipped away from me.

"The berserker thinks he is showing a false face, Mistress," Aglo murmured to Liara. The blade against my neck focused his attention, making him suck in breaths as though they would be his last.

Had he died like this? I lashed out, hoping to catch a glimpse of a memory, and got assailed by them. I couldn't understand or parse it now, however.

Aubin's face was flat. "Am I bluffing, spirit? It was you who said I would come to the right conclusion. I have. Whatever you are, whoever you were, you're not anyone I'd care to rescue."

"If you want him dead, then be my guest." Liara smiled.

"By all means." Aubin drew a knife and hefted it.

My heart beat slow and sure. I pulled down the calm of battle. *I am dead already.* There was no way out of this horror, and my allies knew it. Even now Tuniel held back, able to watch her soul companion kill me right in front of her.

My eyes burnt with tears. I felt the knife close to my throat and watched the blade Aubin held, ready to throw across the distance. Which one would claim my life? Neither could back down from their positions now. Who would? Or would they both stand-off forever?

"Both of you have rescinded your claim on him," an angry voice said. The princess had returned, her mouth twisted in disgust at both parties. "I claim him. Let him go."

"Princess, he's an officer in the Oberrotian army," Gough protested.

"Princess, he is my slave," Liara cried.

Sabatha snapped, "And both of you were going to kill him! His life meant nothing to either of you. It is mine now."

With her gesture, the Artists behind her came toward me, and Liara was forced to step back.

Aglo stood up with my arms locked to my sides.

"Tuniel MasterMage of Oberrot, release his restrictions," the princess ordered.

Tuniel raised her hand, and the armour flowed back into my shoulder. It was terribly sore, and Aglo leant into the pain, mind wiped clear by the white-hot moment of agony.

The princess beckoned to me and Aglo followed her, dragging my feet.

Disappointed you didn't get your second chance at death? I sniped at him. *So good you wanted to relive it, as it were?*

"Silence, berserker."

We entered a cool corridor open on one side, a large courtyard filled with shade and water and green. Aglo blinked, my eyes watering in the light.

He cast about as if he were lost. *"What is this?"* He sounded utterly repulsed.

It's beautiful. I hadn't seen green vegetation since...

"Refreshment?" A servant asked me, jerking Aglo out of his reverie and into an offence stance.

The man cowered. The princess frowned at us.

Aglo bowed my head, the motions rigid. "No. I wish to fast, to purify this vessel."

"Vessel?" Sabatha took a step closer.

Surveying the open space that made anyone crossing it vulnerable, Aglo trembled, keeping to the shade of the corridor.

The princess's hand landed lightly on my arm.

Aglo flinched back. *"The touch of a god!"*

She's a princess, but she will be human. It was calm in this open space, with servants moving quietly here and there, their long white robes trailing behind them. None of the trailing edges betrayed traces of blood, as I'd expected and Aglo evidently anticipated.

"Princess, if I may... what is this place?" Aglo feared to speak, but Sabatha's face creased with concern.

"It's obvious you have been mistreated. You will understand in time that your past is behind you now. Here you will find rest, recuperation, healing and help. You do not need to be afraid anymore."

"Afraid," we scoffed.

"I'm not afraid," Aglo said aloud.

Nor I, I said, but worry for Evyn clawed at me.

Aglo heard. "Where is the Earthian?"

I caught the edges of his dire intent. *No, don't you dare!*

"I gave my life to serve the gods," he snapped back at me. *"The real gods, not this flawed, soft-hearted wench!"*

"The rest hall. This way." Sabatha waved for me to follow. He stalked the perimeter after her, past burbling waterfalls and clever stone carvings harbouring fresh blooms. The air hung heavy with nectar, and he wrinkled my nose. Artists patrolled the palace roof in pairs, their shadows tracing around the edges of the courtyards.

Sabatha kept a few steps ahead of me, and Aglo's steps were firm with purpose. Artists tensed as I passed by. *Stop him!* I screamed at them. *Stop me!*

I could hear laughter. Aglo smiled in anticipation of turning it into screams.

Aglo, stop. Your religion has moved on, your gods are dead or changed by time, you have to stop! You serve the royals, do you not? The princess is right here, she wants the Earthian alive!

His humming drowned me out.

The rest hall lay open to the courtyard so that breezes and scents from the herbs in the gardens would aid convalescence. Beds lined up in rows, covered in crisp colourful linen in soothing blues and greens. The scent stuck in my sinuses, pulling me back to memories of lying dying with someone keeping the skin on my back together, and someone else holding my hand.

Aglo, please. I'm begging you.

"*At last. I was expecting this much sooner, but you broke at last.*"

Don't hurt her. Do what you want with me, I will not fight you ever again, but please, leave Evyn be.

"*I am already in control, whether you fight me or not. You cannot change my course.*" He flexed my fist.

The servant led me past various sick individuals to a more secluded room. Evyn was awake and resting abed, her face pale and her eyes red. A quick survey showed four guards, one at each corner of the room.

Evyn tucked her knees up to her chest. "Thorrn?" she croaked.

The princess stepped close to the bed. "Well met," she said in perfect Oberrotian. "I am Sabatha. It is a pleasure to meet you."

Evyn dragged her gaze away from me to face her. "Oh, sorry love,

I was distracted... Please, that's my soul companion, and I don't think he's well." She touched the deep circles under her eyelids; she looked sallow and sick.

Aglo. No. I marshalled every single corner of my being toward a towering rage. I had to break his control, and I had to do it now!

My heart hardened, the edges of Aglo's resolve clear.

Evyn frowned. "Are you an alt? An alternative version, I mean. If you are, there's no need to be afraid, I'll look after you."

It hurt me to hear her say that when she could barely sit upright, and a soft touch on my sore shoulder sent pain wracking through us both. Evyn had Found me.

She clutched her blankets. "It's you, but... you're acting strangely. How long did Liara have us?" Fear flickered in her eyes as she met Aglo's glare, screwing her fists closed. "Thorrn, is there anything left of the real you in there? Or did Liara torture it out of you? What's come over you, it's like you're possessed!"

Sabatha spun toward me. "Has he ever acted this way before? You can tell me truthfully."

Evyn hesitated only briefly. "No, he's not like this. He's a bit arrogant but he's a sweetheart really."

Aglo took a halting step forward, ready to sing her to the gods as my hands throttled the life out of her.

Now! I threw all I had against Aglo, trying to snarl my legs, to stop my hips, to break every bone in my body, anything other than just sit here! Screaming, I battered against him, but he pushed me away, a cruel smirk twisting his lips.

Evyn cowered, and anger burnt through me so white-hot that all I could see was her fear. *Evyn!*

The princess took a step between us. Eyes blazing, she thrust her hand into my chest. Her fingers slid beneath skin with unbearable pain, tearing into something deep.

Aglo wailed and cut off, as sudden as a snuffed candle. The absence of his voice, his presence, felt like I had been bowed before a savage wind which now ceased to blow. I staggered forward, my limbs all tingling and sparking with pains. My lungs hurt, my throat was sore, my shoulder and my skin throbbed, but worst of all was the pain in my heart at seeing Evyn look at me in horror.

Sabatha heaved back. Black mist coiled around her fist, a dazzling glare that flashed and flared, pulsing in time with my hurried heartbeat. She tugged, and bile lurched up my throat, Aglo's influence trickling out as she weaved the mist around her small ring-laden fingers.

Guards grabbed my arms to keep me upright and prevent me from taking another step. My head dropped forward as Sabatha gave a few more pulls, each one reaching deep into my body and feeling as though she prised strings out from along my bones. Nausea overtook me, and I retched, sagging into the arms of the guards.

With a final gentle twist, Sabatha drew all the black mist she had excised from me and curled it into a ball in her hands.

I could barely lift my head. "Ev—" I vomited again, bringing up nothing but yellow liquid that stung my throat. My chest was whole, no wound and no blood, though it felt as though I had run fifty miles at pace.

Tugging my left arm free, I swung a fist, hoping to connect. The guard grabbed my arm and twisted it behind me.

"Thorrn, stay calm!" Evyn said.

I cannot, I need to fight! I had struggled for so long that giving up now was impossible, not when Evyn was only an arm's length away from me.

"Guards, put him in the cells for now." Sabatha's black hair flew around her head, the mist tracing up and down her arms. She glared at it rather than me. "I need to deal with this."

They already held my arms, containing me. My ears rang, and I swallowed to clear them. When Evyn sat up reaching out to me, I set my stance and resisted the push of the guards, unable to leave her beseeching look, but her eyes rolled back in her head and she slumped to the side of the bed.

"I'll look after her," Sabatha said. Her eyes glowed obsidian as she held the seething mass of mist in her hands.

Whether or not I trusted her, the guards pushed and shoved me out, and I could not stand against them. I tried to fight, my body responding at last to my commands, but I was half-starved, dehydrated and dead on my feet, and they pulled me off them with sickening ease.

They dragged me down into hot clammy cells, the walls bare and scrubbed clean but still bearing scars of crimson with a grille in the centre of the room, the metal rusted red. I swayed on my feet as the knife fighters manacled my wrists and chained me to the wall, tying a gag tightly between my teeth and knotting it at the back of my head.

Not knife fighters – Artists. Some of Aglo's knowledge remained with me. I hoped that was all that remained, but despite my exhaustion I was satisfied that my fingers curled to my commands, my legs moved for me, and the betrayal of my body was over.

The princess had pulled a spiritsight from me. I had not realised Rush had that kind of power over the spirits, the part that remained after death. Perhaps no one did, as Tuniel hadn't mentioned it.

Tuniel. As the Artists left me, my chest shivered with an unvoiced sob. What was she doing here? Perhaps Gough had asked her to come, to try to retrieve me. My king had come down here himself, and I had seen only Aubin and Gerlay there to protect him. Gerlay looked well at least, but Aubin...

He had given me up for dead and been ready to kill me. And why not? I was a dangerous swordsman. Aglo had come close to killing him and would have tried to do so again.

I collected myself, sinking to kneel on the floor, my arms raised. Both Liara and Sabatha had worked or wielded a black smoke which turned out to be Aglo. His departure was cause for celebration, except for our predicament now, the worst case that could have happened in Rush. Liara had given Evyn as a gift, and the princess had taken me for her own. Was Evyn going to be hurt? The princess seemed disgusted at the notion. But what else would someone want an Earthian for, if not their blood?

Tears pressed against my eyes, salt stinging my sun-scoured cheeks. I couldn't feel Evyn at all. She had slept much of the way here, she had to be suffering, and I hadn't helped her at all.

I snuffled with sobs, my ribs aching to voice them.

"At last. There you are."

I looked up, snorting through my tears.

Aubin stood next to the sandstone wall, looking critically at the chains and my gag. He looked well, if a bit drawn, his eyes sandy but every hair in place.

"It's me!" I tried to say. It came out as a kind of gargle.

"Yes. Just calculating here. Looks like you do not have a significant reach. I'll need to come close to get the gag off. Very considerate of Rush to supply me with facilities to interrogate you," he murmured, pacing toward me. "And now the dangerous bit." He drew a blade. "Make a move and I'll stab you."

I nodded, opening my mouth wide for him to remove the gag.

Pulling it free with quick fingers, he retreated. "Good. Well. You said you wanted a few words."

"Aubin," I rasped. "It's me." I ran my sponge-like tongue around my dry mouth.

"Ah yes. Now that you're incarcerated, you're our hero with the silvrine armour, back once more." His gaze did not waver from mine, but I couldn't see anything other than hard edges to him now, his eyes cold, his jaw stiff.

I didn't know what to say to him, how to start. How could I convince him I was myself again? There was nothing I could say or do to prove I was telling the truth. Aglo had had access to my memories easily enough.

I rolled my sore shoulders, wincing. "Evyn is up in the internal courtyard. There's a lot of greenery like the vegetation on Earth.

She's in something called the rest hall, which is in the third court-yard along, in a private room toward the back. She has a bed, she doesn't look like she's restricted in any way, and the princess was with her. They seemed to be getting along." A smile tugged at my lips. "Evyn is charming her, like she charms everyone. I don't think she's in any immediate danger except that she's a known Earthian in Rush. The princess didn't seem minded to hurt her, did she?"

Aubin tapped his hands on his forearms, rapping his leather bracers. "No, she did not. She definitely wants Evyn alive." He grimaced. "Has something happened to change your mind?"

I nodded once. "Liara unleashed a spirit on me, a Rushia fanatic named Aglo. But the princess pulled him right out of my chest." I looked down, still amazed to find there was no blood, even though I clearly recalled her hand plunging into me.

Aubin's eyes narrowed. "Go on."

I settled into a reporting cadence despite kneeling on cold stone with my arms upraised. "Liara surprised us in the streets. I picked up Evyn, and Liara was able to enchant me. I'm not immune to magic when I'm touching her, recall. Then Liara used a black mist, it rushed at me and got inside me." I shuddered, chains clinking and shivering. "After the mob brought down Al Shur we went into the desert. Aglo was determined to harm Evyn, and he told Liara that I killed Waker. She exacted some of her revenge directly against me and meant for the princess to kill Evyn in front of me as the rest, but it did not turn out as either of them expected. Liara was disappointed she didn't get something, and Aglo just wanted... wanted..." My stomach turned again to recall his cold purpose flooding my body with murderous resolve against Evyn.

More tears pressed at my eyes. "She slept the whole way. I think she was exhausted and drained from Liara using her to enchant the whole town but... I wasn't there for her, I wasn't helping her, I didn't lean into the bond, so she's probably even more ill." My chest heaved with sobs, but they were useless right now. I needed to focus.

Aubin would help her.

Aubin moved closer to me, and my heart leapt at the show of trust. "It seems Liara also tried to gouge the armour out of your shoulder." He circled around me, muttering darkly. When he came back in front of me, his hands balled into fists. "I had to leave you with Liara. Everyone was upset about that, but Evyn was weaker without you, and I knew Liara would be using her even more. She needed all the help your proximity could give her." He rubbed his forehead. "For what it's worth, I'm not sorry about that. She might very well have died if you weren't near her." He sounded like he was trying to convince me, amber eyes flicking between mine.

"I... yes. That was sensible."

He dropped his head. "I ... I'm regretful it was necessary that I left you in Liara's hands. She did not look after you."

I shuddered, pain and stress spilling free. "Aubin. Aubin, I need to... I need to..." I bit my lip hard to stop it trembling. "Please, get her out of here."

Squatting down next to me, he lowered his voice. "We're working on getting you both out. It's complicated." Aubin grimaced. "You are both slaves of the princess. We are going to try and bargain for you, buy you back, whatever acceptable method we can use, but if it looks like either of you is in danger, we are going to break you out. That could spark a war, and no one wants that."

I shook my head. "No. Don't cause a war over me, but please, get Evyn out."

Aubin nodded slowly.

I sniffed loudly. He held up a pocket square. I took it with thanks. "What happened to you? How did you escape the mob Liara enchanted?"

"Gerlay and I escaped from Al Shur using the travel mage Tuniel sent. Tuniel came and tracked you using the soul jewel, but we had no way of containing you if we did manage to capture you. When the jewel halted in the desert, Tuniel took us there. We thought we would find your body." He took the small, light green stone out of his pocket. It glowed fitfully.

My chest warmed, overfilled with joy. "You found it!"

He nodded. "Meanwhile Gough has been working on political channels as we knew Liara was heading to the princess. It took the full sennight to get an audience with her, but we were too late, and Liara was shown in at exactly the same time." He grimaced.

"You did the best you could." I sniffled. "How have you been?"

He put his hands behind his back. "Somewhat galvanised. Gerlay and I have been working together to track you, plan your rescue and develop moves to take you down. It hasn't been fun exactly, but it was not entirely unpleasant."

I smiled at him. "See, I knew you'd be a great Ranger."

"Hm."

"If it helps your ego, Aglo had you targeted as the most dangerous from the very start."

"This spirit would have been taking from your assessment, and you have an overinflated opinion of me, so..." His lips tugged up at the edges as I shook my head at him. "Fine. I'll take the compliment." He sat beside me, back against the wall, one leg extended along the floor.

I grinned at him, shuffling to sit, arms still raised. "Put those moves you used against me in the manoeuvre planning."

"Oh, I have been. And I've been sending full morning reports to Barlay. He likes my reports. He calls them pithy." He cleared his throat. "We need you back."

"I want to be back. I need... I need to get back to you all." I tried to hold back another hitch in my breath.

"Can you hold on a little longer? We are trying to find a diplomatic solution. While we wait, I want to investigate those spirits—"

"No." My heart jumped in my chest. "Do not go anywhere near him."

He raised his hands. "I have a theory, and I want to see if it bears out. I will do research and read the records here in Rush. I'm not going to go anywhere near Liara."

I nodded. Library research sounded a great deal safer. "Aubin, do you know why the princess wants Evyn?"

He nodded once. "She wants an Earthian soul companion. My theory is, she wants one to protect herself from magic."

My chest squeezed hard, as if from a blow. *No.* "Please, if you can, please don't let them do that." My heart howled. "She's mine, and I know I haven't been anything near good for her—"

"It wasn't your fault, it was some blasted spirit." He patted my scarred forearm. "If it helps, this is what I felt. Both times, after Waker and Liara."

It did and it didn't help. To know that I was vulnerable did not help protect me against anything. Preparing and pushing hard was the only way to do that. Knowing that Aubin understood my utter helplessness, shame and disgust fixed none of it. All the same, my chest felt lighter, loosening as if to pass him some of the burden.

We had to focus. "Help Evyn. Help me," I begged him.

"I will. You are not alone." He set the stone on Amare. The metal formed around it, and the pain as it moved caused me to bite the inside of my cheeks.

He winced at the damage on my shoulder. "This is going to have to come out."

"No, please, I need it." I bowed my head.

"I will go and tell the others you have returned to us and start to investigate spiritsights in earnest. Meanwhile, Gough and Gerlay will be playing the politics game." He looked down. "He is a good man. Gerlay, I mean."

My heart warmed. For him to say such things about the man meant much.

He gave me some water. "I can return and stay in the next cell along to rescue you in the morning if need be."

The offer made me sit up straighter. "My thanks, but you need to guard the king and scope out where Evyn is first. Make sure she is safe and well. Stay with her if you have any doubts."

He saluted. "Yes, sir." He waved and pinged away, and the light flickered out in the soul jewel.

Alone again, except not. I closed my eyes and felt the tremble of the soul bond, and the more intangible bonds between me, my friends and my liege. Aglo and Liara had neatly severed their importance from me, but they had stood firm and true and come for me. Now I just had to be patient.

CHAPTER 18

I SOMEHOW MANAGED TO CATCH SNATCHES OF SLEEP, SPLUTTERING AWAKE when the cell door banged open and Artists surrounded me.

"Up," they grunted.

I knew I would get no answers from them, so I saved my dry mouth from moving and instead gathered myself. I would need to find where Evyn was in relation to me and how she fared, orientate myself to the palace and assess the security of the inner sanctum. Now that my mind was solely my own again, I could think things through.

I let them unchain me from the wall and stood while they manacled my hands together. They took the chains to lead me through the sweltering corridors to another cell. Surrounded on all sides, I tried to see what I could, but they tugged me forward any time I slowed.

The room was empty except for one chair. "We wait." One of the men glowered. He wore a bandolier of knives, each one no bigger than the smallest finger of my hand, all gleaming in the light. "Sit."

With nothing else to do, I sat on the edge of the chair, the wood creaking under me. Where was Evyn? Closing my eyes, I tried to feel out where she could be, but the idea of encountering anything inside me made my stomach clench. What if I found some remnant of Aglo?

The princess came in, followed by two other Artists who took a station at the door.

I rose to my feet, but the Artist holding my manacled hands yanked me back down. I fell back, head spinning.

Sabatha placed her hands in front of her. "Give him water."

A guard handed me a glass, and I guzzled it gratefully. It splashed on my bare chest, and sudden shame welled up at how sweaty and unkempt I must appear. I was shirtless in front of a princess.

She held herself composed, her face hiding any disgust she might feel for me. "You have nothing to fear here. It will take you some time to believe that, I know, but I want to reassure you." She tapped one of her many necklaces. "I was able to retrieve the spirit that has terrorised you. Your soul companion is safe and well. I've sent word to her that you are here; she will come momentarily."

My arms and legs started to shake. I mastered them, forcing them to stillness. "I... Thank you."

"What's your name?"

I could give that at least. "Thorrn Shardsson, Ranger in the Oberrotian army. King Gough can attest to that, Your Highness."

Sabatha pressed her palms together. "Yes, he has been attesting at length and at volume. Meanwhile, the ex-Sinjorina Majestica of Dinahe Liara said to me privately that you wish to be returned to her."

"No, please. Not Liara." I swallowed as what Liara had done to me pressed into my chest, filling my stomach with bile. I quailed at the mere thought of seeing her again; I nearly retched but mastered myself. "Not her."

She nodded once. "I have ended my dealings with the mage of love. She has vanished now." She sighed. "The other Oberrotian is suddenly asking to name my price for you. This is after he tried to kill you, of course. I will never understand Oberrotians."

"That's just Aubin; he's hard to understand anyway, Your Highness."

She chuckled, but quickly her face dropped into a frown. "This makes it difficult. Liara told me there was an Earthian in distress. I thought that I could have an Earthian soul companion to protect me from the... all magics." I noticed her correct herself. "I had hoped you would give her willingly."

I looked at the Artists either side of me. Although Rushia were smaller in stature generally, these had the build of Daronian wrestlers. "Even if your men torture me, I wouldn't give Evyn up willingly. Not unless she wanted to separate from me of her own free will."

Sabatha scowled. "Torture? Oh, gods. You Oberrotians."

I bowed my head. "I know you could have me killed. I respectfully beg that you release Evyn, please. And please don't harm her."

"What is it with foreigners being so afraid of Rush?"

I glanced up into her hard gaze. "Uhh..."

She waved a bejewelled hand. "Speak your mind."

"The... sacrifice thing?"

Her lips twisted. "I've explained this to Evyn. She seemed to find it sensible once she understood."

"She did?" My heart clenched. "She's not, I mean... she hasn't...?"

She cocked her head. "She's not volunteering. Was there a concern there?"

"No, no, none. Well, maybe a little. My apologies," I said as the princess rolled her eyes. "I... I'm worried about her. I'd like to see her."

Sabatha nodded slowly, her golden earrings waving. "She has described her illness to me, and it sounds debilitating. I have a perspective on it which may help. However." She looked to her guards. "I would like to be in more comfortable surroundings for everyone. Not in a cell, for example."

"Would you know it, I was hoping the same thing."

She chuckled again. "You are very amusing. The other half of your spirit is very delightful as well."

"I know. I love her very much."

She sighed. "I can see that. I would not wish to separate loving companions. I will ask my chief of security what he thinks of moving you back up, but I expect there will be restrictions until you have proved yourself."

"Understandable, yes, I did try to punch one or two of your guards, and thank you. This is … much more than I expected."

"Much more what? Reasonable?" She sighed. "Foreigners."

"I … yes. Happy to have my expectations challenged and my eyes opened, Your Highness."

She inclined her head and left with some of the guards, and I remained sat in place with two guards as company.

This is wildly different to what I expected. Even Aglo had been disconcerted by what he found here, believing he would find a princess as fanatic as himself in worshipping their gods.

My ears popped and the guards snapped into a defence stance. I turned around to see what had startled them. "Evyn!"

My soul companion stood at the door, wearing a white robe and barefoot. Her eyes were wide. "Sabatha said you were in here and that you were yourself. I wanted to see if you were okay."

"Yes, Evyn, it's me, it's really me. I'm really sorry about... wait, stop!" The guards advanced on her.

I stood, an Artist moving to slam me back down. Grabbing his forearms, I twisted and put my foot out, tripping him to the floor. The others grabbed handfuls of knives from their chest straps.

"Stop!" Evyn backed up to the door. "Alright, I've caused a stir. Sabatha says she's sorting something out, so I'll clear off for now. But don't you dare hurt him!" She scowled at the guards. Her gaze softened when she met my eyes again. "I'll be right outside, Thorrn, okay?"

I sank back down. "Yes. Yes, that's fine."

She pinged back out, the guards muttering to one another. I

stared at the door, my heart much lifted, as if I could see through it to her small shape standing sentinel outside. I could barely contain myself, knowing she was close, my half of our spirit longing for hers.

When Sabatha came back, she allowed Evyn in. She ran for me, flinging her arms around my neck, and I tucked my chin into her shoulder, burying my face in her hair as our bond renewed with a soothing wash of relief.

"Let's get you a bath and some clothes." Evyn started to cry. "And a medimancer. And ... and food, and whatever else you need."

"I need you. Stay with me, please."

"Of course." She turned to the Rushia princess. "Sabatha, can we do all that, please? I'll get Gough to pay."

The corners of Sabatha's eyes glittered, and she wiped them quickly. "There is no need for payment. Please, the facilities are yours, although my chief is wary of him being completely unfettered after his attack against the palace guards yesterday."

Evyn opened her mouth to argue. "Yeah, but that was—"

"And just now," the Artist I'd bowled to the floor complained.

Sabatha closed her eyes briefly.

"Evyn, it's understandable," I said quickly to smooth things over. "We can keep the shackles on for now." My arms were in front of me at least.

"I still don't like it," Evyn said, glowering, but when the guard let me stand she threaded her arm through mine and hustled me out of the door.

We walked up two flights of steps, the air getting more breathable as we went up until we came out along the cool corridor. Sunlight lit her tired eyes as she looked up at me. "Sabatha explained that you had one of those ghosts in you, but you're all better now. What happened exactly?" she asked. "I remember arriving into the border city with the guys and... and then waking up alone in a moving cell with you completely different. I wondered if I had fallen into an alternative reality like Evie does. And then, well, when I ping out to see you..."

My stomach fell. "It must have seemed as though I betrayed you. I'm so sorry." Regret and self-loathing still tangled my stomach.

She must have felt it, touching my hand. "I remember Liara cornering us in the street, but that's all. It must have been hard to see her again."

Fear and anger rose in my throat as a ball of rage. I pushed it back. "You collapsed, but I forgot that I'm not immune to magic when I'm touching you, of course, and it seems as though Liara knew that. She was able to enchant me and then she... she unleashed a spirit somehow. She had a ring that looks like the jewellery Sabatha has. He was called Aglo, and he was rather enthusiastic about the Rushia religion. He had complete control over me, doing Liara's bidding, with the first order being to kill Aubin and Gerlay." Evyn had gone pale. "Are you hale? Do we need to rest?"

Her mouth fell open. "Killing Aubin? Gerlay?"

"They survived," I said hastily. "They are here in the palace now; they followed the caravan for a while and then got ahead of it."

"Phew. Okay." Evyn patted her chest.

"We fought, but while they may have had the upper hand to start, my skills turned the tables on them the second time. Aglo would have won if they hadn't fled."

She rolled her eyes at me. "Well. Interesting, I suppose."

I grinned at her, then grimaced. "Liara enchanted a mob using your energy to get me out of the Rushia barracks, and it laid you out for the whole sennight we were in the caravan to get to Rush. Liara knows I killed Waker. She tried to tear the armour out of my shoulder."

"Oh, Thorrn. That must have been horrible."

"It was, but it's over now." Pain and shame coiled in my stomach and chest, sharp and angry.

Evyn touched my hand, and her understanding and acceptance hurt almost as much. "You just went through something terrible. It's okay to not be okay, Thorrn."

I shook my head. "I need to focus. We could still be in danger here. The princess wants you for the immunity from magic, like Torgund did."

Evyn flushed. "Ah. Awkward."

"Yes, but... she wants us to agree willingly. Which I won't, ever, but I still find it strange that she's not going to just kill me and take you."

"Not so strange, Thorrn. Civilised." Evyn glanced up at me. "I had a nice chat with her. Rush has had a lot of misconceptions and just flat-out racism laid against it. Yes, they do hold gods and goddesses in high regard and they have a big respect for life, life lived freely and fully. They respect it so much that when someone is suffering, they send them on to paradise with their gods, right? Even if you're a convicted criminal sentenced to death, you get to go in the light of the gods, not as a punishment but an 'oh, you got it wrong this time, try better next time.'

"Sabatha says Rush has had dark periods like any country where the ruler gets a bit stab-happy, but she wants a fresh start and a new image for her country. Unfortunately, she's battling against prejudices like 'human sacrifice' and stuff."

"Because ... they do, Evyn!" I lowered my voice, scouting the courtyard with quick glances.

Evyn scowled, tapping my forearm. "But not the way you're thinking." Frowning, she lifted her hand to her forehead.

My stomach lurched. "Are you well?"

"Yes. Bit ... bit dizzy."

"Sit here and lean against me."

She collapsed, and I caught her. Immediately a servant hurried up, ushering me toward the rest hall.

"What is wrong?" Sabatha and the guard were passing.

"She's not well." I wanted to clutch her to my chest, but the chains pressed between us. "She is being drained by Liara. Something is making her tired all the time and likely to fall asleep in a heartbeat."

The princess tensed.

I hesitated. What did she know about that? Regardless, I had to secure aid for Evyn now, and without putting her at risk. "Aubin Tabreksson, the Oberrotian who tried to kill me, he's treating her."

Sabatha nodded. "Guards, take her to the rest hall and call for the Oberrotians. Ranger Shardsson, perhaps you would want a bath and to see to your wounds after seeing her there safely?"

I did, desperately. I had several days of desert clinging to me, and I could barely look at my shoulder without wincing.

I oversaw Evyn's installation back into a comfortable bed, and then attempted to undress and bathe myself with my hands chained while being watched by two men. I was used to bathing in company, of course, but not studied extensively as I did so.

New clothes were acquired for me, baggy trousers and some kind of blanket with a hole in the centre. The guards slipped the latter over my head, making a sleeveless garment. The fabric rubbed on my sunburns, setting them alight. I endured it, eager to return to Evyn's side.

When I came back to Evyn and the princess in the rest hall, I was gratified to see Aubin standing next to Evyn's bedside, deep in discussion with a medimage.

I pulled up next to him. "Well met!"

"Thorrn, well met." He took me in calmly. "You seem better looked after."

Sabatha frowned at him. "As if you care. You were ready to end his life."

"Yes, he cares," I told her. "That's why he was going to do it."

She rolled her eyes. "Oberrotians."

Evyn blinked awake. "Oh. Drat. Not again." I sat on the edge of her bed, and she pulled herself up and took my hand, blinking around at everyone. "Hi, Aubin! How are you?"

"Very well, Lady Evyn." He inclined his head. "I'm glad to see you. That puts my fears to rest."

She beamed at him, and my heart swelled, even broken and battered as it was. The bubble in my solar plexus was tempered against the current peril we found ourselves in, but there was no denying that my soul companion felt delight upon seeing Aubin.

Sabatha stared between me and Evyn. She looked down quickly, her cheeks darker.

I straightened up. "If you don't mind me asking, Your Highness, where is Liara now?"

The princess studied her entwined hands. "That I do not know. However, I wish to ask for your assistance in... addressing an error I have made concerning her." She drew herself up. "Evyn seems to think that the Oberrotians, with the support of the Dinahens, will be able to help my situation."

"Yes, we had a nice chat last night." Reaching over, Evyn touched the princess's hand. "But we need Gough, Tuniel and Gerlay in on this. I promise they will be able to help, Sabatha."

Sabatha grimaced. "But at what price?"

"Well..." Evyn looked at me as if checking it was all right to speak. I nodded encouragingly. "Thorrn did say he wanted to tackle it anyway."

"Wait, what? Tackle what?" I sat up. "The Rushia smoke stuff? Are those spirits? Oh no, no no no, I'm not going anywhere near it if that's the case." Except it was draining Evyn. I took a deep breath. "Yes. I have to, don't I?" Fighting something that could take me over in a heartbeat, trapping me in my own body and rendering me help-less... it was impossible.

I squeezed Evyn's hand in mine. If it was the only way, then I would have to throw myself at it.

Aubin put his hand on my good shoulder. "We will think of something. All the best minds will be applied to the task."

"You're right." I did not have to do this alone.

CHAPTER 19

We waited for Gough, Gerlay and Tuniel to be shown in. When they arrived, I saluted my king. "I am devastated, Your Majesty. I was severely compromised. Please inform Captain Barlay that the spirit had access to all my thoughts and—"

"Thorrn." Gough grabbed my forearms. "Lad, you look somewhat better, but you need to rest and recover. Ranger Aubin has it all in hand, and I am in talks with Sabatha about the entity in question." He nodded to the princess, who inclined her head in return.

My stomach relaxed slightly. The king looked care-worn and tired, eyes red with sleeplessness, but they crinkled in the corners as he smiled at me. He was pleased to see me returned, and I was equally relieved to be back under his command once more. I saluted, and he nodded to me before taking a seat.

Gerlay took Evyn's hand briefly, genuinely delighted to see her, before bowing and backing away from the bed. She looked down at the bed covers, tucking her hair behind her ear.

He approached me. "Shardsson, it is a relief to have you both returned."

"Good to see you hale and well, Gerlay."

Tuniel stood at the back of the room with her arms folded. I tried to catch her eye, but she resolutely ignored me. My shoulder gave another pang, the metal cold. Why wouldn't she meet my eyes?

The Rushia princess spoke, drawing my attention from my inamorata. "I have called you all here on Evyn's recommendation. She and I spoke yesterday, and she is convinced that you will be able to assist me."

"Assist Rush?" Gough asked. "Are you acting in an official capacity?"

Sabatha made a face. "No. I mean, will you help me, Sabatha, with the mess I have created. In a way, that will also help Rush." The princess closed her eyes, as if she faced an impossible drop in front of her.

"It's okay," Evyn said softly, holding out her hand.

Sabatha took it, eyes welling with tears. "I need help," she said quietly. "My father is a good man, but he is intractable on one issue: my marriage. He is determined that it would be for political gain. Meanwhile, I wanted to marry for love. I'm not blinded by love, it would still have merit for my country, but it wasn't the alliance he had hoped for."

"Oh?" Gough said, glancing at Gerlay, who also looked interested.

"Yes." She bit her lip.

"Go on," Evyn murmured to her.

"I want to marry..." She paused, eyes seeking Evyn's.

Evyn nodded again, an encouraging smile on her face, and my heart warmed at my soul companion bolstering a princess's resolve.

Sabatha threw her head back. "I want to marry Princess Catherine of Daron."

"... Ah," Gough said.

"Oh," said Gerlay.

Looking around belligerently at us all, Sabatha subsided when no one challenged her. She carried on quietly, "Father was not favourable to Daron as a valuable enough ally, and he did not understand why I would want a woman. He insisted we hold out for one of the other bigger, more brutal countries, and told me I would learn to love a man." A bitter twist to her lips marred her face. "I longed to help my father see, that was all. I was a stupid, silly girl, and I looked for help with matters of love."

"You approached Liara." Tuniel put a hand to her mouth.

Sabatha nodded. "Yes. I sought the advice of the love mage, and she said she knew of a way that involved the Rushia magics that the royal family are entrusted with."

She touched the heavy pendants on the necklaces around her throat. They were a variety of stones, all sparkling with some kind of light in their depths, as if they were very worn-out glowstones. "These are all handed down throughout the royal bloodline, our folly and our burden." She took off one of her rings. "Tuniel MasterMage, as you are a stone mage, you will sense that these are not ordinary ornaments."

"No, they aren't." Tuniel leant forward. "They have a crystalline resonance, as all stones do, but this has... something inside it, ricocheting against the sides of the structure." She held out her hand, and Sabatha dropped the ring into it.

Sabatha said, "These were all formed in the dark days of Rush's history. They are all spirits; two soul companions, the victim and the devotee who sacrificed them. Their opposition to one another creates a kind of perpetual energy; they will always be drawn together but rejecting each other, and can never reconcile and fuse into one whole spirit again." She gestured sadly to the pendants around her neck. "These are all such beings, and what we call a tangle."

All of them? There had to be at least a score of the dark jewels on her person. "Those are all... spirits?" My skin crawled imagining Aglo's spirit swirling so close, trapped in a stone somewhere.

Standing, I snatched the ring out of Tuniel's fingers. "Get rid of them. These are dangerous." I clenched my fist around it, containing it, fighting the urge to hurl it away from us.

Sabatha approached me, hands raised as if to placate me. "Yes, they are. I'm sorry that you appreciate that from first-hand experience." She held her palm open, beckoning for the ring. "There was a spate of tangle creation nearly half a century ago. My grandfather, then part of a lesser branch of the royal family, led a rebellion to stop them from being made."

Her words sparked a strange, disjointed recollection in me. "I can remember, in a way. Aglo, he left... impressions." The stones in her jewellery were all dark precious gems, some red, some brown, others jet, glimmering with a faint light. My stomach rolled. "He killed his soul companion, then himself. Their spirits couldn't fuse; she would not accept his actions." Heartbeat drumming in my ears, I tried not to relive it myself. It was not even my memory!

Tuniel stepped up next to me, facing the princess with me. "Their opposition keeps them from fusing into one spirit as intended," she said, working it out.

Sabatha nodded sadly.

Somehow, having Tuniel beside me eased some of my tension. Even though she had not even looked at me yet, her presence was alongside me, supporting me silently.

Sabatha touched my hand with slow movements, and I loosened the grip I had on the ring. She took it from me, continuing her tale in a low voice. "Liara and Waker both entreated me that these spirits had the power necessary to achieve the aim of changing my father's heart. It did not escape me that, should they solve my problem, they would have leverage over me. The three most powerful mages in three nations working together is unheard of, but they were eager to court my compliance and subservience." Her eyes hardened. "That I would never give, and it showed. I never gained their inner circle, which was... intimate, in any case."

She met Evyn's gaze and seemed to use that contact to shore up her courage. "Under Liara's direction, I released one of them. It... is a very specific one, made from a religious Rushia fanatic with a soul companion from Earth." She turned sad eyes to me.

Aglo. She released him. My eyes widened.

The princess put both hands around the ring, pressing it to her chest next to the other gems in her heavy necklaces. "I am deeply ashamed and repentant. Liara said she would guide me, but while I had control of the magic and could use it to some extent, it scared me. She stood by my side, teaching and supporting me, or so I thought. She returned to Dinahe for a time, but suddenly she called out for me. The Oberrotians were attacking, and the Dinahens had abandoned her.

"I used this tangle to rescue her, but when I gathered it to myself again, the tangle felt... different. I suspect now that she kept some for herself to toy with, to add to her own magic."

Tuniel tapped her lips. "Doable, but she would need a lot of power to do that."

"Check," Evyn muttered, hunkering down in her bedcovers.

Sabatha nodded, gaze low. "When she recovered from her ordeal, Liara explained that she needed to control the spirit tangle to defend herself against the Oberrotians and Dinahens. I refused, of course, but offered her sanctuary here. She then explained that she had found an Earthian enslaved by the Oberrotians. I... gave her resources to rescue this Earthian for me, to free the slave from bondage, but also because I knew Earthian soul companions bestow upon one another an immunity to magic. I wished to save myself from the mess I had created. I asked Liara to bring me the Earthian and in return... I would lend her the other half of the tangle to accomplish this, with more as her reward." She winced.

"You don't need me to tell you that was naïve," Tuniel murmured, but kindly.

"I know. The tangles are entrusted to me as a member of the royal bloodline. It was entirely the wrong thing to do." Her eyes welled up afresh.

Evyn made a soft murmur of distress that echoed in me. "You were scared," she said to the princess. "Lots of people act differently than they would like out of fear. What matters is what comes next. Tell them."

Sabatha smiled through her tears. "I know Liara was heartbroken when Waker died. The mage of love moved against you, Tuniel, but she was also frustrated of her original goal. Perhaps she hoped to secure my support to achieve it, and she would have, if I had not seen you."

I looked up at Sabatha's pause, and found the princess looking squarely at me. "Me?" I asked.

The princess nodded sadly. "When the Earthian was delivered to me, I realised Liara's story and apparent methods did not match. Your condition, how beaten and abused you were, informed me that while the love mage spoke of love, she wielded it for her own ends.

"I dismissed her at once, breaking my promise to her. Unsure where to turn, I found myself baring my heart to Evyn and... here we are." The princess finished quietly, sitting straighter than she had before.

We sat in silence. Aubin's expression was flat, Gough's pensive. Gerlay frowned, and Tuniel looked like she needed a stele in hand to record some observations. I let the princess's testimony settle into me to see how it fit. It suited well what I had seen of the princess since Liara had delivered Evyn and myself into her custody, and it was clear Evyn believed her and wanted to help her. I felt for her predicament. She had reached out for help, but Waker and Liara had used that to manipulate her.

"Do you know what's wrong with Evyn?" I asked into the quiet.

"Yes," the princess said quietly. "You recall that I rescued Liara using a tangle. This was the Aglo-Ellen tangle; a willing Rushia and his unwilling Earthian soul companion. When it returned to me, only half remained. I did not know which half, until now. At the same time, Liara must have changed the spirit somehow, adding her own magic to it.

"I don't know how, but rather as Aglo resided in you, I fear the other half, Ellen, has taken root in Evyn."

Evyn squeezed my hand. "Sabatha and I chatted about this. It's going to be okay, I promise," she reassured me. "She doesn't seem to be taking over exactly, and the bad dreams I've been having, they are from this scared spirit, not my anxiety."

Of course she would be pleased that it wasn't some fear of me giving her nightmares of me hurting her. That was the sort of person she was.

My heart ached with anguish. "It's a spiritsight."

"A type, perhaps," Sabatha said, her voice lacking its usual forthright assertion.

Evyn had a spiritsight. Was it tormenting her as Aglo had done to me? "Get it out of her now, please." It had hurt, but being free of Aglo was worth it.

Sabatha laced her hands together, considering. "I do not know how she is able to resist it, but the Earthian spirits evade me in a way I do not understand yet. I cannot pull her out as I did Aglo from you, not yet."

"Then we will find a way." That rang through me like a new tenet.

Sabatha went on, "We have kept the tangles secure for generations, but Liara assured me they could be controlled and contained. I, like a stupid girl, believed her."

Aubin tapped the hilts of his blades. "Do you have any insight into Liara's target? Why does she want this tangle? For what purpose?"

The princess shook her head slowly. "Only that she seemed certain that she needed it."

"You said Waker and Liara worked together on something else. Did you have any hints at all?" Aubin asked.

"None that I can piece into a clear picture. I heard them mention a 'she.' It made me imagine a cabal of women, perhaps as lost as I, in need of guidance. But the methods they employed, the routes they took…" She glanced at me again. "There has to be another way."

Gough nodded. "Thank you, Princess. An open ledger between us helps us work more effectively together. Where is your father?"

Sabatha flinched. "I used the spirit tangle a mooncycle since to try to bring my father around to my point of view. It did not work as I intended. He has slipped into a sleep from which he will not wake." She kept her spine straight.

Gough clucked his tongue. "That does sound like a problem, one that will need a great deal of assistance. I can help you, one fellow ruler to another, in your interim appointment. I will also lend my Rangers. Shardsson, Tabreksson, your assessment please?"

I rolled my shoulders, wincing at the pain. "Whatever Liara is doing, we will stop it. She is in the city somewhere, yes? Please monitor movements in and out. She can enchant her way past guards, though."

Aubin nodded. "We will need to find her quickly."

Tuniel raised her chin. "I have taken the liberty of setting out watchstones at the guard posts on the perimeter. She can enchant people, but she cannot blind stones. Liara will not be able to leave this city without the watchstones notifying me; as soon as she arrived in the city, she walked into my trap." A cold smile crossed her face, grim satisfaction in her voice. "Next, I intend to set out sequences of watchstones so that she will not be able to navigate the city without touching some form of rock on her journey, and the stones in the sequence will inform me immediately."

"Will that take time to set up?" Sabatha asked.

"Yes. If you have any mages or mancers with an affinity to stone or metal, I could use them."

Aubin tapped my arm, making me jolt. He raised an eyebrow at me. "You should use the time to recover, Thorrn, but I suspect you'll only accept a fraction of what I recommend. You will need to be hale to defeat Liara, as none of the rest of us can get close."

My skin ran hot and cold. "Yes, of course," I said, tamping down my burgeoning misgivings. Facing Liara again, as myself, would I be able to fall back on my training, or would my thoughts freeze me, as they had in the streets of Al Shur? Even thinking of confronting her stirred memories best left tamped down away from interfering with my purpose. "I will have to train."

Aubin nodded once, eyes studying mine. I looked away from his penetrating gaze, lest he see any weakness there. *I will not fail again.*

"I will help you train," Gerlay said.

I clapped his back. I appreciated his support, offered in the way of soldiers.

Aubin sighed. "I suppose I can also be persuaded to train. I want to add the knife-throwing ability of the Rushia guard to my skillset, if I can. It would have been useful to hamstring you from a distance," Aubin told me.

"Indeed. Wonderful." I resisted the urge to rub my vulnerable tendons.

"And so..." He took a big breath. "We will train."

I grinned at him.

Aubin saw and rolled his eyes. "I thought you might enjoy that. You have a lot of work to do, Shardsson. Gerlay and I have already bested you."

"You only won one out of two."

"Two out of two. We're still alive."

"You ran away!"

Aubin scowled. "We have also been busy developing some manoeuvres against you. You have a lot of weaknesses we can exploit."

"I won't cheat and peek at them but, uh... weaknesses? Really? Where?" Surely he was joking.

He put his hands on his hips. "Well, we can't tell you, Thorrn."

"Yes, of course, but, I mean, I'm perfect, so, where are these weaknesses you speak of?"

Sabatha smiled at us, a small sign of hope in her young face. "You will do it?"

"Yes, Your Highness," we said, Tuniel adding her voice alongside mine, Aubin's and Gerlay's.

"I'm sorry," Evyn whispered, squeezing my hand. Her gaze dropped to her covers.

Aubin said, "It's not your fault. I promise you, we will cure you of this."

"Er. What he said," Gerlay chipped in.

I tucked her head close to my chest. "Of course, Evyn." I searched for what she was feeling, but even though she was physically as close as we could be, all I could feel was her shame. She hated being the centre of attention, but this was different, something I could not grasp.

Gough cleared his throat, and my attention swung to him. He said, "Well, personal motivations aside, this would be a large favour that Oberrot is doing for Rush. And with Dinahe, of course."

The princess's cautious smile faded at his words.

Gough's face was composed but kind. "I can see several ways forward. When the Rangers are successful, we may be able to negotiate… a similar trade deal to the one I was hoping to draft in the event of an Oberrotian-Rushia marriage. Additionally, we could also begin discussions with Daron."

The princess's eyes widened slightly. "You would do that?"

"Daron is a small market, but it's the open trade with Oberrot that is of great interest to many. I'm sure your father can be made to see that." Standing, he put his hand on Evyn's shoulder and nodded to me. "I trust such goodwill is worth two slaves?"

Ah. I held up my hands, still bound by manacles.

"Of course," Sabatha said warmly. "You are both free to go."

Tuniel waved her hand, and the manacles sprung open from my wrists.

I rubbed them. "Thank you, Your Highness. MasterMage."

Sabatha smiled, but Tuniel still did not look at me. A pang of regret slid through me.

The princess turned to Gough. "It would be good to discuss closer Oberrotian relations, even without marriage."

Gough nodded. "Yes, it is more flexible, but marriage remains the traditional method of strengthening agreements between nations."

It was Evyn's turn to close her eyes. I had the feeling she wished she could pass out right now.

"First we fix you, eh?" Gerlay said, a sad smile on his face.

"Yes, first things first," Aubin murmured, his expression turned inward and gaze distant, as if focusing on the problem already. *Good.*

Tuniel said to Sabatha, "I also require access to your records, with the help of an Oberrotian researcher, to understand what combination of spirit and stone magic was used to contain this evil in the first place."

The princess held up her hand. "It is not evil; it is human suffering, misaligned and abused, and in need of help." She looked at me. "Just as you were when you arrived. You were locked in terror, and Aglo clung to his decision, for good or for ill, lest he recognise that he had made the wrong choice before. You did not know, but both of you needed kindness. Neither of you were open to seeing another way. You knew only the lonely pain and you held to it for comfort."

"I could not reason with Aglo," I mused. "His heart was not open. But, Your Highness, I wasn't scared, I was mostly angry."

The princess nodded. "Precisely."

I frowned. She did not understand. *Or perhaps I did not.*

"Is that all, princess?" Aubin asked.

"For now."

Aubin clapped his hands. "Then we have our tasks. Research. Develop. Practise. Test."

I smiled at him. "You're loving this."

"Yes, actually. And we will ensure a cure for Evyn."

"Well then, let's slap some books," I said.

Evyn snorted.

"Isn't that what you say?" I asked her.

"It's 'hit them'." She chuckled.

"Same thing in the end."

Tuniel snapped her fingers at me. "Shardsson, I need a word with you."

I straightened up. "Yes, MasterMage." At least she had said *something* to me, but her tone was distinctly unwelcoming.

Saluting to the king and leaving Evyn with them, I followed Tuniel out of the rest hall. She marched down the corridor, skirts flurrying, scattering servants out of her path with the fury in her face. "How dare you drag me, the MasterMage of Oberrot, down for some kind of search mission to find you, one lone swordsman?"

"My... deepest apologies, MasterMage." My head whirled. "I did not ask you to come. I... suppose I can be sorry that spirit contacted you, but in the way that Evyn seems to be sorry for many things; I am regretful that it happened, but I cannot take full responsibility for it."

"Be quiet," she snapped.

I shut my mouth. What was she angry at me for? Hurting Aubin? I hadn't even apologised to him yet for that.

She found an empty room and shut the door with a resounding bang. The anger fled from her face. "Pretend I'm admonishing you severely."

"You aren't?" Now my head really hurt.

Her expression soft, she put her arms up to my shoulders. I winced when she touched Amare, and she drew her hand back. "Thorrn, I'm the one who is sorry, and I mean that in the truest sense. I'm sorry I couldn't find a way to descend on Liara's caravan and kill her and take you back. She deliberately kept to sand, and I am weaker on sand unless the bedrock is close. When the soul jewel stopped moving, I feared the worst." Laying her forehead on my chest, she put her arms around me.

I relaxed into her touch. *She's not angry with me, at least.* I drew her hips toward mine, then dropped my hands, in case I had misstepped. "Tuniel, I... haven't read all of that contract. What does the document say about this?" I gestured toward the empty room, a single simple wooden door the only thing keeping our relationship a secret.

Reaching up, she cupped my jaw in her hands, and her ice-blue eyes swam with tears. "Nevermind any of that now. I thought you were dead." Her lips quivered. "You're hurt and starved, and she took you and kept you from me."

Her sadness spoke straight to my core. I wanted to wipe her tears away and never see her cry for me again. "I stand here, alive. All will be well, Tuniel."

"I'm glad of that."

I drew her into my arms, pleased when she did not protest. "I did not think you would come. The contract said if something were to go wrong on a mission, you wouldn't rescue me."

"Oh, that." She put her hands underneath the blanket I wore, and my breath quickened at her touch. "That was for Gough's benefit. I anticipated he would get his hands on the contract at some point, as Evyn's most likely place to turn to for help with it, so that was to show he couldn't rely on me to pull your irons out of the fire, and he would have to send you prepared."

That made a great deal of sense, but it still irked and saddened me. *If only our relationship could be simple rather than interwoven with politics.*

She traced her hands up my sides. "I need to explain about the armour."

Her fingers sent a thrill through me, as they always did, but Amare had reacted to Aubin's words to trap me. *Which he only used when he needed to.* "I suppose it's a good thing you have a failsafe on me." My voice came out stiff and formal.

"It's not by design; that is just how my magic works." She met my eyes, sincere and sad. "I cannot find it in myself to hurt Aubin, and that translates across to my magic. You will notice it is only he who can say those words and have that effect. I will always have something that protects Aubin in the things that I do."

It was a small easing of the situation, not perfect, but much improved. I struggled to find the words to express that. "Well. That feels slightly better."

She turned her head to survey Amare, sorrow in her face. "What are we going to do about this?"

I smoothed my hands down the back of her dress. I did not have the answers for all the issues that piled against us, but I knew where I could turn next. I had missed her with a deep ache, and every single one of her touches was more precious, perhaps because we could not bestow them on each other every moment of every day as I so dearly wished to do. We would have to find a way to sustain our love in spite of that, and fight for it.

"Engineering later, sex now?" I asked hopefully, leaning down to brush her lips with mine.

She laughed, quietly. I kissed her, pulling at the ties to her bodice as she unbuttoned my shirt with eager fingers.

CHAPTER 20

Afterwards, and much refreshed, we went to find Aubin. He and Evyn were in the library, of course. This library was wide and open, scrolls and books in impenetrable long rows making their own corridors up and down the space, spilling out into the courtyard to entice a breeze down the long aisles.

Small dishes of fragrant rice and meat had been set out on the study tables, and I sat myself near one. "How delightful. Don't mind if I do."

Tuniel settled herself at the table next to Aubin. "While you're here, Aubin, Evyn, let's look at his shoulder. I heard you say it was not looking good, Aubin."

"As if you haven't seen it just now." Aubin gave his soul companion a disparaging look.

Evyn giggled. "Busted."

"Fine, yes, well, keep your voices down," Tuniel huffed.

I opened my shirt, pulling the collar down to allow them to study my red shoulder. Evyn winced, Aubin looked grim and Tuniel contemplative.

"Well?" I asked.

"It looks really sore." Evyn touched the surrounding skin, and the coolness from her hand spread to the area. I sighed with relief.

"It's his magical immunity. It's fighting the magic in the metal." Tuniel tapped her lip.

Aubin nodded once. "If it were solely metal, the body would not fight it. Metal doesn't provoke this much of an immune response."

"Can you move the magic out of the bit that's in his body?" Evyn asked, pointing at where the metal met skin, silver ringed with red, like a receding tide. "Can you leave that bit as normal metal, and then the magic is actually up here in the middle somewhere, not touching his skin?"

Tuniel tapped the jewel in the centre of Amare. "I can store the magic in the soul jewel and immediate surrounds. When needed, the jewel would shove the magic into the metal to deploy." She rubbed her chin. "It means there will be a slight delay."

"How long?" I asked her.

"One or two heartbeats."

"So deploy before the swing, not mid-swing," Aubin told me.

"But that is less dramatic. Yes, of course, that's fine, I'll work with it."

Tuniel's fingers lingered on my bared bicep, her touch sending pleasant shivers across my skin. She smiled briefly at me before wiping her face clear. "It will also mean that if the jewel gets removed, the armour will not deploy at all. It will be a lump of metal on your shoulder."

"I'll protect the jewel," I said.

Her soft touch roamed upwards, skirting the inflammation. "It will need replacing frequently, as that would be a lot of power running through it. There are tiny fissures and cracks that can weaken over time. Stones endure a lot, but they can crumble."

"Oh." A swell of sadness overtook me for the little green stone, glowing happily surrounded by Tuniel and Aubin's bond.

"Don't be concerned," Aubin said. "We have a lot of soul jewels.

It seems every time she turns around, Tuniel makes friends with another rock."

Tuniel flushed, glaring briefly at her soul companion. She shrugged. "It will be nice to put these to some form of use. Unfortunately, you'll have to come see me to replace it."

"Unfortunately. Ha," I said, but quietly, to please her. "Still. This one is special."

"I'll replace it now so it doesn't get damaged. You can keep it. I'll need to load up another stone and such. I should be ready by tomorrow." Tuniel peered onto the table. "What are you working on?"

Evyn gestured to the teetering pile of tomes in front of them. "I'm gathering documents on the Earthian and Rushia tangles. I want to go through these in detail to see what it says about how it was created and contained, and you can help me come up with ideas for how to address it. I'd like to deal with it completely rather than just seal it up again. Something like this shouldn't be a can kicked down the road for future generations to deal with."

"If it can be dealt with. It might not," Aubin said. He held up his hands. "Yes, I won't be a pessimist immediately." He glanced at me briefly, as if assessing my reaction.

I nodded once. Changing one's thought patterns was likely as difficult as learning a new stance, a task that required persistency to progress.

Tuniel picked up a sheaf of papers, thumbing through them. "I would be delighted to assist you, Evyn."

Evyn snorted. "Methinks it will be me assisting you. Your world cheats at physics, but I'm excited to learn." She passed Tuniel a tome. "I can pick out connections, though. That's my one and only superpower."

"It's not your only one at all," I said, and Aubin shook his head as well.

"Okay. Saving Thorrn's life too." Evyn ruffled my hair.

I endured it with heroic stoicism.

Aubin nudged me. "Meanwhile, I'm looking up texts on fighting

Oberrotians and Dinahens. Nothing like getting inspiration from one-time enemies."

I sat straighter, leaning to look at the scroll he held in his hands. "That's a great idea, let me see."

Aubin chuckled. "I knew we'd get him into reading one day," he said to Evyn.

She smiled back, and I felt a small swoop in my solar plexus. *Something from Evyn, and a pleasant sensation to boot.* She wasn't solely delighted with my desire to learn, either.

"I'm going to read a small bit and try it out," I cautioned them. "Don't think that I will be sitting here reading for turns of the glass."

"Still a good start for a love of books," Evyn said, finally tearing her gaze from Aubin.

He looked up at the high, vaulted ceiling, as if collecting himself. "Gough will come by later," he said, voice rougher. "The heads of state are formalising the loan of the Rangers as well as Gerlay to Rush. They are also negotiating some lessons from the knife throwers."

That pleased me, except for the term. "They are called Artists, Aubin. Aglo was one, and I'm not sure yet, but I think he left some muscle memory as well as some others." I grinned widely. "That's what I'm really excited about. And meanwhile you can teach us the Battlemistress blades! This world tour of weapons is coming to fruition, as we arrived and asked them to teach us, and they just might!"

Aubin rolled his eyes, the edges of his lips twitching.

When Gough joined us in the library, he reported his success. "The chief of security will teach you some basics about the Rushia knife fighting, but no advanced techniques." Gough sniffed. "I trust my Rangers would be able to analyse and break down such techniques, anyway."

"Yessir." Getting in to see any form of training would help me understand it much better. Trickling recollections of my hands holding a knife just so made me confident I would be able to apply any learning quickly, but I needed to try it to confirm that Aglo's experience had indeed transferred to me.

Gough continued, "Once Liara has been contained and the tangles restored, the princess will facilitate introductions on her side while I provide those from Daron. Or rather, Oberrot through Daron." He rubbed his hands.

"We just need to defeat an ancient horror show first. No pressure," Evyn muttered.

"Yes. That'll be challenging, but I've no doubt you can handle it." Gough nodded firmly.

I saluted to reassure him, but also wondered what assurances I could give myself. Aglo had overpowered me easily, and there seemed to be no defence against him.

Closing my eyes, I took a deep breath, letting my chest expand. I looked to Evyn, who sat with her chin in her hand, looking at Aubin. *We have to overcome it, for her sake.* There was no question in my mind that I had fought as hard as I was able, so technique had to be the key here.

Thinking of what else was key, I cleared my throat. "Your Majesty, there's one other thing," I said. "The Rangers cannot guarantee your safety here, and we will need to apply ourselves fully to our mission. I recommend you return to the city and Special Forces, sir."

Gough's gaze briefly scanned me. "I've reached the same conclusion, and I will, once I've facilitated these introductions and spoken to Sabatha. Only a few more days, Ranger."

"Very well, sir." I could put a watch rota together for that short a period.

"Except you're on bed rest," Aubin said firmly. "No arguments, Thorrn. You've been thoroughly dragged through the desert and you're no good to us weak with hunger and heartsick. And," he raised his hand, forestalling my protests, "you and Evyn need time to reconnect, to strengthen your bond."

That halted me. "Yes. Yes, of course." I had to fortify her against the spirit she carried around in her heart.

She glanced up at me then away, busying herself with her papers. She gave every impression of wanting to get immersed in her work, but I could feel her trickling embarrassment as she realised she was the centre of attention again.

"Evyn?" I held my hand out to her. "Please?"

She stood with a small sigh. "Alright. I'll be back in a mo, Tuniel."

Whatever Earthian unit of time a "mo" was, I would take any time she gave me. "Then let's make a start." I would strengthen our bond and shore up Evyn against that spirit lurking inside her somehow.

I had to.

CHAPTER 21

Evyn and I shared a room with two large comfortable beds furnished in white linen, curtains draped between to give us privacy. We had barely sat down when a knock at the door proved to be food.

"Let's eat first. I don't know about you, but I'm famished." Evyn passed around the plates, aromatic rice and meat spiced with something that burnt my mouth a little and added pain to the delicious taste.

Wincing, I guzzled water. "Why spoil perfectly good food with something that hurts so much?"

"I love it." Evyn laughed at me, refilling my waterglass. She daintily picked my chicken from my plate, licking her fingers of the brown sauce.

I closed my eyes briefly, exhaustion pulling at me. I locked my spine upright to keep from swaying.

Evyn put her hand on mine, jolting me alert. "You look done in. Go to sleep, Thorrn, we can talk in the morning."

"I'm hale and well, that meal has renewed my vigour. Let's begin." I had to get her to open up to me so she could use my energy to make her hardy and tough. She might be struck down with sleep again, and for an indeterminate period; the previous bout had lasted nearly a sennight, and I would not allow that to happen again.

The sides of her lips lifted, but her eyes dropped down to her hands. She screwed each of her fingers into a napkin to clean them. "I don't really know where to start. I was out for most of it, so it's like... five minutes of stress and then waking up in random places." She tucked her hair behind her ear. "How are you doing?"

"Me? I'm..." *Hale and well*, I nearly said, a trite phrase that rolled off my tongue all too easily, a shield over the top of the things that were not hale or well but that I would make so. I would marshal and command my thoughts and emotions; they did not control me.

Her glance up pierced through me. "Thorrn, you went through something awful, but... it's a bit like what I'm going through right now. You're the only person I know who had a... a one of these." She tapped the side of her temple.

My mouth went dry. "Does it talk to you, make you say or do awful things?"

She shook her head. "No, not at all. It... She doesn't really do anything, I just get flashbacks every now and again."

Just, she said, but it sounded hideously unpleasant. "She." I rubbed my tongue against the roof of my mouth. "Her name was Ellen, the princess said?"

"Yes. That much I managed to tease out of the nightmares, and Sabatha confirmed it, which makes this whole thing that much more real." She wrapped her arms around her chest. "Do you mind telling me about what it was like for you?"

"Of course not." I would charge into death for Evyn; I could certainly say a few words for her. Settling into a seated reporting stance, I composed my thoughts. "Shortly after the spirit infiltrated me, it started moving my body. It spoke to Liara and then she—"

Evyn tapped my hand, interrupting my litany. "I know all that. It's just us here, and we're not in immediate danger." She shuffled closer. "I want to know what you felt, Thorrn, and how you feel now."

My throat tightened. "How I feel? How would that information help you?" I shook my head. "No matter, Evyn. If you ask it of me, I will do it."

She smiled, a genuine one this time. "Not quite so pushy, though. Just when you're ready."

"I am determined to be ready *now*."

She threw up her hands in mock surrender, her grin wide across her face. She sobered to take my hand, lacing her small fingers in between my big ones. "I can feel a lot of anguish, Thorrn. You probably blame yourself for either what you did or for not being able to stop it."

The naming of my coalescing emotion froze me in place. "I... I do feel that."

She stroked my thumb with hers. "There's a hot bite of shame. Again, you probably think—"

"That I should have been able to fight it. My efforts obviously weren't good enough. I wasn't good enough." I clung on to her fingers.

She put her other hand over ours. "I also know you're afraid."

I resisted the urge to jerk my hand back. Instead, I forced myself to weigh her observation, her insight, to examine it for truth, no matter how ugly. "We don't have time for me to be afraid," I whispered. Something tickled my cheeks. I put my free hand up, dashing away the tear that had dared to trace down my cheek.

She pressed my hand between hers. "I caught snatches of fear from you when we arrived at the palace outside. You were in a complete panic, but you stood perfectly still in front of me. It really confused me."

"That wasn't fear. I was trapped in a berserker rage. I was angry," I explained. "I do not panic. When I cannot think, I fall back on my training."

She sat back, still holding my hand in hers. "And when you rage, what happens then?"

I shut my eyes. How should I voice it? How could I frame it so she would not turn from me?

Her palms were warm, surrounding mine. "I've been around two of your rages, Thorrn. One was when we first came back to Oberrot to find Torgund in charge, and the other underneath the Master-Mage's Palais, fighting Rhona."

Her voice washed over me. I matched my breath to hers, breathing in when she did.

"The emotion I got from you, it matches what happens to me when I have a really extreme anxiety attack," she admitted quietly. "What is it like for you?"

I opened my eyes slowly, breathing deeply and evenly. *Evyn understands.* If I told her more, perhaps it would help her, even in some small way. I resolved to try. "The very first time I fell into a rage, a lordling had pushed my sister. I was just over half a score and five, fifteen turns as you mark it. She... fell and hit her head. Seeing her lying there, limp, not moving, it... it triggered something in me."

I met and held her eyes. She deserved to see all of me, understand all of it. "When I woke up, it was two days later. I beat the lordling nearly to death, hitting anyone who tried to stop me, and it took several Regulars to throw me in a cell and a whole day before I collapsed of exhaustion. I slept for another day after that.

"When I came around, there was... blood all over the walls, a dent in the door, and my knuckles were swollen and bloody, my fingernails mostly ripped off. My father waited in the next cell along, staring at me through the bars, and..." I shuddered. Bringing our hands up, I pressed her knuckles to my forehead. Hiding, or clinging on, I did not know which for sure.

"He was so composed but so quiet. I know it changed his view of me utterly, but there was more." I swallowed hard. "Until a score and a half of turns ago, there was a unit of the army called the first fight-ers. They were all berserkers, the first on the field and the first to perish. King Dolobere, Gough's father, abolished the unit, but the saying is 'berserkers are chained, not trained,' because they throw away all their training, all their skills, all their control, in a heartbeat."

Hot tears slid down my face. There was no stopping them. "The lordling's father called for me to be locked away, and I knew it meant I could never follow my father. I would be an embarrassment to him the heartbeat I lost control."

Now my arms quivered. I tried to master them, but they trembled all the more. "You are right. I was scared. I was scared that my sister was dead. I panicked." I had never, ever said as much, not even to my father, who had to deal with the lords and the king, and my mother, who was consumed with worry for a child in the infirmary and a child in the cells.

"My father let me out, and he said... he said that I was never to lose control again. I would work to command every aspect of my mind and body, and it would never waver or slip out of my grasp." My arms stilled. I breathed deeply, calling down the calm of battle. *I am in control.*

Strangely, speaking about it did not force up unpleasant feelings. The remembered terror, the sharp sting of regret, the utter confusion of what had happened, it all swirled in my head, but they were manageable.

"What happened after?" she whispered.

"Gavain helped." I looked up and laughed at her sceptical face. Rubbing away the tears, I nodded. "He didn't draw away from me as some others did. He did all the extra practice and training that Shard had me do, and he knew me well enough to start pushing me, to get me to the brink of anger so I could calm myself down. Gavain could make me mad at him in a way no one else could."

I reached for a pocket square to wipe my face. "But if it was panic, and not anger, then all that training was for naught. I can still throw away all my skills and slip into a berserker frenzy if I am frightened." That turned my stomach. Admitting to fright was tantamount to refusing to fight in my mind; a traitorous thought that could not be harboured or allowed succour.

She smiled, cuddling my hand close to her chest. My heart warmed as the bond between us swelled. Her smile widened. "You're feeling a lot of relief. You must have really needed that."

"I suppose I must have." I squeezed her hand. "Mostly, I am relieved that the bond is strengthening at last. Now, then, what do you need from me? I can push over a great deal, once I am rested tomorrow."

Evyn gently disengaged her fingers. "Let's walk before we run, mm?"

I leant forward. "Evyn, what are *you* feeling?" I could catch swirls of emotion that were not mine, snatches I couldn't name. It was nothing like the immediacy of Aglo's presence, but softer, causing echoes and ripples in me in response.

She pushed her hair back behind her ear. "I suppose it's only fair. I'm thinking about this whole... designation we all have, the 'Patient Slave' stuff."

"What? Oh, you mean how we're classed across time? The Lonely Man, and the others?"

"Yeah."

Shoulders had told me our designation, the Patient Slave, which made little sense to me at the time. "I suppose I was a slave for a short while, or at least the princess claimed me as hers."

She put the chicken down, face pale. "Yeah. It's coming true."

I shifted slightly to be ready to catch her should she be struck asleep. "What were you again?"

"I don't remember. I'll have to ask Evie when I see her."

But I could feel a knot of tension in her. A sick dread. I watched for her reaction as I said, "The Spirit Shaper, wasn't it?"

She put her hands flat on either side of the plate, face turned from me. "Ah, yes, that was it."

"You think that relates to these trapped spirits, don't you?" I touched the back of her hand, sticky sauce or no. "It's important not to make inferences like that yet."

She pressed her free hand to the top of mine, our bond trembling between us. "Yeah, I'm going to let it simmer, let it kind of unroll and reveal itself. Evie wouldn't tell me what it meant on her world." She stared down at our mingled hands. "But what are these spirits doing to me? I'm Earthian, so I can resist magic, but it isn't magic, is it? It's something else." She moved her hand away to tap her fingers on the table, her eyes unfocused, and I lost my soul companion to her thoughts.

A sick sensation moved my stomach, nothing to do with the spices I'd just subjected it to. "There's no coming back from a spirit-sight, Evyn, so we need to get rid of it. Please be careful and don't put yourself in harm's way just on the basis of some sort of weird classification system. It's almost like a prophecy, and I don't put stock in those."

"But yours came true. Aubin's is true," she whispered.

"Anything can come true if you interpret it enough ways. Maybe the stripes on my back from Gough. Perhaps when I was in thrall to Liara. Listen, I wager I can explain spirit shaper any number of ways, and Aubin would be able to do so ten times over." I hesitated. "Perhaps it means the depressed bit of you and the not depressed bit."

A small smile touched the edges of her lips. "Thorrn, they aren't separate parts of me. It's a part of my make-up."

"Well, then, something else. But please don't take this as some sort of sign. We have to get that thing out of you. Do not engage with it alone." I hugged her close to me. "I can't lose you."

"It'll be alright. Thorrn, I'm not going anywhere. I'll be asleep on the couch for the whole thing, I bet." She screwed her napkin into a ball, setting it on our plates.

"No, you'll be much better because I'm back with you." I snapped my fingers, making her jump a little. "I wager I can help! Maybe it needs both of us to act in concert or some such. We're a complete spirit, you and I, Evyn! That leaves no room for halves to come along. We should be able to push it out if we work together!"

My soul companion was not infected with my enthusiasm. Chewing her lip, her eyes unfocused again. "I'll ask Tuniel and

Sabatha. I don't want you anywhere near this, though." She stood to stack the plates near the door, as if the conversation were closed.

What could I say to cajole or convince her? "Evyn, I'm a swordsman. I'm trained to face danger without fear or hesitation."

She turned a scowl at me, but swayed on her feet, and I scrambled upright and caught her before she fell.

Swinging her up in my arms, I tutted at her. "Stop trying to protect me. That's my role," I told her, laying her on her bed.

She snored in response. Of course she would be brave and want to handle this herself. Our shared spirit would accept nothing less. Still, I wished she would let me help.

I rolled onto my bed, determined to keep a light watch that lasted all of ten heartbeats.

CHAPTER 22

I SLEPT LONG AND LATE, SNORTING AWAKE TO A RAP AT THE DOOR. A SERVANT waited in the corridor, offering out plates of cold meats and fruits; I knew the names for them even though I'd never seen such wrinkled, unappetising looking fruits before. Dates.

Setting the tray down, I wondered what else Aglo had left behind. I flexed my hand, wanting to hold an Artist's knife to see if I could feel the balance I was sure would be there.

Evyn yawned awake. "Morning, I hope. How long was I out?"

"I'm not actually sure myself, I've only just woken up." Light filtered in from the window above us, and it had looked to be after dawn at least when I opened the door to the courtyard.

Evyn picked at the meat and took a date. "How are you feeling?"

"Rested." I rolled my shoulder, wincing as my right side sent a wave of pain radiating across my body. "Hopefully Tuniel can take the magic out of the metal today."

"Yes." She reached up to touch my shoulder, and I sighed as coolness spread down my arm. "Although she'll be busy laying out that net for Liara. Today, I'll be holed up in the library, and I'll ask Sabatha some more about spirits." She scowled down at her white convalescent's robe. "I don't suppose I can get some new clothes from somewhere?"

"Ask a servant. They will requisition something." Thinking of where they might be, a clear memory surfaced. Aglo had surveyed the plans for the palace before its construction. "I know just where to find them. I'll ask one to come by, and find Aubin and Gerlay." I rolled up several slices of meat and downed them quickly.

I found the servants station easily, exactly where Aglo had seen it marked in Rushia script on crisp parchment turns ago, and instructed one to assist Evyn. After complimenting me on my Rushia, she hurried away. The barracks were not far away either, the next courtyard over, and so I went there to do some reconnaissance.

This courtyard had four guard posts on the roof above assigned to it, with a large cream tarpaulin pulled across the opening above to shield bodies from the sun and the ancient Art they practised from the world.

A lean Rushia man, weather-beaten with skin darkened by sun and hair roughened by wind, spotted me immediately. "So he wakes at last. Still on Oberrotian time, eh?" He eyed me suspiciously as I approached and saluted him. "Can you speak Rushia?" he grunted.

I entered a ready stance. "Basic Rushia, yes, sir. Are you the chief?"

He growled as he nodded. "Basic Rushia is all you're going to need. Pointy bit of knife goes into the target. There, now you under-stand Rushia knife fighting, as you barbarians call it." He turned away from me.

An open balance book and treating with an open mind was needed here. I was eager to learn; perhaps showing that would be advantageous. "What do you call it, sir?" I knew the answer.

"The Art," he snapped, and it resonated inside me. "It is the only Art. It is Art, and it is beyond those who do not value life to understand."

I nodded slowly. "Sir, with respect, I value life. Special Forces is encouraged to develop a code of conduct that each man holds dear.

In my code I do not kill unnecessarily, especially others doing their jobs. My friend the Dinahen holds to the same, and you will know the Dinahens don't kill in combat."

He grunted. "And your third man?"

"He's working on it. Sir."

He rewarded my attempt at levity with a chuckle.

The courtyard held a few training marks and a small pavilion where visitors could sit to watch. Aubin and Gerlay were in there, drinking water and deep in discussion, Aubin talking and Gerlay leaning forward, intent and shaking his head. When they saw me, Gerlay rose and bowed, while Aubin scowled.

"Well met to you too," I told him.

"Bed rest, Thorrn. That's rest in a bed."

"This is restful to me. I want to see what you're learning." I eyed the collection of small knives piled to one side. "Oh, at last."

Aubin grabbed my wrist. "Thorrn."

"I just want to throw one. One, Aubin. There's something I want to confirm." Hefting the knife, I noted the blunted tip; it would not sink into the target without significant force.

Making sure the yard was clear, I called out, "Practice!" in Rushia.

The knife left my hand and sank into the wooden head of the practice mark.

The chief scowled. "Beginner's grace," he muttered.

Aubin frowned. "Thorrn, how do you know Rushia knife fighting?"

"It's called the Art." My heart thudded so hard it rocked my chest. "These are Aglo's skills. He could use mine, and I can use his, even though he has been wrenched out." There was no doubt in my mind that he had gone; his control was so complete that he would not have hesitated to exert it before now. "The sanctity of life, it's not about not killing, it's to ensure a clean death. The Art is to hit and to break into these small targets with one stroke."

The chief grunted. "We aren't like the pacifist Dinahens. We preserve the sanctity of life through respect and grace, and when there is a need for killing we do so cleanly, with no pain. That is what value for life means to us. With the Art, you can kill instantly and know your target suffered nothing, and he or she was sent to the gods and goddesses with care and respect." His gaze turned suspicious. "Where did you learn this?"

Memories of long painful days sweltering in the desert and frosty nights spent shivering in amongst others filtered up to me. "A spirit visited me."

That seemed to appease the chief. "And you survived. Well then." He settled back on his heels. "Carry on. You might as well teach your men, I am too busy."

"Yessir."

Aubin looked at me askance, but I had a feeling he would get on very well with this.

Meanwhile, Gerlay already looked uncomfortable. I spoke to him in my improving Dinahen. "You don't have to use it to kill. You can learn the precision to, say, hit someone in the leg or ankle, or hit a weapon out of their hands."

"They are still sharp knives, Shardsson," Gerlay said. "Things can go awry and intended targets can be missed, with death caused accidentally. There are large veins in the legs; hitting one will kill."

"Accidents can happen with a staff, too. A blow to the head or body can kill," Aubin pointed out.

"That's why we train carefully to know exactly how much force and how to hold back. No, I dislike this, and I shall stand against it," he said firmly.

Aubin shook his head. "So you keep saying, but sometimes lethal force is the only way to end a threat decisively. I intend to kill Liara to make sure she cannot influence Evyn anymore."

Gerlay flushed. "Lady Evyn to you, and when *I* apprehend Liara, I will make sure she is brought to justice."

"Do you even have the death penalty in Dinahe? How are you going to lock away an enchantress who can just walk out whenever it suits her?" Aubin shaded his eyes against the sun, bright even with the tarpaulin protecting us. "I will add killing quickly and painlessly to my code," he told me.

"That's a good tenet to keep," I said, pleased. A few of the swordsmen and women held something similar, and it now chimed with the Rushia perspective on the issue. "I can see that working well for you."

Gerlay grimaced, and Aubin rounded on him. "Giving people second chances is how you end up dead or hurt. Once they have proven to be ruthless enough to betray you the first time, it is your fault if they are given the opportunity to betray you a second time." Aubin glared at me.

Gavain did betray me again. I rubbed the back of my head.

Gerlay straightened up, staff in hand as he faced Aubin. "Everyone deserves a fair trial. Where murders are perpetrated in haste, in the heat of the moment, everyone loses, the murderer among them."

"So you think Liara deserves a second chance? Maybe an opportunity to explain her actions, which is actually an opportunity for her to enchant us." Aubin made a slashing motion with his hand. "What happens when we try to corner Liara? To get away, she could pull so much energy from Evyn that she dies."

Gerlay's jaw worked. "I have said my piece."

Aubin thrust a finger toward the stone courtyard. "You'd let Evyn die, just so your principles stay pristine?"

That yanked hard in my gut. I had already proved to myself that I would bend or break my tenets when it came to keeping her safe.

"This is a hypothetical situation—" Gerlay fired back.

Aubin talked over him. "Or will you merely stand aside and force me to do it?" Aubin balled his fists. "She's your country's problem, you said earlier, but you do not seem willing to take the steps necessary to rectify it."

I raised my hands. "Both of you, let's focus on this training."

"No, it's important that we decide ahead of time," Aubin snapped. "That's the whole reason behind these tenets, is it not?"

"Yes, so we don't make choices in the moment that compromise how we want to conduct ourselves."

Aubin nodded once, a savage jerk of his head. "I have made my choice," he said quietly, stalking away.

"Aubin!" I called after him, but he flicked his hand in a Ranger signal—*redeploying to the walls.*

"Shardsson, I request a moment of privacy with you." Gerlay gestured toward the pavilion.

Looking around the empty training ground, I shrugged and followed him into the shade.

Gerlay passed me a waterskin. "I hope you are recovering well."

"I'm feeling more myself, yes."

He sat, lips thin, hands resting on his kneecaps. I waited for him to speak, but when he didn't, I asked, "What did you want to talk about?"

He inclined his head. "I wanted to apologise for my ignorance. There is clearly some Oberrotian custom that I am not aware of, and I wish to rectify any damage that my blindness to it has caused."

"Your pardon?" What was he talking about?

Gerlay leant forward. "In Dinahe, it is typical that marriage contracts are simple. I am aware that Oberrotian ones are more complex and require nominated individuals to negotiate on behalf of the marriage partners. Naturally, I assumed you would be Lady Evyn's nominated negotiator, and that I could remain as negotiator for myself." He sat back. "Being part of the Rangers, I should have realised you would be busy, and that Lady Evyn would need to nominate someone else to negotiate instead." He glanced at the columned archway, where Aubin had departed.

Oh, ye gods. "What has he been doing?"

Gerlay straightened up. "Acting as Lady Evyn's representative, he has insisted on multiple clauses being added to the marriage contract."

I rubbed my temples. "Could you give me some examples?"

Gerlay counted off on his fingers. "The ones that come to mind are an extensive list of which flowers never to give her under any circumstances, the exact specifications of the library that she is required to receive no later than one turn after our wedding, and that he is to be her personal physician, despite being employed by Oberrot Castle." Gerlay's nostrils flared. "Do not misunderstand me; the first two are examples of things that I am happy to accommodate, but the latter is rather... unusual." He studied my eyes. "Should I bring this up with Lady Evyn directly?"

I pressed my hands together. "We're all under a great deal of stress. I'll talk to her in a quiet moment." She might have asked him to act as her negotiator, but she would have known that would be cruel, and I was sure she would not have asked it of him.

Aubin was acting on his own. *Yet again.*

Taking my leave, I stalked out to find the tawny-haired man. Where would he be? Redeploying to the walls meant he might be making a survey from them. Consulting Aglo's recollection of the plans, I made my way to a set of stairs and stomped up them.

The city walls towered over everything in the vicinity, given that this was a flat desert and the city was composed of tents that the nomadic Rushia could take down and move at will. This late in the afternoon, commerce was starting up again after the mid-sun break, hawkers starting their sing-song calls announcing bargains.

Aubin surveyed the sheer walls with a scowl. "The walls are not actually that thick," he informed me, pointing accusingly. The glaring sun picked out the red in his hair, the brisk desert wind stirring it up.

I gestured to a pair of Artists roaming the perimeter. "They are patrolled."

"Is it enough, if Liara should call another mob?"

My stomach churned at the idea of civilians being flung against the unyielding walls and the Rushia's Art.

Aubin put his hands on the ledge. "We will watch Evyn for signs that Liara is drawing heavily from her. That might give us warning."

I nodded. "You're always a few steps ahead. That is valuable, in a Ranger." Sidling up to him, I said, "We need a drink, and a talk."

"Very well." He led the way, but when he hesitated at a junction in the corridors, I pulled ahead toward the correct courtyard. Here were sets of seats and ornate piles of stones, artfully arranged with meaning behind them, but that I could not discern. Perhaps Aglo had not been into art either. Still discomfited with the idea of his experiences colouring mine, I gestured Aubin to sit.

He tapped the bracers that held his Battlemistress blades. "Is this a formal Ranger to Ranger meeting, or is there something you need? Some bruswurt? I can see you holding yourself together."

"No, no bruswurt, today or ever again." I leant my elbows onto my thighs, meeting and holding his gaze. "Her own library, Aubin?"

His ears flushed. "He has the money for it," he muttered.

I ran my hands through my hair. "Why are you writing yourself into Evyn's marriage contract?" I asked quietly.

"No one else in Dinahe will be able to treat her if she becomes ill, because of where she's from," he said, voice pitched low. "If she needs herbs for anything, no one else should attempt to treat her, lest they harm her."

That made sense. "Is that what the list of flowers is for, then?"

"Yes. There are plants that she might react badly to, perhaps even have anaphylactic reactions against. Dinahe has more varied farmland than our monoculture. I needed to be thorough." He leant back. "And then there are flowers I think she would not like, based on what I put into the house. Some she speaks highly of, others she barely notices. I gave him a list of the ones she likes."

I nodded. "Aubin, that all sounds three steps ahead, which is you. But listen to yourself. Sending another man a list of the flowers she likes?"

"He isn't going to notice, he's a soldier, not a... a man who notices." He huddled down into his seat.

"Her own library, then. Do you worry he won't notice she enjoys being surrounded by books?"

"No. He understands that already, but..." He shrugged one shoulder as if he couldn't care less. "I saw an opportunity for her, so I took it. What do you want me to say?" His glare dared me to comment.

I dared. "Aubin, I don't want you to talk to me. I want you to talk to Evyn, openly and freely."

He stiffened as if I'd run him through. "The outcome will be the same." His voice was distant. "I've made my choice. I will not stand in the way of this chance for her." He scowled at me. "We have more important things to discuss, like how we are going to trap Liara in this city without her endangering Evyn."

"I've made progress on the first part of that," a welcome voice said.

I looked up at Tuniel as she entered the courtyard. She had piled her long silvrine hair atop her head in a way that reminded me of how she liked to put it up in dishabille. A delightful shiver stroked through me.

A smudge of dirt marked one cheek. I longed to wipe it off with my thumb. "What have you been doing, MasterMage?"

She sat next to Aubin, grabbing his glass from the table and taking a long drink. He raised his eyebrow at her.

Smacking her lips, she leant back in the chair, tucking her legs underneath her. "I have finished spreading out my senses and connected with all the major keystones in the city gates. Unless she climbs over a wall, Liara cannot leave without me being aware of it. To truly corner her, I will make connections at key sites, creating a kind of interconnected web. If she crosses any of the stones, then I will know she is in that area, but in order to do that, I need to walk around the city."

"Hm. Liara might see you first," I cautioned.

"Yes. It would be rather risky."

"Let me think about how it could be done," Aubin said. "Where are Evyn and Gough?"

"Together. I've left a lodestone with them."

If Aubin and I were here and Gerlay was at training earlier… "Damn and blast!" I roared, shocking servants into view. "Move aside, the king is undefended!"

Tuniel raised an eyebrow at me. "Only while I came here to find you. Gerlay came by and is currently on guard, as it were."

It heartened me that the king felt comfortable enough to trust Tuniel. "Barlay will still tear these tattoos off me if something were to happen. Come on." I put my hand to my hip to feel nothing. My stomach plummeted as I remembered Aglo carelessly slinging the blade into the back of Liara's wagon.

Aubin grabbed my forearm. "Breathe. What ails you? Is it Evyn, is she well?" The strength of his grip hurt my inner elbow.

I could barely speak. "My father's sword. I left it with Liara. If we catch up to her, I might be able to recover it." A slim hope.

Aubin looked down. "Yes. Well, we intend to do that."

My father's sword had been steadfast by my side, serving me as faithfully as it served him, and to lose it was heartrending. But we had a task before us, and I would apply myself to it fully.

"You should be on bedrest," Aubin said. "I'll guard the king."

"I feel hale and well—"

"I'll escort you to your quarters," Tuniel said, her voice invitingly low. "We need to get that stone swapped out and the magic moved."

"Yes, ma'am." I hoped I would need to take my clothes off for this.

CHAPTER 23

I was not disappointed.

When we reached the small room set aside for Tuniel, she closed the door. "Take off your shirt and lie back on the bed."

"Those are some lovely words to hear."

She might have rolled her eyes, perhaps. Another woman would have. Instead, a smile spread across her face, a darling blush the shade of shared memories gracing her cheeks. Her eyes studied me as I pulled off the white shirt lent to me by the Rushia princess, that smile slipping from her face when I bared my sore shoulder. She smoothed her hands along my arm, careful of the inflammation. "You truly are not at your best, Thorrn."

"I'll heal. I will also move better once this irritation goes down. Let's hope it works because I've rather enjoyed being held by your... Amare."

Saying the phrase made the armour flow out, agony gripping me. I cried out as I tried to master it, willing my body to stillness.

She arrested the flow, halting it in its tracks, glaring at the metal with a heated fury as if it were a disorderly soldier and she its irate sergeant. Her eyes glittered in the soft light of the glowstones, her chest heaving.

I took her hand. "It will be well, Tuniel."

"No, it's not." She sank to the edge of the bed. "It's hurting you. Amare is... causing you pain, and I think it will be hard for you to bear. It all will be, this relationship, what we have... it will be harder than you realise." She swallowed hard. "Thorrn, when I was four turns old, I found Aubin. He was walking along the sides of the canal with his mother; I was on a business trip with my father on the family barge. Aubin ran into the canal without a heartbeat's hesitation, and with a similar lack of thought I made the canal basin rise up to support him. I manifested my powers then.

"But being the soul companion of a mage is fraught. As we grew older, we were constantly reminded that he was an obvious weakness, the one place I could not defend. We... we came up with the ruse to combat that. Morven, Dorcas, Aubin and I. Dorcas and myself would pretend not to care for our soul companions; Morven and Aubin would remain safe."

She tucked her hair behind her ear. I sat still, afraid that if I moved, she would stop speaking. Mages and mancers fought each other to rise to power, sometimes overtly and other times through power games and ploys. Something about having the elements at one's behest made people more susceptible to taking what they desired by force. A soul companion was an obvious weakness, one that was typically done away with before a magic user left the Academy. Soullessness left the mage or mancer less emotional and less reactive, perhaps more stable. No one wanted someone who could level a mountain to have a bad day. Because they were aligned, both halves of the spirit coming to terms with what needed to happen for their magic-wielding partner to thrive, their half spirits would come together and fuse in the Labyrinth, or so the doctrine claimed. I would never contemplate a way forward that did not involve keeping Evyn alive and well, and my chest warmed that Tuniel had felt the same way about her own soul companion.

Tuniel wrapped her arms around her shoulders. "That proved to be insufficient for my cousin and her soul companion. We will never know for sure what transpired, but Morven is dead and I... I killed Dorcas during my trial to become a Journey Mage. I did it not only because I suspected he killed her, and that nearly killed Aubin... but also because he knew about the ruse."

The walls around us shifted with a low groan, dust sifting down from the ceiling above. I glanced up, and she moved to the wall, placing her palm against it as I would calm a skittish horse.

Her hand was still and pale, her head bowed as she spoke to it. "I have been careful never to let anyone see how much I care for Aubin. Every time I push him away, it is because... I love him." She looked at me, eyes glittering. "And because I love you, I will need to do the same to you, and I don't know if I can bear it. I don't know that you will maintain the patience and willingness you've shown in going along with this ruse, that you will want to. One day you will be at some event, a ceremony or something in your honour, and instead of sitting next to you or applauding you, I will have to studiously ignore you."

Standing up, I went to her. "Tuniel... you are right in that it was... exciting at first, the idea of a clandestine, forbidden relationship. Romantic nonsense." I cleared my throat. "But what you are describing... that would take true commitment."

She sniffed. "I'll still fix Amare and put it away whenever you like. I can load the soul jewels and give you as many as you need, a whole turn's worth, and—"

"Tuniel." I brought her hand to my face. "You do not have to be alone. You are not alone in this."

Her eyes glittered. "It might not be worth it. I can only give you the edges, the peripherals of my attention, but know that you are the last thing on my mind at night, and the first in the morning." She held up a soul jewel, a faint red glow burning in the heart of it.

I smiled. She thought of me more times than that. "You think of me and reach out to Amare, don't you? I can feel it heat occasionally.

That's you, isn't it?" She coloured. I warmed to my subject. "When you're thinking about re-engineering or tinkering or optimising Amare, you're thinking of what it could do for me." I tapped the armour. "This. This care and thought is worth more to me than any number of public sweet nothings, of any... applause at some event. You saw me whittled down to nothing, and you reached inside the molten mass of everything that had happened to me and... reforged me into something new." I put my hand over her heart. "For that, I can put up with some snub."

She breathed in deeply, her chest shuddering. Amare warmed even further, almost as hot as the desert sands, and an itching sensation started up. I held still, trusting that this was something that needed to happen as she moved the magic into the jewel between her fingers rather than swimming in the metal embedded in my shoulder.

She placed the jewel into the centre of the metal. "There. I have moved the magic entirely into the gemstone. There are small fissures and cracks in stones, Thorrn, and this is no exception. A hit in the exact right place can shatter stone. If this gem breaks or is removed, Amare will just be useless metal."

Taking her hand, I kissed it. "I understand. I will protect that stone with everything I have, and I will be sure never to let enemies get close to any fissure." I tugged her into my lap.

Now she rolled her eyes. "I know I might work stone, but it's not a direct comparison! That's rather on the nose. You aren't a fissure."

I shrugged. "Well, I am but a mere swordsman. We speak plain and strike true." I wrapped my arms around her. "You said something about bed rest. What did you mean by that?"

Her ice-blue eyes, cold at first glance, turned into limpid pools of desire which I gladly dived into.

It turned out that Tuniel's definition of bed rest aligned perfectly with my own.

Afterwards, she let me hold her wrapped in my arms for half a turn of the glass. I treasured every single heartbeat, for we could never know when such a moment would come around again.

Eventually, she stirred, reluctance in every line of her. "I should return to the library to find Aubin. Liara will not catch and kill herself, after all."

"Very well. I'll escort you." I yawned, peace and a quiet certainty settling in me. Surrounding me were my allies, all working harder than I to catch her and frustrate her of her goals. I was heartened and determined to match them. A small edge of disquiet surfaced; that I would freeze in fear as I had before when I faced her or, worse, slip into a panic, unable to contribute to our plans or be an active detriment.

I watched Tuniel pull her dress into place and tie the bodice, and that was a happy distraction. When she turned to face me, she smirked. "See something you like?"

"Indeed." I stretched out my hand toward hers. "Maybe we can delay for another half turn of the glass or so."

"Focus, Shardsson." She pulled her long hair over her shoulder. "I've been thinking through what happens if I get enchanted by Liara again. You don't stand a chance."

"We might." I sat up. "We haven't practised yet."

She smoothed her skirts. "There's no telling what I would be capable of. Would Liara want me to capture you alive or kill you? And would I care about collateral damage? If I didn't, I could probably level this side of the palace with you inside. There's no defence to that."

"Would you kill Aubin, though?" I pointed out.

Tuniel pushed her silvrine hair back over one shoulder. "Who's to say? I don't think I would have intentionally hurt him, but if Liara ordered me to, I might." She cocked her head. "If I did care about collateral damage, then... perhaps Gerlay has a chance, a small one, as he doesn't use a metal weapon. I could still open a pit underneath him and contain him. But you would be thoroughly dead."

"I train to fight mages and mancers, though."

"In overwhelming packs. On your own, I can deploy your armour and heat it up. It would melt with you inside, and you would die roasting in it."

I winced. "Uh." Swinging my legs over the side of the bed, I pulled my borrowed slacks on. "Let's talk to Aubin. He might see a way to address that."

Tuniel smiled. "I must admit, it pleases me that you have recognised his talents." She stroked my hair into place. "Now, if only he could see them for himself."

"Precisely! You understand perfectly." Taking her hand, I kissed it. "I figure I'll have to hammer it through to him."

Tuniel's smile turned sad. "He will never be pushed, Thorrn. He can be exasperatingly stubborn and immovable."

"Agreed." Those traits made him hard to work with, but were strengths when our goals aligned, as they did now.

I rolled my shoulder. "The metal feels better already." Sliding the loose shirt over the swelling, it did not twinge or burn. "My thanks."

"Of course." Cupping my face, she kissed me deeply, and this time when Amare gently squeezed, I felt no pain. "We should leave separately. After you."

With reluctance, we left the room, but I wanted to put eyes on Evyn. I had been revelling in my own feelings for a while and found it hard to discern if I was getting anything from her.

As we neared the courtyard that held the library along one side, a rested contentment filled me. *Evyn must be feeling happy.* I picked up my pace.

Evyn sat at the table with Gough, Gerlay and Aubin. Gerlay sat straight-backed, talking to the king, but his gaze stole over to where Evyn and Aubin leant over a tome. She put her hand over her mouth, pointing at something, and Aubin shuffled closer, eyes narrowing to peer at it. I knew his vision was sharper than mine. I scoffed to myself at this transparent attempt to get closer to her.

Still, Gerlay was only there, and such behaviour had not escaped Gough's notice either. The king drummed his fingers on the table.

Princess Sabatha came into the library from the courtyard opposite, Artists hovering behind her. The research party stood, but Evyn wobbled, stumbling into Aubin.

He caught her, and by the time I got there, she was asleep. Aubin swung her up into his arms, an unguarded look crossing his face; a deep worry, yes, and an even deeper pain.

Sabatha laced her fingers, gazing sadly at Evyn. "It was Evyn I came to speak to. I have finally finished the vital elements thrust on me for today, and I had hoped to answer her questions about the spirits and the tangles in the hopes of helping her condition."

Tuniel arrived at the library, books in hand. She placed them on the table, moving smoothly around Aubin and Evyn to stand next to me as if by accident. "I had questions of my own, Your Highness, given that they are stored in precious gemstones. Was a stone mage or mancer involved?"

Sabatha met her honest question with a steely glare. "Master-Mage, forgive me, but I have no wish to see a tangle recreated ever again."

Tuniel folded her arms, a light trickle of pink high in her cheeks. "Understood, of course."

Sabatha inclined her head. "However, I would be interested to see if our combination of magics can assist Lady Evyn." Sabatha waved her hand toward her Artists. "Ask the infirmary to prepare a bed."

One turned to fulfil her request while another approached Aubin, arms outstretched ready to take Evyn.

"I'll take her there," Aubin said in Rushia, moving back a pace.

"Give her to the guard," Gerlay said, voice low. "Shardsson and I will accompany her. You're needed here to protect your king."

Aubin's arms tightened, even though the guards made no further move to take Evyn from him. "The medimancers and mages might need a history of what we have tried from me. There are certain ways of saying things. What could you add to the proceedings?"

I winced.

Gerlay drew himself up, shoulders square. "As her future husband-to-be, I can make sure her voice is heard, particularly as she is unconscious." His hands flexed.

Aubin adjusted his grip on Evyn, bringing her closer to his chest. Her head lolled against his neck. "Thorrn can do that."

Gerlay glanced at Gough, who stood. "Perhaps, Prince Gerlay, in this particular circumstance, Ranger Aubin has the right skills to assist Lady Evyn. In this instance," the king emphasized, levelling a sour look at Aubin.

Aubin dropped his gaze but did not back down.

I held myself tense. Gerlay's politeness would only extend so far and he was already suspicious. Aubin had to admit the truth before it was too late.

Gough turned to Gerlay, a smile fixed in place. "Let's discuss the upcoming nuptials, shall we? Particularly the trade contract I'd like to put before King Gordonne. I'd be grateful for your opinion on it."

Sitting, the prince muttered, "Contracts and more contracts," watching us leave.

We passed into the relative cool of the corridors. "Aubin..." I began.

He picked up his pace. "I'm not going to let her die just to assuage a man's pride."

"I agree with you. I was just going to point out that this is the first sleep episode today that I know of," I said mildly.

His shoulders twitched, as if he had been caught out. He smoothed them down. "She will improve again now that you're back with her."

"That sounded very optimistic, Tabreksson."

"Realistic. Through previous experience and evidence, I know this to be the trend."

I paced alongside him as we walked through two leafy and cool courtyards, past sets of stairs up to the walls. He glanced up the stairs to check they were clear. "Make sure Evyn goes up at least once to see the colourful markets sprawled outside. She will love it," he informed me.

"Ah huh," I said, keeping my voice neutral. He was an intelligent man; surely he could see that we all knew?

In the courtyard with the fountains and herbs, a servant met with us and led us back into the private room. Aubin laid Evyn on the bed, shifting his hands to take her pulse. *At least, I think he's taking her pulse. He may just want to hold her hand.*

"You're not going to be able to let her go," I said, unable to hold it in any longer.

He dropped his hands to the bed. "Will you stop? Why aren't you respecting the choice that I have made?"

"Because what you say and what you are doing are two different things."

"Since when has that been any different?" He scrubbed his face with his hands.

I tamped down my frustration. "Alright, let me clarify. What you say you *want* and what you are doing are different."

Placing his palms flat on the bed, he glared at me.

I squared up to him. I would not back down, not when I could see clearly what he should do. Battering some sense into Gavain and Aleric had been necessary on occasion; if that was what Aubin needed, I was only too happy to assist.

For good or for ill, Sabatha and Tuniel arrived. "We're going to try pulling the spirit out of Evyn," the princess explained. "It may be uncomfortable, so tell us if she is feeling pain."

I wrenched back to focus on Evyn. "I will, Your Highness, Master-Mage." Saluting them, I took up station next to Evyn's head.

She looked so small, slack in sleep and lying prone. At least her chest rose and fell with regular deep breaths, and she seemed contented. Still, the unfairness of it rankled me. *She should be up, being courted, not lying ill and sleeping her life away.*

Aubin stood next to me to watch, his arms folded, and Tuniel moved to the foot of the bed, a small glittering stone in her hands. *Probably worth all the pay a soldier made in his lifetime.*

Sabatha hovered her hand over Evyn's chest. Evyn's forehead creased, but I shook my head; Evyn wasn't experiencing any pain that I could detect.

I tried pushing over strength and determination, feeling increasingly stupid just thinking the words at her. How did it work? What did I have to do?

Or did I have to relax into it?

Something sparked deep inside me. Fear, and a deep ache of worry. I reached for it, snatching as it faded away. That could easily be my emotions rather than hers, but it hurt to think of her being afraid. *I'm here. Don't be frightened.*

Evyn stirred, eyelids flickering, as Sabatha's hand moved closer. "I can feel the spirit, but I cannot dip in as I could for you, Ranger." Laying her hand on Evyn's breastbone, she gently pushed. I started forward, but her hand did not sink in.

Sabatha shook her hand as she lifted it. "It is not possible to get in."

"It's to do with where she is from," Tuniel murmured. She meant that Evyn was Earthian. "Magic does not work as well on her, but that includes both helpful and malicious magic."

I took Evyn's hand. It was cold, a bluish sheen to it. "If I touch her, does that get negated? Same as she does for me?"

Sabatha tried again, but shook her head, earrings swinging. "That does not help."

"It's not an effect caused by your bond, Thorrn," Tuniel said gently. "This is who she is and where she is from."

I nodded. Dampening magic was all well and good, until you needed magic to help you.

Sabatha hovered her hands over Evyn's arms. "The drain of her energy is not benefitting the spirit. Part of it has been tainted, twisted somehow, and it's siphoning it off. Now, if only I could follow that, for I am certain we would find Liara at the end of it."

"But if we could remove the spirit, that would remove Liara's magic also, correct?" Aubin asked.

"Yes. But I cannot grasp the spirit, and I cannot change what Liara has done." She let her hands fall. "I can feel something else, however." Sabatha smiled at me. "You are very open to her. I can feel your spirit flowing freely to her." She stroked Evyn's fringe away from her forehead. "She is still quite closed. I do not know whether that is an effect of the spirit inside her or not."

Evyn hadn't opened up to me fully yet? I balled my fists. All I'd done was talk about myself again.

"I'll try harder," I said, my voice choked as my throat closed.

"It's not about trying harder and faster and pushing, Thorrn," Aubin said, his voice low. "Allow her to open up to you."

But we didn't have time for that. I took her hand. *Please, Evyn. Let me help.*

CHAPTER 24

I DID NOT LEAVE THE INFIRMARY WITH THE OTHERS, PUSHING MY STRENGTH over to Evyn as much as I could. Evyn did not stir. Aubin brought in a meal and took some with me. He would have stayed all night except I pointed out I was here and I would monitor her. Servants brought a bedroll at the top of the night, and I rolled into it gratefully, keeping a light watch and willing her to wake up.

To my relief, she spoke in the grey hours of the morning. "What, stop…" she moaned.

I jumped up and stroked her head. "Evyn? Are you dreaming?"

"Oh." She yawned and, at last, her eyes opened. "Hi. What time is it?"

"You mean what day is it! You slept all yesterday, and it's the dawn of the next day."

"Oh. That's not good." She frowned at her surroundings. "Why am I in the infirmary? Did something happen?"

"Princess Sabatha tried to extract the spirit from you. She was unable to." I did not know who else might be listening, so I could not explain the mages' theory that her Earthian nature was repelling the magic.

"Oh." Evyn rubbed her eyes. "Look, I know this might sound weird, but I'm not sure how I feel about that. Ellen is scared, and I don't want her to go back into a stone to continue being scared for all eternity." Hugging her knees, she shivered. "It's not right."

I gathered her close. *My compassionate soul companion.* "We will think of something, and deal with it—her—properly. You're my priority, though, Evyn. Always." New bony angles pressed into me from her spine. She was wearing thin.

She isn't open to me helping her. Prickles of impatience sparked in my belly. "I'll stay with you today. You need to eat as much as you can, here."

She pushed the food away. "Not straight away when I wake up. Yuck."

"Yes, straight away, you need more energy!"

"Okay, okay, fine. Look, I've got a lot of junk in the trunk, I'll be okay for a few missed meals." She dutifully drank, and my stomach relaxed a little.

She set the glass down. "Right, I feel much better. Off you go to training, I'll hit the library."

She did look better, pink-cheeked and smiling. Nonetheless, I had a goal, and I intended to meet it. "I am not going to training; I'm staying with you all day, and I will not move from your side."

"Er. Don't take this the wrong way, but please go to training." She grabbed my hand as my heart sank. "I didn't mean it quite like that! You just feel better when you've had your exercise. Otherwise, I get this knot of something like tension mixed with an itch, too much energy, and I get frazzled really quickly."

That did sound uncomfortable. "You can feel that?"

"Yes." She smiled. "You come over loud and clear right now." Sighing, she took my hand. "Try not to worry. I'll stay where people can see me, and I'll take a bath with Tuniel." She glanced down at herself. "Sabatha said I could borrow some clothes, as they won't be able to make me any until tomorrow."

"Alright. I could escort you there, and train near the library."

Where I can see you.

"I'm sure the Rushia would be highly amused," she said drily. "If someone started doing push-ups in my library, I'd boot them out."

I straightened up. "Then I shall provide amusement."

"Thorrn." Evyn's eyes went steely. "I don't want this to affect how you see me. I'm not okay with you hovering over me. You have to recover yourself, and you have stuff to do. Fighting Liara on your own is going to ask a lot of you, and you need to be ready, not flapping over me like a six-foot-ten mother hen."

My heart thudded in my ears. Evyn could feel everything, which meant she had felt my reticence, my weakness about facing Liara. "I will defeat her," I asserted, my voice louder than I'd meant it to drown out the trepidation worming its way up the base up my skull. "I will not fail you."

"Oh, sweetheart." She grabbed my hand. "You always think everything is about you. You haven't failed, Thorrn, and you won't. Don't worry, you'll get her. But it might be hard, and that's what I want you to prepare for, not get distracted by me."

I clung to her hand. A rap at the door made me reach for my father's sword at my hip, once again feeling nothing. *I'm not prepared.*

Fortunately, it was Gerlay at the door and not an invasion. He ducked in, staff held loosely in his off hand. "Good morning. I hope I am not disturbing you too early." In his fist he held a book. He thrust it out to me. "I wish to bring this to Lady Evyn, not to hurry her back to work, but in case she feels up to it," he said in Dinahen.

Evyn reached up and took it from him. "Thanks, Gerlay. That's really nice of you." Her cheeks flushed. "Would you do me a favour?"

He went to one knee. "Anything, Lady Evyn."

Her flush deepened into piqued crimson. "Could you take Thorrn for some training? He thinks better when he's all worked out."

Gerlay stood and bowed. "I will certainly train him."

Evyn winked at me. "I'll get discharged after I read a few more chapters. See you later."

Head full, I saluted. It seemed that she wanted me away from her for the time being, but as she assured me, it was not always about me. *She wants some privacy, some space to think without my emotions spilling over to her.* She had always coped better alone.

But you aren't alone, Evyn.

Nonetheless, I could show that I respected her wishes. "I'll come to the library later to see you." Kissing the top of her head, putting my heart in hers, I left with Gerlay.

"She looks well," Gerlay said as we paced down the rows of the infirmary.

Compared to the people here, some lying still, others hunched in misery, Evyn looked well, but she was not as she should be. It was not fair to be struck with something like this just as the prime of life was opening up to her.

I reined in my anger. Maybe training was exactly what I needed to drain this helpless feeling of injustice out of me.

Gerlay looked at my face and nodded. "My apologies. It was a platitude. We will stop Liara."

"Even if we do so, Sabatha still cannot get the spirit out of Evyn." That came crashing down, a weight that sat firm on my chest. "But at least the sleep episodes might stop." Still too many unknowns, and all the while Liara was out there. "What progress has been made on Tuniel MasterMage's keystones?"

"I do not know more than you, my friend. I have not seen the MasterMage this day." He beckoned me. "Come, I must fulfil my promise to your soul companion and train you. Let's get to the training courtyard."

I glanced at the sky. Tuniel might not even be awake yet. "Very well. A quick lesson."

The staff had the potential to be unwieldy and hard to change direction at speed. Gerlay showed me how he changed the momentum of the staff through different fulcrum points in its length. When he passed me his staff to try, I spun it as he had, but it was still slow. "Is it too long for me?"

"It's not, it is actually just right for you. Your mind is too constrained. It expects instant, fast, quick in the moment. This works better if you are willing to think ahead." Taking it back from me, he spun it, changing its direction and orientation seamlessly.

Think ahead. Not something I was particularly known for. Thinking ahead, I could hope that Tuniel's watchstones cornered Liara. Then what? Did I rush down there with no sword, hoping she didn't enchant half a street to throw in my way? She would defend herself, and she would have no compunctions about using civilians to do so.

I couldn't prepare for every eventuality, but I could prepare for some. If Gerlay were enchanted, he might not adhere to his principles, but that would then be his weakness, as he never trained using his full force and his staff would not act as he was used to.

I could engage, and then Aubin could take him down from a distance… Except Aubin couldn't be there either, or risk being enchanted.

I rubbed my temples. One thing at a time. "Have you seen a sword around here I can use?"

Gerlay nodded, pointing toward the practice rack of weapons. The conditions of the blades were good, well-worn but well looked after, but none had the reach or heft of my father's sword.

I will have to accept and adapt. I could not change the past.

Taking a serviceable sword, I faced Gerlay. "Practice bout, first to land a blow?"

Gerlay spun his staff. "Yes."

I circled him and that whirling cane of wood. I could try grabbing it to see what he would do.

Gerlay sank into a defence stance and when I started forward, he whirled his staff around. Raising my sword, I charged. He whipped fast into a jab, and I dropped my sword and grabbed the staff with both hands. Gerlay frowned, jerked the staff and me forward, and headbutted me in the jaw.

"Ow!"

The staff whipped sideways and into my gut, winding me.

"Don't just grab at it," Gerlay chided me.

"Indeed. Don't touch a Dinahen's staff without his permission," Aubin called from behind me. "At least take him to dinner first."

Gerlay frowned at Aubin, but I had to take a break to recover, bent double to breathe from the blow and from laughing.

Sitting back on my heels, I waved to him. "Aubin, join us. This time, let's work together."

With a glance at Gerlay, Aubin shook his head. "It's better for you to train separately. Liara could enchant either of us if we are close enough."

I pulled myself to my feet to face him. "I'm not talking about just Liara, though. There will be other threats once we've dealt with her. We need to learn to work together." I waved again to the space next to me.

Aubin shifted his weight, amber eyes dark. "That won't help you in this current campaign. It's a waste of time and, speaking of wasting time, I've been sent to find you two. Tuniel needs to move to the next stage." He turned away but waited for us to follow him at least.

Why hadn't he started with that? Instead, he had flatly refused to train with me. Was it me, or was it Gerlay? Either way, those excuses wouldn't stand for long. Pushing down a simmering ire, I drew level with Aubin, Gerlay at my side.

Aubin walked in silence to start, moving out of the way of a white-liveried servant and leading us toward the right, into the green courtyard where a fresh breeze cast over my skin, soothing it. As we headed to the library, Aubin started talking without preamble. "Tuniel will explain, but essentially, we need to get out into the city. In terms of defending this place, we're limited in influence here, but from what I've been able to glean from the princess, the—" He halted in place as if suddenly immobilised in the stone of the path.

CHAPTER 25

Casting about for a threat, I put my hand on my borrowed sword. "What is it?"

Aubin's gaze was fixed on the open-air entrance to the Sultanate's library. Sat at the table were Tuniel, Sabatha and Evyn.

Tuniel wore a robe in the Rushia style, beautiful pale green gossamer fabrics that wrapped around her curves in layers. Her pale skin shone underneath, tempting me to tease those tissue-like veneers apart. A most satisfactory present.

My hand slackened off my sword hilt. "Oh, my word."

Evyn wore layers of amber. Combined with the rosy hues of her face and the autumnal browns in her long hair, it created a warm aura around her. Jewellery in the region's darker gold sparkled at her neckline, red henna lacing up her arms like tattoos of her very own. Truly she glowed, beaming at us as we approached.

We walked to the table with something like trepidation. I shot a grin at Tuniel, and she let a small smile cross her face, shifting her legs to uncross them.

I had to lock my knees upright.

Standing, Evyn searched all our faces, especially mine and

Aubin's, the smile slipping from her face. She twined her hair behind her ear. "What do you think?"

I held her at arm's length. "You look wonderful! Does it feel good?"

She nodded once, gaze darting to Aubin.

Gerlay bowed low to Evyn. "You look like a princess of Dinahe."

Sabatha smiled. "Perhaps she looks more like a princess of Rush."

Aubin moved over to the bookstacks, studying the spines of the tomes as if something had grabbed his urgent attention.

Evyn stared after him, then screwed her hands into fists, glancing up at me. "I had nothing else with me, Sabatha lent me some clothes." A curl of her discomfort spiked my stomach. "I know they're off-piste for me, but, well, it's too hot, and—"

"Evyn." I lowered my voice to reassure her. "If you like it, I like it. And you do look like you in this—you seem comfortable in it."

She watched the back of Aubin's head, a nervous spiral uncurling within her, tremulous and tender.

I suppressed a grimace. She didn't want *my* reassurance after all.

Aubin turned around. "We need to talk," he said, voice loud.

The bubble in my solar plexus surged so hard I staggered forward a pace.

Aubin frowned at me. "About the defence. We need to talk about the palace defence." His gaze swept over Evyn to land on the princess. "Princess Sabatha, if you would be so kind."

She looked between him and Evyn. *Even she can sense something is going on.*

The princess complied even so. "I have already informed Tuniel MasterMage and Evyn that we have yet to uncover Liara's whereabouts in the city, but the guards are preparing for their possibly being enchanted. Each guard will carefully quiz his fellows, and they are spread out. Where one acts out of character, he will be secured as quietly as possible and brought inside for questioning, hopefully out of Liara's influence."

"Neither the princess nor I feel any large surges of magic being used," Tuniel added. "If Liara is using her power, she is doing so sparingly, or she is using something else." Tuniel's gaze slid over Evyn.

Sabatha's face fell. "I cannot sense that far, so Tuniel Master-Mage gives me great credit. But I can tell that something is happening to the spirit tangle." She put a hand on Evyn's. "The small part here is resonating with change."

Evyn nodded, squinting up at me. "And I was exhausted for a while, but correlation is not always causation, you know?"

I paced. If Liara was pulling energy from Evyn, she had to be stopped immediately. "Liara cannot leave, you said, Tuniel? Then she has gone to ground somewhere."

"I fear that she's still close," Aubin said. "Maybe even inside the walls."

My stomach churned. If that was the case, we could be attacked at any moment.

Sabatha shook her head. "The palace is watched by multiple guards, each with resonance stones, to signal if and when one group is compromised. Hopefully, any use of her power will therefore signal her whereabouts."

Despite the princess's assurances, I was not sure that enchantment would be caught so quickly.

Aubin laid his hands flat on the table, still not looking at Evyn. "Tuniel needs to walk around the city to set up those stones to narrow down where Liara is hiding, but she might be vulnerable while she does it. I suggest we make a foray into the city, Thorrn, Gerlay, Tuniel and myself."

I frowned. "What, Oberrotians and a Dinahen walking around? Won't that cause the locals to talk about us, and potentially warn Liara?"

"Tuniel and I can pose as Rushia. You're correct in that there aren't many Dinahen or Oberrotian traders around, and you and Gerlay are too tall to pass as Rushia." He tapped his bracers. "We will need another disguise for you both."

I grimaced. "I can't believe I'm suggesting this, but the marks on my back make a great disguise. I can pretend to be your slave," I said to Gerlay.

Aubin cocked his head. "A Dinahen walking around with a slave would be unusual."

"Well, he can be an Oberrotian, as long as he doesn't talk."

"Strong silent type. Yes," Tuniel said.

"And Tuniel and I are Rushia. Alright." Aubin nodded. "We will need some headscarves. A black one for me and a bright one for Tuniel."

Sabatha raised a finger, summoning a servant, and the one who responded listened and rushed to obey.

Evyn shifted uncomfortably. "I don't like the idea of you even pretending to be a slave, Thorrn." She gave me a significant look, lips trembling.

My stomach iced over. *The Patient Slave.* Perhaps it was coming true. But, if so, what did that mean for Evyn?

She looked away from me before I could broach the subject, leafing through the texts spread before her and starting to read. Her quick gaze scanned the pages as I would assess an opponent, searching for useful information, before she settled to read more deeply.

Meanwhile, Aubin's discreet glances at Evyn became more frequent. He kept tight control of his expressions, but something akin to wonder shone in his face. Tuniel looked sharply at him, and I wondered if she sensed some sort of shift within him.

I drummed my fingers on the table. With all the changes that he had wrought in himself, stepping into the role as I knew he could, perhaps he was finally listening to his heart and allowing himself to dream again. Or so I fancied, but imaginings and real life could be far away from one another.

Aubin pulled himself away from the table, holding himself tight around his chest and closing his eyes. *What I wouldn't give to see inside his head sometimes.* He let out a long breath, loosening his arms, and approached Evyn. My heart rejoiced, and Tuniel's eyes widened.

"I want to check the battlements," Gerlay said loudly. "The view from up there is spectacular. Would you like to take a walk, Lady Evyn? With your soul companion as chaperone, of course."

"Mm?" She glanced up, refocusing on him.

Aubin stopped in his tracks, shooting a barbed glare at Gerlay.

Gerlay stood up slowly, gaze fixed on Aubin.

Aubin's mouth opened and closed. I tensed, wondering what he would say, what he would reveal.

"Uh..." Evyn looked between them. My stomach grew heavy, echoing with her discomfort, but before I could be pleased about that, she pulled back from the bond and the feeling vanished. She pushed her hair behind her ear, gaze dropping to the pages before her. "Actually, I'm on a roll here. Maybe later?"

No, Evyn. This needs to come to a head. I flexed my hands, looking between them. Both stood glaring at the other, but hands were far from their weapons, as they should be.

If Evyn made a choice, how would that swing things? I nudged her shoulder gently.

"I'm busy," she said, voice strained and eyes resolutely fixed on her books.

I barely restrained myself from grabbing handfuls of my hair.

"Rangers, Prince Gerlay." Gough came to us with a stark face. "We have a situation," the king said hoarsely.

I snapped into attention, heart racing. "Is it Liara?"

"No. It's Luc."

A length behind the king, sauntering along studying the courtyard with the sun shining full on his face, was what looked like an older version of me. He was another offshoot of King Dolobere, Gough's father and my grandfather, although that revelation still made me hellishly uncomfortable to even think about. Luc was a pain mancer and the self-described guardian of Earth, focused on keeping the ways between the worlds a secret from the mancers and mages of this world.

Deadly focused.

I swallowed hard. "What's he here for, sir?"

"I called him a sennight ago regarding your situation, Ranger," the king said. "He turned up at the doors of the palace this morning and said he had noticed something. He stated he was coming to investigate." Gough fixed Aubin with a glare. "Do not tell him about your ability."

Aubin frowned.

I whispered, "Pinging, do not mention you can do it."

"Fine, but why not?" he murmured under his breath.

"You'll see why not," I said.

Luc drew up to us, brown eyes snapping to me. "Ah. Shardsson. Well met," the mancer said, baring his teeth in a too-wide smile. He looked Gerlay and Aubin up and down. "And a positive welter of masculine energy."

"And me." Evyn squeezed between Aubin and Gerlay to stand beside me. "Hi. I'm not sure we were properly introduced down in the tunnels under the MasterMage's Palais. No one was really in the right frame of mind anyway." She offered her hand. I tensed. "I'm Evyn. Researcher and tourist."

Luc raised an eyebrow at her. "Are you sure you want to do that?"

"Oh, I know you're a pain mancer." She kept her hand firmly in place.

Luc reached out and I couldn't help but put my hand on Evyn's shoulder. When he used it, Luc's magic would reawaken every white-hot moment of pain a person had experienced over the course of their life.

Luc smirked at her as he shook her hand. "Luc. Rogue mancer and self-appointed guardian of our homeland." He jerked Evyn toward him.

I cried out and reached for my sword, but Gough shook his head once, jaw tight.

Luc lowered his voice, speaking into Evyn's ear, but I was close enough to hear. "I hope you've been careful, little girl. You and your soul companion gave an ostentatious display under the tunnels. I did not think it necessary to warn you that the fewer people see a portal, the better," he hissed.

Evyn's eyes went wide.

Aubin stepped up behind Evyn, putting his hand on her other shoulder. "She's careful. We have to close our eyes, blindfolded, hands over our ears," he said.

Of course he would hear that.

Luc narrowed his eyes at him.

My heartbeat quickened, and I had to force myself to breathe in and out deeply.

The mancer let go of Evyn's hand, straightening up. "Very good. I'd hate for someone to, say, pick up the technique from observation. That would lead to only one recourse."

"Understood." Aubin gently guided a grey-faced Evyn back behind him, handing her to Gerlay and then squaring up to Luc.

I unhinged my jaw from its locked position.

"Thank you for coming, Luc, and with all haste," the king said.

"The debt is all yours. You owe me, big brother."

Gough and I winced at the same time, and I put my hand on my sword.

Luc peered at me. "What seems to be the problem with your swordsman this time? Too many blows to the head?"

Gough gestured toward me. "It seems he and his soul companion, who you have just met, have been infected by a kind of spiritsight."

"My condolences. You need me to plan their funerals?"

"No," I said, pushing down the rush of anger. "The Rushia princess pulled the spirit from me, but she cannot help Evyn. Would you have any ideas?"

"Why on Oberrot do you think I can deal with death magic? No, sorry, if there are spirits flying around, I'm out." His dark brown eyes looked me up and down. "Particularly if they can affect people like *us*. Why is the king so close to something like that?"

Colouring, I saluted Gough. "My pardon, sir, but he's right. I've said before that I cannot guarantee your safety here. I strongly advise that you leave."

The king nodded slowly. "I'll make the arrangements. You have it all in hand here, Rangers?"

I saluted smartly. "Yessir. Between me and Aubin, we have it under control."

"Uh-huh," Luc drawled. "Well, I'd say it's been lovely seeing you, except it hasn't."

"Wow!"

We spun at the interruption to see a middle-aged man with lanky limbs and coiffed brown hair making his way into the courtyard.

Luc's jaw went slack. "James!" he hissed. "I told you to wait in the car!"

"Luc, this is immense! I'm not going to miss this." James waved his arms at the open courtyard. "Sun! Oh, Lukey, we said we wanted to get away." He sauntered over to us and beamed at me. "Oh, hello! How are you feeling? Luc came over all worried when he got a message that you weren't well."

"Shut. Up," Luc grated through his teeth.

"And... oh, hello." James grinned at Gerlay.

"Well met," Gerlay said, bowing politely.

James rubbed his hands.

"No, get out," Luc snapped.

James huffed and put his hands on his hips. He surveyed us all, gaze snagging on Evyn. "You okay, love?"

"Not really," Evyn said softly.

James straightened up, all business. "I'm a paramedic. What's the problem?"

"No, no, no! We are not getting involved!" Luc's face went red, his voice thunderous.

"Luc." I lowered my voice. "You two are the closest thing to friendly medimancers that we can trust with this. Please. She needs help. You helped us once before." I went down onto one knee. "Please. I'm begging you. Help her."

Luc's gaze flicked between my eyes. "And what fun helping you out that one time was." Luc threw up his hands. "Damnation, I suppose we can take a look."

I sprung to my feet. "Thank you. I owe you a great debt."

His eyes bored into me. "I won't forget that, Shardsson."

CHAPTER 26

While Luc ran some tests on Evyn, and Gough left via a travel mancer procured by Tuniel, we made preparations to enter the city in disguise. Aubin fitted his dark headscarf and Tuniel was furnished with a bright woman's one. I tried to find a quiet moment with her where I could simultaneously beg her not to discard the Rushia dress while also pointing out that it was highly distracting.

While I stripped my jacket and shirt off, the small stone on Amare glowed; upon touching it, Tuniel's voice filled my mind. *"This is not quite a true lodestone, but I am confident you can hear me; I'll be keeping hold of the dress."* Her lascivious intentions brushed my mind with an impression of satin and skin.

Gerlay put my sword on. "How does one talk to a slave anyway?" he asked in his best attempt at smoothing out his accent while speaking Oberrotian. He sounded like Evyn.

Pulling myself back to the present, I dropped my hand from the stone on my shoulder, rubbing the back of my head and hoping I could explain my red face as being caused by the heat. "Usually barking orders. Just don't get me to do anything humiliating."

"Would we take advantage of you like that?" Aubin asked in Rushia.

"I'd be tempted," I admitted.

"You're a bad person, Shard—slave," he said.

"Yes, that's right." I followed them with downturned eyes and demeanour.

We made our way through the tent city. The tents leant against old weathered brick, enhancing the dilapidated buildings and providing much-needed shade. The area around the palace was lively with trade, Rushia gossiping with each other and pointing out their wares. Guards shooed people away from the palace, and we were more than happy to be shooed out toward the food markets, where the smells tied my stomach in knots.

"Flesh market is that way, if you're looking to sell that slave!" someone helpfully directed us.

"My thanks," Gerlay said, managing to sound Oberrotian.

"Good work," I whispered to him.

"You're supposed to address me as Master."

"You're getting a little too invested in this."

Tuniel needed to walk two circuits around the city, activating a small ring of warning stones about a quarter of a mile from the palace first and moving to an outer ring afterwards. On the map, the sets of three outer stones that she had already activated and the two inner ones that we facilitated now looked like a spider's web. I nearly set off ahead, but then remembered I had to follow Gerlay.

We weaved along the edges of the market, and I caught and automatically translated snatches of Rushia from the market goers, the hurried whispers and hushed theories of why the guards were prowling around the city. They feared the sultan was either dead or edging toward issuing orders for control of the city, but for what reason, they couldn't guess. Stories already abounded that the princess was dead, or that the Oberrotian king had arrived to take her for his bride, and friends counselled each other to watch all foreigners with suspicion.

I stayed in my disguise as a slave and walked behind Gerlay and Aubin, carrying the things we bought. The guards ignored me entirely, seeing the silvrine scars on my back rather than the identification tattoos or the metal embedded in my shoulder. The former were in a sorry state; the one on my chest had the big cross I'd cut into it and the one on my forearm was covered over with multiple slashes that Aubin had laid into me. The only ones intact were my left bicep, and that was easily kept toward walls and awnings away from the guard, and my thighs, hidden under my trousers.

At mid-sun, as the heat approached an unbearable temperature, a fat Oberrotian approached Gerlay and hailed him, wiping his brow of sweat. "Just what I need at last. My slave died this morning. Yours looks strong, what do you want for him?"

Gerlay stilled. "He's not for sale. We're using him."

"Name a price."

I had no idea what slaves sold for.

"He eats too much," Gerlay said slowly, trying to erase his accent. "You wouldn't want him."

The Oberrotian's eyes narrowed. "Where are you from? There's a Dinahen burr there."

"My mother is from Dinahe," Gerlay said, completely truthfully.

"And you won't sell him?"

"I think he might kill me if I did."

The man frowned.

"This one kill him," Aubin said, stepping forward and speaking pigeon Oberrotian in a Rushia accent. "This one bought the slave. The slave is owned by this one. No sale here! No!" He flapped his hands at the Oberrotian.

"Fine. I'll look elsewhere," the man muttered, fanning his face as he left.

Aubin turned to us. "We're attracting attention. Let's find some lodgings."

Strands of Tuniel's silvrine hair were plastered to the side of her face and curling up under her headscarf. "Good. I'm flagging. I'm finding it hard to keep stretching out my senses like this. It's too hot."

Aubin found us a place to sit out the midday heat, hiring rooms where sand had crept into the bedsheets, the air musty and dry. Gerlay sagged onto the bed, and I recalled that Dinahens had an interval in their days to rest at mid-sun.

"I'm not tired. I can keep searching." I was eager to be out and about learning what I could.

"Most people stay in at the heat of the day, Thorrn," Tuniel murmured tiredly. "It would be unusual if we kept walking around."

"Very well." I sat beside my bunk listening to Gerlay snore and to someone singing a sad high song down the street, watching the sunlight flicker outside the wooden slats of the window as lone people walked by. It quietened down, and I closed my eyes and tried to think my way to Evyn. Was she alright? Had she fallen asleep? Was Luc taking care of her?

"I need to do something. Move. Anything." I bounced on the balls of my feet.

Aubin scowled from his bunk. "Don't stink up this room, and it's hot enough as it is. Do some balance exercises."

"We could use some blade tutorials," I pointed out.

"Hm. Well." He held up his blades. The hilt sat in his hand with the blade curved back over his forearm, protecting it but also acting as the offensive instrument. "I essentially punch to the side of people and the blade will slice them as it passes. I've told you that the foundation is built using careful, slow movements to teach body control and awareness and build strength. Then you add explosive power, like the Art. The trick to wielding the blades is fast, powerful movements, therefore you need to have acute body awareness and control, but also power behind your strike." He held out his blades. "Try them. What do you make of them?"

I held the well-worn hilts in my hands. The blade curved backwards and was a little short and low for me, coming to a wickedly sharp point just above my forearm muscle. I was more interested in the grooves in the blades themselves and the intricate delicate metal work around the hilts.

"The bloodletting lines help clear the blade quickly. The hilt is patterned for improved grip," Aubin explained.

"Bloodletting," Gerlay grumbled, sitting up and yawning.

"Yes. No point to a blade if things aren't bleeding after you use it," Aubin said cheerily.

"So you punch and the blade slices." I put my hands up into an unarmed fighter's block. "I like how the hilts feel. Makes the fist more secure."

"Yes, but there's no give, so you could break your knuckles more easily."

"Hm." I tried to hand the blades to Gerlay, but he waved them away. Passing them back to Aubin, I turned to Tuniel. "Do you remember those bracers you made for us underneath the Master-Mage's Palais, Tuniel? With the slashy bits on them?"

She looked up from her book. "I modelled those on Aubin's blades. You didn't like them, as I recall."

"I did like them, I just liked the armour better. Could we have bracers that deploy a blade on the side of them occasionally?"

She bent down a corner of the page in her book, closing it. "Yes. That should be easy enough. I just need some metal."

As soon as the day cooled, we went to the scrap merchants so Tuniel could set the next stone and to look for materials. We passed towering piles of the detritus of industry, tools bent and bowed or unwanted, and she touched and patted pieces as we went. Suddenly she looked up and made a direct line for a pile of scrap swords.

"Found something you like?" Aubin asked in Rushia.

Tuniel dug around and triumphantly held up my father's sword.

I cried out and ran to her, taking it reverently. "I'm so happy I could kiss you."

"Don't, not in public," Tuniel whispered.

"Ah, yes, I meant you as well." I hugged the blade carefully to my chest.

A voice rang out from behind us. "Who's armed that slave?" The Oberrotian from earlier stared at us, hands on his hips.

"He's just carrying it for me," Tuniel said.

"We'd like this one." Gerlay pointed at my father's sword in my hands.

The man sniffed. "So I see. The price is that slave."

"For scrap metal?" Tuniel scoffed.

He thumbed his nose. "That's not scrap metal, I can see it's an Oberrotian officer's blade. By rights I should destroy it. Could be used for nefarious purposes." He looked Tuniel up and down, eyes glinting with appreciation, and I stifled the urge to stand in front of her. She could crack the floor underneath him if she so desired.

"We want to take it to its rightful owner," Gerlay said, again completely truthfully. He was wonderful at lying by telling part of the truth.

"Throw in these pieces here." Tuniel gestured to her small haul of thin metal plates.

"What! I... oh, fine," I grumbled. Aubin and Gerlay could escort Tuniel around to set the rest of the stones without me easily enough, and although the tension between them was not yet palpable, I knew Gerlay would not decline working with Aubin to fulfil the mission.

"Done." The man spat on his hand.

Gerlay looked uncomfortable, but he shook it.

My new master grinned. "Get over here, slave!"

"I'll be back after dark," Aubin murmured to me as he passed.

"You'd better."

The fat man bristled. "I mean now!"

I followed him, keeping my head lowered even though I towered above him.

He led me to a pile of unsorted dirty metal pieces and contraptions. "These all need breaking down and then the pieces need piling in size order."

"Yessir. What tools can I use?"

"That hammer there." He pointed at a sledgehammer against the wall. Next to it was a short chain and a manacle. "Put that on your ankle. You'll wear that while you have that in your hands. Wouldn't want you getting ideas."

"Fine." I snapped it shut and looked at all the work I had to do. I grinned.

"What are you smiling about?"

"I was looking for a way to pass the time. This is a boon, thank you."

He frowned at me and then shook his head.

I fell into the hard, hot work of smashing and bashing pieces of metal into submission, lifting the hammer up high and swinging it down with all my force. Soon I was drenched with sweat. I shook my head occasionally to clear the droplets.

While my body worked, my mind was free to wander and turn over my problems. Evyn's illness being the number one, linked directly to Liara, but perhaps Luc and James could help. Next was Liara herself, who needed to be brought to justice for daring to threaten the Crown of Oberrot. I wished I could bash through them as easily as I smashed this metal; that Evyn would open up to me so I could strengthen her, and I could face down Liara with no issues.

I halted, panting. Being trapped in my own body with Liara and Aglo tormenting me had been torture, but Liara had been struggling. No longer the calm, cruel mage in full control as in Dinahe, life on the run had taken its toll. She had meant to harm Tuniel as revenge for Waker, her lover; she had lost someone dear to her, and was hurting from that as well.

I shook my head. Feeling sorry for Liara was out of the question. She had moved to harm me and mine; she was a threat to the king and the prince, and would be ended.

She probably thinks the same way. So does Aubin. He had felt that Gavain needed to be ended, and followed through, accepting the consequences as he did so.

Returning to bashing metal, I turned over the problem of Gavain.

His health was improving, Gough had said, and he would return to stand trial for poisoning Evyn. What would the outcome of that be? The more severe punishments included banishment, where his tattoos would be flensed from his skin and he would be immediately cast out, shunned from all Oberrotian society. The idea turned my stomach. It was a punishment the condemned rarely survived; staggering around bleeding with no succour from anyone left no quarter. Evyn was the daughter of the king's soul companion, a person of importance. Did that mean the outcome could be banishment? Or even execution? Did Gavain know that he got better every day just to return home to face the noose? What kind of impact would that have on a person?

And did he truly deserve such torture, and such a fate?

Yes, part of me screamed, the part that snarled in rage and fear that he had nearly taken Evyn from me.

No. He acted badly, but he had been horrified at seeing Evyn laid out. What had that changed in him, and what could that lead to?

I shifted a new pile into range, wondering how Evyn felt about all this. Was her compassion coming across to me at last? She had an incredible capacity to forgive, evidenced by me remaining in her life and Teresa finding a way to be friends with her despite turns of torment. Was there a line that, once crossed, Evyn would never understand and forgive?

When I had finished all the piles in range, it was nearing quarter-day. I made sure the broken pieces of metal were neat and sat down, breathing hard.

"Oh." My new master returned, eyes wide.

"What's next?" I asked.

He gaped at me. "Some water. Then I suppose you can get started on tomorrow's piles."

"Great. Thanks."

"You know, you're probably the best purchase I've ever made."

"Glad to hear it." I hesitated for a heartbeat before risking a question. He might not stand for a slave asking him things. "Where did you get that sword from? The ones my... previous masters wanted?"

He wiped his sopping forehead. "Someone abandoned a bunch of wagons in the city. They were stripped down, and everyone knows I buy metal, so they came to me with it. Look, see, some decent metal bars fitted on one." He gestured to a pile where grey bars lay in a heap. I recognised them as the bars around Evyn's wagon while we were Liara's prisoners.

My stomach knotted. Without the wagons, Liara was sure to still be in the city. Part of me had wondered if she had managed to slip out before Tuniel set her watchstones. This confirmed that she was within our sights, and we had only to flush her out.

"Are you feeling well? Is it the heat?" the slaver asked me.

I shook my head.

"Drink some more water. Don't want you dying on me like the last one did, I've learnt my lesson now."

I nodded and drank more, then got unshackled to help him move the piles around, so that new pieces awaiting breaking sat before me in an even bigger heap. I put the ankle manacle back on and got back to it, raising and smashing the hammer down as if Liara was in front of me.

"Keen, keen," my master said happily. "But it's sunset. You can stop now."

Startled, I looked at the red sky. "I could finish this pile."

"Well, my neighbours complain if there is noise much beyond sunset, so you can rest for the night." He gave me a bowl of rice and spicy meat, too spicy but welcome to my growling stomach.

"Are you really a slave?" he asked as I ate.

"What else would I be with lash marks on my back?" I guzzled more water.

He scoffed. "Oberrotians whip soldiers all the time for misdeeds. Had one a few moon cycles back, a sergeant caught out with stuff, tall lad with... with brown hair..." His eyes narrowed.

"Oh, really? Interesting." I replied evenly, taking big bites of my dinner.

"Hm. Well. You'll sleep in the shed. I don't tend to lock my slaves in, but you're new."

"Yessir. That's fine." I finished eating and then levered myself to my feet, feeling the hard work I'd put my body through as a satisfying soreness throughout.

I followed him to a small shelter with a rough pallet on the floor. Laying on it, I stared up at the bare ceiling.

He shut the door, the snick of the lock shortly thereafter.

I closed my eyes. What if this were my life, just seeing these four walls and the compound outside, breaking metal day in, day out, eating and drinking what he saw fit to bring me? And if I had a harsher master, one who took the trials of his day out on me because I was under his power? And harsher again, a group egging each other on to greater and greater cruelty?

I curled up in a ball thinking about it. The next time I saw Shoulders, I'd have to go to one knee and salute him for surviving it, but also give him a hug for what he had endured. I had hope to cling onto, that this situation was temporary, almost a novelty, but in the bare shack, it was all too real.

It's coming true, Evyn had said. Was this truly my destiny?

It was harder to dismiss it as bunkum in the dark of a cell than in the bright light wearing a sword, but I did so.

CHAPTER 27

I jolted awake when Aubin landed lightly on the roof. It felt like one turn after my nap, so I was slightly rested and refreshed. "Took you long enough." I yawned.

"Rush is like Dinerah. All the activity happens at night when it's cool." His voice was muffled. He had to be wearing the headscarf.

"The door here has a lock, I can kick it down," I said, my voice loud in the small shed.

"Oh, very stealthy. Why did you even wait for me? Let me work on it." I heard him now by the door. "He didn't seem a dire master. Are you well?"

"He was fine. I did about three days' worth of labour for him breaking metal." I paced, eager to be off. "Is Tuniel pleased by that sort of thing or not?"

"How should I know?"

"Forget I asked. I'll try it out one day in bed. I'll bring in some scrap metal and a hammer and get all sweaty bashing it to pieces."

"Sounds like the opposite of a clandestine meeting. People will definitely ask questions about noises like that." The door opened and Aubin bowed for me to leave.

I clapped him on the shoulder as I passed. "My master would probably go to the guard to put out a notice for an escaped slave, so I think it's time I get dressed as a Ranger again. I don't want to be strung up against a building."

Aubin handed me a shirt; he had already anticipated as much. As I pulled it on, he updated me. "We're heading back to the palace. Tuniel has set out all the stones she needs. The next time Liara moves, we will know exactly where she is, so we need to plan the next step."

"Oh! Maybe I'll leave my shirt off and watch Tuniel sneak looks at me."

"She has much better self-control than that."

"Want to wager on that?" I buttoned up the shirt over skin that was sweaty and dirty, but that could not be helped.

We jogged back to our lodgings where Gerlay and Tuniel were resting. "Aubin, that took you two turns of the glass!" Tuniel complained.

"I couldn't move until Rush had gone to sleep." Aubin pulled his headscarf off and rubbed his eyes. Deep circles underlined his tiredness.

"As it happens, I could have gotten myself out," I said. "The metal merchant only put one lock on a threadbare door."

"We didn't know that. He could have locked you in his personal torture dungeon," Gerlay said in flawless Oberrotian.

"I'm impressed and concerned that your mind went there. Also, that you can say those words. He had heavy lifting to do and paid for someone else to do it so he could get on with other things. He would not buy me to turn me into meat."

"What *did* he get you to do?" Tuniel asked.

I leant close to her. "Break metal."

She shivered.

I raised my eyebrows at Aubin, and he shook his head.

Tuniel held out my father's sword to me, freshly shone up and gleaming. "I smoothed all the nicks out of it. You take good care of it, but someone used it recently to chop at thick wood and metal." Her nose wrinkled at the idea.

So did mine. "My thanks, MasterMage. I am very pleased to have this back." Pleased did not begin to contain the shades of my elation. Holding my father's blade with its well-worn hilt, I felt myself again, an unstoppable Ranger with no fear. That I was neither unstoppable and I had shown fear hitched my heart.

I would do what I had to. Evyn needed me to stay strong for her.

I pulled the belt on, tightening it. "It was probably used to break up the wagons. I have intelligence; I found the pieces of Liara's wagon at the scrap yard. She abandoned them, so she's likely still here." Somewhere nearby.

Tuniel's gaze turned cold. "We knew that. I set the watchstones as we came after you. Once that witch entered the city, she was mine. Even so, it's not like her to wait around. What is she doing?" Tuniel chewed her lip.

Gerlay sat up. "She could be resting. She was used to a pampered life in Dinahe. Being heartsick and enduring deprivations of the comfort one is used to takes its toll."

I nodded, as I had been thinking along similar lines, but Aubin said, "Ah, yes, let's assume our enemy is lazing about instead of preparing."

Gerlay's jaw tightened. "It was a suggestion."

I stared at them.

Tuniel sighed. "It's been rather... fraught," she admitted to me quietly.

Aubin scowled. "Making the assumption that our enemy is lazy or stupid is a good way to get killed. Liara is neither." He pulled his bracers tight against his forearm. "Do not underestimate the woman, or any woman."

Gerlay's hands curled into fists on his knees. "You asked a question. I provided an answer."

Tuniel waved a hand at them, leaning toward me. "Aubin brought up the gender roles in Dinahe earlier. It did not end well."

"They don't let women think in Dinahe," Aubin said. "It's the one thing that goes against the generally agreeable culture."

Gerlay's hands went white-knuckled. "The men do the harder work. Our women are to be protected." His brows knitted together, jaw working.

My stomach tightened. I had only met male Dinahen traders, soldiers, craftsmen and bureaucrats. "What do the women do, then? How would Evyn be received there?"

His gaze dropped. "They bear the burden of childbirth and rearing. She would have her library, as agreed."

Hot disappointment flooded my chest. "So you'll lock her away?"

"Of course not." Gerlay met my eyes. "She would be shunned somewhat, I fear. I would protect her from that and challenge any man who dared say something in my or her hearing."

"But not the women." Aubin shot him a scathing look. "You have to defend her against all comers, not only the men. Women have the same capacity to be cruel."

Gerlay reached for his staff, deliberately taking a deep breath. Through the turmoil of this revelation, I could see that he was having his own preconceptions challenged, and making him stand alone to answer for the habits of his culture was unfair. It was like asking me to justify slavery. I wasn't sure I could do it, but Oberrot was built on it. How could Gerlay or I change something engrained like that?

Tuniel nudged me gently, producing two metal bracers. "I made these. Let's fit them on and I'll show you how they work."

"Should I take my shirt off for this?" I asked, winking at her.

She sighed. "No, Thorrn."

"Oh. I can, though, if you'd like?" I really wasn't feeling into it, but the levity took my mind off Evyn's latest predicament.

She slipped me a small smile. The bracers slid onto my forearms like the armour, soft liquid metal. "Gerlay wanted the basic bracers to repel attacks but not the modified ones with the sharp fins. What word do you want to use to deploy them?"

"I like the Oberrotian root words you know, what's something like 'cut' or 'knife'?"

"Secare?"

"Yes, sounds thrilling. Secare!" Twin blades slid out from the outside of my forearms. "Very nice. Unsecare to put them back?"

Tuniel sighed but nodded. "Here are the jewels to store the magic in. You'll want to take these off when you aren't using them to prevent irritation."

"Noted. Thank you, MasterMage." I saluted and bowed to her. Then, because Aubin and Gerlay were embroiled in their glaring match, I kissed her cheek.

She smiled at me, biting her lip.

I slapped my thighs and stood. "Mission successful. Let's return to the palace. I can't feel anything untoward from Evyn, but I'd like to confirm all the same." I looked between Aubin and Gerlay, bristling at each other. "Let's get moving before my description starts circulating and I get lynched."

The walk back to the palace was quiet and cold. At night, braziers inside the tents protected against the desert chill, throwing shadows against the tent walls and colours to blaze out, painting the packed dirt streets in reds and blues.

We only had to approach the Artists and were shown in. The palace walkways were cold now, heatstones placed along corridors patrolled by the Artists on duty. Tiredness dragged at my limbs, a soreness from a full day's exercise. Tuniel went to the library and Gerlay said he wanted to walk the walls before turn in time. I made my way immediately to Evyn, not surprised in the least to find Aubin at my heels.

Evyn lay in bed, with James curled up on the chair next to her. Luc surveyed her with sandy eyes.

James waved from his seat. "Good, you're back. Come here."

"I hope wherever you were was worth it." Luc's frown darkened his face.

"What's happened?" I took Evyn's hand.

"She pretty much collapsed when you left and has been in a deep sleep ever since." James shook his head. "This isn't normal."

"Liara must be draining her and planning something large," Aubin said, voicing my fears.

"It's not that. It's because she has some damned spirit nestling up against her heart." Luc stretched his hands out above Evyn. "She will not be reliable as some kind of gauge on the enchanter, because the energy isn't going anywhere, it's staying within her, feeding that spirit. I've never seen anything like it, and neither has Sabatha." Luc put his hand on his soul companion's shoulder. "You will stay away from those spirit things, James. I don't want them infecting you."

James cocked his head at us. "What did it look like, these spirits?"

"Amorphous black smoke," Aubin supplied.

"Smoke?" James gaped. "This is nuts. How can this be real? Magic and... and swords and kings and evil sorcery and stuff."

"Have you not been to Oberrot before, Lord James?"

"I'm not a lord anything! And no, Luc has kept me firmly away from it. Spirits, what a nightmare," James said, rubbing his cheeks. "What a surreal day." He gave me a small smile. "On the other hand, her vitals are fine; I can be at least that much help."

"Can you do anything?" Aubin asked them.

James winced. "This is not anything I've ever come across. I'm good for acute emergency situations, not chronic illnesses."

Luc folded his arms. "I can't reach in to them. So, unless they leave of their own free will, I imagine they are going to drain and kill her."

No. My hand tightened on hers. "I'll strengthen her until you can find a cure, she can use my energy."

"For that, you need a very strong bond." Luc sneered at me. "And you've only just met."

"We've been through a lot. We are close," I asserted quietly.

Luc shook his head. "She loves you. She's keeping this away from you, away from the bond, to keep you safe."

I sat slowly on the edge of her bed. *Let me help, Evyn. I won't let you down.*

"I'm tired. I'm going to find that room they set aside for us," Luc snapped at James.

"Sure thing," James returned, his voice bright despite the late hour. "Let me finish up a few things here."

Inclining his head, Luc left with stiff steps.

When the door closed, James winked at me. "Don't mind him. He's worried." He tucked the coverlet up to Evyn's shoulders.

I nodded. "He's right, though. She's protecting me. How can I strengthen the bond if she's pushing me away?"

James glanced at the door. "Well, I have personal experience of that. Just don't tell Lukey I told you." He settled into the chair next to Evyn's bed, taking her wrist and comparing what he felt from his fingers with a small circular device in his hands. He spoke quietly. "Luc and his mother were travelling entertainers. She had him hide the fact that he could cause pain accidentally through a single touch. He didn't like to bump into others, rub shoulders, anything that might set him off and hurt someone, but part of the work of entertaining is being around people.

"One day, someone cornered them and tried to rob them. They hurt his mother, and all he did was slap one man, but it killed him with a touch. They thought he was a soul searcher and gathered a mob to hunt him. He ran until he couldn't run anymore and screamed for the other half of his spirit to be with him only this once."

No wonder Luc did not want to be around people. I shuddered at the idea of a mancer who could kill with a touch, my skin crawling. Nevermind that he didn't mean it, the capability was there.

But I could understand his pain. How lonely he had felt. It chimed with my recent experience all too easily, longing for Evyn to appear and be by my side at last.

I took her other hand.

James leant back in the chair, balancing it on its rear legs. "I was jogging in a park when he fell through right into my path. I was in uni, studying to be a medic, so of course I stopped to help him. But as soon as I touched him..." I winced, waiting for James to say Luc had hurt him, but there was a wide smile on James' face. "I felt something shift inside me...

"He realised what I was, who I was, but he feared that his touch could cause me great harm. He kept me away from him, kept me ignorant of what we were to each other. I thought I was attracted to him in a traditional sense, except I never wanted to bed him. He felt like my greatest friend, a brother, something deeper than a lover. I wanted to hold his hand, but he shied away from it.

"He tried to leave, but every time, my heart Called him back. He was at war with himself for a good long while, and it turned into a war with me. He couldn't live with what he could do and have me close, so he decided to save the planet I lived on instead. If he couldn't be with me, he would at least make sure that no harm would ever come to me."

My chest filled with warmth. Such dedication, such single-minded purpose. I looked to Aubin, who leant against the wall, head lowered as if tired. I wondered what he thought of this sentiment.

James grinned. "I broke through that. I was dogged and determined myself, and I wore him down. I told, I scolded, I begged, I asked. Eventually I said, 'I *want* your touch. Luc.'" He held out his hand. "'I want you to take my hand. I am not afraid of you, and I never will be.'"

"James," Luc snapped. He had opened the door. "What are you doing? Come to rest now!"

James stood up. "On my way."

Luc turned his steely glare on to me.

I cleared my throat. "That was a very touching story, and I feel—"

"I will kill you if you ever breathe a word of it," Luc said calmly.

My instincts spiked with the threat. It sounded genuine enough.

James picked up his tools, shoving intricate shapes of metal and opaque bottles into a green bag. "Right, yes, absolutely. Thorrn, let me know if anything happens in the night."

Luc grunted. "We are just in the room next door, and I can monitor pain from there."

"Is she in pain?" I bunched the covers in my fists.

"No. Not her pain." Luc turned away. "James, hurry up."

James waved, mouthing goodnight.

"I'll stay," Aubin said, a statement.

I rubbed my face. "Very well." I lay next to Evyn on the edge of the bed. "Please take from me," I whispered to her. "Please." I would need to be determined, to constantly set out my stance on this issue, and never relent in my love for her. I would have to repeat myself every day until she allowed me to help.

If she even has days left.

Trembling with fear, I rolled myself in the covers and pressed her hand over my heart.

Aubin settled on the chair James had vacated, pulling off his boots and setting his Battlemistress blade holsters on the bedside table. "She will. She has to," Aubin said firmly.

It came to something when Aubin was the optimist over me.

CHAPTER 28

When I opened my eyes, Evyn was sat up in the bed. Aubin sat straight-backed in the chair, watching her. The predawn light filtering through the small windows high above laid shades of grey over the room, unable to cut through the black shadows lurking in the corners.

"Evyn?" I whispered.

Aubin tensed, hands clutching the armrests of the wicker chair with a creak.

She turned to me slowly. Her eyes were bloodshot, pink and red. Her irises glowed faintly, a dark carmine.

My chest clenched. "Evyn, speak to me!"

She blinked and rubbed her eyes. When her hands fell, her eyes were a watery blue again. "Oh. Hi."

"Evyn, what happened just now?"

"Hm? How long has it been? Are you on your way out or just come back?" She smiled, but I could feel a pit of dread in her stomach.

"Evyn—"

She slammed her fists into the blankets with a dull thwack. "Yes,

I know! I know something happened, but I don't know what, because I keep bloody collapsing all the time!"

I could not move. The wash of her despair slammed into me, a powerful wave that I could not hope to surmount.

She wrenched the desperation back at the same time as she pulled the coverlet up to her face. "Argh, damn it. I'm sorry for shouting at you. But no, I don't know what time it is, what day it is, whether anyone's coming or going..." Her shoulders shook. "Is this what it's like at the end? Just dreamlessly sleeping, sliding in and out of the lives of people around you? Lying there doing nothing while the world carries on?"

My throat squeezed, pressure pounding against my head as if I were deep underwater. I had no answers for her, no paths forward. *I need to do something. Anything.*

Taking a big shuddering breath, she let the covers fall. "Alright. Have to make the best of it." She rubbed her forehead, red faced but lighter for the outburst. "Can you stay with me today?"

I leapt at the opportunity. "Yes, Evyn, yes, a thousand times yes. Lean on me, take from me. I give anything you need freely, please."

She hesitated and my hope rose, but then she shook her head firmly. "No. This stays mine. There's something I need to do, something she wants me to do." She sighed. "I think."

The soreness in my heart, wanting to help and being unable to, morphed into anger. "Evyn, if you're having conversations with it, tell it to get out. I'll tell it to get out! Go! Leave!"

She pushed me away. "She doesn't speak exactly. I just feel things that aren't mine. She's afraid, Thorrn. I can't push her out if she's afraid."

"It *is* killing you," Aubin said.

Evyn jumped, a spike of fear lancing down the bond. "Oh my life, I had no idea you were there." She chuckled, pulling a hand down her plait and composing herself. "Let me get up and get started. Um. Morning training?" she asked me hopefully.

"Are you—"

Her glower interrupted me.

I stood up slowly. "Yes, but I will not leave your side."

I held to that. On the way to the training quadrangle, I asked a servant to bring us something to sit on, and before too long the small, shaded pagoda had been set up as a relaxation area in the courtyard. "Comfy cushions, ice water, some meats and cheeses," Evyn cooed with appreciation. "Now this is some morning training!" She plumped a pillow and then bent to sit.

I felt her pain as each joint moved, a dull ache radiating throughout her body and pulsing in the back of my head. I held out my arms for her to lower herself down, Aubin's hands shooting out to take hers.

She sighed at us both. "Don't fuss," she grumbled.

Tears pressed behind my eyes, my nose stinging. "Let me help, Evyn."

She covered her face with a hand. To block me out, or collect herself? "Just... carry on," she muttered. "Pretend I'm not here."

I sat at her side as Gerlay arrived, spinning his staff idly in one hand. He looked from me to Evyn, dark eyes widening, then frowned at Aubin standing sentinel behind her.

Gerlay bowed stiffly to Evyn. "Good morning. I hope you have slept well?"

"Yes, thank you." Evyn hid a yawn. "Too much. Hope you had a nice sleep."

He nodded once, jaw tight. He was more tense than usual. Could it be because Evyn was here watching him, and that put pressure on him?

I took Evyn's hand, raising my voice. "I'm going to sit this one out. You two have at it."

Evyn shot me an apologetic look, red-rimmed eyes and lips trembling.

I smiled to reassure her. "I'm looking forward to it. I'm going to wager on Gerlay."

"Excuse me?" Aubin put his hands on his hips.

I reclined against the cushions, as a lordling might when presented with entertainment. "Staff against Battlemistress blades? You won't get close enough to use them."

Gerlay bowed again. "I won't fail, Lady Evyn."

"Oh, jeez," she muttered, sinking down into the cushions. "Don't hurt yourselves."

"Hmm." I leant in toward her to whisper as they went to opposite sides of the practice square. "If he's fighting for your honour, what's Aubin fighting for?"

She gently smacked me on the arm, high spots of colour on her cheeks. "Don't," she murmured.

Gerlay turned his staff over, passing it from hand to hand and making slow arcs in the air either side of himself. Aubin shook out his wrists and flexed his fingers. They circled each other, each pace measured. Gerlay was the taller with greater reach, but Aubin was faster.

"This will be good, actually." I sat back up, arms resting on my knees. "They have to practise in the event one of them gets enchanted, and now they might actually fight for real."

"Over... me?" Evyn squeaked. "Thorrn, no, make them stop!"

"They won't hurt each other." I raised my voice. "Go to!"

Gerlay swung the staff at Aubin's midsection. He had to jump back, drawing his blades in a smooth movement and landing with his right arm raised. Gerlay knocked it aside with a smash that flung Aubin's arm wide, the blade sailing out of his hand.

Aubin clenched his teeth, hissing with pain and staggering.

I'd never seen Gerlay hit so hard before. "Is your arm broken?" I called.

Aubin snatched up his blade. "It's fine," he grunted. "Metal took the brunt."

"Yes." Gerlay ran his thumb down his staff, stopping at a new notch cut into the hardwood.

"It appears Gerlay wants to take our training up in intensity." Aubin sank into a new stance, one arm protecting his chest, the other his head. He had to punch to the side of Gerlay to slide the blades into play against him, which he mimicked by tapping us on the chest to show he could have done it.

Aubin was aiming for Gerlay's side properly now.

"This is getting really good," I said to Evyn, but she had passed out. "Oh. Damn and blast." I whistled. "Alright, Rangers, she's asleep. There's only me to impress now."

"But what if we do get enchanted?" Aubin said. "Don't we need to face off against one another properly?"

"Wise words." Gerlay swept his staff across and then down, faster than I could follow.

Aubin dodged the downward smash and twisted around, arms swinging wide. Gerlay had to raise the staff in front of his face, and the blades thunked deep into the wood, two new notches sliced in.

This is moving into something else. I stood up, hands raised. "Alright, simmer down."

"Stay out of this," Gerlay snapped, twisting the staff and taking Aubin's arms with it. "This is between him and me!"

"Why? What's the problem?" Aubin set his stance and pulled his blades free with a snapping sound.

Gerlay's grip on his weapon went white-knuckled. "I have seen more than enough to challenge you, Tabreksson."

Aubin sneered. "I'm an apothecarist, I'm helping her." He darted in.

Gerlay spun his staff, blocking Aubin's assault. "I'm not talking about that."

Aubin skidded to a halt and Gerlay jabbed. Aubin fell back to avoid a brass end in his gut, panting. "The contract, then. I took liberties like the library, but those can be ironed out during the nego-tiations."

Gerlay swept his staff to the side, glaring down at Aubin. "I'm talking about the looks you give her when you think she or I cannot see. It's disrespectful to me and to her."

Aubin bucked his hips to jump to his feet. "Looks?" He dashed sweat from his eyes. "I'm merely checking on her condition."

Gerlay snarled. "You're *lying*. Those are not the looks of a professional tending his patient." He advanced, spinning the staff. "Why are you lying? Why can't you be honest?"

Aubin wouldn't be able to halt the staff's momentum. He had to dodge and get around behind Gerlay somehow. "It's not part of my make-up. You won't understand, because you've never had to lie to protect someone."

"I don't see how lying can protect anyone."

I did. Tuniel and Aubin lived a lie, and shortly so would she and I.

Aubin shrugged. "Good for you." He backed away as the spinning staff drew nearer and nearer, that brass end whistling past his face.

"Do you love her?" Gerlay asked. "And don't lie to me."

Oh hells. "Lads," I tried.

Gerlay frowned at me. "Don't interrupt!"

"Yes, let him get it off his chest." Aubin backed up until he hit the wall. Unless he scaled it, he had nowhere to go.

"Well? Do you love her?" Gerlay demanded.

Aubin shut his eyes tight, raising his arms in a guard and bracing himself. "Yes," he said, breaths short. "Enough to want the best for her. She needs to be with someone good. Someone who has never hurt her, who will support her, who is a rock with morals and has steadfast dedication. She needs to be with you. I know you'll do well for her."

Gerlay let the spin wind down, pulling his staff up and leaning on it, breathing hard. "At last. I thought as much."

Aubin unpeeled himself from the back wall, glancing at me.

I folded my arms. "I'm staying out of it, as ordered."

Gerlay dabbed the sweat from his brow. "Gordonne wanted me to secure a marriage to a high-born lady of Oberrot, someone well-liked at court. For myself, I wanted someone who could navigate court, for it is fraught, even in Dinahe. When I spoke to Lady Evyn, she seemed suitable, and then when we were seen in public at

Shardsson's… disciplining, I felt I had to secure her reputation. She… grabbed hold of my hands." He flushed. "More than once," he gulped.

Ah. I exchanged a look with Aubin, and he stared at Gerlay as if he'd never seen the man before.

Gerlay went on, "She explained to me two days ago that she did not know what the giving of a soul jewel represented, and she did not realise that accepting mine would lead to marriage. She said she would need some time." Gerlay glanced over at Evyn lying on the pillows, one hand sprawled open. "Did she really not know what a soul jewel meant?"

Aubin sheathed his blades, passing his hand over his eyes to wipe the sweat away. "No, she didn't. She's not from here."

Gerlay nodded slowly. "I can understand making cultural blunders. I know she is not playing us both off against one another."

"She isn't. She's not like that at all," I said.

Gerlay held up his free hand. "Peace. I admit I do not know how to navigate this situation, and I have only my own moral compass to guide me. If I break my troth, then others might think it is because she is ill, and I would never abandon someone like that. Gordonne will be angry if I displease King Gough, and I'll never be trusted with anything of importance again." Gerlay frowned. "But these are my problems. In terms of Lady Evyn, well, she loves you. I can tell by the easy way you are together, but also how she lights when you come into her presence. She doesn't light like that with me. She is uncomfortable because she feels I block you from her." Gerlay put his hand on Aubin's shoulder.

Aubin's head lowered. "She doesn't deserve someone like me. She needs someone good, like you."

Gerlay's lips quirked. "I think she needs to be with someone who understands all of her and can keep up with her. I am but a soldier; her mind is so quick I cannot see the worlds she sees. She needs to stretch and fly with someone who appreciates that in her, who can challenge her and see her to glory. And steadfast dedication? Aubin, you broke enchantments to be with her. You would do very well for her." He sighed.

I cleared my throat. "Actually, the choice is hers as well. Just wanted to put that out there."

They shot me a glare. Gerlay hefted his staff and Aubin slid his blades out of their holsters.

"Yes, fine, staying out of it." I sat next to Evyn. She looked like she had been trying to reach something at the edge of the cushions when she passed out.

Me?

A shadow flickered over my face, Gerlay's staff as he raised it.

CHAPTER 29

I SHOVED MYSELF UP, SLAMMING MY SHOULDER INTO HIS GUT. GERLAY tumbled back, dropping his staff.

Kicking it to skitter out of his reach, I drew my father's blade. "Damn and blast." *They are enchanted!* Liara must be nearby.

Aubin's Battlemistress blades sang out as he flailed them in my face. I parried and shoved them back. He overbalanced—he was definitely enchanted.

I held back, determined to defend for now. Where could Liara be? Watching us? I turned my head to scan the battlements as Aubin picked himself up for a second swing. The blades clashed with the flat of my father's sword.

Then a solid hit across the back from Gerlay sent me barrelling forward, winded. I cursed. *I have two foes to focus on!*

I narrowly avoided Aubin's fist, twisting away from the sharp edges glittering along his forearms. Landing on my stomach, I hooked Aubin's legs out from under him, yanking him to crash on his back. *One down.*

I rolled away to one side only to come up against Gerlay's feet, trapped. I raised my arms in a block as he lifted the staff ready to bring it down into my torso. *This is going to hurt.*

Gerlay tumbled when the ground gave a lurch. Tuniel stood framed in the doorway, her hair mussed in its bindings, and she had swiftly belted a gown around her, for the buttons were still undone. "Quickly. Liara is here." She beckoned me, and I rolled onto my feet. She clucked her tongue at Aubin and Gerlay. "They're enchanted, but I can trap them in here. Where's Evyn?"

"Asleep under there." I jerked my head toward the pagoda. "Liara must be draining her for power." I would put a stop to that. *Once and for all.* "Where are Luc and James?"

"I don't know, their rooms, hopefully. I should not get close to Liara, otherwise she will enchant me as well. I can stay here with them and Evyn." Her eyes narrowed. Aubin and Gerlay had dragged themselves to their feet and staggered toward us.

I sighed. "Give me a heartbeat, I'll take them down for you."

"No. They would be useful if they were nearby if... I mean, when you get them out of Liara's enchantment. In fact, what are they enchanted to do?"

"Attack me?" I waved my father's blade at them. Gerlay's staff started a slow circular movement.

"And what happens if you sheathe your sword and surrender?"

I gaped at her. "Tuniel, this is no time for experiments!"

"You need to find Liara. I wonder if they will bring you to her." Tuniel tapped her chin, then nodded. "Well? Go on then."

With a grunt, I slid my father's blade back into its scabbard. I winced as Aubin and Gerlay closed in, but they put up their weapons and grabbed one arm each.

"Good." A smile danced along Tuniel's lips, quickly doused. "You can face and defeat Liara. I know you can."

I glanced back at Evyn. *I have to.* I would.

I nodded to Tuniel. "Be careful here."

"Of course."

We had no opportunity for a kiss as Aubin and Gerlay pulled me into the building. The sudden darkness blinded me, but the soul jewel on Amare warmed briefly, reassuring me.

They marched me along the cool corridors of the palace to the common area that we were so familiar with. An unnatural hush lay over it, so much so that I could hear the gargle of the fountains. Artists lined the perimeter, all staring with vacant expressions, and Sabatha stood in the middle of the courtyard in the full sun. She struggled against something, muscles and tendons standing stark. *Liara's enchantment.* She was fighting it as best she could.

Liara herself paced in front of her. Nevermind that her hair was undone and her clothing ragged, her visage sent terror into my heart to snare my limbs.

Lifting her chin, her eyes tight, she sneered at me. "Stop," she ordered. "If you move further, I'll kill her." She smirked at Sabatha.

The heavy burden of necklaces and rings were absent from the princess, and in her white nightgown with her feet bare, she looked younger than her sixteen turns. My heart went out to her, fists bunching. How dare Liara do this to her!

Liara snapped her fingers at Sabatha. "Get out the tangles. I need one that's more powerful than the useless one you gave me before." Pushing a sweaty handful of hair from Sabatha's neck, she leant in to hiss in her ear, "Give me the tangles, or your new friends will kill each other."

Sabatha's eyes cracked open, bloodshot.

Liara waved toward me. "We'll start with the swordsman. He's been trained to die. Let's see how accomplished he is at this."

Sabatha screamed. She was fighting so hard to resist her, but Liara held her tightly controlled. Cold settled in my limbs, and I breathed deeply and evenly to call the calm of battle down.

"Bring him," Liara ordered.

Aubin and Gerlay gripped each of my arms tight, forcing me toward her. When we got close, Aubin kicked the back of my leg. I slammed to my knees.

Four Artists struggling with a heavy wooden chest between them entered the courtyard. The dark wood reminded me of Gough's desk —magewood, said to be impervious to magic. They bore it toward Liara and set it between us, directly in front of me.

"Open it," Liara crooned, stroking Sabatha's bare neck.

"No! The tangles are entrusted to me." Hot tears chased down Sabatha's cheeks.

"Very well. If that's your choice." Liara smiled at her. "Aubin, slit his throat."

"No!" Sabatha shouted.

Aubin grabbed my hair, but at least my arm was free. I shoved away from the box and rolled backwards, out of their reach, leaving a handful of hair in Aubin's fist.

Liara's eyes flashed a lurid green. "I suppose they will all die at the same time, then."

The Artists packing the perimeter raised their knives. I cast about. They were slow under enchantment and their aim might be poor, but there were enough of them that I couldn't hope to avoid all the blades, and Aubin and Gerlay wouldn't even try to move out of the way.

Before I could think of what to do, Sabatha sobbed, "Stop! I'll do it." She waved a hand and the box sprung open to reveal the wealth of the Rushia Sultanate: hundreds of gems and jewels on chains and rings and hooks, strings of beads and slivers of crystal, all faintly glowing with malevolent swirls of light. Each and every one a tangle, spirits opposed and trapped together to create a perpetual source of death magic.

My stomach iced over. *If Liara gets hold of these...*

Patting Sabatha's cheek, Liara crooned, "Thank you, my dear." Delving in, she pulled out handfuls of tangles.

She screamed and dropped them as they all glowed red. A waft of burnt flesh struck me, and Liara raised her hands to her face, arms shaking. Her palms blistered, burnt.

Liara toppled as the ground shook again, and the Artists tipped to the side.

"Thorrn, get up," Tuniel called. She stood at the threshold of the room I shared with Evyn. "Get Liara, I'll defend against the Artists."

I gaped. *What about defending Evyn? She's helpless asleep!* But I had to seize this opportunity.

Drawing my father's sword, I paced toward Liara. She was a great evil and could not be allowed to escape again. My mouth dried, limbs moving in patterns they had described all throughout my life, to move now when my mind was too locked in blankness to decide anything.

She cannot hurt me now. She will not hurt anyone else soon enough.

Liara stumbled back, her face ashen, then grabbed into the chest. She pulled out a ring, thrusting it toward me.

I drew to a halt. *She could set another spirit inside me to turn me against Tuniel.* A nightmarish image of me swinging my sword at the woman I loved as she screamed at me to stop choked me.

"Liara, surrender." My voice came out small. I ground my teeth. "Surrender!"

"Never," Liara hissed. "Never to you or to her!" Despite her burnt hands, she scrabbled in the chest for something.

"What is going on?" Luc strode into the courtyard.

Damn and blast! "Mancer Luc, get back!" I roared.

"The hell I will. There's pain spilling out everywhere. What—"

Standing up, Liara thrust a ring toward him. A spear of black arched into his chest. He staggered back a pace, and Tuniel grabbed his arms.

I raced forward. "No! That's a spirit, he's going to be—"

"Got you," he snarled, slapping a hand to Tuniel's cheek. She screamed, writhing in his hands.

"Amare!" I roared, barrelling into Luc. The armour took a heartbeat to deploy and didn't blast him away, but I shoved him to the side and Tuniel dropped from his grasp.

"Tuniel, can you speak? Tuniel!"

She breathed still, but she was senseless, pale from the pain. A quick glance at Aubin proved he had fallen to the floor as well, from the agony she felt.

Luc picked himself up, straightening his collar. "That hurt. Not as much as you will, though. Lashes, Gough said. Lashes to the bone. I'd hate to relive that all over again."

Fear clenched my gut. One touch and I would feel the bite of the lash, like swords slicing into my flesh, all over again and all layered onto each other, and the agony of my pulled and torn shoulder muscles on top of that. It would render me unconscious for sure, and that much pain all at once might be enough to kill me.

Luc flexed his fingers, taking a step toward me.

"Stop."

I kept my stance against Luc, but my eyes widened. "Evyn?"

My soul companion came to stand beside me, wobbling on her feet. Her chest heaved with ragged breaths as she faced Luc down. "I know what you did, what you're trying to do again. I'm not going to let you."

Did she mean Luc? *No, she is addressing the spirit inside him.*

Liara screamed again. "No one needs to die today, but they still could, unless you get out of my way."

Evyn scowled at her. "I'll deal with you in a minute, Liara. Wait your turn. This has been brewing for over two hundred years." Her eyes glowed red. "She won't stand for the pain any longer." She raised her hands, wisps of dark carmine smoke flooding into her palms.

Liara gaped. "You can't use magic! You're an Earthian!"

Evyn shrugged, shoving her hands toward Luc. He jerked as she bathed him in red light and screamed, a wild edge to it.

"Stop it!" James shouted, running up from his rooms. "He's not going to hurt you!"

"He is. He did," I called back. "Besides, Evyn wouldn't hurt him." Heart beating wildly, I flanked her as Evyn took a shaking step forward, then another, pressing her way toward Luc, that red mist curling and coiling around her like steam. I did not want to interrupt whatever she was doing. The air hissed and snapped as if boiling. Another sound built underneath it.

Luc was laughing. "Yes. All this pain! I offer it up to the gods!"

Evyn screamed as Luc lunged for her.

I snatched her out of the way, bowling over with her toward Tuniel. "Evyn, stay behind me. I'll defend you while you do whatever that was again."

Evyn stared at her shaking hands. "Thorrn, what was that? What happened?"

"I don't know but it was amazing, and I'm sure Tuniel will want to study and classify it when she wakes up, but right now we have to save everyone—Tuniel, Sabatha and Luc, especially."

"And end Liara," she said fiercely, curling her hands into fists.

Liara plunged her hands into the chest again and started muttering something, but Luc chose that moment to dart at me. I danced away from his reaching hands, knowing that he could down me in a heartbeat. My stomach crawled with fear.

I held my ground in front of Evyn. He wouldn't pass me.

Liara's movements caught my eye, her hands flowing in a way that was familiar to me. I frowned. *Where have I seen that—?*

A jagged portal split through the courtyard air in front of her. Heat blasted out from it, and at the same time I felt my clothes pulled toward it, hair whipping in my face. A portal. *Liara has made a portal!*

Liara leant backward, her feet sliding in the grass, looking around wildly as if to seek help. When she saw me, she turned again toward the portal in front of her, biting her lip.

"Give up, Liara!" I shouted.

"I will never give up on her," she said in Dinahen, dashing away her tears and leaping into the abyss.

The portal snapped shut behind her, my ears popping so suddenly I touched my ears to make sure they weren't bleeding.

Sabatha collapsed to the floor, unconscious. Gerlay sagged, holding himself up with his staff. "What? Where am I?"

Aubin dragged himself upright. "We must have been enchanted. Thorrn?" He locked eyes with me, Evyn, and ran toward Tuniel on the ground.

"We fought Liara, but it's over now," I reported.

"Ah." Luc held up his hand. "Everyone seems to be forgetting about me." He smirked, eyes flashing black.

Damn and blast. My gaze flicked to the unconscious princess, Artists rushing toward her to help her. She wouldn't be able to drag the spirit out of him.

I drew my father's sword.

"Don't hit him!" James shrieked.

"Only gently," I reassured him. "Rangers, to me. New plan: subdue Luc until Evyn and the princess can help him. Do not use fatal force."

"Yes, sir," Gerlay said.

"Very well," Aubin replied, standing up. "Tuniel will be fine. Evyn?"

"I'm here, I'm okay." She hugged her knees, tears staining her cheeks. "Just a bit freaked out."

"I'm here. It's going to be alright." I winked at her with more levity than I felt.

Luc was a problem. With one touch, he could knock out a swordsman. Aubin, Gerlay and I would have to charge him. He could only unleash his power against one of us at a time. *Still.* He could sense I had sustained the most serious injuries, and I was the weak link. Could I really charge this mancer thinking I might die, and still run fast and true?

The Artists helped the princess up. Her knees buckled once, but then she held steady. "I can help him, if I am close enough," she said.

"Thank you, Your Highness." I signalled Aubin and Gerlay in High Dinahen, *All three attack.*

Gerlay nodded, but Aubin shook his head, flicking me a quick hand signal. *Us two. You fall back.*

I hesitated, and Gerlay and Aubin surged forward.

298

Aubin spun under Luc's outstretched hands, kicking his leg. Luc stumbled but didn't fall, snarling at Aubin. Gerlay swept at his other leg, but Luc danced back.

"He works out!" James called.

"New plan." Gerlay dropped his staff. "Come, Luc."

Luc sneered at him. "You think I cannot see a trap laid plainly before me?" His gaze fixed on me. "I'm saving my power for you. You've endured quite a lot of pain. You will die."

"You'll have to get through me." Gerlay launched himself at Luc.

I winced as Gerlay grabbed hold of Luc's wrists. The mancer tried to pull his arms back but Gerlay was unrelenting, following him and holding on gamely. "Get Sabatha in here, quickly now."

"Get off me!" Luc roared.

I led the princess toward them. Luc's panicked sweat flew wide as he shook his head and snarled at Sabatha. "No, no! I've served well and long!" Luc snarled. "I'll kill her if she touches me; if I send a surge of power into her, she's dead."

James was aghast. "Lukey!"

"This was what I was afraid of." Gerlay took a deep breath. "Very well." He let go of Luc's wrist and touched his cheek. Then the prince screamed in agony, quickly driven to his knees.

Luc pushed him aside easily, cruel gaze fixing on me.

"Now, Luc used his power, he's weak!" I darted in, reaching for Luc's arm.

Luc pulled his sleeves open, baring his teeth. "If you touch me, you are dead!" His breaths were panicked and harsh.

"Luc. You're hurt." James called. "Luc, calm down. It's okay."

Luc shook his head. "No. I cannot be weak. I have to resist you! The gods have a plan. I have to obey. I have to trust."

I guided the princess over, Artists following. She held onto my arm, trembling. "Listen to me. I am Princess Sabatha of Rush. I am considered the voice of the gods; if they speak through me at all, it is through my heart. True Rushia value life. Stop this. It is wrong. You must desist."

Evyn stood up, and I offered her my other arm. "It's terrible, and it's tearing me apart. Angry, sad, frightened Earthians wrapped up together with the madmen and women that killed them; no one can move on, and no one can go back, it's awful." Evyn shook her head. "It stops now."

Luc's panicked breaths stopped as James approached. "Him. Not him," he moaned.

James came behind us, holding out his hand. "I want you to take my hand. I am not afraid of you, and I never will be."

"You should be," Luc snarled, lunging for him.

I slapped my palm against Luc's and was engulfed in pain. Slices across my back, cutting deep and set afire. Bands of red-hot iron encasing my ribs made breathing pure agony. My shoulders ripping, tearing, the bones grinding against one another. A huge ache engulfing my entire body, deep to the bone. I screamed.

The pain stopped. I blinked away tears and sweat. I was on my knees, hand held in Luc's. James held Luc's other hand, and Sabatha stood in his guard, the black mist in her hands.

The mancer breathed rapidly, staring at me. "He's alive?"

"He's alive. Totally alive. Still conscious, even." James nudged me with his foot.

Luc swallowed hard. "He should be dead."

"Well, he's not. I should know," James pointed out.

"I... I have immunity. Evyn," I croaked. My throat burnt.

"Right." Luc relaxed a little.

"I... er."

"Yes." Luc let go of my hand.

I pulled myself to standing, my knees wobbly, when Sabatha screamed.

The black mist erupted in her hands, swarming up her chest. The smell of burnt flesh sickened me.

I grabbed her arms, tearing the mist from her hands.

"No!" Evyn clung onto me. "Don't touch it!"

Black mist roared up like a wall between us and I plunged into noise; a low wail, a high shriek, a moan of pain and despair, and an unfamiliar voice, deeper than Aglo's, laughing. My heart faltered, fear fouling my limbs. I choked on the mist as it thrust down my throat. I panicked, coughing and spluttering.

Gritting my teeth, I reached out with my hands. *Evyn!*

But the new spirit turned their attention to her as well. *"The gods demand a sacrifice."*

No!

"They need her!"

I fought to stay me, to rise above the rage. *You won't trick me this time, spirit.* I breathed deeply. I had done this all my life, always learning new ways to control different types of anger and fear that manifested in all-consuming berserker rampages. I could do this!

Surrounding me was the black mist, howling and screeching, turmoil turning and tossing it into a strong current. If I touched it, it would sweep away me, but it was separate from me at least.

Yes, it's working!

Opening my eyes, I loomed over Evyn. Both hands were poised at her throat, but the fingers on each hand were extended, shaking as I kept them from closing. I held them there with all my might.

Evyn took my palms, eyes glittering with tears. "Thorrn, I know you're in there."

I could only grunt between my gritted teeth. The spirit inside me howled. I refused to move, I couldn't trust whether it was me or this new thing giving my body orders.

"Give it to me. I can handle this." Evyn beckoned.

No. It wants to hurt you!

She smiled. "You saw what I did earlier. Let it go, don't be afraid."

I *was* afraid, but I trusted her. Keeping my fingers outstretched, I turned my attention inwards. *You heard her. Get out!*

Threading through the screams and howls, slowly becoming louder, was a soft sigh. The sort of sigh Evyn gave when I set a cup of tea next to her, or when she turned a page in her book and found the answer she was looking for.

Peace. My mind cleared.

The bond that Evyn and I shared twanged with pain, deep and sharp and cutting. Her face creased, and she sagged against my hands.

"Evyn, no! Evyn, what's the matter?" She did not respond to me, eyes staring straight ahead. "Evyn, we have to do this together. Let me help!"

Her gaze snapped to me, wild with fright. She tried to rip away from me, but I held on.

"Fine," I growled. "I'll just have to take it." I wrenched the rage into myself, away from the bond, away from her, taking as much as I could and swallowing it, feeling it grow and build as pressure inside me, a scream ripping my throat.

Fear and anger all in one, soul companions locked in opposition and attraction, a constant surge of feeling that would never abate.

I screamed, holding it all tight inside. *You're staying with me!*

"Don't, let go! I'll take it, give it back!" Evyn wrenched at my hands.

I couldn't see anything except flashes of black and red, I couldn't see where she was. I held on tight to the pain, keeping it far from the bond. *I have to keep it away from Evyn!*

"Give it back, it's hurting you!" Evyn, screaming and crying.

She had carried it long enough, protecting me from it. It was my turn to carry it.

My legs were knocked out from under me. Impact with the floor winded me, breath rushing out with a gasp.

My vision cleared to see Aubin, above me, close enough to touch. Gerlay stood behind him, staff in hand; he must have tripped me. Tuniel lay dazed an arm's span away, rubbing her head, and the princess was kneeling, arms wrapped around herself, surrounded by Artists. She would not be able to help. Where was Evyn?

The spirit thrashed me against the ground, my head slamming back against the cobblestones.

Aubin grabbed my shoulders, and the spirit used my fist to punch him in the face, laughing as he reeled away. "A new vessel, a mobile vessel! We won't be trapped in gems anymore."

Aubin slammed my upper back into the ground. "Amare prohibere!" The armour deployed, cold where it touched my over-heating skin. I shuddered. My arms sealed to my sides; the spirit tried to pull and jerk them free, my shoulders screaming, but my upper body was stuck fast.

Aubin straddled my chest, knees on my upper arms. His watering eyes searched mine, growing colder as a dark certainty crept into them. "Get out of him, or I'll kill this new vessel of yours."

I bucked my hips to dislodge him. "You can't bear that burden! It will destroy you."

Aubin was calm, his face emotionless. "Gerlay, hold him down!"

Gerlay laid on my legs, the man trembling with uncertainty.

Aubin's amber eyes searched mine, his jaw tightening. "You think you can hurt them, and I won't do anything about it? You think you can take them away from me, and I'll just let you be?"

"Kill him then. Brother to brother is a pleasing offering for the gods!" my voice crowed.

Aubin, help me!

Aubin's eyes flickered.

He shoved my head back, catching under my jaw so I couldn't work my mouth. His other hand sealed my mouth and nose, pinching my lips and nostrils together in a white-knuckled fist. I couldn't breathe.

"I'll make you leave," Aubin hissed.

I couldn't draw breath, I couldn't breathe! Pain thumped in my head from the pressure. He held on as the spirit struggled, driving my head into the ground as I tried to escape. His face pressed against mine, studying me with a cold clinical detachment. "You won't get him! Either of them!"

This had to be a bluff. Yes, I had to trust Aubin. *I do, I will.* I dug my fingers into the ground and held on tight, feeling my tendons creak. He wouldn't hurt me.

"Get out."

Tears forced out of my eyes. So much pressure! My lungs worked desperately, my chest heaving on nothing.

"Brother to brother. Oh, the sweet pain!"

Gerlay sat up. "Aubin, stop. Stop it!"

"Not yet. It's not done yet!" the spirit exulted.

Aubin glared down at me. "I won't lose. I won't back down. You won't win."

"The gods will delight in this offering!"

Aubin. I trust...

Darkness crawled across my vision. The black mist? Was it leaving at last? Aubin's face went indistinct, and I was so very exhausted, as if all the exertions of the sennight had caught up at once. My arms and legs tingled.

Aubin's face went slack. "Thorrn?" he asked, before he went dark as well.

CHAPTER 30

Pain wracked me. Someone was hurting me. Pain was generally not something I ran toward, unless it was exercise related.

"Thorrn!" Sabatha's voice, faint, but added to it were others, obscuring it.

I was forgetting something important, but there was one thing I could never forget. *Evyn?*

"Thorrn." A soft sigh. "Come on. Come here. Come—"

A shot of pure pain lanced through my chest.

"There! Luc, that's done it, his heart's beating. Come on, Thorrn!" James shouted above me. "Get back here right now!" My chest hurt badly; something thumped broken ribs repeatedly.

My throat burnt and ached. An obstruction held my mouth fixed open. I blinked rapidly and tried to cough, and pain travelled and burnt from my throat to my chest.

"There, there! Good, come on, big breaths. That's it. Don't try to move, just lie there." James pulled the blockage out of my mouth to release my jaw and I heaved as a long tube snaked behind it, disgorging from my sore, dry throat.

James sat back on his heels, wiping his sweaty forehead.

Someone had opened my Ranger jacket and torn my shirt open; Luc lifted one hand from the centre of my chest and the other from my left side. I lay flat on my back, staring up at the blue sky.

Sabatha stood to one side, clutching hands with Tuniel. Both had tear-streaked faces and Tuniel smiled when I looked at her.

Between them a gemstone sparkled with swirling black light.

"Yes, we got it contained," Luc said tersely. "Well, the worst bit of it, anyway."

"Ev... Evyn?" I coughed.

"Here." Her small hand slipped into mine. Relief took me like a wave from the Serene Sea.

James leant over me, shining a light into my eyes. "Responsive pupils. Brain functioning. Can you talk, Thorrn? Can you understand us?"

Nodding, my neck ached. I winced.

"He's okay. Phew." James fanned his shirt collar and smiled, then frowned. "Aubin? Aubin, where'd you go?" He looked over my head. "Ah, there you are. Come see, look, he's fine."

I didn't feel fine, I felt like I'd been hit by a car beast.

Evyn kissed the side of my head repeatedly. "He nearly died, none of that was fine."

I took in deep ragged breaths, each one whistling out. "Yes," I croaked. "Except for the part where you were trying to protect me. We tried to help in our own way, but we need to work together, Evyn."

She flung her arms around my shoulders, sobbing. "Okay, Thorrn. Okay." The bond renewed, sending a surge of happiness over a twist of anxiety in my belly.

"There you are." My contentment mingled with hers. *At last.*

I sat up slowly, Evyn helping me. My whole chest and neck hurt. Gerlay smiled broadly, and I tried to smile back. "Aubin?" I rasped.

"He's over there having a freak-out." James waved wildly. "Hey. He's calling for you." James shook his head. "Aubin's in shock," he told us calmly.

"I'm fine," Aubin snapped from the edge of the courtyard.

"Come here," I ordered, as loudly as I could.

He walked into view, looking at us both carefully, studying our faces.

"Hi," Evyn said.

He swallowed, eyes welling with tears.

"What's the matter?" I asked.

"I killed... I killed you. I did it like it was nothing. It was a task I had to do." He thrust his shaking hands behind his back. "What am I?"

"You're a Ranger." The words caught on my throat, and I coughed.

He winced.

"It helped unseat the Rushia spirit," the princess pointed out. "I wasn't prepared for him to fight me. He would have hurt Evyn, and when Thorrn took it all into himself it bought us some precious time to come up with a way to contain it." Sabatha bowed to Tuniel. "Then Aubin's quick thinking drove it out, straight into our workings."

Tuniel handed the red gem to Sabatha. "Put that down a well or something."

"Or destroy it." Evyn shuddered.

"The tangles cannot be destroyed," Sabatha said sadly. "We must carry the burdens of the errors of the past. The best we can do is to protect against them ever being used." The jewel winked in Sabatha's hands.

"Does that mean the Earthians are back in there with the Rushia?" I asked.

Tuniel and Evyn exchanged a look. Evyn twisted the hem of her robe. "Uh, well." She cleared her throat. "You know that thing I did, with the red stuff? Apparently, that was me acting as a conduit."

"I have never seen such a thing," Sabatha murmured. "It may be because of where you are from."

Evyn clung to my arm. "Ellen wanted some payback, and she

used me to do it. I've offered to take her through onto Earth so she can see if there's a next life there."

"She is still there with you now?"

Evyn bit her lip. "So, let's get her situated, shall we?" She lowered her voice to whisper, "I can ping from our rooms or something, just quickly."

Nodding, I closed my eyes. I took in deep breaths, marvelling that I could. That had been close.

My hearing was still sharp. Underneath the pad of feet as the Artists and servants dashed about and Evyn's breathing right next to my ear, I could hear the creak of Ranger leather on marble. I sighed. "Aubin, I can hear you trying to sneak away."

His footsteps stopped. "I need time to think."

"You will have it, but let's see to Evyn first." I rubbed my still aching throat.

James was quick to dispel my fears. "That will get better. I'm amazed you lived, though. It was a very outside chance." He raised an eyebrow at Aubin. "You're a medic too, aren't you? You knew that."

Aubin turned his face away, shoulders quivering.

Tuniel stood, buttoning up her dress and scowling. "Aubin and I will take a moment. We will not tarry long, and then we will glean clues of where Liara went."

I watched as Tuniel led him away. He had to be struggling for Tuniel to feel it and react. The memory of his closed face and still features sent cold racing down my limbs. He had reined in his emotions and thoughts and replaced everything entirely with someone who would complete the dire task in front of him, forcing the spirit out of me in a bluff where no one could back down. He was the only one who could follow through with something like that.

Servants fluttered about trying to restore the courtyard to normal and I felt we were very inconvenient to them. Standing up with help from Gerlay, I leant on Evyn. Either she vibrated with a strange kind of energy, or we both did, and my teeth rattled as if I was cold. James and Luc huddled up behind us, James patting his green bag and grinning as though it had all been a wonderful adventure.

James waved at Luc. "Thank goodness Lukey was here. He makes a great AED."

"Enough." Luc sounded as drained as I felt. "Let's just get home. We're leaving."

James pouted. "Yes, it is a bit hot, but can't we say goodbye, Lukey—"

"The more we stand around here, the more likelihood there is of something bad happening." Luc pointed at Evyn. "She's a magnet for lost spirits. One of them could infiltrate her and turn her insane any moment now."

"Wait, what?" I asked, staggering to a halt.

"He's being extremely pessimistic," Evyn murmured.

"I sincerely hope so." I doubled my hobbling pace.

We filed into the room that Evyn and I had been given, but it was Luc who barked orders at the threshold. "Dinahen, out. I'm not having you see this."

"Very well." Gerlay nodded.

Luc closed the door on him. "Eyes shut, Shardsson."

"Yessir." I complied, and a wave of tiredness swept over me, threatening to drag me under.

"Hey, just a bit longer." Evyn swung my arm. "Then you can take a nap."

"Mm."

Luc handled the portal creation, and Evyn guided me through. Opening my eyes to bright sunlight, I turned around slowly on the spot. We were close to the sky, on the tallest hill for miles around. It was warm, but not in a dry heat way as Rush had been. I scanned the perimeter, looking over the stone walls; below on one side were glittering towers next to a shining sea, and from the other came the snarls and hoots of car beasts, clawing their way up the incline past wide palaces surrounded by grey rivers of roads.

We were next to a castle, or at least something that looked like a castle. I cocked my head at it. "It's got walls we can run right up to. It's so squat. And what's this moat? It's empty."

Evyn grinned at me. "I know where we are. This is Montjuïc Castle, in Barcelona."

"What's the point in having a drawbridge which doesn't draw?" I muttered, dismissing the structure as non-defensible. "Where's Barcelona? Is it close to your lands?"

"We travelled far to get to Rush, right? This is in Spain, a different country to Britain." She cocked her head. "Like Oberrot, Dinahe, Rush and Skien, they are all different countries."

"Earth has different countries? Goodness." I peered back over the edge. "This looks substantial. Is that your biggest city?" James gave a single "ha". "I assume not then."

We walked around the walls, drawing little attention to ourselves because so many other people were running past us. Evyn pointed down the hill. "The cemetery. That place is beautiful. We'll do it there."

"And we will say our farewells here," Luc said stiffly. "I don't want James anywhere near that parasite when it finally emerges."

Evyn pursed her lips as if to argue, and I bowed quickly to forestall her. "Well, farewell, Mancer Luc, medimancer James." I saluted them. "Thank you for all your help. I am sincerely grateful."

Luc did not look impressed. "You've misplaced a dangerous mage. If I find her first, I'll end her."

My stomach tightened. "We will, if only we knew her objective."

Evyn laced her fingers in mine. "I think she wants to get Waker back. She opened a portal, a new kind we haven't seen before."

Luc drew in a breath.

"But you have?" I asked him.

Luc scowled. "If she tore a way between the worlds, then she is likely dead. Very few people can survive there, and there are strange powers beyond even my understanding."

"Such as?" I ventured.

His eyes unfocused slightly. "Someone who can pull what they need from across the worlds, and, worse, someone who can see the impact of that and guide it." Luc shook himself and scowled. "I will handle it. You get back to your... things."

Evyn nodded, eyes round. "Thanks. Give us a shout if you need any help."

"I think you've done enough," Luc said quietly.

I saluted Luc and James as they walked away.

"Well, that wasn't cryptic in the least," Evyn muttered. The early morning sunlight winked along golden strands of her hair. "But first things first. This is getting seriously uncomfortable."

I could not feel any pain from her. "What can I do to help?"

"Just... stand guard when we get there." Evyn led me toward the cemetery. Like the one in Oberrot City, this one clung to the side of the hill, rows of markers lining each gradient. It was not as brightly coloured as home, but it contained a stillness that invited reflection.

"Here is good," Evyn said, drawing me to a halt.

"Yes, ma'am." I surveyed the wide stone steps and out of the corner of my eye watched Evyn.

She closed her eyes and cupped her hands in front of her. The red mist rose again, but it seemed like it came from her chest, percolating through her shirt and pooling into her palms. "It's alright," Evyn said, and even I settled, a wave of fulfilment washing over me from the bond.

The mist dissipated, swirling away in the still air. Evyn let all her breath out in one long exhalation, her creased face smoothing as if she let down a heavy weight. "Ahh. That's better. She's really excited to be free."

I stared up at the sky. "Aglo and Ellen are separated by worlds now. Their spirit will never be whole, they won't find each other and be complete."

Evyn pushed her hair behind her ear. "Irreconcilable differences is a thing, Thorrn. Sometimes you have to separate." She scrunched her nose. "I had to get her away from him."

"Mm. Well done. That is a good thing you did for her, I suppose, even though she was hurting you. I would not have been so kind." Her heart knew no limits, endlessly patient but also stern when needed. She would always stand up to those who needed help to fight back. That resonated deep inside me, feeling like another tenet, something else I could swear to with my whole spirit. "I'm glad she has found peace, and even more glad that she has left, as this likely means Liara has no foothold within you anymore."

Evyn nodded, still staring into the sky. "Hopefully."

I jiggled her hand. "How do you feel?"

"Could do with a cup of tea, or six." She squeezed my fingers. "But really, she wanted someone to listen to her and help her stand up for herself."

"Speaking of, I really want nothing more than to do the same for you, Evyn." Gesturing to a nearby stone seat, I settled myself first, an immovable object. This world was a great deal colder, and the stone sapped my warmth even further.

"Thorrn, we're really tired. Now might not be the best time."

I leant back, rubbing my neck. "There's never a good time, Evyn, but right now we aren't being chased or attacked or racing against time. In fact, only one person back in Rush can come disturb us, and I don't think we would begrudge it if he did come find us and join us."

Evyn nodded, slowly lowering herself to perch next to me, ruching up her simple gold dress.

The view of the sea was arresting, but I closed my eyes, waiting, leaving myself open to whatever she might want to impart. A cool breeze hissed through the nearby grasses and ruffled my hair, sending strands of hers into my face. Spitting, I bolted upright.

She giggled as I fished them out of my mouth. "Sorry." Curling her hands around the edge of the bench, she lifted her gaze toward the glittering waves on the horizon. "I talked to my dad the most. I used to tell him everything, good and bad. As I got older, it... tended towards the bad." She quivered, and not from the cold. "One day he told me how sorry he was, that he had passed on what he had, even though the genetic link isn't clear. He blamed himself. It was an extra thing he had to bear. If I'd been a cheery and happy daughter rather than me, maybe he wouldn't have felt so bad."

I rested my hand on her shoulder, to reassure her I was there and listening. Her story hurt, and it had to be hurting her more.

"Mum said me and you, we'll balance out. She didn't say as much but she hopes you'll fix me, and I'll be just like everyone else. But if we balance out that means you'll... you'll get some of this. I wouldn't wish this on my worst enemy, Thorrn, let alone you. You'll change, and I don't want you to change. And one day you'll resent me for making you less than you are." She hunched lower, and this time the wind sent a deeper bite of cold into my core.

I put my arm around her shoulders, turning over her words. "Evyn, we will balance out and complement one another, and I welcome that. A very clever person told me that we have to accept and adapt. We all of us change through our experiences to be more than we were before, and I can't wait to become the person we are going to make together, standing alongside you. And if that means accepting the dark as well as the light, well, the light is worth it. Already you've shown me patience and compassion wins through more times than assuming I know everything. You've even helped me with my rage, and I've been dealing with that for turns. So yes, I do want to change. Come change with me."

Evyn nudged me. "Don't sell yourself short. Confidence counts for a lot."

"Overconfidence, though?" I grinned at her. "I have enough and to spare of confidence. You're welcome to the overspill."

She pushed herself back onto the seat, fitting herself close to me, her warmth radiating out along my side. Blooming between us was the bond, a gentle ebb and flow, and I fancied my heart and hers beat in time. There was still fear there, an unspoken need as a shadow on her contentment.

I took her hands in mine. "I won't leave you, Evyn."

"You can't promise that," she whispered. "No one can promise that, and you're a soldier. You're in harm's way a lot."

"Alright, then. I won't leave you voluntarily." My spirit half would linger near the Labyrinth, waiting to reunite with hers to make our whole.

"Mm. That will have to do." She put her arms around my chest. "Thank you."

"Anytime." I rested my chin on her head.

Evyn took another deep breath, this time to steel herself, and a calm certainty settled in my stomach. "Now it's my turn to stand up for what I want."

"Oh?"

She nodded, jerking my head up and down. "I bet Tuniel is going to arrange magical transport. As soon as we get to the city, I want to go shopping."

I snorted. "Well, this is where we diverge. I'm having a bath. A big one."

"Well, okay, that first. Then will you come with me?" She smiled up at me, and a sure determination thrummed through the bond.

"Of course. What are you so intent on buying?"

She grinned. "A soul jewel."

That warmed me even further. "Oh! Well, good for you."

She threw her shoulders back. "You were right, life is precious, Thorrn. No time like the present, and now there's nothing sucking out my energy, I have enough strength to finally do stuff!"

"Not without benefit of marriage, you don't," I teased.

"Oh! Not like that!" She blushed.

CHAPTER 31

WHEN WE JUMPED BACK. AUBIN WAS WAITING OUTSIDE THE ROOM, ARMS folded tightly around his chest. He did not look up as we stood next to him.

"Aubin?" Evyn asked.

He looked away.

Tuniel and Sabatha were coming down the corridor. The princess waved to us, finally fully dressed and looking better already. She had put on her assortment of jewellery, and the burden that the Sultanate carried looked heavy around her thin shoulders and delicate wrists.

I nodded to her, glancing at Aubin. "I'd wager this is going to improve Oberrotian-Rushia relations tenfold," I ventured.

He took a step away from me.

He was truly struggling. I put my arm around Evyn's shoulders and we exchanged a quick worried look.

Tuniel and Sabatha drew to a halt just in front of the door. "Thank you for assisting me with containing half of the tangle," Sabatha began. "Is Ellen...?"

"Ellen promised to disperse and not hurt anyone. I believe her, she just wanted to rest somewhere safe." Evyn beamed. "Thanks for helping."

"No. Thank you, Spirit Shaper," Sabatha murmured.

Tuniel looked between them. "We highly recommend that you stay in close correspondence with Sabatha, Evyn. We will need to investigate that ability you showed."

"Was it magic?" Evyn held up her hands and turned them over. They did not look any different.

"We're not sure yet," Tuniel said. "I do not have enough information, but, given that you are Earthian, I think I could classify it as an ability."

Evyn grinned at her. "Thinking of writing another paper?"

"Of course not, I could never publish this." Tuniel put her hand on Evyn's shoulder. "But it will be fascinating."

I inclined my head. "Before you ladies get entangled in the science or whatever this is—what?" I asked Evyn as she winced. "What's the matter?"

"Entangled, Thorrn? Too soon."

"What? Oh, the tangles, yes. I did not mean to do that."

Evyn gently swiped at my arm. "You're always making puns, of course you did."

I shook my head, unable to defend myself. "Regardless, we still have Liara to deal with. Gerlay, Aubin?" I said, calling them over. Everyone had grim expressions except Aubin, who stared off to one side. I pushed ahead anyway. "Where did she go? What was that?"

"It was some kind of portal. A door between the worlds." Evyn chewed her lip.

"Will she come back?" Sabatha asked in a small voice.

"I cannot say for sure. Did she achieve her aim?" I asked.

Sabatha nodded sadly. "She took some of the tangles. I've been through them all, and she has taken some powerful ones as well as middling ones. She should be unable to use them, but she might find someone who can, someone who has an affinity with death magic. And if she breaks them, the spirits will be released and can cause damage." She shook her head sadly. "I'm so sorry, but I had no choice. I didn't want innocent blood on my hands."

Aubin refocused on her with a sneer. "That is unlikely now. As soon as Liara uses those things, the disaster that follows will be your doing."

Sabatha recoiled. I glared at Aubin.

Tuniel patted her shoulder. "You're young. Your ability to turn away from suffering in front of you has yet to develop."

"For the record, if that happens again, sacrifice us," I said.

"Thorrn!" Evyn put a hand to her mouth, but Gerlay nodded eagerly.

Aubin said nothing.

"What did she want the tangles for?" I asked.

"I do not know," Gerlay said, and no one else volunteered anything.

I grimaced. We had lost her again. "Then it's a dead end, at least until she reappears, or we try to follow her somehow."

Evyn shook her head firmly. "I can't open a portal to nothing, and that place didn't feel good, did it? Maybe the alts will know more."

"And we are at the whim of their visits." It galled me, but there was nothing further to be done here.

The king agreed when I updated him and Barlay via lodestone, and Tuniel arranged magical transport. Travel mancers and mages arrived in less than half a turn of the glass, and before long we were back in the castle.

"That's much cooler," Evyn said, exhaling.

We all dispersed for the afternoon; Gerlay went to the public baths while Aubin, Evyn and I went up to our apartment, Aubin wearing his Asmar headscarf. He went into his room as soon as we arrived, the door closing firmly behind him.

Evyn and I glanced at each other. "He needs time," we both same at the same instant, and I couldn't help the smile that spread across my face. She grinned back.

I bathed quickly and then let Evyn in, mentally sorting through my tasks for the day. I would need to report in, and then I could take Evyn to the city if she still wanted to do that. Looking forward to doing something normal with her, I yawned. Feeling the exertions of the last few days throughout my body, I lay down just for a moment to await her.

When I woke up, it was dark. Cursing, I rubbed my eyes. I had fallen straight to sleep for who knows how long.

"Hi." Evyn's voice floated out of the darkness.

"Well met. My apologies, what time is it?" I groped around on my bedside table for the glowstone.

"Oh, midnight, something like that," she said quietly.

"I'm sorry for falling asleep on you."

"That's my line." She went quiet. "Want me to turn a light on?"

"Please." But instead of a glowstone on the side of her bed, a soft white glow emanated from her hands, throwing stark light on her face. "Oh! Is that a soul jewel? Oh! It must be ours, correct?"

"That's right." She stroked it gently, coming to sit on the pillow next to me.

I levered myself upright, cupping my hands to receive it. "I'm sorry I missed it."

"That's okay. I think I've had enough sleep to last me the rest of the year. I mean turn. I left you to it, you looked knackered." She passed me the jewel. It was small in my palm, the edges smooth and pleasingly rounded. "I went to a gem shop and this one shone out at me. It's an agate."

"Oh?" I smiled at it.

"Yeah. I looked it up in the library, it helps with a few things, apparently; concentration and enhancing perception, but it also heals inner anger and anxiety. It strengthens relationships."

"Sounds... yes. This is our stone." I chuckled.

She didn't join me. She continued speaking, her words in the reporting cadence. "I... I came straight back here. I saw Aubin in the kitchen and... and I couldn't wait. I gave it to him."

My heart surged, but then fell. The evidence of how that had gone rested in my hand. "... And he didn't accept it."

She curled around my arm, making herself small again. "He didn't take it. Said I had dithered too long, that I had played off my suitors against one another. I said you can talk; you were lying about loving me. He said... He said he never lied, he never said he didn't, but things had changed." Burying her face in my pillow, her chest heaved as she tried and failed to contain a sob. "So I just came back up here."

"I see." I swung my legs over the edge of the bed. "I'll be back momentarily."

She grabbed my arm. "Thorrn, don't do anything. It's within Aubin's right to not want a relationship with me."

"No, see, this is him punishing himself for nearly killing me. He feels like he shouldn't have been able to, but, in actuality, we needed him to do it." I closed my fist on the jewel.

"He didn't say that, though—"

"This is how he's getting you to stay away from him," I explained. "I need to talk to him anyway."

"Do it in the morning. He's probably asleep by now."

I cocked my head, listening. A tap downstairs. "No, he isn't." Throwing off the covers, I stalked down as quietly as I was able.

The yellow moon hung high tonight. Beyond the dark walls of the castle twinkled the lights of the city. A shadowed shape stood at the balcony window, hand on the latch.

"At least use the stairs," I said.

Aubin turned his head but did not hail me.

I folded my arms. "Seriously, climbing the castle walls at night in a headscarf is not to be recommended. Especially if it's your first time trying it."

"I'll take that under advisement." He picked up his backpack from the table.

My spine turned to ice. "Where are you going?"

"To think."

"And you need a pack for that?"

"I need time and some space."

I nodded. "I said I would give you that. I bet we have some leave from Gough due."

He took a breath, but then let it out.

I took a step toward him. "I... I do want to stop you. I don't want you to go. I want us to talk about this. I want you to run to us instead of away from us. We need you just as much as you need—"

"I don't need you," he snapped. "I've just proven that rather spectacularly. It is James's skill that enables you to stand before me right now. I did the task we needed to do to get the job done." His voice was cold and cutting. "Is that what you need me to do? To be?"

"Well. Yes." I ran my hand through my hair. "We needed you to do it and you did. Your instincts were correct! It was exactly what was required. We needed *you*."

Aubin turned his face away. In the dark, under the headscarf, he was utterly unreadable to me. "Yes. You did. But that doesn't mean I want to be that person."

"Then let's work it out. Let's talk."

"No, because the heartbeat you convince me it's actually fine that I killed you, I know I might be asked to do it again. And I will be able to kill my friends. I murdered you. No matter what fancy tenets I put around that, when it comes down to it, I am a killer."

My heart sank. "And... and you don't want to be." I could kill when I needed to, when my tenets agreed that it was the right and only course of action left to me. Aubin's tenets were cloudy, half-formed and malleable. If only I could explain that!

Aubin inclined his head. "Correct."

"Aubin... I froze, in front of Liara. I had an instant where I could have ended her. If I'd have been like you, able to act anyway, maybe we could have eliminated her there and then."

He scoffed. "You don't want to wish yourself anything like me, Shardsson." He tugged at the backpack straps. "So. Are you going to stop me?"

There was nothing I could say to match him. His course was set, and he would see it through. I shook my head slowly. "No. Because we love you."

He let out a breath.

"Go well, Aubin. Find your way back to us."

"Goodbye, Shardsson." He hitched up his pack and left out the front door.

AT MORNING TRAINING, Captain Barlay grunted a greeting. "Sounds like you had somewhat of a successful trip. I had a report from Evyn."

"My deepest apologies, sir, I fell straight asleep, I have no excuse."

"Oh, I assumed you dictated it to her." He looked behind me. "No Asmar this morning?"

I shook my head, sadness pulling at my heart. "He's on leave, sir. I request a bit of time for him."

"Granted." Barlay leant in. "You should take some leave as well, Ranger."

I drew myself up. "Maybe a few days, sir, but let's see what shakes out of this Rushia campaign. I like to be kept busy, and Liara is still out there somewhere." Maybe between the worlds, causing who knew what kind of havoc. And for what? What was her ultimate aim?

As Special Forces and their soul companions gathered, Evyn ran up from the castle. She hurtled to the front and saluted me with a grin. I beamed back at her.

"Someone is full of vigour this morning," Barlay noted.

"Yes. No longer sick, sir."

"Punched the thing that was draining her into submission?"

"Actually, sir, treated part of it to a bit of compassion. And then incarcerated the bit that wasn't amenable to that."

Barlay nodded, smiling. "Perfect, Ranger."

Evyn threw herself into the exercises. "This feels so easy now!" she told me excitedly. She raced through the stances and could follow along with the exercise Barlay set us.

"Hm. Might be time to get you a training sword," I said as I passed her.

She rolled up her sleeves. "Oh, I want to ask Tuniel for bracers like yours. Those were really cool; I can wear them all the time and then I can learn more of the Skienien Battlemistress blades."

"Yes." My stomach fell.

Evyn pulled her hair back from her face. "He needs a bit of space right now. We can give him that."

"Indeed."

After Evyn and the other soul companions were dismissed, I helped Barlay with manoeuvre development. I noticed some moves incorporated a Dinahen staff stance or a rapid Rushia movement.

I raised my eyebrow at Barlay, and he smiled. "Some good stuff in here, Shardsson. Keep it up. Skienien Battlemistress blades next?" He rubbed his hands.

"Yessir. But he's on leave for a bit, sir," I reminded him. Already Aubin was sorely missed. *Does he realise that?*

After training and bathing, I found Evyn in the library. Gerlay sat nearby, leafing through a volume. She pointed out something that she had been reading, and he nodded politely.

"All for the mess hall?" I asked.

Evyn closed her book with a small smile. Her hands did not shake as she picked it up, and my chest lightened. She was hale again.

Gerlay cleared his throat. "The mess would be good. Shardsson, I'll be going back to Dinahe tomorrow."

I bowed. "It was an honour to serve with you."

"And I you. And it was nice to get to know you, Lady Evyn."

"Thanks, Gerlay." She cocked her head. "Oh, before you go, there's someone I'd like you to meet."

"Oh?"

"Mm-hmm. I'll arrange a little get-together in our apartment later, a *bon voyage* party."

"Thank you. I deeply appreciate it."

They remained perfectly polite on the way to the mess hall and Evyn rushed off to talk to someone once we arrived. As Gerlay sat, he patted his breast pocket. "She gave me my jewel back. We have together decided not to proceed."

I nodded, studying his face. "For what it's worth, I think it is for the best."

He looked a little sad, but mainly tired, with grey rings under his eyes. "It is, but I worry Gordonne might be disappointed. My brother was hoping to strengthen relations with Oberrot or Rush. Now, both are out of the story." He stared at the food in front of us.

I clapped him on the shoulder. "I think our relations are strong enough without anything like that, but just so you know, Oberrot does have a few pretty girls lying around." I waved my hands around at the courtiers and soldiers filling the hall at mid-sun.

He looked up. "Mm. Like that one, talking to Evyn?" Gerlay jerked his chin behind my shoulder.

"Who?" Turning in my seat, all I could see was my sister.

"Tall, legs for days, nice... deportment."

"I don't see any..." I blinked. "You mean *Sylvia*?"

"Is that her name? It has a musical quality."

I grinned at him. "Yes."

"Sylvia. Mm." He straightened up in his seat. "And what is she like?"

I tapped the table. "A very skilled courtier, I think she speaks Dinahen, but I'll check. Dances. She's well-liked here at court. She has a significant downside though; a very protective younger brother. You have bested him in a fight, so you'd have nothing to worry about."

Gerlay frowned, and then gasped as he worked it out. "Oh, she is your sister?" He slapped his hand to his mouth. "Oh, Shardsson, I'm so sorry, I did not mean anything inappropriate."

I took a bite of my roll, chuckling. "I'll tell her you liked her deportment. She'll be tickled."

A messenger approached me. "Ranger Shardsson? The king would like to see you immediately."

I stood up. "I'm on my way. Gerlay, see Evyn back to the library, would you?"

I jogged lightly up to the royal apartments and flashed my tattoo to be granted entry. Special Forces frowned at the slashes and scars all over my forearms. "Yes, I'll get the Lorekeeper to redo them. They are still valid, though."

Once they let me through, I knocked on Gough's office door. "Sir. You wanted to see me?"

Captain Barlay sat in front of the desk, and Gough looked up, a smile crossing his face. "At ease, Shardsson." The smile faded. "What do you know about the other Ranger's departure?"

I had to catch my breath a little from the wave of worry over him. "Sir, he needed... time. It was out of the ordinary, I know, sir, but he gets very... Anyway. I asked for leave on his behalf this morning and Captain Barlay granted it." I nodded to him. "I'm sorry it was out of the usual order of ask and wait for permission, but he was very uncomfortable. Sir."

Gough's brows bunched. "Leave?"

"Yes, sir." I searched his eyes. "He's... He's due leave, correct, sir?"

"Yes, he is, you both are. But this isn't leave." Gough stood, handing me a sheet of paper. On it looped Aubin's precise handwriting across a few terse statements.

As always the words tumbled away from my understanding, but this time the paper trembled in my hands as well. I stilled them with an effort. "Sir." My voice was occluded. I tried again. "What is this, sir?"

Gough came around the desk to stand beside me. "That's his resignation from the Rangers, Shardsson. I take it you didn't know," he said quietly. He slid the paper from my nerveless fingers.

"No. Sir. I... I thought he only needed a bit of time. Some leave." I forced myself to take a breath, expanding my lungs fully to try to clear them.

"This has come as a bit of a shock to us all, then."

"Yes. Sir." I swallowed.

"Thorrn," Gough said softly. "Take a seat."

"Thanks, sir." Sinking down into the padded chair, I put my head in my hands.

"He's gone, then," Barlay said gruffly, passing me a glass of water.

"Yes. He left last night. Evyn tried to give him a soul jewel, and that may have pushed him over the edge."

Gough made a small murmur.

I sat up. "She's returned Gerlay his jewel, sir. We still have strong relations with the Dinahens, sir, what with this joint campaign."

"I was hoping to have further ties," Gough groused.

"We may yet, sir; Gerlay was commenting on my sister's fine deportment."

Gough brightened up considerably. "Ah. Yes. Very good, Shardsson, I hope that goes well."

I wrapped my hands around the cold glass. "Yes. He's a good man. Aubin didn't think he measured up. But the thing is, sir, we don't need good men all the time. Gerlay wouldn't have thought to force the spirit out. Aubin did. That's what's troubling him. He doesn't want to be that person. But... that's who he is."

And who we love anyway, regardless. If only he would come to terms with that.

Gough nodded slowly. "So he's quit. Ordinarily you cannot quit Special Forces, but he was never part of the Forces, so there's nothing I can really do. He's officially dead besides. Any idea where he might have gone?"

Where could he go? "No, sir. Tuniel MasterMage might know." Did she? What would she think of his precipitous departure? Was she in support of it?

Gough rubbed his chin. "It might not be best to ask her. I'll leave that up to your judgement."

"Yes, sir. Thank you."

They dismissed me shortly afterwards. My head spun as I walked slowly back to our apartments. *He left us.* He left me and Evyn. Evyn would be devastated.

I hesitated outside Aubin's door before I opened it. His bed lay neatly turned down, the smell, once sharp lyneal and bitter somnus root, drained and faded already. A folded Ranger's uniform and the pile of books the Assassin had penned studying the effects of bruswurt sat on the desk. On top of that was a dark green jewel.

It remained unresponsive to me as I picked it up, holding it up to the light. There was a flaw deep inside, a fissure that could crack at any time.

I could not find a note. He had nothing more he wanted to say to Evyn or me.

I sat on the edge of his bed and let the tears stream free.

"Thorrn?" Evyn stood at the door.

I had no words. "I'm sorry. I was wrong." I sucked in a deep breath, steeling myself. "He has left us."

Evyn rocked back a step, then raced up to me and flung her arms around my neck. "I'm sorry. It's my fault. I pushed him too far."

I wrapped my arms around her. "I pushed him too hard. The fault lies with me."

"Aubin did what he had to, what he thought he had to. As it turned out, it was the correct course of action." Her shoulders slumped slightly. "I don't know how he's going to square that circle without help."

Without us, what was he going to do?

A rap at the door made me startle. Evyn wiped her face. "Messenger, probably."

Perhaps it was a message from Aubin, or maybe even Aubin himself, turning back because he recognised he had to work through his pain with us rather than away from us. I wrenched the door open eagerly.

"Message from the king," the lad said. "Not urgent but important."

"Yes?" I nearly danced on my toes as the boy passed me the note. Had Gough forgotten a detail?

I spun around, nearly bumping Evyn to the floor. "Whoa!" I steadied her. "What is this? Can you read it for me please?" I wouldn't be able to, not wound up as I was.

She pulled it open, hands shaking. Her eyes widened as she scanned the contents.

"Well?"

She let out a low breath. "Gough says he's just received word. Gavain is well enough to travel." She looked up at me, eyelashes heavy with tears. "He'll be in the city within the month."

EPILOGUE—THE GUARDIAN AND THE WAYKEEPER

Rubbing my eyes, I peered at the Waykeeper's screen. Lines bisected and crossed it, all the various meetings and turning points in lives. Sometimes it was hard to remember that, seeing them reduced to little more than the London Underground map.

"So, as you can see here," the Waykeeper said, nail-bitten finger on a junction between multiple green lines, "this is a problem."

I sighed. "Could you explain it a bit more, dear?" I smoothed his messy tawny hair. He had inherited his father's hair colour, but not its seemingly supernatural ability to always look swept back like a supermodel. The messiness probably came from me.

He nodded eagerly, tapping again at the screen to show me four lines in parallel and then one branching off. "Their Aubin has left them. That's a bit of a disaster."

"Quantify 'a bit.'" My husband approached, hands on the hilts of his Battlemistress blades, as if he would need to use them at any moment.

The Waykeeper ran a hand through his hair, messing up what I had just set right. "Like, sticks-a-spoke-in-the-wheel type of disaster. And we have a loose Liara tearing up the place."

Aubin sighed. "What do you think, my love? Time for the cloak-and-dagger routine again?"

I pursed my lips, looking at my various disguises, not least a Rushia man's headscarf. "I'm sure we can kill two birds with one stone here. Let's plan, but after lasagne. And," I said, holding up a finger, "you must also eat some of the salad."

"Yes, Mum," the Waykeeper intoned.

"Good boy. Then we'll think about how we fix the king's swordsman's timeline."

THANK YOU SO MUCH

Thank you so much for reading. I hope you loved it as much as I loved writing it! I hope you'll come along for the next instalment of Thorn and Evyn's adventures.

If you enjoyed this book, will you please review it? It really helps independent authors like me – and I do truly want to hear what you think. It only takes a few minutes, and it means so much to me. Thank you!

My free gift to you - learn how Gavain and Thorrn's friendship started. Grab your exclusive copy on my mailing list – you won't find *"Dough Boy"* anywhere else. Go to: https://www.beckyjamesauthor. co.uk/subscribe

Acknowledgments

A massive thank you to my wonderful beta readers, Kristen Braddock and Cristen Faulkenberry. I genuinely couldn't do this without you!

As always, all my love to my soul companion across all the worlds.

And to you, my readers! Your support keeps me writing and improving. I hope you continue to follow along with Thorrn and Evyn's many adventures to come. You will not have long to wait!

About the Author

Becky James is the author of The King's Swordsman series and coauthor of the Dark Tides series. Based in the UK, she has a deep love of the British countryside, canals, and all things fantasy; she devours anything that has magic, swords, good friends and good times. She is a massive extrovert, but nearly all her friends are introverts, so she knows how not to energy vampire them. She will still talk your ear off though.

Her series can be found wherever books are sold, and she is often floating around on Facebook and Instagram - follow @beckyjamesauthor.

https://www.beckyjamesauthor.co.uk/